Igor Savelyev where he still lives and works as a crime reporter for the local news agency. He has a degree in Philology from Ufa University. His short novel *Pale City*, based on his own hitchhiking experiences, was shortlisted for the Debut and Belkin prizes in 2004 and published in France. Critics have noted his "masterful, finely chiseled style based on brilliant counterpoints like a virtuoso music piece." "Here realism is bordering on phantasmagoria, a striking sample of new-generation psychological prose."

Irina Bogatyreva, born in 1982, grew up on the Volga. She has seven novels to her name and has won several important literary prizes, including the prestigious Debut Prize for her novel *Auto-Stop (Off the Beaten Track)* which came out from a major publishing house in Russia. Bogatyreva spotlights the most topical issues of Russian life and enjoys both readers' and critics' acclaim.

Tatiana Mazepina is the latest winner of the Debut Prize for a travelogue about her Eastern travels. She is a member of the Society of Free Travelers and works as a journalist writing on religious matters.

"An unusually gifted generation is entering Russian literature. Literature has not seen such an influx of energy in a long time. This new generation – both the individual writers and the phenomenon as a whole – deserves great attention." – Olga Slavnikova

GLAS NEW RUSSIAN WRITING

contemporary Russian literature

in English translation

Volume 52

This is the third volume in the Glas sub-series presenting young Russian authors, winners and finalists of the Debut Prize founded by the Pokolenie Foundation for humanitarian projects in 2000. Glas acknowledges its generous support in publishing this book.

OFF THE BEATEN TRACK

Stories by Russian Hitchhikers

Igor Savelyev

Irina Bogatyreva

Tatiana Mazepina

GLAS Publishers
tel./fax: +7(495)441-9157
perova@glas.msk.su
www.glas.msk.su

USA and CANADA
Consortium Book Sales and Distribution
1094 Flex Drive
Jackson, TN 38301-5070
tel: 800-283-3572; fax: 800-351-5073
orderentry@perseusbooks.com

In the UK
CENTRAL BOOKS
orders@centralbooks.com
www.centralbooks.com
Direct orders: INPRESS
Tel: 0191 229 9555
customerservices@inpressbooks.co.uk
www.inpressbooks.co.uk

Within Russia
Jupiter-Impex
www.jupiterbooks.ru

X000 000 044 2062

Editors: Natasha Perova & Joanne Turnbull
Front cover photograph by Anastasia Perova
Design by Tatiana Shaposhnikova

ISBN 978-5-7172-0092-9

CONTENTS

STORIES ABOUT HITCHHIKING

Igor Savelyev

THE PALE CITY

1

The same question must have tormented everyone who ever sat down with a blank piece of paper in front of them: where should I start? Logically, of course, it would make sense to start with a bit of history. But I'm no good with historical data and wouldn't do a particularly good job of describing the city where I was born and used to live. To be honest, it's probably just as well. You don't need to know that this story happened specifically in Ufa, capital of Bashkiria. All you need to know is that it's set in a moderately industrial city in the Urals, on the banks of the Volga, with a population of just over a million, five theatres and a state circus. How many museums? I can't remember. See, I'd make a terrible historian.

How would a proper historian describe the city today? He (or she) would probably start by waxing lyrical on the subject of the rivers, and how they "carry their abundant waters past the white stone walls". Well, I'm going to start at the city limits, where a sign saying UFA lets you know you're entering a built-up area. Please refrain from sounding your horn, driver – you're not on the highway now.

Incidentally, the sign is bilingual; Ufa in the Bashkir language is 'Ephe'. Not the most attractive name for a city, I'm sure you'll agree, but we're used to it. And since we live in Ephe, are we modern-day Ephesians?

There's nothing between the sign and the police checkpoint, and this is typical of Ufa. Anyone who's ever visited one of the other regional capitals in the Urals – Chelyabinsk or Ekaterinburg – will know what I mean. In both these cities there is a cemetery running alongside the road at this point, like a kind of tribute to city life: rows of white headstones, apparently made of breeze blocks… There's nothing remotely depressing about these cemeteries. They're like miniature replicas of the suburbs. Everything about these sprawling metropolitan churchyards seems to say, "Greetings and welcome, dear visitors!" It's always amusing when the city authorities hang a banner bearing words to this effect on the fence separating the cemetery from the road, and you're never quite sure whether you're being welcomed to the city or the afterlife.

At least the cemetery isn't the first thing you see as you approach Ufa, and that has to be a good thing, right?

So, what else can I tell you? There are basically two sides to the city. The first is the centre, where everything's very charming and picturesque: cobbles, boutiques, shop windows, bright lights, and plenty of people strolling about. The main street is named after You Know Who. Sometimes when you notice the street signs you can't help remembering that Vladimir Lenin chose his pseudonym in honour of the river Lena in Siberia, where he served his exile. Imagine the alternatives: Amurin, Irtyshin, Enisenin… He had plenty of rivers to choose from!

To put it into context, the names of nearly all the streets in the centre of Ufa are connected in some way or other (most of them directly) to all that Marxist-Leninist nonsense. It's the same in every ex-Soviet city. At least Ufa doesn't have a street named after 1937, like they do in Saratov. The peak of the Great Purge. But seriously: Twentieth Anniversary of October Revolution Street, that's what it's called.

Anyway, as I was saying, there are worse places to hang out than our city centre. You can buy ice cream here on every street corner, and on a hot summer's day there's nothing like it. You take your cone and the ice-cream seller hands you your change, which is also kept in the freezer for some reason. A few frozen coins. It's nothing, really, but it's a nice feeling.

The rest of Ufa is industrial – home to the major Bashkir

oil refineries (plus a dozen or so derivative petroleum factories) and whole districts of squalid, soot-covered Khrushchev-era apartment blocks, which are inhabited by blue-collar workers with bluish faces. It's nothing to do with chemical poisoning – they just drink too much. That part of the city is where the famous rock singer Zemfira comes from, by the way. Zemfira: the leading exponent of Russian aggro-rock. When she launched her first album (like a missile), the cover was a photographic image of dilapidated factories and crooked chimneys in a haze of pearly-white chlorine cyanide smoke. Views just like this could be seen from anywhere in the centre of Ufa. The locals knew the best vantage points and were always happy to share them with visitors, who would never fail to be impressed by this evidence of our connection to the world-famous rock star.

This imposing industrial zone identifies our city as part of the Urals; you don't get views like this in any of the other cities along the Volga. When I visited Samara I saw just one tall chimney on the city skyline. It really stood out. I found out later that it wasn't actually a chimney at all but an enormous rocket-carrier, a monument to Sergei Korolev, a key figure in the Soviet space programme.

To give you a better feel for the city, let's take a walk around and eavesdrop on a few of the locals.

An elderly spinster, looking up at a billboard…

"That's Sandra Bullock! A famous actress!" she exclaims before adding, profoundly, "I used to look just like her…"

The local recreational park, early evening…

Two friends are larking about, smoking grass, wandering around one of the glades and urinating wherever they feel like it. Already stoned, they're squealing with high-pitched laughter. A middle-aged man carrying two bottles of wine hears the laughter coming from behind the bushes.

"Would you like some company, ladies?" he calls out.

"There aren't any ladies here, old man!"

A girl suffering from claustrophobia, her first time in a solarium... Before clambering into the sarcophagus she turns to the nurse and asks in a panic, "What's your name? Just in case..."

"Why do you want to know? I'm not usually on first-name terms with the clients. Weird... Well, since you ask, it's Larisa, and I finish at half past five!"

A conversation in a food shop...

A drunk rushes over to the counter of the wines and spirits section.

"Now for the most important purchase! I need a bottle of vodka. Just the one, but make it a good one, the kind you'd give to your son!"

"I'd clout my son over the head with any vodka bottle!"

The drunk is speechless...

The next customer is a young man of about twenty who looks like he doesn't give a damn. Prominent cheekbones, dirty shoulder-length hair, scruffy old clothes... that pretty much sums him up. Yes, this is where you get to know one of our main characters. Officially his name is Mikhail, but everyone calls him Squire. Everyone, that is, except his university professors and a couple of other clueless old fogies. Like his parents, for example.

"A large can of Shikhan lager, please. Yeah, extra strength. Thanks..."

His parents are out of the picture. They still live in Sibai, a small Bashkir town in the middle of nowhere – a typical provincial backwater.

Squire arrived in Ufa four years ago to take up a place at the Aviation Institute. He started his course, and everything was fine, but he wasn't really interested in studying... From the very first day he was blown away by the metropolis, charmed and smitten, once and for all. The city had it all! There were lots of places to hang out, like the 'pipes' – underground passages that had attained a kind of cult status. They were neglected and filthy, covered in Dutch tiles and full of soggy cardboard; he could spend hours in there, screwing up his eyes as he emerged into the unexpected sunlight. Nobody bothered him or interfered in his business. In fact, the only thing missing in Ufa was anyone who cared what he got up to, and that suited Squire down to the ground! A big city is never dominated by any one group – that's the curse of provincial backwaters.

Mikhail's new friends regarded him indulgently. His naïve enthusiasm amused them, and initially they even took to calling him 'The Squire from Sibai' for comic effect. Absurd juxtaposition.

Squire himself, meanwhile, grasped 'city life' with both hands – he couldn't get enough of it! Buskers in the underground passages, taxis splashing through puddles inches from his stoned face...

Ufa is full of people like Squire. They come from the provinces to take up a cherished student place, pooling their money to rent squalid shared apartments, and their lives are identical from one year to the next: endless drinking bouts, an ever-growing arsenal of empty bottles in the communal kitchen, absenteeism and the ongoing (and exhilarating) threat of expulsion. It's all so familiar and predictable that I'm sure I don't need to go into any more detail.

To be fair, I should point out that Squire wasn't one of those student layabouts who drink their futures away. Even students at prestigious universities can be lost from society and trust me, plenty of them are. No, Squire exercised moderation in everything. He was a notorious loner, someone who felt the lure of the road and the constant need for a change of scene. He spent several summers hitchhiking, travelling all over the country, and the apartment he sublet became one of Ufa's legendary squats. These squats are basically informal doss-houses, where hitchhikers arriving in the city can spend a night or two for free. The addresses of these squats are circulated on scraps of paper and over the Internet, and visitors are always turning up unannounced. How many strangers have stopped at this apartment on their way through the city? Too many to count. A blur of casual acquaintances, faces, names, addresses scribbled hurriedly on the wallpaper...

Squire left the food shop with a bag containing his large can of beer and a packet of dubiously grey pasta, the cheapest you could buy. Standard weekend supplies. "I'm going to end up with a beer belly at this rate. But who cares?" he thought, as he headed home.

The sun was setting and the sky had already turned red, decorated with a panorama of clouds illuminated from below. Evening in Ufa: it was like the backdrop to a battle scene. The fact that it's Ufa is irrelevant, really. It's just another Russian metropolis. One of the few points on the map where two state highways intersect, in this case the M7 Volga and the M5 Ural.

2

"Hang on a minute, you said 'we'... but who's 'we'?"

"Me and my friend Nikita. We're travelling together. We left St Petersburg three days ago."

"But there's no one with you!"

"No, you don't understand. We're hitchhiking separately... I mean, who's going to stop and pick up a couple of guys? There aren't many drivers who'd be mad enough to do that... But we're *travelling* together. He probably hasn't got much further than Bavlov."

"How do you know? Maybe he's overtaken you. I'm not driving very fast..."

"No way. You don't know Nikita. He always takes forever."

"Hang on, how can he 'always' take forever? I don't understand. You're hitchhiking... Surely it's down to luck?"

"Yeah, you're right. It's weird, though, I can't explain

it... He looks perfectly normal, and even if he wasn't drivers can't tell from a distance. But for some reason Nikita's always slower than me – there's always a breakdown or something, he has to take loads of different cars... I don't know what it is. It's just something about him."

"He doesn't wear glasses, does he? And carry a funny blue thing?"

"His sleeping bag. Yes, that's him. See, you didn't pick him up, did you?"

"No, I didn't."

"Why not?"

"Well, I don't know..."

"You see?"

This last was declared in a particularly triumphant tone of voice, as if to say, "There you go, you've just proved me right!"

Even if the driver had wanted to he wouldn't have managed to find room for a second passenger. It was a middle-of-the-road foreign car, a few years old but still reasonably presentable, and the boot was so full it was held shut by a piece of rope. The entire back seat was piled high with blankets, bags, a vacuum flask and so on. There was every indication that the car had a long road ahead of it. A long road behind it, too, judging by the state of the driver. The red eyes, the drooping eyelids... How many lives are lost on the road? I'm not talking about the little crosses and makeshift memorials you glimpse fleetingly at the side of the road, forgotten and covered with dust, banal in their familiarity. I mean the lives of the drivers who travel across entire time zones without stopping to sleep or rest. Thousands and thousands of kilometres... Every evening when the sun flits sideways behind the trees, making it hard to see the road, these drivers ask themselves the same question: shall I grab a couple of hours' sleep or just keep driving? Unfortunately, it's often the latter. I wonder how many strokes and accidents the road has on its conscience.

The driver was barefoot. Maybe it gave him a better feel for the car or something. The cold pedals were probably helping him stay awake. His feet were small and swollen. His destination was somewhere in the Far East. The hitchhiker in his passenger seat was heading for the Urals.

"So what's the big deal about Ekaterinburg?"

"E-burg is great! We've got friends there. Well, some people we met over the Internet... They've invited us to stay. There's a place there – a 'dam' they call it, like a kind of city square, where there's going to be a huge get-together. We're bound to meet some interesting people there. Have some fun."

"Do you travel round the country a lot like this?"

"Yeah, I guess so. When I make it to E-burg I'll have done nine thousand kilometres."

"Wow. You know, I envy you, son! If only I had your youth..."

The hitchhiker's name was Vadim. A lot of people think this isn't a Russian name, that it's a relatively recent foreign import, like Ruslan. I must admit I was quite surprised when I came across Vadim the Bold, one of the first Novgorodian princes and something of a hero back in the ninth century.

Our Vadim was from St Petersburg, birthplace of three revolutions and cultural capital of Russia to this day. A city that is proud of its ornate railings. Incidentally, one particularly frosty winter when he was a little boy Vadim got his tongue stuck to the legendary railings in the Summer Garden. Not every schoolboy can boast of such a thing!

Generally speaking, Vadim was a perfectly normal young man. Reasonably cheerful, reasonably nonchalant, reasonably unkempt... He'd failed one of his exams at St Petersburg University, but that didn't stop him from setting off on his travels around the country. "It'll all be sorted out in the autumn, anyway," thought Vadim, pleasantly alarmed by his own composure. "Either I'll retake it or they'll kick me out, and that's pretty unlikely over just one exam..." His parents didn't need to know. They didn't need to know about anything.

"My daughter's about the same age as you," said the driver, with a sideways glance. "Maybe a bit younger. If I thought for one minute..."

He gave a lopsided grin. Vadim knew what he meant.

"If you thought for one minute she was hitchhiking?"

"Yeah. I'd kill her."

They fell silent. The car overtook a lorry. The driver concentrated on the road, manipulating the pedals with his bare feet. Then a dark blue sign swam past, telling them how far it was to various places. Vadim knew that the information given on road signs like this was unreliable at best, and sometimes completely arbitrary. This one said Ufa 72km, Chelyabinsk 489km.

"I live with my daughter. It's just the two of us."

This was followed by another silence. In situations like this, the hitchhiker doesn't even have to respond. If they want to, they'll tell you more. It's a kind of unspoken rule that the driver is allowed to interrogate his passenger on the most personal subjects (and usually takes great pleasure in doing so), whereas the hitchhiker has no right whatsoever to poke his nose into the driver's business. Does that sound a bit unfair? Well, they're doing you a favour by giving you a lift, at the end of the day. It's their prerogative.

"Her mother was a whore. We split up six years ago."

Vadim immediately adopted his most understanding and sympathetic expression, whilst simultaneously thinking to himself, "Nice one! He's a talker. At least he won't hassle me."

"We were classmates. I studied history at college. Gave it all up later, though... Anyway, they sent a group of students to work on a collective farm, and that's where it all started. I bet they don't send you to collective farms any more, do they?"

"Of course not! Some friends of mine at teacher training college had to go, though."

"We went out together for about three months. Her parents were against it, and so were mine. Her mother was a real bitch. She had gold teeth and everything! She didn't even come to the registry office, can you imagine that? But we had a party for everyone in our course... A real Komsomol wedding, it was. You know what I mean?"

"I can imagine. With vodka in the teapots?"

"Exactly! That sort of thing. Then we got a flat, had a baby... Then the arguments started, the bickering and the rows... Maybe it was that old cliché, just a 'clash of personalities'... Probably. You know what annoyed her most of all, what used to really wind her up? This'll make you laugh... Me not putting the lids back on."

"What?"

"Seriously! I was always forgetting to put the lids on shampoo bottles and toothpaste tubes after I'd finished using them. Same with the shaving cream. It used to drive her absolutely insane!"

"That's a bit..."

"Then she started going out with other men, drinking too. 'You carry on, sweetheart,' I said to her. 'As long as you're having a good time, eh?' Eventually we split up. And do you know what sums it up? Marinka was only little, and when I asked her who she wanted to live with she chose me. Can you imagine that? What kind of... How bad does it have to be for your own daughter to..."

They were silent.

"While we're on the subject, Vadim, let me give you a word of advice. Whatever you do, don't rush into marriage. You're a young lad, your hormones are all over the place... You're bound to fall in love sooner or later. Fair enough. But whatever happens, don't let her drag you to the registry office! It'll only end in tears. Student relationships always do!"

"I wasn't planning on getting married just yet."

"And if you do get married, don't get her pregnant. Otherwise it'll be a disaster. Make sure you tell her right from the start that you want to live together for three years, without any children. And don't give in, even if she cries or tries to persuade you!" The driver paused for a moment before saying, "You must have a girlfriend. Do you?"

"No!"

Vadim always answered this question, which came up quite a lot, with a look of casual indifference and a stupid half-smile. As if to say, "So what if I don't? What's the big deal anyway?"

The driver turned to look at him.

"Why not? What's the matter with you? How old are you, anyway?"

"Here we go," thought Vadim. He began to change his opinion of the driver. His face continued to bear an expression of calculated nonchalance, though it was now mixed with a kind of helplessness. No one likes to be thought of as past it. He couldn't bear the thought of justifying himself or entering into a complicated explanation.

"Let's just say that I just haven't found the right person yet."

This cliché and the pause that preceded it indicated that the subject was closed. The driver got the message and turned his attention back to the road. He threw a quick glance at Vadim.

"You're taking the whole business very seriously, aren't you?"

The way he pronounced it, 'the whole business' was loaded with innuendo.

You might be wondering whether Vadim had ever been in love… Oh, he had – head over heels! She was in his class, a languid girl with beautiful eyelashes and curly hair. And as for stupid romantic gestures… At 5.00 a.m. one morning when his chosen one, along with the rest of the city, was still asleep, he took a can of paint to the courtyard of her building and stood beneath her window with the intention of leaving her a message on the tarmac: "Good morning, my love!" – the eternal greeting of all would-be Romeos.

The outcome was so comic and humiliating that he preferred not to think about it any more. There was no happy ending to this particular love story. Vadim was caught in the act by the yardkeeper, and this is how it happened...

The sun was already up but the city was still empty, full of echoes. Vadim felt as though he were in some kind of parallel universe. It was a revelation, being out in the city this early in the morning, and subsequently he would make a point of getting up at first light, just to go for a walk. But on this particular day he was on a mission. He sneaked into the courtyard and marked his message out on the tarmac with chalk. Just as he started going over the enormous letters with paint, the yardkeeper turned up! No one could have predicted that he would start work so early. He was a big strong man with bad teeth, a hereditary alcoholic, and, more importantly, he didn't have a romantic bone in his body. Vadim could still remember the sound of the yardkeeper's voice as he yelled at him, and his own swift departure! He didn't see the yardkeeper attacking his handiwork with a stiff broom. The letters "Good m..." hadn't even had the chance to dry.

As he mooched about that morning the thwarted young Romeo decided to drown his sorrows, but even that mission was doomed to fail: at 6.00 a.m. the 24-hour bars and kiosks were decidedly shut. Fate was not smiling on him. He could remember how the streets had been illuminated by the slanting rays of the rising sun... God, how many years had passed since then!

The car approached the city. Interspersed among the heavily laden long-distance lorries were an increasing number

of suburban Moskvich and Zhiguli cars, full to bursting with
family members, with the occasional rusty old barrel strapped
to the roof. Why on earth did anyone need a barrel like that in
the city? Or in the suburbs, for that matter? Ufa's industrial
landscape was painted crimson by the setting sun and crowned
with smoke from the factory chimneys.

"You're a good lad," said the driver, giving Vadim an
appraising look. "Shall I just drive you straight to Chelyabinsk?
It makes no difference to me where I spend the night. I can
manage another five hours, and I can just set off a bit later
tomorrow. What do you say, eh? Shall we just keep going?"

"Thanks, I really appreciate it, but you should get some
rest. I'll be fine here – I've got the address of a good squat. And
anyway my friend Nikita will never catch me up if I carry on to
Chelyabinsk! So, thanks but no thanks... Are you stopping at
the police checkpoint? You can drop me there."

3

The last lorry drove past, rumbling with the sound of
disappointed hope. There's something unpleasantly predictable
about heavy-goods vehicles when you're standing by the side
of the road. They make such a noise when they rush past that
even seasoned hitchhikers experience a moment of panic – will
it squash me like a fly?

The last lorry drove past and then the road was empty,
apart from a few cars in the distance. Nastya lowered her arm.
It was a long time since she'd been stuck like this in the middle
of nowhere! Bloody lorries. Mind you, the cars weren't exactly
falling over themselves to pick her up either.

Everything was quiet. You tend to be more acutely aware
of silence out on the road, maybe because it occurs so rarely.
"Oh, well!" smiled Nastya, resolving to take a philosophical
approach to her misfortune. Walking away from the road,
towards the grass, she squatted down near her rucksack and dug

out a lighter and a packet of cheap cigarettes. She took a drag on her cigarette and looked around. The silence was serene and interminable.

A little further away from the road was the edge of a forest of gnarled pine trees, but there were probably other species mixed in with them too. The fringes of the forest had been littered with old tyres and empty canisters, poisoned by petrol fumes and polluted by the urine of countless travellers. Strange as it seems, these roadside forests are quite wild – hardly anyone ever goes further than two metres into them. There may even have been mushrooms growing in the impenetrable heart of this forest, unseen and undisturbed. Amongst the rubbish was another regular feature of the highway: a flattened corpse, kicked to the side of the road. The body of a dog.

Nastya was used to it by now, but the first time it was always an unpleasant discovery for a novice hitchhiker. She could remember being dropped off about 70km from her home town of Tyumen, about two years ago, and the first thing she'd seen was a squashed cat. Poor thing, it obviously hadn't realised what had hit it. Quite literally. The cat hadn't been merely knocked down but completely run over, and its flattened insides lay neatly to one side. It was horrific. It had taken Nastya half an hour to compose herself sufficiently to be able to hitch another lift. She still cried over things like that back then.

On the other side of the highway stood a couple of ramshackle wagons, crumpled and repainted to within an inch of their lives. A roadside café. There are plenty of these throughout the Urals, all more or less identical. Smoke curled above the metal trough that was being used as a makeshift grill for *shashlik*, and a couple of KamAZ trucks were parked to one side. Silence and serenity reigned here too.

Does it seem strange that nobody would stop to pick up a young girl? Sometimes that's just the way it goes, albeit not very often... The thing is that female hitchhikers don't tend to have an overtly feminine appearance. This is a deliberate tactic, employed for various reasons – for example, it helps to avoid attracting any unwelcome advances and is also a way of distinguishing oneself from the roadside prostitutes. Practical considerations also come into it: travelling clothes need to be comfortable and functional, and that's all that matters. Nastya was wearing heavy boots, jeans and a lightweight yellow waterproof jacket. She wore her hair cropped short, so she didn't need to bother tying it back. It was just easier that way. She wasn't wearing any make-up, but that wasn't just because she was on the road – Nastya never wore make-up in town either. She couldn't care less what other people thought. As long as she was comfortable, that was the main thing.

She stood on the roadside verge, smoking and thinking. She looked up at the sky and thought... about what? She spat and threw her cigarette butt to the ground. A heavily laden car approached and Nastya raised her arm, but she'd already given up hope. She'd resigned herself to going back to the *shashlik* café – it obviously wasn't her night.

It was nice out here in the woods, though. The air was fresh, and somewhere out there in the distance, beyond Ufa, beyond Dyurtyuli, were the steppes. The endless, open steppes...

In the quarter of an hour that she'd spent standing by the side of the highway, nothing had changed in the café. The same faces sat at the same tables. The girl behind the counter was obviously a local. She can't have been more than about sixteen years old, but already her eyes betrayed a terminal boredom. The wheezing old speakers were playing the kind of song that was always popular on the road – 'driving music', they called it, but the lyrics were composed of prison slang! Why did they always sing in prison slang? These people at the tables, the long-distance drivers, had they all been inside or something? You can learn a lot about the Russian penitentiary system simply by travelling across the country.

The table furthest from the door was occupied by the owner of the establishment. He was middle aged but powerfully built and had an imposing presence, like all elderly natives of the Caucasus. He sat there leafing through some paperwork, effortlessly in charge.

"So you're back, are you? I knew you would be!" he said, his accent faint but perceptible. "You're not going anywhere tonight. Sit down! I'll bring you something to eat."

Nastya sat down, put her rucksack on the floor and stuck her elbows to the oilcloth table covering, which featured a pattern of cute little cartoon drawings. That was one of the distinguishing features of all these roadside cafés, the incongruous little traces of domesticity that managed to tug at your heartstrings when you were least expecting it.

What else? Walls made of plywood, indefatigable speakers positioned up near the ceiling... A few solemn and burly long-distance drivers at the little tables, eating their dinner. Refuelling on instant coffee.

The owner returned from the kitchen carrying a plate with steam rising from a double portion of *shashlik*. He placed it in front of Nastya. He was revelling in his Caucasian hospitality, she just knew it. Plying this hungry girl from the highway with hot food, watching her devour it ravenously – that was obviously how he got his kicks. Or maybe she was just in a bad mood because she was so tired.

"Thank you."

"So come on, then. Where are you from?"

Conversations like this are the hitchhiker's cross to bear.

"My name's Nastya," she began, with a little sigh. "I'm travelling from Tyumen to Moscow. I've been on the road for two days already, but it's my own fault it's taking me so long. I overslept yesterday, and what with one thing and another by the time I'd got my things together and got out onto the road... Basically I only made it as far as Ekaterinburg on the first day.

So today I've been trying to make up for lost time. Tomorrow I'll take the M7 out of Ufa. That'll be the quickest way."

"Why do you want to go to Moscow?"

"Why not?"

"Have you got friends there, or family?"

"No. I just felt like it. I haven't been to Moscow since I was a kid. I'll find some friends when I get there. I've got a few addresses written down…"

"So, basically it's just some stupid idea you've got in your head."

"*You* might think it's a stupid idea. I don't."

Nastya spoke quite sharply, letting him know that the subject was closed. Just because she was eating his *shashlik*, that didn't given him the right to start lecturing her!

"Aren't you worried about travelling alone? It's so dangerous out there. A young girl like you…"

"I know it's dangerous, but that doesn't bother me. I can't explain it."

"What about your parents?"

"What about them? We don't talk much. They know that I travel all over the place. They say I've got 'itchy feet'. There's nothing they can do about it!"

"What does your boyfriend have to say about it?"

"I haven't got a boyfriend. Not since May. I'm young, free and single!"

Nastya said this with such a desperate, angry smile that even the café owner knew to leave this subject alone.

He started bustling about, then went back behind the counter and flicked a switch. The café lights came on. He seemed to have complete dominion over this modest empire; he was in charge of everything, down to the humblest light-bulb.

"You're not going anywhere tonight. It's already dark."

"But it's not that late…"

"You are not going to spend the night on the road! I won't

allow it. I'll get someone to make you up a bed in the box-room."

"But I…"

"You're spending the night here, and that's the end of it."

Nastya wiped the last traces of the *shashlik* from her mouth with the back of her hand and smirked. Wow! She hadn't expected such steely insistence from the café owner. Of course, she could have predicted that things would take a similar turn…

"Thank you."

The café owner got up from the table and went off into the kitchen, presumably to bark a few orders. Meanwhile one of the long-distance drivers stood up and walked towards the exit. Refreshed and refuelled, he was ready to continue his journey. Nastya stood up as well.

"Are you going to Ufa?"

The long-distance driver nodded. Excellent! She pushed her plate back, picked up her rucksack and followed him. Ciao, little roadside shack! Nice knowing you. Nastya left without a backwards glance, grateful that she'd managed to extricate herself from yet another predicament.

What next? The dark cabin of a KamAZ truck. For some reason it really seemed to feel the bumps in the road. At first the cabin would rock and sway, then the trailer would rumble behind them. The driver let her smoke and, tired and silent, they both took long drags on their cigarettes – two glowing red dots in the darkness. The blind headlights reached into the night, feeling for the tarmac and the uneven verge.

"I've driven across Siberia," said the driver, breaking the silence. His voice sounded muffled. "One night it was really, really dark. Pitch black. Then suddenly I saw something…" He flashed his headlights for emphasis. "Something lying in the middle of the road. I thought it was a sack that had fallen off a lorry, so I slammed on the brakes and swerved… At least there was no one else on the road. I just missed it, thank God. It was a man's body! Someone must have hit him, then just driven off and left him there. It can be pretty wild in that part of the world. So I just started the engine and drove off."

This was followed by another silence. Nastya gave a bitter laugh. That was a pretty depressing story. A pretty depressing attitude, too. But hey, that's life. *Memento mori...*

They continued their journey along the nocturnal highway of the Urals, breaking the silence only rarely to make the occasional remark, but always aware of one another's presence in the dark cabin.

The kilometre markers – a constant reminder that they were on a federal highway – floated out of the darkness, reflecting the headlights. It was strange to see these flashes of glowing blue light emerge from the night, like a series of spectral apparitions. Each one seemed to approach slowly, then in a flash it was gone, taking its number with it. Four hundred and twenty-three... Four hundred and twenty-four...

4

The days are long in July, and the evening sky feels enormous. It's all that exists. It's easy to ignore the city sprawled out beneath it, strung with chains of barely perceptible street lamps. But the sky... It keeps changing. First it's a curious peach colour, then it glows red and then... it goes out altogether, and the precise outlines of the buildings form a stark contrast against the background of the recently extinguished sky. Charcoal on metal.

People hurry home from work, calling in at the shops before storming the buses. Windows light up, some more invitingly than others.

Turning awkwardly, the trolleybus scatters sparks over the roof of a car. I wonder whether they'll leave scorch marks.

Squire was sitting in the middle of his room on the broken and slightly singed sofa, mending his jeans. Actually he wasn't mending them so much as 'restoring' them by going over the drawings and signatures that had been scrawled all over them a long time ago in red and black marker pens. A *very* long time ago, judging by their sorry state.

The apartment itself merits a detailed description, even if you've been in one like it before. It's a studio apartment sublet from the legal tenant, and it hasn't had any work done on it since... Well, it's probably best not to think about that. The wallpaper is torn and faded and has witnessed a great deal over the years. There's hardly any furniture, just a few items left there by the owners to be 'run into the ground' – an ancient chest of drawers, a couple of shelves (used more for CDs and cassettes than for books), the aforementioned sofa... No TV set. Such a luxury would be completely out of place here.

As is often the case in such apartments, the kitchen is not for the faint-hearted. Well, it's hardly surprising when you've got a gas cylinder and a gas stove competing against one another in a confined space, year after year, and the resulting soot and greasy sediment and methane deposits are cleaned up only rarely and with great reluctance. Wheezing and panting, the decrepit old fridge adds to the atmosphere of filth and neglect.

It might sound like some kind of squalid dump unfit for human habitation, but it's just a typical apartment and it suits Squire down to the ground. Not to mention his numerous friends, all the overnight guests, the passing hitchhikers from all over Russia... Actually, there's one of them here right now.

Our friend Vadim from St Petersburg came out of the bathroom. He was naked from the waist up, and he was drying his long hair carefully with a towel. Long hair isn't really compatible with hitchhiking. You can tie it back to stop it getting too dirty, but even so... You can't wait to wash it whenever you get the opportunity.

"I've washed my socks and hung them in there on the line. Is that alright?"

"Yeah, no problem. They'll be dry by tomorrow."

"Are you redoing the colour?" Vadim nodded at the jeans that Squire was working on. "Have you just washed them?"

"Yeah, right – they'd fall apart if I washed them! I haven't washed them for two years."

"You're kidding. How come?"

"Well, I don't wear them much any more. When I do I try and look after them. So, like, I never wear them out when it's raining, only when the weather's good. And I wear underpants now. When I was younger, seventeen or so, I used to like going commando. But now, I'm an old man!"

They laughed. Vadim had never met Squire before (this was his first time in Ufa), and they had the whole evening ahead of them to fill with conversations and the mutual exchange of stories. It started predictably enough, with Vadim looking through Squire's music collection. The ensuing exchange ("What have you got?", "I haven't heard this album before", and so on) is unlikely to be of much interest to us, so let's leave it there and resume the narrative at the moment the doorbell rang.

"Oh, that's probably Nikita," Vadim exclaimed happily.

"Is that the guy you're travelling with?"

"Yeah. He's always slower than me… I was worried he wouldn't make it to Ufa tonight!"

"It could be anyone, you know…" Squire went to open the door. "It's half nine, still early…"

From the stilted tone of Squire's voice in the hallway, it sounded as though 'anyone' was an unexpected and unwelcome guest. Vadim was instantly on his guard. In theory, anything could happen here – normal rules didn't apply, because a squat wasn't like a home or even a real apartment. Everything has its price, including a free night's accommodation. If you're going to risk your life on the road, you might as well risk your life by dossing down in strange places. Vadim had spent the night with a bunch of drug addicts once. Well, they weren't really drug addicts, just pot-heads, but they'd stayed up all night partying and he hadn't been able to get to sleep. Vadim wasn't really worried now, though. He knew he could stand up for himself.

A police officer entered the room. A regular police officer, and evidently a fairly junior one too. Unlike many others of his age and generation Vadim had no automatic antipathy for the forces of law and order, but he did take an instant dislike to this particular individual. He was short, with badly pock-marked skin, and his grubby, ill-fitting jacket gave him a slovenly look. But what Vadim found most offensive was the fact that the police officer hadn't removed his shoes. Of course, they probably weren't supposed to – after all, they had to be prepared for anything. But still, he and Squire had bare feet!

"Right then, Mikhail... yes? Renting the room from a Mrs Hassanova... yes? Living in Ufa temporarily as a student, originally from Kumertau..."

"From Sibai. Please, take a seat."

Vadim decided that he must be a divisional inspector.

"So, Mikhail... I was here in April, wasn't I? Did I not tell you then that the rent... the renting... the rental arrangements of this apartment are incorrectly formulated?"

"You did. But you need to talk to Mrs Hassanova about that."

"Fine... But what about these complaints from the other tenants?"

"What complaints?"

"Same as last time! Noise, disturbances, non-stop partying... Dodgy types turning up at all hours of the night. I've had four complaints already this summer!"

The inspector stared at Vadim. "He probably thinks I'm going to panic and make a run for it, or try and climb out of the window or something," thought Vadim. He tried to keep a straight face but couldn't help smirking. The inspector took exception to his smirk.

"Can I see your documents, young man?"

"No problem." Vadim bent over his rucksack then turned to Squire. "The traffic cops here are as bad as ours. I've already had my passport checked twice."

"So you're not from round here, then?"

"No."

"St Petersburg!" declared the divisional inspector. "Are you staying for a while?"

"Just passing through."

"Ah, I see. Another freeloader, sponging off other people... There's something wrong with you lot. You're all as bad as one another!"

Vadim shrugged. He wasn't about to argue. The inspector carried on inspecting his passport. St Petersburg passports were quite a novelty! Eventually he put it down with a little sigh. He had no axe to grind with this visitor. The student, on the other hand...

With a triumphant air about him, the divisional inspector produced some forms from his zip-up document wallet. He straightened the crumpled corner of one of them.

"Alright, let's draw up this report. I've had four complaints this summer. Gross infringement of the norms of communal living, committed by an individual living in violation..."

The inspector was having trouble finding the right words. He paused , then appeared to lose his train of thought.

"I'm living in violation?"

"You do not have the correct paperwork relating to your tenancy of this apartment. So we're going to draw up a report in Mrs Hassanova's name. We're going to have to draw up a report in your name too, unless..."

The inspector paused, pen in hand. Squire chuckled, stood up and shuffled into the kitchen. It took Vadim a while to figure out what was going on. He didn't get it even when his host returned carrying a large can of beer, dark and heavy.

The divisional inspector looked from the beer to the report form, to the beer and back to the report form. He wasn't weighing up his social responsibilities, though. Oh, no! It was just that he'd already started filling out the form. Eventually he capitulated, declaring, "Damn, I wrote the wrong date!" He screwed the paper up into a ball and threw it into the corner, as though he lived there. Social responsibilities, indeed.

Before leaving (with the beer under his arm) he seemed to cheer up a bit. He even attempted a few friendly remarks, although they came across as rather patronising.

"So you're from St Petersburg, are you?" he asked. Then he smiled, although neither of the others had said anything. He almost seemed to be talking to the passport, which was lying where he'd left it on the sofa. "So what's going on up there?"

"Nothing special," Vadim answered with a shrug. "Same as always."

"Mmm, I went to St Petersburg once, on a school trip... Or Leningrad, as it was back then. Nice place! Yes, I remember it well... The Hermitage, the Aurora..." His face suddenly changed, becoming sad and pensive. After a pause he added, "You're still young... You can travel... Ekh!"

At the door, he reverted to his stern official look.

"Sort the paperwork out properly with Mrs Hassanova!"

"I will."

Vadim expected Squire to be angry. He can't have been happy about giving away his beer like that! He felt a bit guilty, too. Although the situation with the inspector wasn't directly his fault, it was because of others like him... So Vadim was quite surprised when Squire came back into the room and burst out laughing.

"What a leech! That's the third time he's been round here. Last time I got off with a bottle of vodka, and now... You saw what he was like, didn't you? Looking around to see what he could get his grubby paws on. Typical Tatar!"

"I thought everyone here was Bashkir."

"Yeah, right. As soon as drivers find out I'm from here they always ask, 'So, are you a Bashkir?' There aren't many proper Bashkirs here, you know. It's mostly Tatars. Anyway, who can tell the difference?"

Squire went into the kitchen. Should he put the kettle on? Where was it, anyway?

"Well, that bastard has left us without any booze! I'll have to nip out to the kiosk. It's only a couple of blocks away. Have you got any money?"

"Yeah, of course, but... Well, not much. And I hadn't really planned on spending any of it in Ufa."

"I don't need much! I know the girl who works there. She sells me out-of-date beer for ten roubles a litre. Better than dying of thirst, isn't it?"

"Yeah, of course! Great..."

"Excellent. I'll be able to buy my student record book back too!"

"What do you mean?"

"She's had it for six months. I left it with her as credit for something, I can't remember what... Ha, what am I saying? It must have been beer!"

They both laughed.

"So what's so important that you have to get to E-burg for?" Squire grumbled half-jokingly. "Stay here for a bit! We can go out, have a few drinks... It'll be a laugh."

"I can't, sorry!" Vadim laughed. "We've got loads of online friends there, and they've lined up a whole programme of events for us. I might even meet a girl there..."

As he pulled his customised jeans on, Squire started complaining that he couldn't wear them in the winter, because dirty jeans are no good in cold weather. Why was that? When they were both dressed and putting their trainers on, there was another ring at the door.

"That'll be Nikita. About time!"

"Let's see…" Vadim heard Squire turn the key, then he called from the hallway, "Wrong again! This time it's a beautiful stranger!"

"Are you Squire? Hi, I'm Nastya from Tyumen. Remember? We exchanged emails earlier this week…"

"Oh, yeah. Come in."

Once she was in the apartment Nastya dropped her heavy rucksack to the floor with a thud. Finally! She'd made it to Ufa before nightfall. That in itself was a minor victory, and everyone knows that they lead to major ones.

She had brought with her the smell of the road, or rather, the rank smell of the cabins inhabited by Russian lorry drivers.

5

Nikita Marchenko was twenty years old. When he was ten, half his lifetime ago, he wrote the following entry in his diary: "Today I went shopping with mum and dad. We bought wellies made in 1991."

Yes, Nikita was a bit odd. He was also a straight-A student and came from a family of St Petersburg intellectuals with an illustrious scientific pedigree. Grandfather Marchenko, a physicist and member of the Academy of Sciences, was still mentioned in school textbooks. He had died in the late 1980s, and all that Nikita could vaguely remember was the prickly feel of his beard. His father was also a famous physicist – not as famous as his grandfather, but a professor and Head of the Department of Physics at St Petersburg University, as well as director of the university's scientific projects. The mantle of academia had long since been exchanged for the respectable suit of a state functionary. And so what if it had? He had a good salary, status, an office with a secretary, and even a black Volga to take him to work in the mornings.

In July the Volga would overheat in the sun (being black,

of course – it was physics at work!) A mini-hell on wheels! The sun would beat down mercilessly on the roof, the bonnet and the windows, reflecting off the surfaces like a scuffed and faded version of itself. Professor Marchenko would overheat too, in his official suit, but he could not dress otherwise.

Nikita's mother worked at the same university, although she was only a senior lecturer in philology. She was renowned for her short temper and her long hair, which she wore in a plait. Nikita had never thought of his family as a happy one. It was a long story, but basically since childhood he had been accustomed to living in an atmosphere of... unpleasantness. This wasn't helped by the fact that his father's first wife lived in the same block as them. There was nothing they could do about it – the apartments were owned by the university, and they were all colleagues. He went back to her once and lived a few floors below them for about six weeks, about the same time that Nikita's mother had to go into hospital. If only this first wife had never existed! Even if she hadn't, things still wouldn't have been right. Every morning the black Volga would drop them off at St Petersburg University and they hurried to their respective floors, desperate to escape from one another. It goes without saying that Nikita was a student at the very same institution.

This atmosphere of oppressive formality, the home library, the glances exchanged over dinner, was what Nikita Marchenko, at the age of twenty, was running away from at any available opportunity. He didn't care where he went, he just had to get away. He ran to the highway and beyond, across the vast expanses of his native land.

He was currently jolting along in the cabin of a loaded MAZ truck, nearly two thousand kilometres from his home town of St Petersburg. They were already in Bashkiria, as he had realised when they passed the town of Tuimazy and the village of Serafimovsky. The landscape was increasingly rugged, and quite beautiful. They were driving alongside the enormous Lake Kandry-Kul – in some places overgrown with reeds, in others an impressive sight to behold – and the water seemed to be lapping the edge of the road. It was a warm, sunny evening and there were rows of cars lining the lake, while their passengers enjoyed a swim. How Nikita envied them! After all day on the road he was hot and sweaty and covered in dust... But he couldn't risk losing this ride. If Vadim had been here, he wouldn't have thought twice about it – it was just the sort of thing he would do. Nikita peered at the bathers. Was Vadim there? He couldn't see him.

There were some wind turbines on one of the hills, obviously imported. They were brand new, gleaming white and graceful. Symbols of austerity and power. There was something surreal about the sight of the turbines slowly turning against the backdrop of the sky as evening fell.... It was like a modern version of all those old paintings of Dutch windmills. New Holland... Come to think of it, there was a district by that name in his home city.

The truck was struggling up the hill. Nikita suspected that it might be quicker, and less stressful, if he were to walk. The truck was fully loaded with various food products, stewed meat or something. The driver had told him, but he'd forgotten.

"You might be better off getting another lift," said the driver, reading his mind. He slapped the wheel, as though apologising for his lack of speed.

"No, it's fine. At least I'm guaranteed to make it to Ufa tonight."

"With a bit of luck!"

Several icons had been strung across the windscreen right in front of their faces. They were there to provide protection, the automobile variety. Nikita looked at the faces of the saints and they seemed to be looking back at him, right into his very soul.

Religion had become one of the main issues that divided

the Marchenko household. Their spiritual inclinations were
as follows: Nikita... Did he believe in God? Maybe, but like
most of his peers he didn't really give the matter a great deal of
thought. Nikita's father, like any physicist (any Soviet physicist,
at least), was a materialist and staunchly atheist. Not only that
but he expounded his beliefs with the kind of zeal commonly
exhibited by members of fanatical sects. Nikita's mother, on
the other hand, suddenly became conspicuously devout. She
took to all the rites and rituals like a duck to water, and she was
at home in the suffocating clouds of incense of the little local
church.

Oh, the fights that took place in their house! The 'crusades'
they mounted against one another! There was something almost
sadomasochistic about his parents' fights – they both seemed to
thrive on the energy of discord. For his father it was a kind
of 'holy war' in which he made it his mission to shatter his
opponent's ideals, to destroy her faith. Nikita wouldn't have
been surprised to see smoke coming from his nostrils. As for
his mother, she revelled in the role of martyr, walking through
fire for her faith. At the end of the day, it was essentially a
kind of spiritual exercise for both of them – gymnastics for the
soul, an exchange of passion that made them feel more alive.
They would go to extremes to prove a point, too. During Lent
Nikita's father, who suffered from stomach ulcers, would eat
salty and spicy food just to spite his mother. His mother would
listlessly chew on her porridge, sick of trying to talk him round.

Nikita had a clear memory of his mother coming home for
lunch one dazzling January day, wearing a scarf on her head
and carrying a large chemical retort. Incidentally, the apartment
was full of these retorts even though his father was a physicist,
not a chemist. They used to store pickled vegetables in them.

"Look!" his mother announced triumphantly. "Holy water!
It's Epiphany today, and the priest blessed an ice-hole. I'd been
waiting there since seven o'clock this morning!"

She proceeded to explain reverentially what was so special about the water and how it should be sprinkled in all four corners of the apartment, to banish evil spirits.

At first his father put up with it, but the assertion that holy water would keep forever finally pushed him over the edge.

"It's just river water!" he exploded. "Have you completely lost your mind? You're an educated woman. With a PhD!"

Basically, Epiphany ended with one of their usual arguments. Nikita didn't fully understand his father's fury. Neither did his mother. Displaying admirable self-denial, she refrained from sprinkling the water anywhere in the apartment. Maybe she had decided to keep it for a rainy day. Either way, she felt as though she'd done her duty and the retort was duly stored away in the darkness at the back of one of the kitchen cupboards, between the bottles of oil and vinegar, and everyone forgot all about it.

One fine day, a couple of years later, the apartment filled with Marchenko Senior's joyous cries. God knows why he'd been rummaging in the depths of the kitchen cupboards... Maybe he was after the vodka? It didn't matter anyway, because while he was groping around in there he'd discovered the retort, which he now dragged out and presented to them. There was something floating in it, a kind of gelatinous clot... basically, the holy water had gone mouldy. His moment of triumph had finally come! The inveterate atheist took great delight in celebrating such a resounding victory. The enemy was defeated, once and for all! Drunk on his discovery, the triumphant victor shouted at his wife for such a long time that she developed high blood pressure. And they all lived happily ever after... Yeah, right.

The truck came to a stop with a heavy groan, and Nikita woke up. He pressed the button to illuminate his watch. Shit, it was already late, especially considering that local time in Ufa was an hour ahead of Samara. "Vadim's probably been asleep for ages," he thought. "And I've still got to find the squat!" In the distance he could see a police checkpoint, flooded with orange lights. The gates to the city. He would have to walk a little further to get to the city itself.

"Thanks a lot!" Nikita finally came to his senses and started rummaging about in the darkness, getting his sleeping bag and his rucksack together. "I really appreciate it. Have a good trip!"

"You too. Good luck."

"Hey!"

Nikita turned round. The driver leaned across the cabin to call out of the window, "You've dropped your cap!"

"Oh yeah, thanks!"

His cap lay on the ground next to the wheel. As he bent down to pick it up, Nikita suddenly felt the vibrations of the enormous, intimidating vehicle against his cheek, and it freaked him out. When he'd straightened up and moved away, the truck drove off. The noise of its engine grew fainter, and its red lights receded into the distance... And then they were gone. It was dark and quiet. Nikita was alone on the road and alone in the universe, or so it felt. He stood there for a minute, just listening, and he was overwhelmed with a sudden, primal fear. Brushing this feeling aside, Nikita hurried along the empty road towards the distant checkpoint. He looked rather peculiar, a solitary figure half-running through the darkness with his rucksack and his sleeping bag... If there was a God, he was probably watching him right now.

The policemen weren't interested in Nikita's sudden appearance, and he positioned himself at the roadside beyond the checkpoint, to be closer to people, to the lights. The floodlights at the checkpoint were so bright that the July night was virtually banished from the feeble roadside forest.

A pair of headlights approached. Nikita raised his arm apprehensively. He didn't like hitching at night. All kinds of thoughts would enter his head, scenes from horror movies and the like. It really is quite scary when a car pulls up and you open the door… You never know what's going to happen next.

The inside of the car was dark and smoky.

"City centre? Thirty roubles."

Nikita sighed and took his rucksack off. It wasn't worth spending the night on the road just because paying for a lift was technically against the rules of hitchhiking. It felt strange being so low down after the truck, and as he sat in the passenger seat watching the trees fly past he resolved not to speak to the driver. Well, it served him right! Once he'd made this decision he relaxed and started feeling better. At least he'd made it to Ufa. He was already in the Urals!

Actually, credit where credit's due – the driver gave Nikita detailed instructions to help him find the squat where he was supposed to be spending the night, although it was the middle of the night already. It was 1.00 a.m. local time when he eventually made it to the Khrushchev-era apartment blocks and started searching for the right address. He didn't like wandering about strange cities at night. In Penza, a few nights ago, he'd been approached by a group of local lads who looked like they were in the mood for a fight.

"Which block are you from?" they'd asked him.

Nikita would have been less surprised if they'd asked him which planet he was from.

"Oh, you're not from round here, are you?"

Then they'd left him alone. It was a district of newly constructed apartment blocks and apparently these 'blocks' were their equivalent of courtyard gangs. So nothing had come of it that time, but the Ufa crowds might turn out to be less tolerant. Nikita noticed a group of three lads under a tree. They all seemed to have stopped talking and were looking at him. He increased his pace. The night wind was agitating the leaves on the trees and blowing rubbish about. Large moths flew at the street lamps, colliding audibly with the glass.

When Nikita finally found the right address, his happiness and relief knew no bounds. The stairwell stank, there was dirt everywhere and the cats he'd disturbed narrowed their eyes at him, but still – he was so pleased to be there! He found the right door and hesitated for a second before ringing the bell... What was his name again? Squire? Something like that...

6

A hitchhikers' squat at night is a peculiar place... The people who spend the night here are just passing through, and they never stay for long. Their thoughts are already far away – memories of a hard day on the road, the blazing sun, a succession of stuffy cabins, and tomorrow more of the same, back into battle. You might expect them to take refuge immediately in their sleeping bag cocoons, to make the most of every available hour of sleep. But no, they have to sit and chat! Squats are meeting places for like-minded souls, people who share the same outlook on life, which means they don't mind talking half the night away. At times like this even bitter out-of-date beer can taste like nectar!

They don't drink too much beer, though, maybe just a couple of large cans shared between them, to keep the conversation flowing. It's understandable, really – what with the early start, the long road ahead and the blazing sunshine, a hangover and dehydration are the last things they need. In any case, it's rude to fill someone else's car with stale beer fumes. That's the driver's privilege.

So here we are... It's the middle of the night, the whole city's asleep, and the only sign of life is in Squire's appalling kitchen. The bare light-bulb burns too brightly. As a rule, apartments like this don't tend to be overly well-endowed with lampshades. No curtains either – they've been burnt, soiled and long since discarded. That's the level of comfort on offer in this apartment, where the nights are often full of acrid smoke and guitar music.

All four of our main characters are sitting at the kitchen table, passing round a can of beer. Squire knows exactly how to tilt it to avoid pouring out any foam. A skill honed by years of practice! What are they talking about? If we disregard the conversations about music (I don't want to bore you), essentially what it comes down to is 'travellers' tales'.

Every hitchhiker takes a dozen or so stories from each journey. They're mostly other people's stories – many drivers love to make confessions and often launch into them as soon as their passenger is on board. Or their own stories, happy or unhappy as the case may be. Each tale circulates until it becomes a kind of folklore, and every retelling is interrupted with impatient comments such as, "Well, I...", "Once I..." These 'travellers' tales' are a kind of competition, with everyone keen to have their say. "Well, you won't believe what happened to *me*", "I've got an even funnier story", "I've done that loads of times"... In other words, "I'm better than you".

It's Squire's turn to talk. Squire is an experienced hitchhiker. Squire flicks his hair over his shoulders, to stop it falling in his beer.

"So there I was, stuck in Chebarkulb, of all places. Only 300 km from home and I had an exam the next day. I couldn't even remember what subject... So I was thinking, 'Shit!' It was taking forever. I kept getting all these battered old trucks, which would take me five kilometres, fifteen at most. I was getting sick of it. So in Chebarkulb I wrote UFA on a bit of card in massive letters and stood by the side of the road. I stood there for half an hour, an hour... The long-distance drivers just shrugged, even the Bashkirs. 'Shit, come on!' I was thinking. 'Somebody, just stop!' Suddenly this amazing jeep pulled up. I'd never seen anything like it. Get this, the speedometer was kind of... it was, like, projecting onto the windscreen!"

"Cool!"

"So this bloke got out. He looked at me really carefully

They'd already forgotten about the beer.

The girl looked Nastya up and down in search of obvious injuries.

"Keep walking along the main road until you get to the second bus stop. Then cross the tram ring and follow the fence."

"Thanks a lot!"

"Look at the state of her!" the girl thought about Nastya, amused rather than annoyed as she usually was. "Dressed like a tramp, and not a scrap of make-up on! Who goes out without make-up on these days? There must be something wrong with her…"

She herself was done up as though she were going into battle. Effectively, she was.

Coming out onto the kiosk steps, Nastya panicked, thinking he'd gone… But no, a shadow peeled away from the wall. Vadim was holding a paper napkin to his broken nose.

"There's no point!" He was still weakly protesting against the idea of the emergency clinic. "It's just a broken nose! Feel it yourself if you like, it's not even dislocated."

"Don't be stupid. What if you've got concussion or something? You're going to be out on the road tomorrow. You might die out there… in Systert or some other godforsaken hole."

"Oh, what delights await me!"

He grinned, and Nastya grabbed his hand and started pulling him along behind her. Meanwhile Vadim kept up his protests.

"OK, look, I'm not registered as an Ufa resident, am I? And I left my passport at home… I mean, at Squire's place. My blood's full of alcohol. And anyway, it was a fight! They'll have to report it to the police!'

"Oh, just be quiet!"

There was a pause, then he laughed and said, "You're dragging me along like a little boy!"

"What choice do I have, if little Vadim doesn't want to go

and see the nice doctor? Oh, he can be a stubborn little chap when he wants to be. Look at him, digging his heels in and everything!" Nastya started laughing and Vadim played along, pouting and pulling a face like a toddler having a tantrum. Now they were both laughing, and the tension of the situation was diffused. Vadim didn't put up any more resistance. It was just a shame, the way things had turned out in this damn city! He should have spent the night on the road.

The napkin was wet through and he had blood all over his fingers. The blood had started clotting inside his nose, so he had to do a lot of sniffing and spitting to get rid of it.

"Shit! That was bad luck, wasn't it? Where did those bastards come from anyway?"

"Just a street gang!" Nastya shrugged. "We should've stuck to the main road. You know what city courtyards are like at night... Never a good idea." She paused. "I was attacked, you know, a few months ago, back home in Tyumen. They broke my nose too."

"Really? They attacked a girl?"

"What's the difference? Anyway, they weren't after me, it was my bag they wanted. They came out of nowhere, punched me in the face and ran off. It was one of those drawstring ones, and I'd customised it... You should have seen it! It looked like a general's uniform."

"What do you mean?"

"It was covered with badges and medals. It started when I found a few vintage badges – you know, with revolutionary slogans on, stuff like that – and pinned them on. People noticed, and someone gave me a medal commemorating the Fiftieth Anniversary of Victory Day. It wasn't actually that special, but I pinned it on anyway. And that's how it started. It's amazing how much of that old stuff people have lying around at home. They just kept bringing me more and more! My best friend Luda's grandfather died. He was a really good bloke, you know...

Anyway, she gave me some of his medals and even promised to give me his Soviet order, but... well, there's no point now."

"Hey, I'm sorry you lost it... Maybe I'll have a go at making one like that myself. But why on earth were you wandering about the courtyards on your own at night?"

"I wasn't on my own. That's the whole point. That was the worst of it."

Nastya's mood suddenly changed and she retreated into herself. They continued walking in silence along the empty avenue, which was flooded with toxic orange light from the street lamps. The only sound was Vadim forcefully clearing the blood from his nose. Finally they came to the tram ring, which was empty at 4.00 am, of course... The trams were all at the depot, sleeping companionably side-by-side, just like their passengers. There was a white fence on the other side of the ring. Excellent! They were nearly there. Intending to share this with Nastya, Vadim glanced at her then decided against it. "We might not appear to have anything in common," he thought, "but we're in this together. A boy from St Petersburg and a girl from Siberia."

Tyumen! He'd never been there. Maybe he'd go there one day, maybe he'd make it that far... He tried to imagine the city – grey snow piled up along the sides of the roads in winter, minibus taxis, smoke from the factory chimneys a blurred trail in the frozen air. Rows of identical nine-floor apartment blocks, home to Nastya and her best friend Luda. And Luda's grandfather, once a merry soldier.

There had been hundreds, thousands of men like Luda's grandfather – full of vigour, optimistic, 'thoroughly decent chaps'. Who remembers now the military operations in which Luda's grandfather was wounded and displayed his valour? He and his kind were immortalised affectionately in Soviet literature. Then he became a grandfather, proud and wise, with medals on his jacket and grandchildren on his lap. The same merry soldier. He even had a smile on his face as he lay in his coffin. It was an eerie and pitiful sight.

Then his medals were pinned onto Nastya's bag. She was even more of a hippy then than she was now... For example, like a lot of young people in Tyumen at the time she used to wear a swastika in her left ear. And the first badges to adorn the famous bag were also in the form of Nazi helmets, though over time they were hidden by the Soviet medals.

You don't think I'm criticising her, do you? It's certainly not my place to say, "*O tempora! O mores!*" It's more a case of Turgenev's "eternal reconciliation and life without end".

Suddenly the emergency clinic swam out of the night – a squat breeze-block building, with its very own moon. Seriously! A flat, round lamp hung over the entrance, flickering weakly and casting as much despondency as the real moon. It was a lonely beacon in the night, attracting only big grey moths and other unpleasant nocturnal insects.

"Looks like there's a light on in those two windows," said Vadim after a pause. They'd been looking at the building for a long time. "Huh! I thought there was no one there at first."

"I thought it looked like a morgue."

"You're right, you know. That's exactly what it looks like."

They approached the building. The surrounding area looked serene.

"Ufa must be a fairly calm place!" said Vadim, with a dry laugh. "I thought they'd be queuing round the block..."

"Hey, don't speak too soon! Maybe they're all inside."

Vadim cleared the blood from his throat.

But it was just as quiet and empty inside. The only sign of life was a nurse in a dirty robe sitting behind a desk at the end of the corridor. She glanced up as they came in and continued speaking in a bored monotone into the telephone receiver that was clamped to her ear.

"Just stop it, Gleb. You're crazy. Gleb, you're behaving

like a child. I've told you over and over again, and you never listen, do you? Gleb!"

Because she was frequently ill as a child, or maybe because she had overprotective parents, Nastya had spent a lot of time inside Soviet medical institutions. As a result, she had come to hate them with a passion. And here she was again! The cheap linoleum floor stained with various bodily fluids, bloodstains on the deathly pale fabric of the bench... But the main thing was the smell, that sickly smell of disinfectant. It was unbearable.

"I'll wait for you outside, OK?"

The nurse looked pointedly over at the door of the doctor on duty, indicating that Vadim should go straight in. Honestly! She couldn't be expected to drop everything to attend to every long-haired hippy that came wandering in with a black eye... Not when she was in the middle of an emotional crisis.

Nastya came out onto the steps and spotted a bench. On closer inspection it was spattered with blood, as though it had come from a torture chamber. She had to sit on the back of it and hunch over, with her feet on the seat. So, what was going on? It had been a particularly bad night, and now there was no chance of getting a decent sleep because she'd have to get up early if she wanted to make it to Nizhny before the following night.

It was that dead hour just before dawn, when you can walk the streets without meeting another living soul and roam the darkest courtyards at your leisure, safe in the knowledge that all the local thugs are tucked up in bed, dribbling onto their pillows and dreaming their innocent dreams.

There was an apartment block behind the emergency clinic, one of those enormous breeze-block monsters built in the late Soviet period. There wasn't a single light at any of its numerous windows. Surely someone somewhere was awake... No. The entire building was devoid of life.

What was she doing here, alone in this strange, hostile

city? She was always alone, always running, running away from herself.

Nastya sat on the bench and cried bitter tears. She felt utterly alone in the universe.

9
Vadim's Story

I started listening to 'alternative' music when I was fourteen. I started with the easier stuff – Mumiy Troll, Spleen, Zhanna Aguzarova's later stuff, Zemfira's early stuff. I can remember my mum listening to a couple of songs and saying, "It's awful! You can't make head or tail of it. What a load of nonsense!"

I was deeply offended, even though I didn't understand the words any better than she did. But I didn't need to understand them! I just knew that those meaningless words expressed a certain view of life. You didn't really need words at all. Why not just sing a rhythmic collection of sounds? Or sing in Latin, or something... Why not? I couldn't believe that nobody else had thought of it. I was a musical genius!

When I was fourteen, or rather, the day before my fourteenth birthday, we went out to the country. It was a beautiful sunny evening. You could hear the sound of an electric saw humming. I picked a daisy and started pulling the petals off one by one, trying to work out whether or not I would fall in love at fourteen. I remember picking another daisy and doing it again, because I really wanted the answer to be yes. Why? I wish I knew. My head was so full of nonsense back then.

I think it's a cultural thing. I mean, just look at the kind of popular culture kids are exposed to these days: 70% of books and 90% of films are about love. Every single pop song is about love, as are most rock songs, and I somehow knew that all the 'nonsense' I was listening to was about love too.

I had such a romantic idea of love when I was fourteen!

Now I'm twenty, and I'm standing under a street lamp in a strange city kissing an amazing girl called Nastya. We're kissing cautiously, because we've just been to the emrgency clinic about my nose. It's not broken or anything, but it's still pretty sore. We even had to go to a kiosk and buy an ice cream in a plastic wrapper for me to hold against it. So now we're taking our time, kissing carefully, and our tongues are made for each other.

I didn't have a clue about kissing when I was sixteen or so. My first kiss wasn't a particularly pleasant experience. I was acutely aware of my sudden proximity to a gaping void, an alien vacuum… then my teeth caught against hers. It was a girl from my class, a straight-A student. She had curly hair and there was something vaguely ethereal about her, and I was head over heels in love with her.

I used to wait for her after school. I kept calling her and telling her how I felt about her. I wrote "Good morning, my love" outside her apartment – or rather, I tried to. Now, of course, I understand why we could never be together. I was a gawky teenager suffering from acne, and I had a stammer too – basically, not much of a catch. Anyway, I managed to gather a few crumbs of happiness from the experience, so I can't really complain.

One good thing to come out of it was that I suddenly understood all that 'nonsense' I'd been listening to! Whereas before I had just liked the sound of Zemfira's voice, now the lyrics, apparently the same nonsense, made perfect sense. It was quite a shock to realise that every single word was about me, that every word perfectly articulated the way I was feeling. It wasn't like Latin at all.

When I look at Nastya – I can't believe I'm actually kissing her! – my head is full of song lyrics, the kind of nonsense that now makes sense. But the real paradox is that when you're in love you're the one who doesn't make any sense. Your thoughts are all mixed up. Only someone else who feels the way you do can understand the rubbish you're coming out with, and that's basically the point of all that 'nonsense', the way it all works. Simple, really!

I understand it, and she seems to understand too. At least she's thinking along similar lines... She seems to be talking about her ex-boyfriend now, why they split up, all that stuff, but I'm not even listening. It's a good thing I'm not jealous of the past. After all, she didn't know she was going to meet me! But still, I'm curious to know how many boyfriends she's had. Not many, by the sound of it.

I've been with a couple of women – girls, technically, I suppose – but it didn't mean anything. It was just sex. When we were students it was something you went along with, something you did because everyone else was doing it. Someone's nicely furnished apartment, expensive vodka poured into a set of matching shot glasses... all very contrived. There might not have been enough snacks to chase the vodka with, but there were always plenty of candles casting shadows that flickered on the walls and made me feel uncomfortable.

When everyone started to pair off and head towards the beds and sofas, not having sex would have been like an insult to the others. I remember one time... It would have been rude to move away afterwards, so I had to go to sleep with my arm around her and my face pressed against her back. It was July and the nights were unbearably hot and humid, and I spent the whole night covered in sweat.

No fun at all, but it was a long time ago. And more than two thousand kilometres away.

Nastya's walking along beside me in the semi-darkness. The street lamp we're walking past isn't working, so I can see her features clearly outlined in silhouette, like a classical sculpture. Her slightly aquiline nose... Her forehead... Her cropped hair...

She lights a cigarette. I admire her profile with the tiny glowing ember.

"D'you want one?"

I don't really smoke but I have the odd cigarette now and then, if I'm drinking. Or if I'm in a really bad mood. Right now I feel capable of rising up above the tarmac and soaring through the sky. At least I'm experienced enough to take a drag without properly inhaling, so that I don't start coughing.

We walk and smoke in silence. The city is completely silent. I'm starting to feel a bit rough from the beer, but it's no big deal – I'm just a bit dehydrated. My mouth feels sticky and I can taste my own teeth. The cigarette is adding an aftertaste of prunes... Sorry! That's more than you need to know about the state of my oral cavity.

I kiss her again. She presses herself into me. She runs the fingers of her free hand through my hair, and it feels amazing.

"So what's the distance between St Petersburg and Tyumen, exactly?"

Of course the atlas is in my rucksack, and my rucksack is back at Squire's squat; I roll my eyes, trying to work it out. I call to mind an image of the Russian Federation.

"About three thousand kilometres. Maybe a bit less."

"That's a long way," she sighs.

"Tell me about it!"

"And think of all the people in between – millions of them! It's amazing when you think about it, we might never have met."

Instead of answering I just hold her more tightly.

"You know," says Nastya, suddenly pulling away from me. "One of my friends married a German guy two years ago. Seriously! She moved to Germany. I can't remember which city. She writes to me quite often. She misses it here... The German guy came to Tyumen specially to meet her!"

"Bit weird, was he?"

"Why do you say that?" Nastya is offended. "There was

nothing wrong with him. He was about eight years older than her, but basically just a normal bloke. He was a bit bald, though… Actually, I've noticed on TV too, German men always lose their hair early. Why is that? Is it because of the radiation, or something?"

"Maybe it's their hormones."

"German hormones? Don't make me laugh! Anyway, when this guy showed up he was beside himself with excitement. 'Siberia! Siberia!' he kept saying. I'm surprised he didn't bring a fur coat with him! It was summer, and due to the hole in the ozone layer over Siberia it was about thirty-five degrees. Probably not quite what he was expecting…"

I suddenly become aware that I'm smiling indulgently and quickly straighten my face before Nastya notices. Tyumen was pretty remote, and it must have been the first foreigner they'd ever seen. An understandable reaction!

The ice cream that I'm holding to my face has almost melted and is sloshing around inside its wrapper. Tracing an arc, it falls to the tarmac and lands wetly, like a frog. It occurs to me belatedly (as usual) to offer it to Nastya.

"Don't worry about it. I don't eat sweet stuff."

Just like me. We're very similar. I keep thinking that. Both inside and out. You can't really see it right now in the pale light of the street lamps, but the right-hand side of her face is tanned from standing on the side of the road. The unmistakable hallmark of a hitchhiker.

Nastya lights another cigarette. She smokes too much.

A car drives past us on the avenue. It might be the first one we've seen the whole time we've been walking. The wide avenue is generously illuminated by the street lamps and completely empty. It would be a good place to come rollerblading in the middle of the night, or early in the morning. This vast expanse of smooth tarmac, completely deserted, the wind whistling in your ears and not a care in the world.

"Wait... Let's just stand here for a bit."

"Why?"

"Just because."

I stopped obediently, although at first I didn't understand why. Then I realised. It was so that this magical night would last as long as possible.

We put our arms around one another and kissed. Nastya buried herself into my embrace, her whole body shivering, and I warmed her up. With her face muffled in my arms, she still managed to cover me with frenzied kisses – my neck, my chest (through my T-shirt), my shoulders. When her lips touched my arm above the elbow, I remembered the conversation over the table at Squire's place (just a few hours ago, but it seemed like a hundred years!) and tensed my bicep slightly. She kissed it.

"I thought I wasn't your type! I don't have 'wings'..."

She burst out laughing and bit my arm.

"That's not true. I was just being stupid. You do have wings... The best kind."

The city sky above us was as full of stars as a city sky can be. My head was full of song lyrics, all jumbled and chaotic... I was happy. I'd found my happiness here, in this strange and distant city. So my journey hadn't been in vain, after all. After all that travelling, I'd finally found it.

10

Just before sunrise everything in the city faded to grey and seemed to swell up and fill with shadows. Even Squire's apartment was full of transparent silhouettes and unreliable outlines. Everything seemed exactly as they'd left it a few hours ago. They tiptoed straight into the kitchen, so as not to wake the others.

Nastya poured herself a glass of cool water from the kettle. She was dying of thirst. It was the dregs from the very bottom, and lime-scale deposits swirled thickly in the glass. She would have been able to see them if it hadn't been so dark.

Vadim went over to the window.

The street lamps were waning against the sky, which had started to grow pale. There were no lights on in any of the windows. It was just after 5.00 a.m.: the deadest hour. When it grew a little lighter, the birds would all start singing simultaneously and then it would seem strange that anyone could sleep through such a racket. But this moment was yet to come. For now, silence reigned and the only movement was the swaying of the trees in the grey half-light before dawn.

"It's so strange..." began Vadim, clearly unable to get over the way fate had brought them together. "Meeting you here, in this random city... In the Urals, in Asia..."

"Actually, we're not in Asia," laughed Nastya. "Ufa's still in Europe, but tomorrow – today, I mean! – on the way to Chelyabinsk, about two hundred and fifty kilometres from here, you'll pass a funny monument. It's like a massive slab of stone, saying Europe on one side and Asia on the other. It's so weird! Wait till you see it. It's really off the beaten track. The Ural Mountains... The road twists and turns like a snake – it's all rocks and ravines, and you won't come across another living soul. The enormous electricity pylons are the only sign of civilisation. And then all of a sudden, out of the blue, you're at the border between two continents! It's like something out of a sci-fi film."

Vadim stood at the window, crushed and helpless. He was barely listening to her inspired speech. It wasn't her description of the Urals that had this effect on him.... "You'll go past," she'd said. "You," not "we".

"So you're saying that tomorrow – today! – we're going to go our separate ways?"

This was followed by an awkward silence, during which Vadim couldn't bring himself to turn away from the window and Nastya couldn't work out what to say.

"Well… you're travelling from St Petersburg to E-burg, right? And I'm travelling from Tyumen to Moscow. Neither of us is going to change our plans. We're each going to stick to our own path. It'll be better that way. Trust me."

"But why?" He turned to her, distraught. "Why does it have to be like that? I'll change my plans for you, if you want me to! I'd be happy to turn around and go to Moscow with you. I don't care where I go…"

"But what about your friend?"

"What about him? He can go to E-burg by himself."

They fell silent. Desperate to find a solution, Vadim found himself clutching at straws.

"Or we could stay in Ufa together! Why not? It'll be like, I don't know, a kind of impromptu honeymoon! When we got here yesterday evening, we didn't know any of this was going to happen… Then we found each other."

"And you got your nose broken."

"Well, at least you're wrong about that!"

A forced smile. They can still bring themselves to joke about it! The human spirit is truly remarkable.

"The thing is…" Nastya's voice suddenly sounded extremely tired and hoarse, from all the cigarettes. "I split up with someone recently, you know. Someone who meant a lot to me. I thought I meant something to him too, but he turned out to be a total bastard. It's… I don't really know how to explain it, but it's like everything inside me is scorched and barren. I felt as though I had nothing to live for! I tried to slit my wrists and cried for months. I can't go through that again. Getting involved in another complicated relationship right now would be like throwing myself back into the fire! I simply don't have the strength to fall in love again. Can you understand that?"

Vadim didn't know whether he understood or not. He didn't really have a clue what was going on. Since yesterday evening nothing had made any sense.

"See, you say that you'll go with me to Moscow…" Nastya suddenly became animated, her words tumbling out erratically, emotionally. Her cheeks may well have been flushed; it was impossible to tell, because it was still quite dark. "I don't care about Moscow! I just want to go somewhere, anywhere! It doesn't matter, as long as it's away from home, as far as possible from everyone I know! I need new places, and I need to keep moving… The main thing is not to get attached to anyone. I know I'll meet people along the way, and that's fine – I just don't want them to stick around! I need to be alone. It's my way of healing my broken heart. And I can only be truly alone when I'm out on the road. Drivers don't count – they pick you up, they drop you off, and you never see one another again. But I don't want anyone else trying to get to know me, asking me who I am or where I'm going. Freedom and solitude – yes, that's what I need right now. Nothing else."

Vadim didn't respond. He rested his head on his arms, and to anyone else it might have looked as though he were sleeping. Nastya had nothing more to say either, so the dawn broke that day in complete silence.

Finally there were movements in the living room and Nikita shuffled into the kitchen. Still half asleep, he stood and stared at them in the weak morning light.

"What the hell are you two doing? Are you out of your minds?" He scanned the kitchen for a clock, but there wasn't one. There never had been. "I can't believe you're still boozing. We have to be on the road in a couple of hours!"

His disapproval was obvious from the way he pronounced "boozing". He was right, none of them should have been drinking in the first place. They were all dehydrated. Nikita turned the tap on and bent his head down to it. The pipe made a loud noise and started shuddering as though it were about to explode. He had to turn it off quickly so as not to wake up the entire block.

"Yeah, you're right," declared Nastya. "We probably ought

They used to congregate at Squire's place, and now he'd been conscripted they would have time on their hands and plenty to think about during the long winter evenings. Or maybe they'd just find somewhere else to hang out.

In fact, Squire's friends did have something to occupy them right now, besides wandering aimlessly around the town. They had come up with a plan to sell Squire's hair. Now, I should probably explain... As we all know, Squire would have his head shaved as part of the army enlistment procedure. In other words, this precious asset that he had been cultivating for over three years would be destroyed by an electric razor in a matter of seconds. They couldn't allow it! So they decided to cut his hair themselves and sell it to the highest bidder, so that it wouldn't "fall into enemy hands". They had to salvage something from the situation.

There were plenty of buyers in the city. Squire's friends dragged him round, gathering contacts and haggling.

They stopped by a lamp-post to investigate yet another flyer proclaiming 'We Buy Hair!' This was followed by the dubious but even more familiar assertion: 'Best Prices Paid!' The wind had picked up, causing the edges of the advert to flutter. Squire seemed to be the only one not showing an interest in any of it. His attitude was one of complete indifference, while his friends crowded around the advert, arguing, calculating, showing off their business skills – how their teachers would love to see them now!

"Shit! Is that how much they're paying these days?"

"Read what it says next... They'll only pay that if the hair's thirty centimetres or longer."

"Damn! His isn't that long yet."

And it never would be.

The situation was complicated by the fact that hair shorter than thirty centimetres was accepted by weight, and weighing this particular asset while it was still attached to Squire's head was clearly going to be a challenge. There were a number of other issues to contend with, as well – for example, almost a third of Squire's hair would have to be combed out because it was of inferior quality. The whole business was enough to make your (unshorn) head spin, and the owner of the relevant 'commodity' was the only one who simply didn't care enough to try and understand it. He just listened to his friends when they specified the days he ought to wash his hair, because a certain amount of grease would make it heavier.

This ridiculous aspect of his enlistment was probably what Squire found most alarming. The longer they spent hanging about by the advert, the more he began to wish that they would hurry up and cut his hair off so that everyone could finally stop going on about it. This thought was enough to induce a wave of panic – he'd been growing it for so long! Oh, but what did it matter now? He himself had been growing for even longer, and look how he was ending up.

Meanwhile it was decided unanimously that they would call the number on the flyer. The number was duly copied down onto the palm of someone's cold, dry hand, and they set off in search of a phone booth. None of them had a phone card, so they decided to try and borrow one from someone once they'd found a phone.

In the event, they didn't have to try too hard. They approached a booth they'd spotted, which was making a soft, metallic noise in the wind and the snow. Just at that moment a pretty girl stepped away from it, wrapped up against the cold, and she kindly lent them her card. This group of strapping lads in leather biker jackets must have made quite an impression on her. They reacted with a great show of enthusiasm – with the possible exception of Squire, who suddenly felt like a 'non-person'. Why was this happening to him? Why?

Was there any point trying to understand it? Was there any point tormenting himself by thinking about his future and what it would be like? No. There was no point to any of it. He'd messed things up, and now it was all over.

The flat that he'd been subletting had already been returned to its legal owner, Mrs Hassanova, a corpulent, taciturn old woman whose clothes were always covered in the husks of sunflower seeds. On Sunday, his last night of freedom, Squire collected his old posters, his cassettes, the material trappings of his former life, and took them out to the rubbish tip. New tenants would be moving in and redecorating soon – they wouldn't want his old junk lying around. Squire thought of the confused stares that would greet countless young hitchhikers from all over Russia, who would mutter their apologies before crossing this address from their notebooks.

Towards evening the temperature dropped, and the chill in the air officially became a frost. The park was partially illuminated by the few street lamps that remained intact. Although the paths were empty there was every chance that they might run into one of the street gangs, so perhaps they should have chosen a different route... Never mind! Squire and his friends walked through the park, chatting quietly, the hair had been cut off and sold. Are you wondering what Squire looks like without his hair? Well, I can't tell you, because he's wearing a woolly hat. And he's walking in silence.

His friends continued their half-hearted conversation – discussing how much money they'd made, how much they could have made, how much had been combed out, how much it weighed, and so on. But none of it mattered any more – the deed had been done, and the bottles were clinking in their bag.

They sat down on a bench under a street lamp. This place was just as good as any other.

Squire produced the first bottle of vodka. It was a good one, too – none of that lethal fake rubbish from the workers' districts.

Their disposable plastic glasses crunched like the snow.

"So, what are we drinking to?" His friends were determined to remain optimistic. "Let's drink to things working out OK for you!"

They didn't clink their glasses, but this was purely out of practical considerations – when the air is so cold sometimes all it takes is an awkward touch, a tremble of the fingers, for the plastic to shatter in your hand.

If you have to drink vodka outside in subzero temperatures you might as well not bother, because it doesn't have the slightest effect. It doesn't get you drunk. You can't even feel it! But they had to drink, and that was what they were doing day after day in the run-up to Squire's departure – an inevitable and compulsory ritual.

Squire heard the jackdaws squawking aggressively and looked out at the darkened park, at the illuminated façade of the House of Culture... The street lamps lining the main road disappeared into the distance, and the factory chimney was adorned with red clearance lights.

Squire cried in his sleep.

12

The alarm went off at 7.00 a.m. and Squire hit it with a groan. At 7.10 a.m. the plumbing system broke into a cheerful grumble as Nikita began his morning ablutions.

Maintaining your oral hygiene can be quite a challenge when you're on the road. Most hitchhikers tend to solve the problem with chewing gum: minty fresh breath in seconds! But that wasn't our Nikita's style... Even if he woke up in a forest somewhere, chilled to the bone, after a good stretch he would ceremoniously extract his toothbrush and squat down by a ditch. As for rinsing his mouth out, well, why do you think he carried a bottle of mineral water? It had the added benefit of preventing terminal dehydration on a hot day on the road.

While we're on the subject, Nikita's washing accoutrements really were something to behold. Particularly in contrast to Squire's filthy bathroom, with its grimy surfaces, stray hairs everywhere, and the cracked toilet seat. Nikita Marchenko always carried a plastic wash bag containing his shaving equipment, his deodorant, a travel toothbrush in its own little protective case, a bar of soap and a barely dented tube of toothpaste. He even had a pair of nail scissors. Good for him! A snagged nail is enough to ruin a holiday.

Nikita belonged to the glorious generation of hitchhikers from good families, with smart clothes and plenty of pocket money. Their life's path was already determined, and there were no potholes to navigate – just a nice, easy ride.

These boys took to the road, to the anguish and dismay of their doting parents – when they knew about it, of course. You should read Nekrasov's *Russian Women*, about Princess Trubetskaya who followed her husband into the depths of the Siberian wilderness – it's exactly the same impulse.

At 7.15 a.m. Nikita was still brushing his teeth. He knew that he was going to be successful, to get on in life. He knew that it was worth preserving a perfect, white smile, because it could be a valuable asset in years to come.

At 7.20 a.m. all four of them finally sat down at the table for a breakfast of boiled pasta without salt or butter, or any particular enthusiasm on their part. They couldn't tell whether it was tasteless because Squire had overcooked it or because it was cheap pasta. Either way, they had to eat it. They needed the energy.

"I don't suppose you've got any ketchup, have you?" asked Vadim, who was having trouble swallowing.

"I'm not sure... Have a look in the fridge. Maybe someone left some."

They continued their breakfast in complete silence, lost in their own thoughts. They all felt apprehensive about heading out to the highway. In their minds they were already out there, on the road, so they didn't feel much like talking. Or eating, for that matter.

At 7.30 a.m. they began making their final preparations, rummaging around in their rucksacks and tightening the straps on their sleeping bags. Then just one tradition remained. Nikita went up to Squire.

"Have you got a bit of paper? We'll leave you our addresses in St Petersburg."

"Just write them on the wallpaper over there in the corner – see?"

Nikita went over to the corner and saw pictures of naked girls mixed up with scrawled addresses, names of cities and so on. He carefully wrote out his address. He always carried a pen with him.

"Vadim, shall I write down your address?"

Vadim nodded and Nikita wrote it on the wall. Then he looked at Nastya and raised his eyebrows questioningly, but Nastya shook her head. He shrugged. Fair enough.

Meanwhile the city was bathed in bright yellow sunlight, and a new day had begun. The buses were full of people. Drivers squinted, giving themselves extra wrinkles, as the low sun shone right into their eyes. They searched for their sunglasses and put them on. A man drove briskly past on a tractor. An old man set out for a walk, carrying a stool. Scenes from an ordinary morning in a big city.

A stout gentleman comes out of a building. Before getting into his posh car, he looks around furtively and leaves a bag full of rubbish by the front door. At that moment a window bangs open and an old woman sticks her head out. This is precisely what she'd been waiting for! She's not going to stand for it.

"Young man! Who's going to tidy that up?"

"You are," he replies, as he walks towards his car.

"The bins are over there!"

"Thanks for letting me know," he retorts, and then he gets into his car and drives off.

These days, squabbles on public transport are a thing of the past. Oh, how sparks used to fly! There was always such a crush, people pushing and shoving... that was communism for you! They have been replaced by a new phenomenon – GAZelles.

GAZelles essentially operate as shared minibus taxis, following set routes, but they're so much more than that! They're a kind of subculture, and they follow their own rules – crossing abruptly from the third lane straight into the first, sudden starts, 'emergency' stops and so on. Their drivers' psychology is different too – they need the money! You must have witnessed it. For example, when a GAZelle minibus approaches a bus stop it watches for the slightest movement to indicate that anyone wants to get on. So the potential passengers sit there waiting, trembling nervously and watching one another's reactions. All it takes is the twitch of an eye and the GAZelle screeches to a halt. Another example... A lilac GAZelle approaches a stop, and a boy who wants a good seat runs alongside it, grabs the door handle and leads the minibus to a complete stop, like the boy holding the reins in Petrov-Vodkin's *Bathing of a Red Horse*.

No, you can say what you like, but in the city GAZelles are a way of life.

Another peculiarity of GAZelles is that they all have three or four rear-facing seats at the front, just behind the driver's seat. If you end up sitting in one of these seats you have to put up with everyone else staring at you, and there's nothing you can do about it! You look pointedly out of the window, deliberately ignoring the boy over there who's devouring you with his eyes. That's if you're a girl, of course...

That's where Nastya was sitting, right in the firing line. The minibus was virtually empty, so it wasn't too bad, but the other passengers were staring straight at her. They were probably trying to work her out... What does she look like? Why isn't she wearing any make-up? She's dressed like a tramp... And why's she got that huge rucksack with her?

Nastya couldn't have cared less! Let them look. She was used to it. People were always staring at her as if they were in a zoo. She concentrated on looking out of the window, though the minibus was going so fast she could barely make out the view. It was heading to the Zaton district. Squire had written directions on a piece of paper for the police checkpoint in Zaton, which was the starting point for the M7, the Volga highway.

Nastya had already checked their progress with the driver a couple of times. Unusually for a hitchhiker, Nastya had absolutely no sense of direction. She found it impossible to get her bearings in the city. But they weren't in the city any more! They were driving past trees and forests.

The GAZelle took a turning and pulled up at the side of the road, raising a cloud of dust.

"The checkpoint's that way," said the driver, indicating with his hand. "Keep walking for about three hundred metres and you can't miss it."

"Thanks!" Nastya held out her fare. The coins had warmed up in her hand.

"Don't worry about it," winked the driver. "Hitchhikers travel for free!"

Nastya thanked him sincerely. She jumped down from the step and set off, without a backwards glance at the other passengers, who were all watching her through the windows... Their curiosity had tripled.

It was nothing, really. Literally six roubles. But still, it was a nice feeling.

She walked along the roadside verge feeling cheerful, energetic and almost happy.

Meanwhile the boys were heading out onto the Ural highway, and their mood was very different. Squire had helpfully written down all the minibus taxi routes for them too, and as they travelled across the city Nikita tried to lift his friend's spirits. Gazing out of the window at the city outskirts, he sighed and said, "We didn't get to see much of Ufa, did we?"

Vadim nodded limply, but his thoughts were elsewhere.

So it was in silence, wearily and reluctantly, that they came out onto the highway, to the same spot where they'd been dropped off the previous day. They ambled across the wide intersection, two tiny figures laden with rucksacks.

The highway was virtually deserted. Just as they reached the verge, a lorry rumbled past at high speed, its canvas covering flapping enthusiastically on both sides.

"It's from Chelyabinsk, that one." Nikita nodded at the disappearing truck and added good-naturedly, "Bastard... He could have stopped!"

"Seventy-four... is that Chelyabinsk?" asked Vadim, perking up a little. "I ought to remember that... What's Sverdlovsk?"

"Sixty-six."

They walked a little further until they reached a reasonably straight stretch of road, then they stopped. It was time to split up.

This is probably the hardest thing about travelling as a group, when one says, "OK, I'll stay here," and the others say, "See you later." Gradually the group gets smaller and smaller, until each of them is standing alone by the side of the road. I seem to remember a fairy tale like that, where all the characters say goodbye and disappear, one by one. Can't remember what it's called, though.

One of them had to go first. Nikita wanted to make sure it was fair.

"Go on, you go. It's your turn."

"I couldn't possibly! Not with your track record... If I get a head start as well, you'll never catch up with me! It's best if you go first. Go on!"

"Let's hope we both make it to E-burg tonight!"

They shook hands and Vadim walked away – to be honest, with a sigh of relief. Nikita was a great guy and didn't ask too many questions, but right now he needed to be alone.

Vadim stopped about two hundred metres further along the road and looked back. He could still see Nikita, and the city in the distance. He could see them clearly because he was standing with his back to the sunrise – they were travelling east. There weren't many cars.

Half an hour later Nikita finally got a lift – a young couple in a Moskvich, as far as he could tell. Nikita managed to wave apologetically through the window as they drove past. And then Vadim was alone.

I'm going to let you into a little secret. Vadim never turned down the chance to go last, and not simply out of comradeship. He had come to look forward to the overwhelming sense of melancholy that envelops you when the door slams, your friend drives off and you suddenly realise that you're alone on the bleak and endless highway. The realisation is always sudden and strong enough to take your breath away. The sense of solitude is striking, almost palpable, and infinitely more intense than the loneliness you feel in the city.

Maybe this is what it all came down to. Maybe this feeling – this vivid, exhilarating feeling – was the reason Vadim liked hitchhiking so much.

Many words and expressions used by Russian hitchhikers have been borrowed from English, but the roads, the solitude and the melancholy are quintessentially Russian.

Translated by Amanda Love Darragh

Irina Bogatyreva

OFF THE BEATEN TRACK

We are footloose and fancy-free wayfarers on roads without end, friends of long-distance truckers and drivers, their amulets, talismans, their guardian angels. Even the cops leave us alone. They know us for who we are and where we are going. We may not know that ourselves, may laugh and gesture into the sun, but the cops know. They swear, shrug, hand back our ID, and send us on our way. There is no stopping us, but why that should be they don't know.

We are legion, dots scattered along the road, romantic followers of our guru Jack Kerouac, members of the same mendicant order, and the motto on our crest could read, *In via veritas* or, more simply, "The Road Is Always Right". Our destinations differ and the routes we take, but we are as one in our sense that only here, on the road, are we truly free.

We are twenty years old, give or take, do not yet have a past, do not look to the future, and in the present have only the road ahead, the asphalt, and the jubilant knowledge that everybody else has lost track of us.

We set out only recently. Soon we'll be everywhere. We are on a high and embrace our road, anticipating its gifts, not knowing where it will lead us.

And you, capricious road, now smiling, now incensed, how are we to detect the moment when your mood changes? You are life, and destiny, the unique instance of all possible combinations. Right here, right now, with this person, and we know no alternative.

Africa / (Rastafari)

We get out and set off along the soft verge of the Moscow outer ring road at pedestrian speed. The nearest turning for the city is three kilometres away, and it would be good to know the area, friend, the area we are in now. It is good to know where you are, and especially like now at night, in the rain, walking along the verge of the ring road, the verge of the whole of Moscow.

The rain sheets down and we feel underwater, walking on the seabed. The ring road hurtles past, headlights probing the darkness, teeth clenched against the speed, and all it can see is night and rain and red lights. Water shatters against blunt windscreens, foams beneath wheels leaving white silhouettes on the asphalt. A car passes and the silhouette holds for a moment before white foam drains to the verge and us.

"Tolya, the speed limit here is a hundred kilometres an hour. Do you hear? They simply can't see you!" I have turned to look back and shout into the darkness. The silhouette of Tolya, pissed as a newt, is shimmering back there behind the wall of rain, his arm outstretched to thumb a lift. "Forget it! Come on!" I urge again.

We are tree stumps, milestones on this godforsaken highway, our speed is nothing compared to theirs. They can't see us, friend, can't see these three wet stumps with rucksacks. We have nothing even to reflect their light, and still have so far to go before we will be home.

"What's the hurry, you bastards?" Tolya's drunken larynx shreds the night air. "Stop, you maniacs!" Night is shredded into shriek. I glance at Roma. He is cool, plodding along with just the hint of a smile, his lips repeating his song. "Titch, just mind he doesn't fall over," he counsels.

Titch is me. It's what they call me, not on account of my height or size but just because I'm younger than the rest of them. I turn to look at Tolya. He seems to be walking okay, lurching, of course, staring at the ground, his rucksack not straight, but at least he's walking, laughing about something, even apparently talking to someone.

The night rushes by, the ring road rushes by, with us as its milestones. Something clicks in me, as sometimes happens, and suddenly I am seeing everything at once, not from inside myself but from above, as if from a bridge or a cloud: three figures walking: Titch (me), Roma Jah, and Tolya, artist and poet, but right now just a straggling drunken pal. The ring road is a Ferris wheel illuminated by coloured lights. The cold is making a thousand and one bunches of hair stand on end on Titch's (my) head. Leftover brown greasepaint is streaking Tolya's shaven head making him look like specialforces out on a jungle mission. Roma, our ginger-dreadlocked Roma Jah, is now so wet and thin, so cool and pitiable, that he looks like Jesus Christ. A Rastaman Jesus with scrawny dreads sticking to his face, he bears his rucksack full of tom-toms, and the smell of ganja hangs in the wet air behind him. Roma always smells of ganja. That's why he is called Roma Jah.

"Are you coming?" I turn round to yell at Tolya, but collide with him and his smell, a smell of cadged rum and expensive brandy recently downed. You are truly bladdered, friend, and now not even the cold May rain can clear your brain.

"No need to shout," Tolya says quietly. Even in the midst of all that noise and water you can speak quietly and be heard if you are nose to nose. "Move on!"

He takes a step in my direction and I jump back and move along. I hear him shouting, "Roma! Hey, Roma! Did that song even have an ending? You know, the one we were thumping out for the last hour back there?" Roma smiles and plods on. "Come on, Roma, say something, will you? How did it go? 'Rastafari...'? Roma!" Tolya tries to remember the words and gets them wrong, bawling away behind our rucksacks.

"Will they get wet?" I ask Roma, nodding at our packs.

All the African drums we have are in there: a djembe, tom-toms, a large kpanlogo. They have thick mahogany bodies and white leather drumheads and look like casks, wooden stools or the tables of an outdoor café. They smell of Africa and ganja. Actually, no. It's Roma smells of ganja and the drums just belong to him.

I wonder whether they have downpours like this in Africa for drums to get exposed to. Roma smiles, says nothing, mouthes his endless Rastaman song, his endless Rastaman mantra. Jah will give us everything, eh, Roma?

I love his songs and his drums. Roma is always very, very cool. Even when he's stoned he is cool and a bit pensive, with no giggling or antics. He's a real, meditative Rastaman whose constant ganja meditation has taught him the truth of the greatest insight of Rasta: Jah will give us everything. I like him for that.

The drums appeared at the beginning of winter. Our commune is a vast, Stalin-era apartment on Yakimanka near the centre of Moscow, with endless corridors and ceilings, which anyone can rent. How many people live there only Roma knows, because he is the landlord. He sublets it and lives in it, in our room; more precisely, of course, in his room, but besides him there are four other people there, including me. I sleep in the gallery. In that kind of apartment the gallery is like an intermediate floor and I like it there.

All through the winter our room was learning to pound out African rhythms on the drums. Tolya and I were the ablest pupils, learning to beat out the basic rhythms, which Roma ornamented with beautiful, non-repeating, unexpected rhythmical patterns. All winter long we treated our neighbours to this and, when the snow melted, migrated our little piece of Africa to the pavement of Kuznetsky Most to make some money.

We were discovered within a fortnight. A plummy woman

came along, put a hundred roubles in Roma's ginger-coloured hat, beckoned him over and said, "Are you a permanent group or have you just now got together?" "A permanent group," Roma Jah confirmed swiftly. "Give me your phone number. We organise corporate parties and our theme next week is 'Natives'. We'll invite you and your group to play." Roma nodded and gave her our Yakimanka number.

Madame didn't call the next week, but two weeks later she did. It was a Saturday and our entire commune was at home. Tolya was having a creative crisis over his pictures and moaning that he needed to get smashed but hadn't any money, and I was reading Kerouac up in my gallery. It was no problem for Roma to get us together and take us on the metro out to Shchelkovskaya. What a corporate party involved none of us had any idea. In the metro the drums clunked against each other in our rucksacks. Tolya asked Roma Jah whether there would be drink.

Next to the metro station, near the Matrix Cinema, a black Volkswagen was waiting and drove us far out beyond the outer ring. I sat in the back with despondent Tolya, while Roma tried to make conversation with the driver. Talking to drivers was a hitchhiking habit of his. The latter remained impassive, however, not even responding to direct questions. "Actually, he was a shaved gorilla," Tolya opined afterwards.

We drove up to an impenetrable white wall, one section of which tipped over and admitted the car to a clean, empty courtyard. The white walls of a not spectacularly large house were surrounded by a hedge, which was still bare and unwelcoming. Glass doors in the porch slid back at our approach to reveal two bronze borzois, restless and lean, light and life-sized. Everything in the interior of the house was white and understated, but with a particular, gilded kind of understatement.

We were taken through to a large room almost entirely

occupied by what looked like a triple-sized table-tennis table on which sat slender, beautiful girls. They were tanned to the point of swarthiness and had had so much ointment rubbed into them that their skin reflected the bright lights. One was a genuine mulatto. They were lightly dressed. More precisely, they were scantily clad in scraps of cloth suggestive of the attire of African natives. A dozen very professional-looking men and women were doing their hair, applying make-up, manicuring them, pedicuring them. The girls were putting on costumes, laughing, and talking loudly. As we entered we were dazzled by this riot of gleaming, sophisticated, fragrant, chocolatey beauty.

"Bloody hell!" Tolya exclaimed. Someone asked, "Who are these?" "Musicians," someone else answered on our behalf. "To make-up!" we were instructed, and proceeded to a corner of the table.

"You are negroes," the woman who had discovered us on Kuznetsky Most announced. She was plump and a product of the most chocolatey of solariums. Golden rings and bangles jangled on her neck, arms and legs. She was large, loud and ready to party, like a fertility goddess in a drought-stricken rainforest.

"Will there be food?" Tolya enquired, looking around tentatively, like a proletarian under arrest on the eve of the Great October Revolution.

"Later." The woman checked him out cursorily. "Two hundred dollars, shall we say?" she informed rather than asked Roma Jah. "Those are very good," she said with a nod towards Roma's dreadlocks. "Pity about that one." This in respect of Tolya. "I shaved them off yesterday," he bumbled.

"You will have costumes." She eyed me. "Do her hair the same way," she concluded after a moment's hesitation. "Do you dance?" I shook my head. "Cover her up," she decreed. Roma was already having brown greasepaint applied. "I don't suppose that's shit, is it?" Tolya enquired warily, sniffed the jar and with a sigh closed his eyes. "Go ahead. What won't we do for money!"

"You need wax to make it go like that," I said, indicating Roma's dreadlocks, "but I'm not up for it. I'd lose my day job." The make-up artist nodded and started braiding my short *gamin* haircut into a thousand and one plaits. I was issued a green linen tunic, then painted almost black, and ribbons of various colours were braided into my plaits. My arms were stained up to the elbows and I was urged not to raise them or the loose sleeves would fall back to my shoulders. Looking at myself in the mirror I saw the reflection of a charred hedgehog.

"Go, Rastas, go!" Tolya commanded in a scary terrorist voice and, festooned with tom-toms, we proceeded to the performance space. We had no idea what was going to happen to us and my palms were sweating. Only Roma Jah was cool, his ginger dreads bobbing over his painted forehead to the beat of music playing inside him.

We sat down on the floor of a large reception room and started playing with practised ease whilst surreptitiously taking in our surroundings. The hall was decorated as a hut in the jungle, but this was evidently the hut of a leader of all the tribes of Africa, who had long ago sold half his subjects into slavery. Wooden carvings of giraffes and elephants were positioned around the floor, ritual masks hung from the walls, and everything was painted in strong African colours. A divan and the floor were strewn with imitation straw. We sat beneath a real palm tree in a pot and played, while the skinny girls we had already met listened.

We played and nothing happened. The girls yawned, popped grapes and pieces of fruit into their mouths, sent text messages and chatted among themselves. I couldn't make them out at first, but then just got used to them. They were ordinary girls, most likely studying somewhere. There was one I quite liked. She wasn't tall and had almost no tan. She had big eyes and a little mouth with peculiar, almost predatory teeth, which gave her a slight lisp. She jiggled her foot in time to our rhythms. Her toes were bare, and the thin strap of her shoe was twined around a slender ankle. The little white heel of her shoe jogged rhythmically in front of my face, like a tooth amulet. We exchanged a smile and nodded to each other and I stopped worrying, concluding that the girls were as much part of the furniture, beautiful, exotic pieces, as we were. It just wasn't clear for whose benefit all this was being put on. There was no sign of an audience.

Madame entered all a-jingle, rolling her sun-kissed waves of flesh. She instantly sized everything up – the girls, us, and the other elements of the setting. She came to Roma and said, "Play louder and make it last. Don't use all the music up at once. They're dining now and will come through afterwards. We've got some other musicians for later. You're the support act."

Then she whispered something to the girls and opened a door in the far wall. A babble of men's voices and the smell of food drifted in. Tolya strained over his drum to look. More time passed, the girls started turning off their mobile phones, adjusting their expressions, then shimmied over and disappeared through the door. Swaying slightly and with his eyes half closed, Roma began a simple Rasta song. Tolya and I picked up the rhythm and began to enliven it.

Rastafari – will be forever – love and Jah. – And Rastafari!

The girls began coming back, their heels clacking, laughing, their myriad pendants jingling prettily. Men in business suits followed them in, still chewing and continuing unfinished conversations. The girls sat on the divan, then stood up and started to dance, trying to get the men to join in, but they were still deep in their business discussions and not yet inclined to dance.

My girl was the liveliest of them all, running over to photograph us with her mobile phone. She laughed and asked me, "Is that difficult? Don't your arms get tired? Did you study it somewhere?" I smiled back and she ran off, laughing some more. She had a pleasant, open face. I pictured her in jeans, a T-shirt and baseball cap and decided we could become friends. I was looking at her so much I lost track of what we were playing.

"Roma, does this song ever come to an end?" I heard Tolya whisper. Roma carried on swaying and singing, his eyes completely closed. They say there comes a point where you don't need grass any more, you are just high all the time. Jah will give us everything, eh, Roma?

Madame finally came swanning back in with a smile and much jangling, her tan glistening and her teeth gleaming, and whispered to Roma to wind it up. He stopped instantly, rose and walked towards the exit. We finished off with a drum roll, in some confusion.

Our place was immediately taken by other musicians, real negroes, and we could only gape in amazement: these were serious jazzmen, international celebrities. "How many bucks do you need to get these guys to come back to their roots?" Tolya chuckled, when he did finally stop gaping. "Hell, Roma, we've sold ourselves too cheap here." Roma looked at him smiling, the song still on his lips.

Tolya had underestimated them: these cats were playing real jazz. We, the waiters, the maids, the make-up artists and the cooks in their aprons crowded round the partly opened door to the hall and listened. The people who worked here were comparing this party with earlier ones. We quickly ran to wipe off our make-up and came back. Tolya had lost no time in getting in with the cooks in the kitchen and the waiters from the bar and was strolling around with a full wine glass. A little later he invited us to the 'dressing room' where dinner awaited us on disposable plates. "Learn from me, Rastamans," he said exultantly, "and Jah will give you everything."

While we were eating and listening to African saxophones, Madame came floating in, slipped Roma two hundred-dollar bills, and headed back towards the door. "Madame, when are we getting a lift back?" Tolya called after her. "It's getting late." She turned round flinty faced, but said finally, "The driver is going home. Find him. He'll give you a lift to Moscow." Tolya whistled. "Well guys, I'm off to find the driver, or before you know it..."

We went back to the door. At that moment I was feeling insanely jealous of the girls. There they were sitting cheek by jowl with real jazz greats! These were major musicians, living classics! Did they have any idea how lucky they were? It was a double door through to the hall and there was a gap. I wished I could squeeze through and see everything, the musicians and the enraptured face of my girl. I was sure it would be enraptured.

I slowly worked my way forward and had just reached the gap when the crowd gasped, "They're coming!" and everyone rushed to get out of the way. I had the gap to myself but only had time to see clothing an inch away. I jumped back and managed not to get my head hit by the doors as they burst open. One of the men came out of the hall with my girl. She was holding his hand by the little finger.

There was an inconspicuous door opposite which led to stairs to the first floor. With two steps they had crossed the corridor and disappeared through it, but in those two steps my girl flashed me a dazzling smile with her predator's teeth. She wore her smile like a queen might wear a marriage diadem before her wedding, a fixed, glittering smile of triumph. She started climbing the stairs and I heard the clatter of her amulet-heels.

"Roma, grab Titch before the driver goes without us!" Tolya was drunk but more firmly grounded in reality than I was. It was the same driver, but in his own new indigo Lada-6. He was as uncommunicative as ever, although with Tolya sitting in front now he did acknowledge that they were namesakes. This new Tolya was from a Moscow suburb, somewhere on the other side of town. He drove us until our ways parted, then dropped us on the outer ring road and drove on towards the exit. He dropped us at a bus stop, not registering that it was one in the morning and raining. The exit he was turning off at was another three kilometres down the road. He evidently thought he was doing us a favour, our new Tolya.

"I say, young lady! You really shouldn't be hitchhiking. Men will be trying to pick you up!" Tolya is convulsed, laughing at Roma. With the wet dreadlocks framing his face, Roma really does look like a girl. He has maidenly brown and very clear eyes, but beneath his nose is unshaved ginger stubble.

"I say, young lady! Perhaps you could all the same just raise your regal little hand? After all, you are the professional. Perhaps you could just flag down some old jalopy for us, you soul of Rasta mother plucker!"

Tolya is talking sense: Roma Jah is fully familiar with the open road. Every year he hitchhikes down to the Crimea or the Caucasus or wherever. In May he collects three months' rent in advance from his tenants in the commune and takes off for the summer. He's got a girlfriend down there and a son who must be three by now. I saw a photo: a strange little creature with a scorched face and hair bleached by the sun. It was completely unkempt and now you probably couldn't run a comb through it. Historically that's where dreadlocks came from – tangles of hair, matted over a lifetime. Roma never tells anyone anything about his non-Muscovite family. All I know about them is that they exist.

"Listen, dude, what is it you want?" Roma says, suddenly turning and speaking quietly right into Tolya's face, in order not to have to yell through the rain. "Have you any idea how much they would fleece you for taking you to the city centre? Do you want to hand them everything we've earned tonight?"

"What do you mean?" Tolya asks in surprise, stepping uncertainly to one side. "Can't we just say we haven't got any money, if you grudge paying?"

"You don't understand. Hitching is not a way of travelling for nothing because you're a cheapskate. You don't tell lies on the road. On the road you have to be open with everyone, understand? But what sort of road do you think this is? Do you think these are long-distance drivers on a job? This is Moscow, man."

He turns away and walks on, but we immediately hear, "Well, I hate Moscow!" Tolya's voice explodes in a shriek. "I hate this Moscow of yours, this greedy, gorging, stinking Moscow!" We turn round. He is standing there like a giant humpbacked bird with broken wings, his arms hanging down under his rucksack, water dripping from them.

"Do you hear? You! I hate Moscow!"

"Sure, we hear. So why were you so keen to come to Moscow?" I shout into the rain. I can feel he is beginning to get to me too because we still have a long, long way to walk, we're not even sure where we're going, and he has to choose this time and this place to let rip. "Why didn't you just stay in Petropavlovsk? What brought you here?"

"I'll screw this place yet! I'll screw all of them, you know?" Tolya yells. "Have you seen the map of Moscow? Come to our showroom, we've got these maps of mobile phone networks on the wall. Have you seen them? It's a spider's web! This is a spider's web and we all fly here and get stuck like insects. We are stuck, struggling and just waiting to be devoured. Only that's not going to happen! That's why I came here: I'll screw them all yet, do you hear me? I'll screw everyone, and you too, everyone, everyone!"

Tolya lives in our room and sleeps under the piano. He makes pictures out of beer caps, fragments of glass, small change, broken bits and pieces, and rubbish he finds in the street. He comes back with boxloads of trash and keeps it under the piano, then crafts it all on to a thin layer of modelling clay on a board. He can recreate the crowds in the metro, the view from our window on to the garbage skips in the yard, the Red October Chocolate Factory, the statue of Peter the Great conjuring the sea on his embankment... an urbanist world evoked through its own refuse. Tolya knows what he is doing.

Roma goes up to him and shakes his shoulders so vigorously that insubstantial, drunken Tolya is almost lifted up in the air along with his rucksack. "Let's go on," Roma says quietly. Because of the rain I can't hear the words but I guess them. Tolya gives a sob.

"Roma, take my share of the rent out of that money," I say when he catches up with me. "Only don't give Tolya his, okay? He'll drink the lot and just get kicked out of his job." "No, he won't. Not now."

We go on. My trainers have soaked up all the water they can, and now with every step I take it squelches back out. "Roma! Hey, Roma. You didn't say whether that song ever comes to an end." Tolya catches up with us and falls into step, a figure bent under the weight of his rucksack, the same as us.

Roma gives a slight smile. We plod on.

New Spring

Hi, Julia, skinhead girl with a twisted smile, given to mild swearing. You saunter out, look your public over with that sneer of yours, hands in your pockets, clenched in tight fists. There's just you and an audience, Julia, and who's to say they are all on your side? You smirk, put on that husky voice, close your eyes in the spotlight, strike that guitar and sing about getting drunk on Saturday nights.

"*And h-ooow I luvvit!*"

After the gig you turn up your nose and tell us about sweaty guys who smell of overpriced vodka and cheap aftershave trying to pick you up, inviting you to the bar, swearing they only come to this dive to hear you and otherwise they drink exclusively at Blizzard.

"It's your image," Producer says. "Cut out the cussing and the songs about booze and you'll find a different crowd around you." You take no notice of what he has to say. You might if he were a proper producer, but what has he done for you? Nothing. He comes up with projects for albums and tours but you're still doing the rounds in bars and nightclubs, like everyone else from the old Moscow underground scene. Julia, girl of great talent, now starring in the beer bars of Moscow. Where the hell did Sasha find her?

"Where did you find her, Sasha?" I ask, but I'm not ready to listen to his long rambling explanation about some festival and running into her in a snowstorm. Like Pushkin's Silvio, Julia appeared out of a snowstorm but ended up in our commune.

No, Julia, you are a Moscow girl, not destined to live here with us on Yakimanka, although you'd be hard pressed to find a better place to rehearse. The walls are thick, you've got Roma here on bass guitar, Sasha to play any pipe or flute you can think of, and Lenka for backing. You've got a group! We admire your talent, and our perpetually pie-eyed Tolya crawls under the piano and holds his breath whenever you come into the room.

Those rehearsals were the highpoint of a fever which rampaged through our commune. We were like charged particles, attracted to each other, colliding, repelled, in a constant state of flux. That cruel fever blew our minds and we lived in the moment not knowing what we were doing.

But already we had a presentiment that soon it would all be over. You and I, Sasha, are on the road and have no alternative path. No traffic either, because what sort of a road is this? It's a narrow track to a village where some people are supposed to be expecting us. How many kilometres is it to the village, Sasha? Oh, what the hell! We should make it by dawn.

Our house is full of people, all playing games with each other. They might not agree, but looking down on them from my gallery I know best. My home is full of kids, all playing at love.

Lenka started it, blonde-haired, blonde-browed, green-eyed Lenka as brazen as the devil. She introduced the bacillus of March madness to Yakimanka. Old Artemiy, our communal scarecrow stuck permanently beside the kitchen radiator, said it all the moment she arrived. "You've got the devil in you, girl," he told her. "Cool," Lenka replied.

There are things which are powerless over the mind. It is powerless, for instance, to figure out what caused two beings as dissimilar as Lenka and me, Titch, to collide. Collide we nevertheless did, in the metro where she was handing out leaflets and I was rushing along one of my courier routes, my endless routes which, starting from a particular place, are guaranteed to take you back there, again and again. So it was. Lenka and I collided again and again, a dozen times, until finally laughter spilled out of our eyes and we were bound to be friends.

"This is one crackpot city we live in," I said, sipping fruit juice through a straw. It was our lunch break. "Right," Lenka nodded. "And we're doing the most crackpot jobs it could think up." "Right," Lenka nodded, eating chocolate with a beer chaser. She is so hooked on sweets she won't eat anything else so as not to put on weight.

Lenka had come to Moscow, was living with an aunt, studying somewhere while doing a job, the same as me. Her aunt kept coming down on Lenka, not letting her flower. "Everybody has the right to live how they please," Lenka protested, "But this despot has got it into her head she has to mother me. That's not what brought me to Moscow!"

Her appearance on Yakimanka was pre-ordained. Even though we were the same age, no one ever thought to call her what they called me. "This chick means business," Tolya said admiringly. "Look and learn, Titch!"

Yakimanka, our rented communal paradise, adopted her and here she found the nurturing environment, the saturated solution of cynicism, two fingers to the world, the permissiveness her youthful schizophrenia needed to grow and flourish. She told everyone she was schizophrenic, found a book on forensic psychiatry and compared her symptoms. "Manic-depressive syndrome triggered by alcoholism," she proudly diagnosed her condition. But you, commune, our shared home, are never shocked and only laugh. So many people here talk like that. There's no knowing when they're serious and when they are joking.

It was only old Artemiy who saw her demon straight away. Later I saw it too, one night, looking down from my gallery. I love watching people while they are asleep. You immediately see something important. Lenka looked scared in her sleep and there was a restive little brownish-grey creature beside her, like a kitten. In the darkness I couldn't see what it was. I raised myself on my elbows, the creature pricked up its ears, tensed, jumped back into Lenka's head and was gone.

Here Sasha and I are on our way, on the road, walking along a strip of asphalt through the woods. Around us it is May, the first green leaves, the first butterflies. After the winter we crawl out of Moscow into the big wide world as blind as moles, crusted with fungus and mildew. We can't think straight, we blink in the light, dizzy in the fresh air. When you see that first butterfly, friend, you know you've survived another winter. "Hey, Sasha, have you brought anything to eat?" "They'll have food." "I've got bread, and water." "Great. We're sorted then. They should have something."

We have a tent and a couple of blankets. "Did you arrange where we're going to meet up?" "Nah. Reckon we'll find them?" I nod. Something in me clicks, and I try to see everything, looking down from above – us, the lake, the guys we are looking for. "I'll be right back. You get thumbing," Sasha says, dropping his rucksack and jogging over to the ditch. I put mine beside his and look into the empty distance. "Sure," I say. "Someone's bound to stop for me now, a chick with two bags."

"Eh? What chick with two bags?" Sasha asks from the bushes. "Nothing. I'm just talking about myself. Hey, hurry up, a lift!" He jumps out, buttoning himself, and we raise our thumbs. A saloon car with rounded contours, foreign, like a shiny golden pie, stops. Sasha leans down, speaking in his polite, breathy voice. Being polite always makes his voice go like that. The driver is a woman and she lets us in the back, along with our packs.

Lenka told us that back home, up in the north, she would drink nothing other than vodka. In Moscow she learned to drink beer. I saw a gap in her education and on her first day, to celebrate her moving in, we bought a bottle of champagne and a coconut, sawed it open with a rasp, quaffed it and by the time Roma and Tolya came back in the evening, were lying on the piano watching the shadows flitting over the ceiling. We thought all the shadows looked like elephants. "The girls have been partying," Tolya said, turning on the lights and instantly banishing the elephants.

It wasn't that night I saw the demon but a few days later. I decided not to get drunk with Lenka again, because if the elephants were enough to keep me happy, they weren't enough for her and it took her just fifteen minutes to run to the shop with Tolya for more booze, so that in no time at all the whole kitchen knew who had descended on us.

"She's just getting to know people," Tolya said at the time.

"I grew up in this village," the woman at the wheel tells us. She looks like the owner of the travel agency for which I run errands, not old but tired. She asks where we want to go and Sasha says something vague about the pier. "There are two," she tells us. Shortly after, she brakes and sends him to buildings about a hundred metres from the road to ask about the people we're supposed to be meeting. "This is the first pier," she says.

Sasha runs over and comes back with the news that they aren't there. We drive on through the village, which has high fenced cottages which look like holiday dachas. The woman lets us out and points to some buildings far away. "That's the second one." As she drives off, I appreciate just how warm it was in the car. "Hey, Sasha let's pretend we're detectives on someone's trail."

At the boat station dogs come running at the sound of our boots and the sight of our humped figures. They bark and wag their tails. "Yes, your friends were here but they've taken a boat. Where to? The islands." "After them!" Sasha says. We count our money. We need 200 roubles to hire a boat and between us have just 230.

"How are we going to get back home, Sasha?"

"They've got money."

Lenka was good at playing the guitar and singing the songs of rock legend Alexander Bashlachov with deep, not to say hysterical, emotion. She could talk about herself for hours on end without boring anyone, and could wear totally incongruous, oversized, weird clothes and make it look like this was the younger generation rebelling against society. Her greatest talent, however, was for falling in, and being in, love. "Look and learn, Titch," Tolya told me. "Look and learn. You're really stuck in that infantilism of yours."

He was in raptures over Lenka and it was mutual. For the first few days she lived with him under his piano until, mutually fulfilled, they parted amicably and Lenka moved her talent on, causing turbulence in our commune.

Her dazzling, ditzy personality induced a state of intoxication or mild nervous tension in men. Even those who avoided looking directly were forever stealing glances at her. Their women became more attentive and loving, a little jumpy, and nearly all lost weight. Lenka taught everyone to play games and the commune became a fevered place.

"We tried it a hundred times but each was like the first," Julia was to say later. I think she was talking about surgical spirit, although she could equally well have been speaking of Lenka. I realised she was contagious when, out of the blue, Sergey from the room next to mine sent a text message one morning declaring, in Latin script, "Ya teba lublu", which reduced me to fits of hysterical laughter. I suddenly realised why I kept running into Sergey, why he was always coming into our room, sitting silently by the locker and gazing up at the gallery. He was a violinist at the Bolshoy Theatre, with the broad face of a peasant in a medieval tapestry and small, sharp teeth. His teeth put me off me. They struck me as unhealthy, and I could never think what to talk to him about. When I got his text I realised that his misspelled 'lublu' must have cost him a great deal. I laughed uproariously, until Roma Jah told me Sergey had asked him the day before if he could move to another room which had access to my gallery. I took a hammer and nailed the offending door shut.

Our commune's hammer is inscribed "Use appropriately". That really is very sound advice.

We take a boat and push off from the shore. The white cat which followed us from the office leaps on to the rock furthest from the shore and sits there staring after us. We are already far out and the land and the cottages merge with the darkness until only the white cat is still visible on its rock, alone, in the night.

The kind of heavy silence you get over water plugs our ears. It is the first time I have ever been in a boat but I don't want to let on. I can't swim. I look down into the water. It is black. Nightfall rapidly swallows up objects, warmth, and any desire to talk. It is a large lake with a lot of islands. It would be good to know which is the one we are looking for.

"There's a campfire," I say quietly. Nightfall has also swallowed up my ability to feel pleased. We row over to the island where a fire is such a flickering, venomous red you can't believe it is natural. We don't see any people but sounds travel readily over water and we hear music. It is not the kind of music the friends we are looking for could be listening to.

"I can hear an axe," I say even more quietly, and we head for a different island and the distinct sound of someone confidently chopping logs. I picture Producer at it, raising his skinny arms above his head, the full weight of his body behind the axe, the body of a top student of Bauman Technical University, a clever boy in glasses.

"Julia!" Sasha calls into the darkness, facing the island, very loudly so as not be scared. "Julia!" "What's Producer's real name?" "No idea." "Pro-du-cer!" I shout. Somebody is chopping wood in the forest. "Let's go closer." We do. We can already make out reeds by the shore, dry and yellow, that have survived the winter. "Pro-du-cer!"

It is so cold the water seems like black ice. The moon is bright and there are stars in the sky and the water. Our boat bobs on a surface between two abysses. We listen intently, for a long time, to the silence and the cold. "You know what, Sasha, I think this must be how people die." "We'll moor the boat, get a night's sleep, and go look for them in the morning."

The boat gets stuck in the reeds. Our legs disappear into cold water. I have no idea which direction we are going in through the bare stems surrounding us on all sides. We get to the shore and walk towards trees. They have branches, we will have a campfire and be warm. May the forces of light be with us.

The bacillus proved highly contagious and Sergey was not the last to succumb to it. The symptoms of infection were not always immediately evident, as I had realised after I brought Sasha to the commune.

He was a courier too, for a firm in the entry next to my travel agency. I had seen him many times before, but it was inevitable that we should meet up during the fever. He was drunk and reciting poetry. He was standing in the archway between our two entrance halls, stooped and as thin as a reed and swathed from head to toe in a lurid scarf. His eyes blazed with the fire of inspiration and he swayed to and fro as he recited early Mayakovsky. It turned out he was the courier with a poetry magazine. His audience was two friends with a bottle of brandy, an alley cat, and me. After his pals had made off with the remains of the brandy, the cat disappeared and I dragged Sasha back to Yakimanka.

"The Soviet generation of engineers has been replaced by a generation of couriers!" Tolya pronounced when he caught sight of Sasha. "You will shortly have a statue erected to you in our courtyard. We live in gone times, friend. What more could you ask?"

The commune turned out to be just what Sasha needed. He was from a distant Moscow suburb and only went home at weekends, staying with friends during the week. Relations with his friends got strained, and on what he got paid the commune was the right place for him. A more suitable berth was not immediately available, so Sasha was accommodated in the bathroom.

He was skinny and drained by alcoholism was Sasha. His knobbly knees were like shrivelled pumpkins and brought tears to my eyes. He had huge thick glasses which concealed the withered face of a man who has been dumped by three wives in succession. He had some innate logical deficit, which meant that listening to simple stories about his life entailed plunging into impenetrable thickets of personal and world history until you were totally disorientated. Nevertheless, I listened to them. We started off in our room when we got back from work and finished in the kitchen at dawn. Still there was no end in sight. We skipped college, and soon every aspect of reality began to fuse in my mind into total nonsense.

Sasha had a ridiculous, endearing, blind vulnerability, and an ability to get on with absolutely anyone. He was kind and undemanding, so I listened to him and hung out with him while he was living in the bathroom. If there was any suggestion of infatuation in my feverishness, then only because I had caught it from Lenka, like 'flu. It was, nevertheless, a relief to see my temptation terminate one evening when Sasha and Lenka went off together to the nearest drink kiosk, returned after midnight and ended up together in Lenka's bed.

That was the night I saw the imp on her pillow.

"Hey, Sasha, let's play Robinson Crusoe and imagine no one will ever come to rescue us." The campfire dries us and we warm up. We cut bread into thin squares, sprinkle them with salt and toast them on twigs. Our tap water is sweeter than wine. Sasha has an old canvas tent. All night we keep warm by hugging each other, then lying back to back. The blankets are too thin for a May night on a lake.

I dream of Producer. He is sitting in a boat fishing. A wonderful new guitar is floating on the water, its strings gleaming. "Is this all for me?" happy Julia sings on the beach, jumping up and down and clapping her hands. Julia is a child, a girl with pigtails. She doesn't yet know she will sing songs and rescue the underground rock music of Moscow from the ruins. Will everyone there be her friends?

I wake up hungry. Warmed by the sun, the tent has become as muggy as a swamp. We crawl out. "Sasha, do you really not have any food?" "We'll meet up with them," Sasha says. We strike the tent and get going, munching bread and salt.

"Look, we can see the whole island. It can't be that big. See, it's round. We'll find them. "Julia!" Sasha yells towards the woods, although no sound is coming from that direction. I try again to see everything at once and from above: there we are, there are the woods, there is lots and lots of water. I see nobody else.

"Sasha, let's play at being eagles catching gophers in the open." The woods are still wet and bare and they haven't warmed up. Nobody lives here. We walk through them like orphans. "Julia!" Sasha bellows like a moose. "Pro-du-cer!" I yell. "Hey, Sasha, why aren't we shouting for Lenka?" Sasha's face darkens. Even when there are three of them, what Lenka wants Lenka gets, and Sasha knows it. He says nothing. We finish the bread. That's it, man, now there's nothing left to fuel your jealousy.

"I still have some sugar," Sasha says. Sugar and water are good, only we've finished the water. We come to a swamp. "Sasha, do you remember where the lake was?" "No. Hang on a minute." He leans over and fills our bottle. We drink the water and eat the sugar. "That's better," Sasha says and stretches contentedly. "First time I've drunk swamp water!" "It's pure," he says. "There was a toad in it. Toads never sit in dirty water."

They both changed suddenly. One mania fused with another and Sasha entered a state where he could not let Lenka out of his sight. Lenka liked that. They stuck to each other like differently coloured pieces of modelling clay on Tolya's recycled picture boards. They had a long and happy life together. Really long by Lenka's standards and really happy by those of the commune. When love becomes dependency, however, the children forget to play by the rules. As luck would have it, this was the moment Julia showed up.

You were not destined to live with us, Julia, but your songs, drunken, crazy, toxic, were about all of us, the waifs and strays of Yakimanka. That is why we loved you, Julia. That is why you were one of us, and in our hearts each of us would have followed you to the ends of the earth. Every age needs an idol, and as we don't have one right now, why not you, Julia, star of the Moscow beer bars? We were at one with you when you were singing about us and for us. You didn't sell out, and anyway, who would have bought you?

Sasha brought her to us. She started singing rap in the autumn, and by midwinter her Producer had materialised. It looked like her creative career was coming good. The commune as a whole, however, not yet back on an even keel, succumbed to a new bout of fever. Roma Jah hesitated for a moment, frowned like an old wise Indian and said, "It's all over!"

His pronouncement came after Sasha, not sparing himself, had run all over Moscow sticking up posters for Julia's concert, while Lenka tattooed on her arm from wrist to elbow the word 'Producer' in runic script.

We are playing associations. Tolya is leading and I am answering. Everybody listens, punctuating a fraught silence with laughter.

"Piano," says Tolya. "Lame dog."

"Alarm clock." "Peevish schoolkid."

"Lenka." "Little girl lost." (I see her laughing and biting Sasha's ear with delight.)

"Sasha." "Boy reading with a torch under the bedclothes at night." (I see Sasha wants to say something, but he is too slow.)

"Julia," Tolya says, getting the bit between his teeth. "Girl looking forward to New Year presents." (What a pity you aren't here with us, Julia.)

"Titch, all your associations follow the same lines. That's questionable." "They aren't associations, they're what I see."

"Okay then. What about Producer?"

"Producer, erm, er... He is..." For the first time I am having to think. It is a pity he isn't here either for me to glance at him. "No, I can't see him. For some reason I can't see anything."

Producer was pale, thin, and wore jeans with holes in them, socks with holes in them and shirts with buttons missing, but he knew the right people at the right clubs, and seemed even to know people in higher and classier places too. He said nothing, though. He waited. He was good at waiting, was Producer, bluffing but with a Joker in his pocket. Or had he?

In the meantime, he showered advice on Julia. They would come back together, Julia would sing the way she always did, and then Producer would say what ideally she should be doing. From my gallery I could see his eyes – blue-grey, intelligent – and I could understand Lenka. From my gallery I could see Julia's lips – thin, with a twist of indifference and a little white lower tooth, and I could understand Sasha. From my gallery I could see absolutely everything, and it all got terribly mixed up.

Madness was building up in the commune again. It built up all winter and by spring had the power of a hibernating atom bomb. Lenka and Sasha made up and broke up, moved on to a brother-sister relationship, then fought and gave each other purple love bites. Julia and Producer continued their quiet, steady relationship and I watched them from my gallery. The light from a nearby bulb dimmed in my eyes because I couldn't see both couples at once. My home is full of children who have forgotten they are children but all want games to play.

They started putting on concerts. Money came in. If they had had love everything would have been sorted long ago, but everything remained as it was and in late April Producer said, "Let's go to the lake for the May Day holiday."

He made it sound like a challenge to a duel. You go to the woods when you are strong and free and most urgently desire to be with the one you want. How they would get on in the woods not even old Artemiy could foretell. The timer clicked and the seconds started ticking away in the time-bomb. I saw their agitation and wanted only to immure myself in my gallery in order to survive the explosion.

We wander on for as long as our legs hold out. We come to a glade where the sun has warmed the moss, and lie down without a word and feel good.

"Sasha, what do you make of Julia?" "She's cool." "And Lenka?" "Little furry animal." "Producer?" "Don't give a toss."

"No, but what do you make of him?" "I haven't looked." "What about the two of them." "God only knows what's going on." "Do you know when I saw her as she really, really is?" "Who?" "Julia. When she stayed overnight with us one time. I looked at everyone then to see what they were like asleep. Her face was so child-like and vulnerable. I wanted to stroke her hair. That's what she's like, Sasha."

I quickly try once again to take in everything at once, looking down from above. I see us, the woods, the lake. But where are the people we are looking for? And who are we looking for anyway? They... for some reason I have a sense that we are too late. I wonder what for, but we are already dozing off in the heat. The sun is setting, warm, glowing. The birds are singing and Sasha begins to snore.

I dream about a dog with a ginger coat. Someone has killed it.

Would I ever have come down from my gallery? What was there for me to do down there if these kids were so keen to play and beat up and torment each other. But May arrived. It was cold. Roma Jah swathed himself in his long ginger scarf, knocked at the door of my gallery and said, "Hey Titch you really ought to go with them." "Why don't you go? I'm not one of their crowd." "I've got 'flu." "So what?" "You go, Titch. Otherwise..."

We agreed to meet up at Savyolovsky train station and go to the lake, but the only people who met up were me and Sasha. We arrived at the spot we'd agreed and ran to the platform only to see the train waving its stumpy tail at us as it disappeared. Sasha looked after it like an abandoned dog. I could swear he was thinking Lenka had done it deliberately. "We know where they're headed," he said. "Let's go after them."

We wake up when it's already dusk, pitch the tent, light a fire and warm ourselves at it. "Lenka asked me immediately whether I would allow her to love him," Sasha tells me. "I said, go for it!" "Who?" "Producer, of course. I told her, go for it. The type he is, it makes no difference whether you love him or not." Sasha takes out his pipe and lights up. "It's good here," he says. "What more could anyone need?" The fire is reduced to a pitiful heap of ash. We climb into the tent. Shelter.

"Sasha, why don't we just sleep all day tomorrow and not go anywhere. "You'll croak, Titch." "Go on, Sasha. I know everything that's going to happen tomorrow anyway. Want me to tell you?" "Go on, then." "Tomorrow's Victory Day. We'll meet up with some people, and the very first man we meet will pour you a vodka to drink to the Victory of 1945. He won't pour me one, only you. You'll get drunk and we'll hitch back to Moscow. On the way we'll spend our thirty roubles on food." "Fine by me. Let's do it all the same."

I sigh. We cling together for warmth. "Sasha, let's pretend we're soldiers killed in the war, here in the swamps, and nobody will ever find us." "You're nuts, Titch. Go to sleep." We hug each other tight and sleep all night, freezing cold.

In the morning we come upon a narrow gauge rail-track and wonder who extended it on to the island. We follow it and reach a village. Everything happens as I said it would. The first man we meet has a bottle and pours Sasha a vodka, but his empty stomach means he's immediately unsteady on his feet. No, friend, with you in that state I'm not going to play any games.

We come to the store and I send Sasha in. I sit on my pack, shut my eyes, and see red spots jumping in the darkness of my eyelids. The fever will be purged from our commune by the spring, the cold, hunger and swamp water. I should have told Roma to ventilate the place thoroughly while we were away.

I open my eyes and out of the dancing sunlight two figures walking down the road materialise like a mirage. I blink and see it is Julia and Producer. Julia's red setter is running ahead of them. I sit there smiling. They go into the store, and the dog runs over to me wagging its whole body.

Producer comes out, sees me, nods and sits down on Sasha's pack. I smile but we don't speak. He is very suntanned, Julia's Producer. He is stripped to the waist and the colour of oatmeal cookies. He sits beside me and I try to get a look at him to see, smell, sense whether anything has changed during his two days and two nights with Julia. It turns out Lenka wasn't with them, and that just strengthens my feeling that I have somehow missed the boat.

Well then, friend, where's your child? The one we all carry within ourselves from childhood? Sasha comes out. He gives me a biscuit and eats one himself but he's woozy. Julia has a half-smile on her lips, she's lolling about with a man's T-shirt over her bare breasts. She looks at Sasha with her invariable hint of mockery. She tells us where they were, where they waited, but we know very well what happened and how. You go to the woods when you want to be with the one you want to be with. Julia laughs. She knows now how much Sasha will put up with for her sake. Hunger, cold, vodka, brackish swamp water...

"What's your name?" I ask Producer. "Ivan," he says, and winks twice.

Farewell, Revolution!

"Any time you leave you are leaving forever. It can't be otherwise, because it is impossible to return forever."

Such was Grand's first rule. He gave it to us the morning we met, an early morning as freshly washed Sretensky Boulevard was waking. We saw it was a good rule and decided to leave Yakimanka that same day. By then the air was stale there and we could see it was time to get out. We ran away without a word to anyone, because Grand's second rule was, "Cover your tracks". We did, without a word to anyone and leaving the same day we met him, both of us, I, Titch, and Sasha Sorokin.

It was our flight together to the East. That is what Grand said: "Go East", and Sasha and I acted on it. We knew immediately that we would leave, although at first we mumbled something about needing to think it over. What was there, though, to think over when the light of summer dawns was failing. Yakimanka was sound asleep and all night Sasha and I had been up walking our iron, tracing circles on the boulevard ring road and seeing Cara off.

Cara, Cara the Black, Cara the yawning night. On the road I will dream when I'm wide awake that your gleaming eye, in which nothing reflects, is fixed on me. You watch me and draw nearer, your fearsome beak touching my open hand, you nod three times and loudly call out your name. Cara, Cara the Black, the raven which put out the light of Yakimanka.

If there is happiness or unhappiness on earth, you alone, Cara, know their ins and outs. If there is joy, anger, hatred, or sorrow, to you alone they are of no account. You came to show us the path and in all probability we shall see you no more, so more power to your wing, Cara, heiress of the ravens of the Tower.

That evening we had taken the iron for a walk and didn't want to go back. We walked on doggedly and in silence, with Cara's shadow circling above us and our dolorous memories. We saw night taking over Moscow, and Moscow gambolled in delight, greeted us in the laughing faces of women of the night, raced by in shiny cars, thundered her music and closed the barriers of metro stations like the pale wings of moths. We walked, chatted with cops, smoked in silence with morose characters we came across, talked to the homeless, bought beer and fruit juice at 24-hour kiosks, drank it looking at Moscow, and went on our way, saying goodbye to our own personal night before it flew away forever.

We both knew we were saying goodbye to Cara but made no mention of the fact.

Then on dear, familiar Sretensky Boulevard we met Grand. He was sitting on a bench towards which both of us were impelled by the force of our loss. When he saw us, Grand knew it was us he'd been waiting for.

"My friends!" he said, looking neither at me nor at Sasha but somehow between us to where our humble iron was coyly hiding behind my leg. "All night long I have been walking through this city unable to leave its streets, because a feeling was constantly with me that this night would bring me companions with whom to begin my journey to the East."

Or if he did not say that, he might have done, strange Grand, a breeze blowing freely along wide roads. He told us hitchhiking was his life, and that hitchhiking was about always moving on, that he could not endure stops, but that this time Moscow had not let go of him and he had understood that someone would come to him, someone the road was expecting. "Hey, Stalker, how much to take us into the Zone?" I quipped and we all laughed.

Grand is a lone hitch-hiker, but there comes a time when any sage takes on disciples. We all realised this was our destiny.

We recognised it when we saw it, because we knew the road, and you learn to see destiny, friend, when you have gone out on the road.

"We've never hitched that far before," Sasha and I said. "I will be your teacher," Grand responded. "Here is your first rule: Every time you leave, be prepared for the fact that you may be leaving forever."

We returned to the commune buoyed up and with the iron clanking quietly behind us. We returned with a sense of clarity and confidence as to our way, because we knew that Cara truly had changed our world.

Cara came to me in the Yakimanka courtyard. She came like a shadow suddenly incarnated as a bird. She flew down from a tree to perch at the end of the bench I was sitting on, arched her neck, swayed and repeated her name three times.

It was a lovely, warm June day and the poplars were clapping their new leaves above my head, but if a black raven sits beside you, friend, you can be sure your life is about to be turned upside down. Anyway, how often have you had a black raven sit beside you?

That day I had given up my courier job. I'd passed my last exam the day before and now in summery mood wanted nothing to do with travel agencies ever again. I left the office and came back home, my head light with a dizzying sense of freedom. Nothing now held me in Moscow. I felt so much space around me I could have flown up in the air like a balloon whose thread has broken. My knees gave way, I sank to the bench and Cara flew down.

A raven is a messenger of fate, and that day it was my fate. I brought big black Cara back to the commune, a free gift from Providence to all on Yakimanka. They reacted to her as Babylon might have. Ashen faced, shocked, they filled their lungs and all together began shrieking hysterically. Before we had time to do anything, the instant we entered the invariably crowded hallway of the commune, there was such a commotion that Cara soared to the ceiling and began swinging on the lamp-holder.

"Unbelievable!" Yakimanka ranted. "Unheard of!" it concurred with itself. "It's against the rules!" "Why isn't the landlord doing something about it?"

"It'll steal our belongings!" "It will foul everywhere!" "Where's the landlord!"

"Young people are getting completely out of hand!" "I've wanted to have a dog to guard my sofa for a long time but it's against the rules!" "Landlord!"

Cara swung and uttered the curse of her name over the lot of them until Roma Jah did finally show up in the kitchen. Everyone fell silent, because he is our landlord. Everyone does as he says, even though his hair is in dreadlocks and he carries perpetual hippy springtime in his heart. He is always calm, and for us lunatics that is a sign of wisdom and good judgement.

Roma Jah stayed calm, and when he saw my Cara swinging on the lampholder said softly, "Titch, you know the rules don't allow people to bring independent animals into the commune." The rules were unwritten. Actually, they used to be written but were soon torn down by someone in a fit of pique, but they were remembered and generally known by being passed on to newcomers. One of the rules was that animals were classified as independent if they could find and eat things or leave the space allocated to their owner. That ruled out cats, dogs, ferrets and excessively frisky rabbits, but did not rule out caged mice, rats, hamsters, fish, reptiles, or Madagascar hissing cockroaches.

After that it was hopeless trying to defend Cara. It remained only for me to bring her down from the lampholder and for us to leave with our heads held high. The denizens of Yakimanka scuttled off to hide, barring their doors. I put a chair on a table and climbed on top. Lenka ran in, opened the window to give

Cara somewhere to fly out, and jumped up and down, laughing loudly to give her something to be frightened by.

I found myself on a level with her. Balancing precariously, I stood up straight and reached for her. Cara looked at me almost reproachfully, turned her head and cawed distinctly, "Caa work!" Thereupon she abandoned the light fitting and flew off down the hallway, instigating a small tornado in the heart of the commune.

"Well, well, well!" muttered old Artemiy approvingly, or perhaps disapprovingly. "Hurray! Welcome to the Psychiatric Clinic!" Lenka shouted in delight and ran after her. Stilling a trembling in my knees, I climbed down and ran to our room, because straight down the hallway is Roma Jah's and my room with the piano and my gallery.

The window was wide open and the room alive with street sounds. Lenka was sitting on the windowsill, holding the flowerpot with Sasha's chilli plant above the courtyard. Lenka and Sasha's destinies within the commune had jointly ordained that at this time he was again living in the bathroom while his chilli, a small green plant, was growing in our room. That was what held him in the commune, that and Lenka's lunatic eyes, which were presently staring out the open window down the vertical drop to the courtyard.

On the day Sasha planted his chilli, a swollen husk with a white proboscis, he had been rushing round the room until Lenka could stand it no longer and said heatedly, "What are you hanging around here for? Go and do something useless. Why don't you take the iron for a walk." Sasha obediently said: "Okay," I lent my support, and Lenka burst out cackling. She couldn't believe we were really going to do it.

From then on we went for a walk with the iron every evening and Lenka renamed the commune 'The Clinic'. At first, we only took it out to the grass near the house, but then Sasha found a skateboard. We tied a lead to it and fastened the iron on, so that now we could take it for longer walks outside the courtyard. Lenka gleefully shouted from the window, "Loonies!" as we turned out through the archway into the street.

"I wonder how long it would take to land?" she mused, sensing that people had returned to the room. "Has she gone?" I asked and my heart shrank.

"No way!" Lenka said with a shrug and returned the chilli plant to the piano. She leaned against the window frame and put her nose back in a textbook. I turned round to see Sasha standing on the locker from which the ascent to my gallery begins, and looking inside my home. "Oh, what kicks, what kicks!" he intoned.

I got up on the locker beside him and looked. There was Cara, crouching by the far wall next to my book towers and sleeping bag, which was rolled up because it was daytime.

"Roma," I said. "Is it all right if she leaves the commune when it's the right time for her?" "We will all leave the commune when it's the right time for us," Roma responded from his corner. "I will soon be leaving. If she stays after that you won't be able to control the riot." "So be it," I agreed.

A red plastic sign on our window reads, 'Emergency Exit'. Lenka put it there. She met up with a young punk and in the evenings they would walk around building sites, from one of which this icon came to enliven our commune. The window is always open here and how delightfully true that is. Lenka sees things very precisely, which gives her whimsical ideas a slightly existential touch.

Like a harbinger, Cara, you know about time and when your own time will be up. You strut around our room, your claws clattering like horseshoes, not deigning even to glance in the direction of the open window. The Emergency Exit is for the future, and for the present you are here, Cara, changing our world.

That wasn't my idea, it's what Max said. Max is a strange

being, everybody's friend and yet nobody knows anything about him. He is a visitor to the commune. He comes in like a shadow, almost unnoticeable but tangible. He photographs us and all kinds of odd stuff in the apartment, talks to each of us about things personal to us, and goes away again. After he leaves, we always find sweets in unlikely places, but he never admits to bringing them. He is a Muscovite and it seems to be like a visit to the zoo for him, or more precisely to a safari park where you can see animals in their natural habitat.

He is older than me and like an elder brother. I have known him for a long time, in fact he brought me to Yakimanka. Nobody knows what he does for a living, but he has the confident manner of an all-round professional. He has already made his way in life, unlike the rest of us who live in the commune, and that seems to give him the right to be unfathomable and keep his cards close to his chest. That's all I know about Max.

He visited us the day Cara arrived. His eyes lit up and he had his camera pointing at her the whole evening. "These creatures arrive to change our world. As you know," he said when he was leaving.

Cara would stroll round our room and Yakimanka's hallways would throb as people listened to the clatter of her claws. She was against the rules, but how can you change the world without breaking rules? "Anarchists!" old Artemiy grumbled when we went into the kitchen.

Cara likes to crouch motionless and stare for a long time at the bookcase glass which protects Roma's books. If you squat down and pat your knees, she will come nearer and touch your outstretched hand with her big, polished beak. She loves to play, to roll crumpled paper over the floor, throw it up and catch it. She invites you to join in her volleyball by fluttering around and tapping your legs with her beak. It doesn't hurt, although it's a little frightening, because if nature contains anything really alien to human beings it is surely birds.

She is a fussy eater and her favourite fish are very pale, scary caplin. Sasha and I were at our wits' end at first about how to feed her. We placed different foods near her beak. "Craap", Cara would say unambiguously and move away. She found only the caplin acceptable. She would twitch her head, give the fish a shake and swallow it so fast we could never see her do it.

Sasha and I looked after Cara, Roma shook his head, and Lenka took to answering the phone with a deadpan, "Psychiatric Clinic". The caller would ring off. Lenka would cackle, jump up on a stool in the middle of the room and recite, *Exegi monumentum aere perennius...* and continue to the end of the text. This was an indication it was exam time.

When you go to sleep in my gallery, Cara, you move away as far as you can, tuck up your feet and roll back your eyes, covering them with a frightful membrane. I watch you for a long time and can't get to sleep. You inhabit a world as remote from our own as it is possible to imagine, and yet so close, so near to us. Who can say that is not totally miraculous?

Even from my gallery I could hear the hallways filling with ill-natured gossip. "You may not be able to see your neighbours, but always remember they are there," says the Yakimanka rulebook, and how diabolically true that is. Even if your neighbour is out of sight, don't overlook their existence. Even if you can't hear them, remember they are aware of you.

All of them were only too aware of Cara and me, and nobody more so than Sonya Muginshteyn.

Sonya was the fourth person living in our room after Sasha's expulsion. She was sane, which didn't fit in with Lenka's idea of a psychiatric clinic and led her to conclude that Sonya's arrival was a simple mistake. I didn't expect her to last long either, but we had underestimated her. She stayed and stayed and showed no signs of moving anywhere else. In fact it was Tolya who was crowded out. She was studying piano at the

Conservatory and when she came home would practice on our piano. Tolya complained he could not sleep under it afterwards because she had so stirred up the instrument's innards, which for many years had slept the sleep of the just, that it buzzed and groaned all night after Sonya had done with it. So he said and so he believed, and accordingly he ratcheted up his efforts to find himself a girlfriend with a place he could stay. He evidently succeeded, because there was no sign of him in the commune all the time Cara was there.

Sonya was normal which, by the commune's rigorous criteria, was synonymous with dull. For us a dull person was anybody totally ordinary. If that was not true of Sonya, we had no way of knowing it because she was very secretive, not to say uptight. She suppressed her emotions and feelings, never revealed whether she liked or disliked anything, and the result was that we assumed she disliked everything. The only expression we saw on her face was one of toleration. She seemed angular, as if all her movements were inhibited. People who look like that usually have stomach trouble. Giving them a hug would be as unpleasant as trying to cuddle a large white fish. When Lenka and I tried imagining what she wanted from life (and picturing nonsense like that was our favourite pastime) we quickly got bored and went to the kitchen for a cup of tea.

We could not understand how Sonya could live as she did, however, so we didn't lose interest in her. We observed her as a bizarre creature which in some ways resembled us but was in fact basically alien. She was incredibly hard-working and held down three jobs at the same time, which our indolence found deeply repugnant. She was economical with everything, even food, and would cook herself a bowl of plain porridge before retiring for the night. She drank a glass of tea in the morning and went to work. To people as self-indulgent and wasteful as us that seemed weird, and we speculated she must be scrounging meals at work off someone else. She was modest to the point of priggishness, wondered how we could live in the same room as boys and, after a first night spent on a fold-up bed in the middle of the room, told us her back hurt and she couldn't sleep like that. At the time Lenka was sleeping in the bed for old times' sake. She sniffed and relinquished it, and the same day Sonya brought a folding pink screen, which meant that now only I could spy on her sleep from my gallery. Sonya wore heavy pyjamas at night, which we children of the commune found very strange.

For all that, we could not fail to notice Sonya's aura of determination, tenacity and courage, and began to wonder whether all this self-denial was a means towards a goal of which we knew nothing. That dawning insight did not, however, make any real difference. For Lenka, with her susceptibility to nutters and punks, for our rampantly insouciant commune in general, Sonya was an outsider and knew it. We were never unkind to her and treated her like any other member, but she became increasingly uptight and, as a result, even more heroic.

"We are delivered into the hands of the Pharaoh," Sonya might have said, but she didn't and the millennia of endurance of her people towered behind her scrawny figure. Our commune, however, took no interest in peoples, and indeed rarely showed any concern for its individual members. Cara, however, had come to change our world, and she began with Sonya.

Sonya was extraordinarily tidy and had very few possessions. The wardrobe might spew clothes from our shelves, but Sonya's things were in neat piles, as if on sale. She had almost no books but a few Snickers bars huddled forlornly on her locker shelf. She had a weakness for them and always kept a stock. Everybody in the commune had a sweet tooth and the concept of private property did not extend to food, but we never allowed ourselves to misappropriate Sonya's chocolate. It was a matter of principle.

Not for Cara. Somehow she sensed its presence and started

helping herself. None of us ever saw her prising open the locker drawer, extracting Sonya's treasures and making off with them. Nobody knew a thing about it, and Sonya said nothing.

To her, Cara was an annoying pet, introduced on a whim for the purpose of giving her grief. When at home Sonya wore prim, long black skirts. Cara would jump happily up and down and hammer her beak on the hem as it brushed the floor. "Girls, do please keep your bird under control," Sonya would say as she tugged her skirt away.

When she played the piano, Cara would sit at the end squinting at the keys as Sonya depressed them. Sonya had big hands and long, thin fingers with flat white nails. Cara would sit for ages peering intently, and heaven only knows what she was seeing at that moment. "Girls, I can't practise like this," Sonya would finally say, getting up. "Your bird is disrupting my studies."

Unfortunately Sonya always complained in a way that made you not want to help her. She said nothing at all about the Snickers, and we would never have known about them if I had not been delving into the far end of the gallery one time when they came showering out with unmistakeable signs of Cara's liking for them. "Oh, shit!" Sasha and I groaned and rushed out to the nearest kiosk for replacements, but that didn't help.

"Girls, please take these sweets away," Sonya said that evening, laying our purchases out on top of the piano. "As you have evidently decided to feed your bird with my confectionery, you may as well be consistent about it." Sonya enjoyed stoically suffering adversity and we understood the tragic nature of her people's history, but she had fanned the flames of Yakimanka's displeasure with Cara, and Yakimanka demanded Roma should intervene.

"Hey, Titch," Roma Jah called, knocking at my gallery, to which Cara and I had retreated to weather the storm. "Titch,

I'm leaving tomorrow. You promised. There are rules, I told you."

The last rule is: "All of You – Love One Another. Let Your World Remain Yours and All Will Be Well."

Oh, Yakimanka, you seem to do everything in your power to make it difficult for people to love each other. A miracle flew in and you want to drive it away. A miracle flew in the like of which you have never seen before or ever will again but you don't want it and want to drive it away.

Cara looks calm. She knows everything. Outside the gallery Lenka's head can be seen bobbing up and down with two lynx-like tufts of hair pointing in opposite directions. "Look, look!" she exclaims, brandishing Bram's *Lives of the Circus Animals*. "The Great Raven can easily be trained to talk and even uses words intelligently."

Some day a miracle is going to fly in and say to you in human language that we are all up shit creek, and your response is going to be, "What a well-trained bird!"

"Sasha, we're not going to turn her out, are we?" "Don't worry about it, Titch. Everything will sort itself out."

He lovingly loosens his chilli's compost.

Before everything could be sorted out, however, we needed another problem and that problem was that our only bed got broken. After five phone calls which got no further than the Psychiatric Clinic, the mother of the under-age punk got through to the commune and threatened to report Lenka to the police for child molesting if she didn't stop seeing her son. "Loony," Lenka snorted as she put down the receiver, and the next day she and her punk had their farewell tryst in the commune.

When I came into our room I saw Lenka raising the legless frame of Sonya's bed upright. "We were rocking and a-rolling," Lenka explained. "Never mind. She can sleep on the mattress." The bed had long lacked one leg and rested on a solid circular dumbbell weight. Generations before Lenka, and indeed Lenka herself and Sasha, had ridden far from the wall on this bed in the course of a night and just pushed it back in the morning. The surviving legs had, unfortunately, not been able to cope with the punk's onslaught.

Lenka's eyes gleamed feverishly. "We shall make an offering. Having the raven here will be perfect!" Cara and I consented to the rules. The bed was adorned with artificial flowers, fairy lights, and Lenka's drawings of the Slavic deities. Milk, bread and cranberry liqueur were placed beside the altar and we knelt before it. Lenka was already the priestess of Devana and Cara started the proceedings by devouring the caplin sacrificed to her. We drank to the glory of Devana, but when Sasha also reached for the liqueur Lenka admonished him. "Draw back! This is a ceremony of woman. The gods will smite you!"

Sasha withdrew in confusion, grumbling like the spirit of the hearth and went off to smoke a pipe with old Artemiy. The summer twilight was already filtering through our window as we continued to drink to the glory of all the gods of the forgotten ancient pantheon. The taste of the cheap liqueur separated unmistakeably into sour cranberry juice and mean-spirited alcohol. Cara perched on top of the altar, one eye on us and the other looking towards the door where Roma Jah's rucksack stood ready for the road. Were you really thinking about that too, Cara? Were you really thinking?

And then, right in the midst of our celebration, just as the moment was approaching for us to leap up and start beating the tambourines, Sonya Muginshteyn came in and switched on the light. "Hey, Sonya, come and drink with us to the glory of Rod and all the gods of Slavdom!" Lenka exclaimed, proffering her a toothglass.

The memory of her forebears' valiant struggle to enthrone the One God and their wanderings in the wilderness shadowed

Sonya's stolid face for a moment, but only for a moment. "I don't drink," Sonya said. "The gods will smite you," Lenka said knowledgeably, but Sonya remained silent. Frankincense smouldered on the altar and I seemed to see the smoke of the fiery furnace of Babylon. "I shall destroy you!" Lenka screamed in a frenzy. "I shall sacrifice you on this altar to the glory of Devana, to Rod and all the great Slavic gods!"

She shrieked so loudly and with such conviction that Sonya and I both believed her. That very day Lenka had bought a souvenir ritual knife which was tapered, ornately carved, and had a ring on the handle so it could be worn round the neck. It was extremely sharp although no larger than a bodkin. "The altar must be consecrated with blood," Lenka said very calmly, cutting the palm of her hand. Ritual red drops dripped into the milk without dispersing. "To the glory of Rod!"

"Girls, can we finally close this window?" Sonya asked. "I am catching cold, and if I'm going to have to sleep on the floor now that can only make things worse." She took a step towards the window, but Lenka leaped to intercept her. "Dare not! Can you not see that is an Exit? It is not yet time. We must wait!" A tornado of scandal, long developing in our room, began to stir and finally to whip up the air. Cara hopped on to the wardrobe and loudly declaimed a collection of her words. "Karvarmant! Upkarts! Kampostors! Kartel! Kargather!"

"This is all too much!" Sonya exclaimed, a note of irritation creeping into her voice for the first time. "This place is a madhouse! It's all too much!" She left abruptly, while Cara swayed to and fro cawing, "Kalinik! Kalinik!Kalinik!"

"Hurray! She's learned to talk!" We jumped around jubilantly, but suddenly went quiet.

We went quiet and a sudden sense of something ending came over us, through the crimson intoxication of the cheap liqueur, the outburst of outrageous behaviour and celebration. We were quiet and had a sense of time running out for this place, our rented home, our commune, our clinic, our temple of pagan mayhem.

"Perhaps her name is Sarah really," Lenka said, "and she just can't pronounce the 's'." "No," I replied. "Sasha told me Kara means 'black' in Turkic languages." Cara, Cara the Black, impassive messenger of destiny, it was at this moment, when a sense of doom came down upon our inebriate heads, that your time came.

She glided over the room, strutted over to Tolya's paintings propped up in the corner, looked them over with one eye and pecked out of the clay some crackers with which Tolya had inset his latest work. With her powerful beak Cara thumped them against the floor and gulped down the fragments. As if in a movie, at just this instant Tolya returned from his latest binge and appeared in the open door.

I thought he would go ape over the picture, but he went ape over something else. "I know you, Sulfat Melyukov!" he yelled, stamping into the room. Cara cawed and immediately flew to the top of the wardrobe. "What brings you here, my angel?"

"Who are you talking about?" "Sulfat, my dear friend, come on out!" Tolya groped around under the piano. "I know you've turned into your bird, you tricky old alky! I thought you'd croaked long ago, but here you are like a phoenix from the ashes!" "Who are you talking about, Tolya?" "Seiful Melyukov. Don't you remember him, sitting by the pet shop on the Arbat with his animals, a raven and a monkey? They brought in the money to keep him in bread and vodka, and he was so pleased with life and told endless tales about Tamerlane."

We were dumbfounded. We knew who he was talking about. We remembered very well the weird wino who at one time haunted the Arbat. The monkey would dance and the raven would pull out fortune-telling cards. You could be photographed with them. Then he vanished. The Arbat changed. The street musicians and hippies vanished, to be replaced by a lot of pricey food and pseudo-Soviet mementoes. We stopped going there. As I looked up at her on top of our wardrobe, though, I did wonder whether it could have been our Cara whose malign eye followed passersby on the Arbat.

"She can talk," Lenka chimed in, and Tolya's whole demeanour changed to that of a zealous entrepreneur. "You've struck gold! How can you risk keeping the window open? This is treasure, Klondike, and you're on the verge of throwing the gold away together with the sand!"

"Cara means 'black' in Turkish," I reflected. "Could she be that very one? Tolya, perhaps we should give her back? She's his livelihood." "You are so not with it, Titch! Melyukov is dead, so it's foolishness to want to meet him. Tomorrow it'll be us on the Arbat, and we'll tell the fortune of anyone willing to part with 50 roubles!" He legged it over to the window to shut it. "She will no longer be just Cara, but Cara the Black, Bird of Omen, Descendant of the Ravens of the Tower of London!" Tolya was on a roll. "Risking my life I climbed up to steal eggs from a raven's nest and raise this bird! She first ate meat from my own hand!"

Opening and closing the window in our room was a multi-stage process. First, everything had to be removed from the broad windowsill and then the piano had to be moved because it obstructed the window. He was doing all that as the realisation dawned on me of what precisely he was proposing. Having dawned, it became a thought, having become a thought it became a shriek of rage.

"No way!" Tolya did not even turn around. "No way am I going to let you do that! She flew to me. She was looking for friendship, and you want to exploit her all over again!" "Titch, I knew you were impractical, but this is pure sentimentality!" I jumped over and grabbed his arm. "Stop right there! It's supposed to be open. It's Cara's Exit. Roma said she can't stay. This is her last day here." "Roma won't mind if we bring him in on it." He flicked me off his arm like a raindrop.

"Are you so short of money?" "I'm short of an interest in life." "You clown! You sad waster! No way am I going to let you abuse Cara." We hauled each other back and forth from the window. Cara took it all in, and then jumped down from the wardrobe and on to the windowsill. Tolya froze.

"Don't breathe, Titch," he said, interposing his broad back between me and Cara. "Fly, fly away, my Cara," I enjoined her from behind his shoulder. "Fly, girl! There's nothing here for you now!" "Shut it, Titch!" Tolya moved in very slowly, Cara showing no interest in him. She pecked casually at *The Life of Circus Animals*, then peered at him and suddenly leaned forward as if she might be about to fall. She squawked right in his face: "Goodbye, Revolution!"

Stupefied, Tolya stopped in his tracks. Cara walked along the windowsill, stepped on to the piano, pecked at the root of Sasha's chilli, felled it, and gave it a good shake before tossing it out the window. Tolya opened his arms wide to lunge for her, but Cara shot up to the ceiling, impacting with the light bulb which dangled there from its flex. It swayed wildly, shattered and rained shrapnel down on us. In the sudden gloom I saw the shadow of Cara slip out, silhouetted against the blue sky and green June poplars.

"Stupid little idiot," Tolya said without emotion, shaking tiny shards of glass from his hair. The dark blue sky of evening filled our room. Somebody knocked at the door and Sasha looked in to invite me to take the iron for its evening walk but his voice broke off in the twilight as he saw what had happened. "She's gone, then?"

"Yes, and taken your chilli with her," Lenka retorted.

What is there to be said about that? What can we say, Yakimanka, other than simply leave you to get on with your destiny as you leave all of us to get on with ours? So we went out, Sasha and I, to take for a final walk our big, heavy old communal iron with the vestiges of light fabrics baked to its soleplate. A strange feeling came over us. We were wordless and stared up at the sky where a shadow of vague foreboding flew above us like a remembrance of Cara.

It was a long walk. We came to Red Square, we came to the Arbat, we strolled along boulevards, and the first intimations of dawn were appearing when we came upon Grand, who invited us to go East. We all but agreed on the spot, but said we would have to think about it first. What was there for us to think about, though, when we both knew it was Cara the Black who had led us to him. For it had been the shadow of Cara, we both believed, which had glided down to the bench, only when we ran over she wasn't there and instead Grand was. Neither I nor Sasha at first told the other what we had seen.

We went back to the commune, but our room was still sound asleep. Only Roma Jah was missing. The window was wide open, my somnolent roommates huddling in their blankets as warmly as they could.

I sat on the windowsill and looked down at asphalt still wet from the street-spraying truck, at the playground and the grass where dogs were already out walking their owners. Lenka came and sat beside me and dangled her feet over the edge too. She yawned, her eyes still only half open, her blond hair matted, and oh, how fresh and joyous it was to sit there with Lenka as she was now!

"Well, we don't need this any more," she said, tearing off the 'Emergency Exit' sign and skimming it like a boomerang. It rotated a few times before falling inelegantly into the courtyard. I smiled, remembering that at 10.00 Sasha and I had a meeting with Grand, and before that I needed to pack my bag. I felt as if I could have spread my wings, launched myself from the windowsill, and left behind forever the open window of Yakimanka, the communal paradise which let us all grow up.

To the Lake

"Life is about moving on," Grand said, and my summer exploded and raced so fast there was in any case no question of stopping.

There had been Yakimanka, and it had been left behind in the smog of Moscow. There had been Sasha Sorokin, and he was left behind the moment I told him I wanted to go with strange, mysterious Grand, away from here, onward to the East. I had never experienced hitchhiking like that, so easy, spontaneous, impetuous, so passionately impelling us towards a destination known only to Grand, shimmering in infinity.

"Always look them in the eye and say 'Stop!' to yourself," he instructed me, peering towards the horizon. Grand the Wayfarer, who looks like a pirate with his black bandana and shaggy beard. His skin loves the sun, his eyes love distant horizons, and who knows what is in his mind?

"Does that really work?" Grand could teach the birds in the trees, the sunbeams, the waters of a river. Perhaps that's why he is on the road: the road loves those who know what they are bringing with them. And what do you bring with you, friend, other than your willingly borne eternal solitude? "What do you mean, 'Does it work?' You are giving them an order. They hear, 'Stop!'"

I am going to learn from this man, taking in his every word and gesture. Before a day has passed I am walking the way he walks, and within three I have adopted his way of smiling his silent approval, where back on Yakimanka we would have exclaimed, "Cool!" or "Really gone, man!", our voices ringing with delight. What he is going to teach me only God and his messengers know, but Grand radiates a power which attracted me the moment we met, and if anyone thinks he might suddenly just stop and decide to put down roots, I would be the first to lose interest in him.

"Can you see their eyes at that speed and distance?" "It makes no difference."

If we stop near a roadside café, Grand sends me in with a pot in which dry buckwheat is rattling and I come back with porridge, tea and two buns, leaving behind no more than a good mood. I had no idea I could do that.

"No, I do understand, only it doesn't seem likely to work every time." "Don't look at appearances, look at what things mean. Everything that happens to us is a sign. If that car didn't stop for us, it means something." "It means there will be another one along which will stop." "That too. But who will be in the car? Look at those people and learn. These too are signs, lessons. Why has the road sent you these people and not others? What is it inside you that person is responding to? Learn to see it."

I learned and saw. I was pleased the road had sent me this particular kind of man, and I cooked the food when we stopped. I asked questions and Grand always answered them in detail.

There was only one question Grand did not answer, and that was where we were going and why. For some reason that caused a feeling to grow and ripen in me that there was more to my journey than met the eye, and that Grand had had everything planned long ago.

You raise your thumb, half-close your eyes, and how desperately I wish I knew what you are seeing at that moment, my friend, when you look at the road, trying to spot reflections from a windscreen.

Sometimes we got a lift, sometimes we just stood at the roadside. At first it was mostly standing. Moscow had us in her grip and didn't want to let go. We yawned, facing the traffic, looking towards the capital we were leaving and with our backs to our journey, which seemed in no hurry to receive us. We were like stones in a tight catapult someone couldn't pull back far enough to fire us at the East.

We didn't yet know each other. We looked and tried to work out what we could expect and how much we meant to each other, but also how much of that talent for communing with the road each of us had.

In the evening we passed through Shatsk. The last people to stop for us were Greeks in an old black Audi with a foreign number plate. With great difficulty they explained they needed Russian money and offered to sell us a gold ring. With great difficulty we told them we had no money and didn't need a ring. Disappointed, the Greeks drove off, leaving us puzzling over whether it wasn't obvious why we were standing at the roadside.

"Well, not too bad for the first day," Grand said, already surveying our surroundings and wondering where we should spend the night. "Moscow is a big magnet. It's not easy to escape a pull like that."

All day a quiet frustration had been building in me. Grand was not the culprit because I still had faith that my destiny had brought us together, but getting almost no lifts, being ineptly unable to get on our way, was making me tetchy.

"What matters most is our *intention*," Grand said. He pronounced the word as if it came from another language. He kept repeating that all day, looking at me, only too obviously sizing me up, while I did everything in my power to look as if I was no stranger to the road and knew all about hitchhiking.

I held up my thumb and leaned towards every car, but only succeeded in looking like a scarecrow planted by the roadside. It got to a point where Grand enquired how I would feel about our splitting up if need be. "Extremely negatively," I muttered, fondly remembering Sasha with whom I had already split up. He would never have made that suggestion, but then again, it was I who split up with him. Grand just shrugged.

I desperately wanted to do something, and in my irritation the most unexpected thing I could think of was to go over to the black and white striped kerb separating the roadway from a steep-sided ditch and wobble along it, waving my arms about and balancing fairly incompetently. Grand looked on indulgently. I thought he even nodded. I jumped down and turned to face the roadway. It was empty. The fiery sunset was so tranquil and classically crimson you wanted only to think about eternity and forget all about lifts and roads.

"A Gazelle!" We raised our thumbs in unison and a minute later were in the van. "Where do you guys want to go?" The usual question. "As far as possible." The usual answer. "Fine! I'm going to Togliatti, but I need to push it to get there before they close the dam at 6.00 am, otherwise I'll be cooling my heels on this side till Tuesday." The catapult had been fired and we were on our way.

We flew all through the night with a driver who played his one and only cassette on auto-reverse. Music on the road is a topic in its own right. You immediately know what kind of person is giving you the lift. You usually end up listening to a lot of underworld songs and pop, but this driver was young and serious, very focused. His music was electronic hard rock. Wisps of white mist rushed to escape the headlights.

After midnight, the driver passed us a couple of pillows and Grand there and then gratefully fell asleep. I stared in horror. Had he not read Anton Krotov's *Questions and Answers*, the hitch-hiker's bible, which clearly states:

"Sleeping during a lift is STRICTLY PROHIBITED"?

I decided to be stoical. The driver glanced sideways at me and asked why I wasn't sleeping. I stared glassily into the darkness, nodded and smiled, as if to say everything's just fine. I could see he hadn't read Krotov either.

As dawn broke and all around was damp and misty, the massive bulk of the Lenin Hydroelectric Dam in Kuibyshev loomed up around us, a statement comparable to the pyramids, ziggurats or other monuments of long forgotten civilisations.

Paying proper respect to a bygone age, the driver dropped his speed, crossed the Volga, then put his foot down and we were off again. He soon stopped at a junction, we jumped out, and our kindly Gazelle drove off into the city.

It was damp and misty and the long-distance truck drivers who had parked for the night at the roadside café were waking up and setting off in their mammoth vehicles. A flock of gleaming black rooks were circling the road, landing on the asphalt and not flying away. One rook was prostrate near the parking lot and the others were strutting over and trying to get him to fly with the rest of them. He struggled but couldn't take off. Vehicles were driving by very close, so close their gigantic wheels could have snagged his beak but there was not so much as a glint of fear now in the stunned bird's eyes. We stood watching, I in horror, not daring to approach, and Grand grimly.

The long-distance truckers departed, neither taking us with them nor touching the bird, until Grand said, "This is clearly a sign, only what does it mean?" He took a sheet of plywood and moved the rook back to the kerb. It opened its beak, moved its feet, tried to prop itself up on its wings, but couldn't fly. Its black relatives circled, cawing, and in each of them I seemed to see the spectre of my Cara. When we moved away the birds again flew to the injured bird, trying to get him to fly. "A curious sign," Grand repeated.

A sleepy family in a Lada-6 gave us a lift as far as Samara. We bought yogurt and went down to the beach, to the Volga. The sun had already dispersed the mist, but there was nobody there. I went into the water, and the river remembered and welcomed me. "Hello, sister..."

Afterwards I lay on the sand and fell asleep. The sun rose higher, became hotter, but I carried on sleeping, listening to the lapping of the Volga, to the sounds from the town above, to the motorboats, and Grand snorting like a horse after his swim. He came out and lay down beside me and he too fell asleep.

Grand is footloose and fancy-free. Fancy-free and weird. I know nothing about him. Tell me, sister, what kind of man has the road given me as my companion?

"Grand, tell me where we're going." "To where the sun rises."

Having once picked us up, the road carried us on steadily and swiftly. In Samara I woke up on the sunlit beach horrified, thinking we were late, but Grand said you can never be late for your next lift, the one and only lift destined for you. The simplicity of that wisdom impressed me. I believed him and before long we met up with a Gazelle loaded with cherries.

The driver was an Armenian heading to Oktyabrsk, near Ufa in Bashkiria The whole way Grand chatted to him about the price of fruit and vegetables, the best way to buy them and sell them before they went off. Loud music was being played and I could hardly hear them. I ate cherries and threw the stones out the window.

He dropped us off and before we had time to see the roadside a Lada Samara hatchback stopped and took us on to Ufa. The driver was a young guy who laughed at the jokes on the radio and talked to Grand about the price of petrol. Bashkiria, green, bright green and expansive, clean and friendly rushed by the window. On the distant hills we could see the silhouettes of idyllic grazing horses and miniature oil pumps like shadoofs at a village well. I felt I was almost in fairyland.

We bypassed Ufa, by which time it was almost evening. It was almost evening, and we remembered that in the last 24 hours we had skipped two hours ahead. We put our watches forward, checking them with a timer on the recorder in a police car, which cheerfully gave us a lift to the next junction on the bypass.

I wanted to take a breather. It had been a long drive and I was feeling dizzy. Grand's eyes were shining wonderfully bright. We had a glass of tea in a café, washed our hands, surveyed the sky, pigeon-grey from the sunset, and got a lift in a Lada off-roader driven by an Orthodox priest.

He was in a hurry and knew the way well. He smoked, blowing the smoke out of the side window only for the smoke to blow back in on me. He told us he was on his way to the funeral of the abbot of a monastery near Ekaterinburg. A sullen sceptic, it was a puzzle how he had come to be ordained. Grand talked about church services, fasts, pilgrimages and the monastic life. He said he had worked in a monastery and intended to become a novice himself but changed his mind. It was the first time I had heard Grand say anything about himself.

"We went to Sarov a month ago," our buddy the priest told us, gradually thawing out. "We walked there from Kazan. That's a holy place, where Saint Seraphim lived and worked, and it is good to go there. It is good to go there and you too, when you feel the call in your soul, should go to Sarov, to pray in the holy places. There are springs there, and water... It is good to go there."

He was so carried away he didn't bother to stop when a cop raised his baton. He lowered the sun visor, which had 'Monastery' inscribed on the reverse, and drove on muttering, "Scoundrels, the lot of them".

In the darkness we could make out a gloomy forest along the road. I could feel the breath of night coming through the air vent and was preparing myself for another sleepless passage on the road when our benefactor said, "I'm not driving through Sim. You need to know the road there in the dark. You hear the devil's fife playing in the dead cedar trees."

Grand nodded. We pulled up at a log-built coaching inn, there was no other way to describe it, with a high porch and fretwork architraves. This roadside refuge in the forest gave off a sense of great antiquity, with the Ural Mountains all around and a solitary yellow lantern swaying above the car park. The priest invited us in, meticulously washed his hands at a washstand, and then ordered beer and soup for himself, and tea and fried eggs for us.

He hunched over the table, looking down into his plate, eating and drinking in silence. He had a bushy beard the shape of a shovel, an unsmiling face and the broad back of an old-fashioned carter. The inner room was brightly lit and empty and the light made Grand and me look pale and haggard.

"Well, don't give in to sin, children," our priest adjured us, sending us on our way. "You are young and temptation is always near at hand." I had already picked up my bag when Grand went over to be blessed and bowed deeply before him. After that we went out to the dark road and were picked up by a taciturn insomniac KamAZ truck driver who took us over the Urals in six hours. I found out then all about Sim, a steady ascent by hairpin bends where the stars become ever more numerous both above and beneath us.

From near Tyumen we hitched a ride with Muslims: two fast-driving Azerbaijanis with two new Ladas in which green discs with a tassel and a gold monogram reading 'Allahu akbar' swung behind the windscreen. As soon as Grand got in and saw this talisman he greeted them with the same words and from then on the conversation never deviated from a discussion of festivals, traditions and the Qur'an. The driver in our car was called Roma and told us that when Arabs had come to Tyumen, commissioning a factory of some description, the first thing they asked when entering a new building was which way was east. Roma thought they were brilliant. He thought Grand was brilliant too, and was constantly phoning and talking about us to his wife at home or to his partner in the other car. After this the other car drove up parallel to ours and its driver shouted something cheerful and hospitable through the open window. They sometimes exchanged cigarettes, a lighter, food and water bottles through the window in just the same way without stopping.

They were reluctant to say goodbye, gave us their telephone numbers and insistently invited us to drop in on them for kebabs on the way back. Grand agreed, and I could tell from his expression that he really would visit them any time he was returning along that road.

From Omsk to near Novosibirsk we were driven in a passenger Gazelle from Krasnoyarsk with a Moscow number plate. Two drivers were taking it in turns to drive. The one who had the day off sat in the back with a bottle of vodka. I was in there with him and our rucksacks, and Grand was in the front. Judging by his by now very thick beard, the strange look in his eyes, and some singular Siberian propensity of their own, the guys decided Grand was an Old Believer and asked which community we were heading for. The whole way they were preoccupied with the Church Schism and wanted Grand to tell them why it happened and why some had refused to accept the new faith 400 years ago. At first Grand just smiled, but then he started talking about the oneness of God, freedom of choice and predestination. He didn't deny being an Old Believer.

We drove for a long time before making a stop. The men produced something along the lines of a Primus stove but couldn't get it to light. They splashed petrol over it and ignited it. The stove burst into flames. We were shocked, but the guys said that when the petrol had burned off their stove would work well, and in next to no time they had cooked up Siberian *pelmeni* dumplings on their contraption.

During the second part of our journey with them, my companion finished the vodka and lost interest in philosophy. He kept beckoning me over, pressing his vodka wetted-lips to my ear, and asking over and over again, "You sure you know where you're going? How long've you known this character? Come on, you can tell me, aren't you afraid? Oh, what a pretty state of affairs. Young people have their eyes shut. Can't you see he's making off with you? Abducting you!"

I forced a smile and moved away. The geezer dozed off, opening his eyes now and again to give me a knowing wink, then drew me over and whispered, "Where do you come from yourself? Go back home, lassie. Come on, I'll give you the money for the ticket. Want that? Ohh... no-o... Come on, I'll give you the money. You've no idea where you're going, no idea. You're sectarians, I can tell."

I said nothing and moved as far away as I could. The road seemed endless. Grand carried on talking about the Schism, freedom of choice and the spiritual path. I had never asked him about his faith, and he had never before volunteered any information about it.

Grand said, "Women are infinitely more gifted than men. A woman needs only to be given impetus and direction for her then to guide her teacher forward." I longed to be a woman like that. I longed for a teacher to give me direction and then everything else could go to hell. For some reason, though, nothing I did ever impressed Grand. He took it as only to be expected. In the tales he told, girls who were remarkable were either witches or wise women, or at the very least 'gifted'. I never advanced beyond 'Titch'.

Then suddenly on my road the witch appeared, hung like the sword of Damocles over my head, and my days were full of anxious, dispiriting anticipation. She appeared when, for the first time, Grand gave more than a vague answer to my repeated question of where we were going. "East", he said, and then added, "We are going to a Lake. Someone will meet us there. I think it will be right for them to come with us."

My heart sank. In that genderless 'someone', as Grand always referred to everyone, I suddenly saw unambiguously that this would be a girl, and not just any girl but one I (and Grand) had come the length of Russia to meet. I wanted and at the same time was reluctant to ask about her. I wanted and was reluctant to set eyes on her. She had become our goal and my question of 'where' had now changed to 'who'. Every time Grand answered, I tried pathologically to detect something that would tell me more about her and about what kind of woman Grand was in such a hurry to get back to.

I pictured her as wise, calm, someone who knew life's reality, someone with a warm, open smile, a gentle light in dark eyes, imposing, engaging and attractive. In other words, I pictured her as much the same as Grand, only even better. She was, after all, Woman, the embodiment of everything in the world that is beautiful. When I thought of her like that my very soul couldn't wait to get the road behind us, the sooner to exult in this meeting.

Alas, I then immediately imagined Grand and me meeting Her, and wondered where I would fit in when she was finally there. I, after all, am me, Titch, the eternal teenager, a puppy with big eyes, the spirit haunting the gallery on Yakimanka. What was there in me of real Woman. How could I possibly stand alongside Her? In any case, what need would there be for me next to Grand when she was there? Thinking along those lines, I stood at the roadside like a weary donkey and not a single vehicle saw fit to pay us any attention.

One of those nights I had a dream: a very tall, bespectacled girl, plump and chubby, approached, towered over me, held out her hand and wanted to introduce herself. In my dream I was horrified. I woke up totally perplexed, recalling that within a day, or at most two, I would be meeting her in the flesh. If we didn't wait for Sasha where we had agreed, it could be even less. She was already expecting us. I knew that because Grand had had a text message the day before which put a smile on his face like none I had seen before. He started replying, a dozen times erasing and re-typing every word. I bristled like a hedgehog and retreated to the tent.

I decided to take definitive action to resolve everything once and for all. It might kill two birds with one stone by demonstrating to Grand how remarkable I am, and at the same time at last reveal to me something about Her. I resorted to subterfuge. I was so scared that Grand with his shrewdness would immediately see through me and felt I was throwing myself in desperation into a whirlpool, but my curiosity got the better of me.

"Last night I dreamed we had arrived," I said and paused, watching Grand out of the corner of my eye. We were having breakfast in the tent because it was overcast outside. He said nothing, knowing I would continue, which I did.

"We met a girl," I said, keeping my eyes on him. Grand munched. "She came over to shake hands," I ended pointedly. Grand finished what he was eating and asked, "What did she look like?"

I didn't want to tell him the truth: the lanky creature in my dream could not possibly be Her, I was sure. I started making it up, watching his expression. "Well, she was tall... Maybe not as tall as you, I'm not sure, but taller than me for sure. And she wasn't skinny but neither was she fat. Average. She had long hair – dark or brown – I don't remember. And glasses." I broke off. Never mind if some of the fine detail didn't fit, I would be able to see that straight away and get a better picture of her. It wouldn't bother me at all if he laughed and said, "No, she does not wear specs, and her eyes are blue, she has blond hair, and in any case... Come on, get ready. This is all just drivel."

Something really did light up in Grand's eyes, though, but it was hard to tell quite what. He said, "What else do you remember?" "Oh, nothing." "Perhaps she said something? Introduced herself?" "Hmm," I prevaricated mysteriously. "I think she did. Yes, I remember now. She did tell me her name." "And?"

I was certain he had seen through me and that by now I

was playing by his rules. I felt like putting a stop to it, but I also felt, what the hell. "Nastya," I blurted out, and Grand's face flickered and changed in a barely perceptible way, like when a stripe runs down the TV screen: the picture stays the same, but something has changed nevertheless. I could see I wasn't going to get anywhere.

"Mmm, yes, that I do remember. She came over, held out her hand and said, 'Hello, my name is Nastya'."

Grand put down his mug and left the tent. I could have cried with frustration. Two days later, though, I discovered he had simply had nothing to add. She was called Nastya.

She was called Nastya, and she was tall, neither thin nor fat, and had small steel-rimmed spectacles which made her look like a laboratory assistant in a Natural Science department. Her hair was long and of a colour so common in Russia it doesn't have a name. Just dark. A person with thin, almost honed, features, cheekbones, eyebrows, the slant of her eyes, nose, lips; they lay symmetrically in ribbon-like lines and stretched when she smiled, not changing their shape. In those first days I was amazed that her body language seemed barely to reflect her emotions. I found her face inscrutable, as inscrutable as Asian faces are said to be to Europeans.

Hurtling along above the speed limit, viewing the world as an endlessly repeated gift, we burst into the city, and found it unwelcoming and grim. "A witch lives in this town," Grand said. "She is gifted but I think you will be able to help her in a number of ways." "It would have been good if you had told me beforehand. What will I need to do?" "Nothing. Just be the way you are."

The way I am. Me, Titch, with a rucksack on my back and tattered sneakers on my feet. I am walking through a new town, glancing into the faces of passersby, wearing my inconstant, crazy hitchhiking smile, so what am I going to be able to reveal to your witch, friend, other than how to brew tea over a campfire till it's just the way you like it?

We stood across from Moskovsky train station under the awning of a large hotel with dark walls which reflected us. It was hot and the busy street, full of traffic, flowed past us like lava. We stood in the shade but nobody walked in this cool, inviting space. They steered clear of these two odd, dusty strangers.

We burst into this city and our hearts were pounding as fast as our progress, almost four thousand kilometres in four days. We burst into the city, bringing with us all the same gifts we had given in each car: love of life, freedom from care and an enormous smile – but had suddenly to stop as we realised we had to wait. We waited, we took it easy, and my excitement, which had reached the level of hysterical palpitations, deflated and was expelled like air when you exhale deeply and are left empty and ready to take in a new breath. Those were Grand's words when he was teaching me to understand the art of breathing, and now I understood them.

I was empty, turned round, and saw Her. Grand had not spotted her yet and was staring vacantly ahead although she had already come round the corner. She was coming towards us but still he didn't see, or didn't recognise her. I knew that was Her and got up from our bags. She approached in a stiff, almost business-like manner and my self-confidence grew steadier and firmer with every step she took. There was nothing about her to justify all my anguish these last days. There was nothing about her I needed to fear.

An instant before she approached, holding out her hand, I knew what she was going to say. "Hello, my name is Nastya." Then she'd turn to Grand as if I were no longer there.

How hard the climbing was at first! It was hard for me because I wasn't used to it and I lagged behind. Nastya was up in front, with Grand following her. Sasha was miles back down the path. Nastya viewed the two of us with a sense of superiority. I could feel every blister on my feet and didn't give a damn about anything else.

Then suddenly everything changed. The open hills, the sloping meadows turned gradually into dense taiga forest. Bizarrely shaped boulders began to peep from beneath the moss. It was a forest of dark pines and larch trees. Now Nastya started falling behind while Sasha and I ran on ahead. We put our best foot forward and the trail seemed no more than a Sunday stroll.

On the third day it became obvious we were lost. Nobody said as much, but we all knew it. We hiked on, but our mood was less buoyant. Grand said nothing either, but started cutting back on the rations. "We can always scrounge food off somebody else," Sasha said nonchalantly, but nobody replied. We hadn't seen a soul during our trek.

Sasha was looking like a wood-goblin. A faraway smile appeared on his face as he dug about in the grass, smacking his lips with satisfaction. In behind his glasses his eyes were spotting things the rest of us overlooked: wild strawberries and allium, cranberries hidden deep in the shade; honeysuckle on bushes, and occasionally gooseberries and a variety of mushrooms. He would pop up to one side of us, in front of us, be catching us up from the rear, festooned with leaves and twigs, bearing the fruits of the forest before him in a plastic bag. When we stopped he would brew herbal teas and braise mushrooms in their own juice in the pot lid. I clambered through the bushes with him.

We gnawed the fibrous white alliums. They were sweet, but with salt and dried bread they were delicious. Sasha could conjure food out of the ground. "Sasha, how come we were so hungry at the lakes?" "Because it was spring, of course, Titch. May."

Sasha and I went far ahead of the others, gathering things to eat. Nastya looked on as if to say, "This is just what I expected.

It's all you are capable of. Now let's see you get us out of this mess." She didn't eat our mushrooms and grumbled that, if we were going to stop at every bush, we would never get anywhere. Grand was more and more unsmiling and had ever less to say. He began taking a serious interest in the extent to which these gifts were a real alternative and supplement to our rations. He trusted our instinct in respect of unfamiliar mushrooms, but did cut some open himself. If they didn't darken he would know they were poisonous. Sasha and I hadn't a care in the world. We gathered honeysuckle. It was delicious if you added it to porridge made with dried milk.

"What do you think, Sasha, are we going to get anywhere?" "Who cares, Titch. Look what a great time we're having."

Forest-covered mountains, boulders combining different colours nestling among moss-covered tree trunks. There were unexpected expanses: we might emerge to find ourselves on the edge of a precipice and hold our breath at the height and the noise of a river raging down below in the gorge, or come across fields covered with strawberries. More forests, streams with the hoof-prints of unshod horses on their banks. Every time I gazed ahead I expected to see our lake shining mirror-like in the distance.

"Grand, where are we going?" "The only direction worth travelling is towards infinity."

Grand is an experimenter. He plays games as if compiling chess problems. He puts the pieces on the board and watches to see how they behave. He changes the disposition and looks again. He adds new pieces and looks again, evaluating, as if seeking the optimal progression – or is it just that he likes experimenting?

Right now, however, he is in a muddle. Something in his chess game is not working out. He doesn't know what, but it is already too late to change the configuration and looks as if someone other than he is moving the pieces. This someone else seems always to get the calculations right, even though they don't agree with Grand's.

He is at a loss. He doesn't know what to do next and doesn't notice that he is himself on the chessboard now, along with us, his chess pieces.

You took me on a walk through Chelyabinsk one night and taught me only to look at the shadows. The shadows of trees, of branches in leaf. Thin, knotted, light, obedient to the breeze, they came alive and spoke of the town, the warm night and the dusty air. Shadows of fences, benches and posts were patterns on the asphalt, the monumental memory of the town. Shadows of the infrequent passersby blurred and disappeared. They possessed sound, colour and mood. Shadows revealed the world to me.

"Everything around us is signs which you can learn to read," he said, and the world opened like a huge book. The world became alive and immense, it began to throb, breathe, be heard – and all that was external to me, independent of me, here and now, right beside me.

You taught me to trust the Earth, to walk backwards without looking round. You taught me to listen and hear, to look and see. You taught me that the world is greater than we know or can know.

How then is it possible, friend, that you were unable to see something as simple as the ordinary love of a woman?

They suddenly turned into incredibly adult and boring people. They turned into a ball and chain on each other's legs, trudging wearily with eyes unfocused.

We had already been waiting three days in the city for Sasha who had got stuck somewhere on the road, and meanwhile we were living with Nastya in an apartment piled high with old furniture and smelling of decay. Its owner was an ancient deaf woman who moved from one room to the next like a spider, slowly and silently. She didn't shuffle and seemed long ago to have become one with the walls, to have dissolved in the shadows, to be part of the dust on the furniture, of the mildew on the ceiling, of the dim lamps, of the books with faded bindings, the paintings, the figurines, the crumbling decor and fittings which retained their value only in the eyes of their mistress.

The old lady is probably no longer in this world, but even then she seemed to be not wholly there. All of us who were temporarily living in her apartment tried not to notice her and treated her like all the other objects in it, with care because they were decrepit, but trying not to come into contact with them more than necessary because they made us squirm. We ignored them because they were irrelevant, because their time had passed. They came from a world to which we did not, and never had, belonged. They were like the glimpse into the past afforded by a faded, yellowed photograph. When I recollect her now the old woman is more alive for me than she ever was when I lived alongside her.

A hearing aid shrieks in her ears. It shrieks incessantly, at very high frequencies, and the louder it shrieks the more quietly we speak or even stop talking altogether. We suspect she turns the sound up the better to eavesdrop on us, the young, the living. We grudge her that. We don't want to share our strength with this creature which is already crumbling into dust. She sneaks up to closed doors almost inaudibly; she tries to hear the sounds we make, even our breathing.

"Nastya, why is it so quiet in here? Why aren't your friends talking? Really, Nastya, you know I can't bear silence," she says finally, coming in to us. My eardrums cannot bear the squealing of her earpieces.

It is impossible to stay in the apartment so we go out for a walk, but as if fulfilling an obligation or doing a chore. We walk, describing circles through the town until our legs can carry us no longer. Grand and Nastya talk, walking side by side, staring down at the asphalt. I feel like a child next to them. I can't walk that slow, and run on ahead, play on the swings, chase dogs, make the pigeons fly up in the air. Nastya adopts a pained expression when I come close, so I try to spare her feelings by giving her a wide berth.

"Step on the side and Lenin's just died," I murmur a children's rhyme as I try not to step on the joins in the paving slabs. "Step on a crack and Hitler comes back," I recite, making the task more difficult, and have to slow down and be even more careful about where I put my feet. Nobody in our kindergarten wanted Hitler to come back. No matter how slowly I try to walk, I still catch up with them.

"So what do you do for a living, when you're not travelling?" I hear Nastya enquire. "The road is my life." Grand's favourite answer. I stop and look around, wondering what to do next. "Walking, walking down the street, thinking where we put our feet," I recite as I proceed along a kerb, my arms outstretched like a tightrope walker.

"How you've changed!" "That's only natural. You've changed too." "No, somehow you have changed completely." "My quest hasn't changed." "Oh, you and your quests. That's all so insufferably abstract!" I don't want to listen to them.

"Zooom, plane coming in to land, request permission to land, charter flight Moscow-Beijing..." I roar past, darting between the passersby and hear from behind me, "Oh, this is impossible. It's like a kindergarten!"

For Chrissakes, does she think I don't know what she's up to? God and all the envoys of light know I know perfectly well, but my role here is to be myself, to be Titch. That is the purpose for which Grand dragged me from one side of Russia to the other. The only question is: how was he able to see that dawn morning on the boulevard that I, sluggish, half-asleep Titch, was the person whose mere appearance would jolt Nastya out of her indifference to him?

She clings to him, doesn't take her eyes off him. She has measured, weighed, probed him with her eyes, studied him from top to toe to ascertain the differences between the Grand she knew and the Grand who has turned up now with silly, infantile me in tow. She looks at him and tries to figure out what we have in common, how I come to be here with him. She would never just ask him that straight out, so I will carry on playing my role to the end, and then who cares what happens?

Sasha Sorokin will come to the rescue.

Mountains, larch trees, swamps. I never realised you get swamps in the mountains. We trek on, looking where we are treading, seeing only the rucksack of the person in front. Above are branches and a lowering sky, but if you look into the distance you see beyond the forest, rocky ranges as sheer as walls. At their summits there are glaciers. You can't see them behind the clouds, but I know they are there. That's why it's so cold at night.

It has been raining for three days and any time now we will turn into mushrooms, get covered in moss and mildew, and settle down here to live forever. You really don't want to move. You just want to stay immobile in the tent and sleep, burrowing deep into a warm sleeping bag.

Grand does not allow us that pleasure. He gets us up and forces us to go on, into the rain and the mud. He says that as long as we are on the move we are in some measure heading towards our goal, whereas if we stop we just eat, and our rations are running low.

We trudge through the swamps following a narrow track, not seeing each other, not knowing each other. We are just backs carrying a rucksack, stooped, our feet squelching in the mire. When we stop we say little, and lie down quietly in the tents to sleep. In the morning we get up to go on, and not to see, not to know, never to get to know each other.

Sometimes I stare at the way she walks, at her figure under that rucksack, and when we stop I stare into her eyes. I stare at her, trying to make her out, but her face remains as inscrutable as the bronze faces of Buddhas. Her body is tense and hard and she puts her feet down almost without flexing them. What she wants, what she hopes for is hidden away, sealed. She's not going to tell anyone, probably not even herself. Sometimes, especially in the light of the campfire, I seem to see her face crumple, to sag into wrinkles, and she begins to look like the old lady with the parchment skin in whose apartment we were living. Nastya had met us by the station and taken us there. She talked incessantly, recalling her time with Grand, once, long ago. As we got to the door she had got to the moment when they parted.

"My friends who saw you put me on the train asked afterwards, 'Who was that, then? Is he a friend? Your boyfriend? A relative? Your guru? What's the relationship?'" she said, inserting the key in the lock. It rasped. "I told them, 'He's all those things.'" As she pulled the door open, she turned round, looked me straight in the eye and said, at that moment just for me (and never had anything to say to me again), "After all, that's how it is." Her eyes finished the phrase. "Isn't it."

Yes, it is, as we both know. And since that is how it is, since that is how it is for both of us, why can we not just be friends? Why is there no understanding between us and why do we behave as if there is something we don't want to share, something we are afraid of losing? No, neither of us has anything. Grand is footloose and fancy-free, and if he did suddenly put down roots I would be the first to disown him.

Sasha Sorokin had come to the rescue, materialising on Grand's mobile as unexpectedly as people do when hitchhiking. We went immediately to collect him. They went, but I rushed full tilt and fell on his neck, rubbing my face against his hedgehoggy ginger cheeks. "Hey, Titch! Steady on. You'll knock me over."

He was swaying under the weight of his rucksack. Unslept, dust-laden, he smelled of Yakimanka and the road, or rather, of beer and fags which of course is the same thing.

Grand and Nastya joined us rather primly. Sasha, always sensitive to other people's moods, became formal too and shook hands with them. We returned unhurriedly to the apartment, but I was capering around him like a little dog, babbling away, "At last, at last you've arrived. I've missed you so much, and all the stuff that is going on here, but you'll see that for yourself, you'll understand."

Unshaven, intoxicated by food after famine, Sasha had sat round-shouldered in the kitchen, talking excitedly about the trials of his journey. Even the old woman's auricles were silent: Sasha rattled on so loudly and enthusiastically she could hear him clearly even from her room.

A month later, when we were lost and a search party was sent out for us, the old woman told the cops we quite certainly belonged to a sect and the unshaven one with the ginger stubble must have been our leader, because we had been waiting for him for several days and been silent the whole time.

"Grand, tell me where we are going?" "I told you already, Titch. We are going to where there is power."

If only they would talk to each other, but they say nothing. More precisely, they talk endlessly but it's all just nonsense. They have said nothing of any substance which might, for example, clarify the mystery of why Sasha and I are separating them. I sleep in Grand's tent and Sasha sleeps in Nastya's.

They look as if the person they knew before was someone else, as if they had been waiting for that someone else but a different person has been substituted for each of them. They look as if they don't know what has happened. It would seem that only Sasha and I know that, but because they are silent we are silent.

What they were like before, Nastya and him, what they meant to each other I can only surmise, try to read in their eyes, in their moods and silences. I think sometimes I might be able to do something if I knew the situation for sure, but I don't, so all Sasha and I can do for now is be, and hike on to our Enchanted Lake. It is a role we perform faultlessly.

I never had any idea before what getting lost in the forest must feel like. I still can't really see how it came about that we got so lost. We were following tracks the whole time. So what if sometimes the track disappeared and Sasha and Grand started arguing about whether anybody had ever gone along it or whether it was only an animal track. So what if we hadn't met a single other person in all that time. Nothing too terrible was happening to us, and if anything distinguished our progress from an ordinary hike in the forest it was only a disagreeable, oppressive feeling that we were lost and didn't know where we were going.

That was enough to make the forest seem more grim, claustrophobic, and indifferent towards our fate. It was all around us, growing in on all sides, and seemed to be deliberately opening up before us in order to lure us on, further and further, and when you turned to look back you could see no sign of your own steps. The trail behind had already been overgrown by the forest.

We started seeing things. I could have sworn I saw an old man with a beard. It showed in the rocky profile of the mountains, in a bend in the river, in the patterning of tree bark, in mud which had dried fantastically on our trail. His hat was trimmed with fur, his big lips had sunk into his moustache, his brows overarched his eyes, and he had a fleshy nose and large birchbark earrings.

I first saw him when, deep in thought, I was gazing at the intertwining of the veins in a rock, a large, white, patterned stone which had remained cool and slightly damp in the heat of the sun. His face appeared and became clearer. Even after looking away, I immediately found him again, so naturally did the lines come together to form his image. Now I see him anywhere I look.

We were sitting silently round the campfire, drying our things over it, while above us every now and then it started to rain. For us, though, even marginally warm clothes were welcome. The glaciers exhaled their cold breath but were still far away. As, indeed, was the Lake. Grand had seemed particularly alert today as we trekked on, often looking around, staring at something. I knew he was looking for signs as to why we couldn't find the right path, what was hindering us.

"These mountains are full of spirits," he said suddenly, looking into the fire. "Good or evil?" Nastya asked. "Spirits aren't good or evil," he replied. "This land is theirs and we are their guests. We need to remember that and behave accordingly." "I know," Sasha interjected. "There are wood sprites here. They point the berries and mushrooms out to me." "Do you treat them with respect?" Grand asked. "Yes, I always thank them." This was perfectly true. I'd seen Sasha myself, bowing in acknowledgement of every mushroom. "Good," Grand said nodding and fell silent. We were all conscious that he had brought us here, and only he could lead us out again.

That night I dreamed. A tree was stooping over the tent, muttering. It was a huge, spreading spruce. In its outline I begin to recognise the familiar features, the old man, his head in a hat, his hairy face, his earlobes distended by the oversized earrings.

I heard a voice: "The mountains are misleading you, misleading you. The branches are poorly linked, they fall apart. You have no single goal or vision. You have nothing to give but you want to get. The mountains are misleading you."

"The mountains are misleading you ... They are misleading you ..." I mumbled as I woke up because Grand was shaking me by the shoulder and shining a torch in my face. I was still uncoordinated, unable to think clearly, and he was shaking me. "Tell me who you are?" "Whaddya mean? It's me!" I parried. "Who were you? Who were you talking to?" "I was dreaming, it was a dream!"

His face was hard, almost brutal, as if he had just let someone slip whom he had been pursuing for a long time. I felt distraught. I told him the dream, what there was of it. "Yes, I see." He was pensive. "Yes, yes, I see." He looked upwards and said to someone not in the tent, "Thank you." He turned off the torch and snuggled back down in his sleeping bag.

We are standing beneath a huge larch tree. It is growing on the edge of a cliff, alone. There is a clearing beneath its branches, the perfect site for a couple of tents. We light a fire before it starts raining. We haven't heard the sound of the river for some days now, the one which was leading us to the Enchanted Lake.

"Well then, Grand, when do we get there?" Nastya asked rudely. "When we change." "What do you mean, change?" "Stop behaving in the old ways and become different." "So how are we behaving?" "Badly. We keep trying to guess what is coming next, we're waiting for something and hoping." "Well, what should we be doing?" "We should be living here and now. Rejoicing in what is around us, in what is happening to us." "Oh, Grand! My feet haven't been dry for days, we've been frozen for nights at a time, we fall asleep at dawn then drag ourselves off to who knows where, eat those disgusting swamp mushrooms. What is there to rejoice about?" "Rejoice nevertheless! See everything as a trial, a lesson, and be glad that you have an opportunity to change."

"Grand, it's just talk for you but I really am frozen, and

I really am sick and tired of all this! You keep teaching us but nothing changes in the slightest, and it's completely unclear where we're supposed to be going!"

Quite what happened next neither I nor Sasha really saw. While they were talking we were trying not to look in that direction, to make as little noise as possible and get on with cooking our porridge. All we saw was that Grand seemed suddenly to pounce on Nastya and she sprang back, as if he had sent her flying, to the larch tree. She looked scared but Grand was already quietly coming back to the fire. "You're right," he said flatly. "Words don't change people much. The Zen masters had good reason to carry a stick." I thought Nastya would be in a big snit, but she came over and behaved just like us, and we were pretending nothing had happened.

Then he hit Sasha because he was in raptures at finding orange milk mushrooms and rattled on, as he usually did, telling us tales of things that had happened to him in the past when he had been out looking for them. Nastya got it in the neck one more time for refusing to take her glasses off, even though she knew she didn't need them and her eyes needed a rest. After that Sasha was deprived of his glasses too, and I got a not very serious kick for talking a lot of stuff about reading Tarot cards and coffee grounds. In the end I found I agreed with Grand that I'd been talking a lot of nonsense.

We became less boisterous and more disciplined, and kept a closer eye on what we said and did. Perhaps this, at least, would bring us closer to the Lake.

"Grand, would you like me to tell you all about her?" "Go ahead, Titch." "You met on the road. More precisely, it was the road brought you together, somewhere around here, in these parts, and you both went West. Am I seeing that correctly?" "Yes, so far you're getting it right." "The hitchhiking was easy and swift. You taught her to understand the lessons the road offers and to see the signs around her. In the towns you showed her the right way to walk backwards and look at the shadows on the asphalt. Right?" He smiled.

"Then you came to the town where you live and let her into your home. She lived there long enough to get accustomed and attached to you, to learn your weaknesses and remember what you like. But then it was autumn and you didn't feel like going on the road, right?" "The autumn was warm, Titch. We could have gone anywhere, but things didn't turn out that way. We just strolled around a bit in the woods near the town."

"Okay. Then the rain came. It was time for her to go back, but it would have been grim for her to try hitching a long way on her own. You very civilly put her on a train and you parted. You corresponded. From her letters you saw how attached she was to you. You hadn't expected that. She wrote to say she wanted to see you again. You doubted that was a good idea but then decided you could, as long as you were not on your own. That way her attention would not be focused solely on you. At which point Sasha and I came on the scene. Am I right?"

"Yes, on the whole, yes. From her letters I saw that one year had been long enough for her to forget everything I'd taught her. She'd lost the goal. But I also recognised that I was the only man in her life she had fallen in love with."

"Splendid. See how well I have learned my lessons! I won't forget a thing. Only, you know what? As I've been such a good pupil, just promise me, Grand, that I won't find out on the return journey where you live."

The rain has stopped during the night and the morning is sunny. We crawl out of the tents and warm ourselves. We begin enjoying life, laughing and joking, something we haven't done for a long time. Twenty metres from the tents we find a low rock shelter among the boulders suitable for making a fire to enable us afterwards to dry our things on the heated rocks. Next to it is a large flat boulder which I immediately proclaim to be our table and lay our mugs and plates out on it. Sasha and I start making breakfast.

We play at home comforts, forget the rain and the damp, and almost forget we are lost. The forest begins to seem hospitable. It fills with birds and we can hear the distant roar of a river we couldn't hear yesterday.

Sasha takes his clothes off and repairs to the shelter and its fire. He sits there in his underpants and hiking boots, grunting with pleasure as if he's in a bathhouse. I imagine clouds of steam coming off him. Nastya arrives, looks round and sits down, frowning in the sunlight. She gives me a smile. Everything is so fine today that we're prepared to like each other. A little distance away in the glistening bushes I find a few small dark raspberries which I proudly bring back and place on our table.

Suddenly Grand jumps out of the bushes. He is oddly rigid, his eyes fiery. He looks demented, like a lion (if you can have a demented lion). He leaps on to the rock and stares round at us as if about to reveal something. I am pleased to see him and say jokingly, throwing up my hands in mock horror, "This is our table, Grand. Why are you standing on it?"

Before I have finished, the lion leaps down on me from above, pushes me in the chest and knocks me over. I fall backwards and just have time to see his furious, fixed stare, his pitiless frozen eyes and I quail in terror. I flee to the niche under a rock where Sasha is and don't move. Grand stalks off. It is quiet, as if nothing has happened.

I jump up and run. I slither on the sodden ground, terrified at first that he may be coming after me, but he isn't. He has done all he wanted to, only why? What had I done wrong? I run, bawling. Not with pain but from incomprehension and the sense of hurt. What had I done to him? Who is he? I've come the devil knows how far and he starts fighting the moment anything is not just so! That's it! Sod him, I'll turn back and leave him to it. Alone? So what?! Hitchhiking? No problem! Only I know I won't be on my own: it only needs one person to rebel and they'll all leave him. He can go alone on his travels as far as he likes but I'm out, I've had it up to here, he's nothing to me and nothing will change for me except that now I'll never see the Lake! Except that I'll never...

I stop, dumbstruck. After all, what is it I'm travelling for? For the Lake. It's nothing to do with Grand and his games. No, my goal is the Lake. A wonderful, pure mountain lake reflecting glaciers like a mirror. That's what it's all for. What have I got? What do I stand to lose? Nothing, except my goal.

My emotions subside, and in the stillness I suddenly hear the bubbling roar of water from somewhere seemingly close. Very close. Behind those bushes. I only need to climb up this slope and there will surely be... Well, I might have to climb a bit further up there and then I'll see it. Or a bit further... and a bit more... I'll get to it quickly, before they even notice I've gone. It's somewhere here. It's so loud it must be nearby. It's thundering, boiling, it must be a huge waterfall. If it still isn't here, how it's raging in the place where it is! It really must be huge. I'll see it any minute now. Now. Just on a little further. Here, here...

I scramble and climb, there are no trees, there are no longer any bushes, all that remains is the stones, the scree, grey, tetchy, they slip away under your feet and you slide down with them, and the roar is deafening, but now I emerge at the top, at the top of a sleep slope and... there's nowhere further to climb, I stop dead in my tracks, looking down.

"Jesus," I whisper. "Get a load of that..."

Like a gigantic excavation, a valley lies before me in the shadow of the surrounding mountains. White snowcaps sparkle dazzling and frosty bright in the sun, reflected in a round, perfectly smooth Lake as still as a mirror. Dwarf pines line its shores. To my right a foaming river roars as it bursts out of the forest and seems, like me, to have come running to this place, scrambling and struggling at great length before leaping out and hurtling down with a thunderous roar of exultation.

"I've found it," I whisper. "I've found it." I take a deep breath of air as pure and icy as the waters of the Lake and yell at the top of my voice, "Hey, everyone! I've found it!!!"

The roar of the river becomes deafening.

Chachkan

That evening, when it became clear they were going to leave in the morning, we gathered up the food and shared it out fairly, given that they were going back down to the world while we would be staying here. Their share was a little barley and maize grain. Carefree and happy, they poured it all together into a tin and all evening Sasha walked around playing it like the maracas.

It hurt me to see their unrestrained delight at the prospect of getting away from this place. It was as if they had already left and forgotten all about us who were staying. As prickly and cantankerous as an old hedgehog, I disappeared into the tent without saying goodbye to them. In the morning half asleep I heard them talking to each other, packing their belongings, but even then I didn't emerge. It was plain that from now on we were following different paths: they, Sasha and Nastya, would go down, while I would stay here alone with Grand, strange, inexplicable, scary Grand crashing through the bushes in search of invisible spirits.

If you have ever in the mountains parted with a friend whom you once loved, you will understand how I felt. If nothing of that kind has yet befallen you, may God grant it never does.

They packed up and left and we stayed behind. Waiting until their voices had faded, I came out of the tent. Grand was sitting by the fire, leaning over a pot, grimacing as he tried the contents, blowing on the spoon. Nastya and Sasha had been cooking porridge from some of the grain we gave them yesterday. They hadn't finished the job and left with no breakfast, evidently in a hurry. Now Grand was fiddling about over what they had left behind. I went down to the water's edge, to a place we already, after just these few days, took for granted. Our tent was pitched ten short steps from the water but I took them slowly, looking all around as if for the first time at this paradise which for once was bathed in sunshine.

The water in the lake is limpid and azure. At dawn it is so calm it reflects the sky, the mountains, and the cold, majestic glaciers. The opposite shore is pure scree with never a tree or a bush, as if someone has dumped the stones there. Our shore is forested, with cedars growing all the way down to the water. If we sit very still in the grass, chipmunks making clicking sounds come down from the branches and start inspecting our campsite.

There is stillness all around and stillness within. No thoughts. They seem to have been overwhelmed, forced out by this air, this tranquillity, this silence of the mountains.

Those mountains know more than we can imagine. They know more than we can take in.

Human beings are fluid and inconstant. They are like water with their thoughts, emotions, sensations. You blink and all that is no more and the flow rushes purposefully on inside you. But these mountains, these rocks, the bed of this chill, crystal Lake... Down in the valley eras and empires come and go, but they remain, unshakeable, calm, eternal. What can a person think as they look at them? Nothing. You can only sit and contemplate and dissolve in the timelessness.

The morning turns out surprisingly warm. All the days we have been here, in the vicinity of the glaciers, with the untiring voice of the river plunging as a waterfall down the precipice and into the Lake, the weather has been the same. The sky has cleared only occasionally and more often we have had rain or hail or snow, or some other form of precipitation for which we didn't know the name. We would have left sooner if I hadn't found my right ankle swollen and turning blue.

It happened the evening we reached the Lake, coming down from the ridge and setting up camp. I discovered it only by chance because my foot hadn't hurt at all during the day. "It's sprained," Sasha said, tut-tutting. "Bruised," speculated Grand. Nastya said nothing, just pulled a wry face. They examined my foot in the firelight, their faces anxious. I looked up at them and felt guilty.

"The road is saying you should stop here for a while," Grand said. "For some reason that is something you need right now." He was joking but the others looked grave. An oppressive feeling, as if we were doomed, descended on us. How could I know why this had happened to me, friend? Who can?

I suddenly started, staring into the forest. "There's someone there." They all turned. On the hillside behind the tent Grand and I shared, we saw the silhouette of a short woman. She didn't move. "Hey!" Sasha called. Still the woman did not move or answer. "Hiya!" he called again, with the same lack of result. Grand jumped up and in two great bounds was beside her. "It's a rock!" he shouted back, and we joined him.

There really was a stone pillar standing in the bushes which looked like a rather stocky girl of fifteen or so. Through the tracery of lines, cracks and chips you could make out her facial features, hair and clothing. It was spooky standing next to her in the growing darkness. She just looked too human.

"It's a local shrine," Sasha said in a low voice. "She looks like a shaman," Nastya said. "This is a good omen," Grand announced. "This is an interesting place. There may be many spirits. A good place to hunt them," he added with a grin, pleased. I winced with pain. "Help me get down," I said, and leaned on Sasha's arm. From a thundercloud invisible in the darkness, cold, white grain started pelting down on us. Such was the welcome we received from our longed-for Lake.

But now they had packed their things and left. Travelling light, in the sunshine, down they gaily tripped. In just a couple of hours they would be past the Lake and come upon a well trodden path. They would follow it along the river which plunged downwards and soon spot a couple of tents some way off the track but they would see nobody around. They would stop, take off their rucksacks and rest, but no one would appear and they would hike on.

From the first people they met Sasha would scrounge a cigarette. He would stand, his eyes half-closed with pleasure, exhaling smoke through his ginger bristles while Nastya asked the way. She wouldn't really need to because it would be obvious and straightforward. A little further on they would come to a backwater with a campsite which had a bathhouse and even a shop selling tinned food, beer, cigarettes and bread. There they would buy some tinned stew. They would talk the bathhouse attendants into letting them both in for the price of one, and be treated to free beer by the people camping next to them that night.

In the morning they would go on. The people they had attached themselves to last night would give them sugar and tea, and before they left give them pasta which they would eat with the meat they had bought the day before. They would again be travelling light in the sunshine, and the lower they went the higher their spirits would be. At noon they would have trouble getting across a river, rest on their rucksacks, then stray from the path but soon after meet rafters who would give them directions and also biscuits and a tin of condensed milk. Very pleased with themselves, they would continue on their way.

I sit looking at shadows, the shadows of clouds which succeed each other on the glassy surface of the Lake, rushing on their way and disappearing. Why should I bother to keep track of our friends when they've already forgotten all about us? Why should I care what's happening to them and what will happen next? The shadows of the clouds cover the Lake again and the part of the shore I am sitting on, but then they scud off, following the river down into the valley.

I'm becoming part of this landscape. Incapacity has separated me from my companions, and now it seems to me that my inner speed, the speed at which feelings flow inside me, will soon be comparable with that of a cedar or the bush I am sitting under. Other people move immeasurably faster than I do. My friends were evidently frustrated and impatient and that made it impossible for them to stay here for more than three days. I didn't notice them wearying of this place and now I have no choice but to be here and wait.

This break in my onward movement is teaching me to see the world differently. From up here, in a ravine in the mountains, with the frosty breath of the glaciers, looking out from the roots of cedar trees, I have a larger and broader view of the world than you get down there in the towns and the valley. There the view breaks down into a hustle and bustle which obscures it, while here it is limpid and clear, and fussing is seen for what it is, mere dust on the surface of eternal things. I see people, their cares, what prompts them to act and what blocks them on their path. I see the interweaving of roads I have yet to travel or which I am destined never to travel. I find it easy to track the movements of those who have left us and, by looking further, to see others below who have lost and are looking for us. I see my own road too, and believe I can see deep and wide with clarity, since the very source and on, and it is only fear and superstition which prevent me from looking far ahead, into dark mists, to the very end.

Here thinking about death comes easily and not at all like it does in the town, not about the death of a particular person or myself, and not even really about death at all. It is easy here to think about the grass which will some day grow on all our graves. It is not frightening, even though in the town we want what comes after to be different, yet as near as possible to how it was. Here, though, it is ineluctably clear that there is nothing different, only all the things which surround me now and what will come after them.

I will be no more, others will be no more, all cities and states will disappear, but the grass and the trees and mountains will remain and grow, and it won't matter to them that we are no longer. They are life and they are eternal and I am not afraid of becoming them. Is it not through our awareness of the eternal life of everything, that we cross over, that we overcome the death that is in us?

At night it was colder than it had been the whole way here. We shivered and huddled in our sleeping bags, trying to keep warm, putting on all the clothes we had in our rucksacks, but that was at best a partial remedy.

Every night our tent was stormed by mice. They jumped on to it and slid down, then jumped again, and again slid down, so interminably that we fell asleep before they finished. They jumped so high it seemed someone was deliberately throwing them at the tent. That idea was enough to make things a bit scary.

"It's her way of playing with us," I joked. "That girl we've got standing out there. She is the ruler of the animals here, the Siberian Diana." We lay there, peeping out of our sleeping bags, looking at the shadows on the tent walls and listening to the games the mice played. We barely moved, and spoke in whispers.

"Chachkan," Grand said one time. "That what she's called. Chachkan means mouse for the peoples who have lived since time immemorial in these mountains."

"Ah, right. Mouse."

Their path will lead them to a boggy meadow and they will lose their way again. Grass waist-high and water underfoot, trails fanning out in all directions but leading nowhere and disappearing. They will wander about before coming to a stream, and follow it in a straight line, sometimes walking in it, until they again come to a forest and a rapid descent with a well trodden path they will have to clamber down like steep steps. They will speed up and not even their wet feet will spoil their mood.

When there are no clouds here you can get a tan, but when it's heavily overcast and windy you feel cold even if you pull on a sweater. As a result I am constantly shivery, but I've got used to it. I sit and watch the water lapping against the shore, steadily, at intervals, as if the Lake is breathing.

Grand gathers firewood, disappearing for a long time and bringing back whole armfuls of dead branches and thick logs. We already have enough for a campfire. If I ask him whether he's planning to melt the glaciers he will half smile without replying. He likes this place. He's always doing something, although he doesn't say what. He'll go off in one direction and come lumbering into the clearing from another, and his eyes are like those of a cat after a successful night's hunting. I once asked him, "Grand, what are you up to?" "Tracking the power" was his answer.

Some time earlier, barely able to contain his laughter, he told me he was trying to catch spirits in the gorges, but every time he called them, Sasha would emerge from the bushes with some twig or other in his hands.

Grand didn't need anyone to hunt with him, so he didn't find our stay here at all tedious. Sasha had also been busy studying the local flora, and said that almost every plant we encountered on the way was also to be found here. Only Nastya was grim-faced and made it plain she was bored by the lack of anything to do. She tried to avoid me, wandered around aimlessly between the tents or on a fifty-metre stretch of the shore. I looked at her and wondered whether the road had given us this break precisely so that she and I should get to know and understand each other, but we exchanged barely a word in the course of the days they were here.

I didn't see it happening, but suddenly they were close. Sasha is like a piece of soft clay: he readily assumes any shape and doesn't stick to your hands. For the whole of his life he has played just one role, smoothing the sharp corners in any group of people he finds himself with. So now, encountering Nastya, he instinctively set about plastering over the cracks between her and us.

They talked in the evenings by the fire. Sasha would return from his daily quest before Grand, light a fire, and busy himself making herbal tea and vitamin-rich soup. Nastya had little alternative but to come and warm herself there. Dusk fell rapidly. No sooner did the sun disappear behind the mountain on the opposite shore than the air thickened, turned greyish, and everything became more contrasted: light objects became bright and prominent, while anything dark became part of the background. Such sounds as there were became muffled except for the shrill cry of an evening bird which punctured the stillness as it flew over the lake. I carried on sitting by the water, and from the direction of the fire came the sound of Sasha making quiet, calm, sensible conversation.

As he had to me in times gone by on Yakimanka, he was talking about his life and his friends, all of whom to the last man and woman were singers and poets; and as I had been on Yakimanka, Nastya was bewitched by his manner of narrating, his voice and the interminableness of all his stories which flowed smoothly on one from another. Turning, I could see Sasha's back and Nastya's profile. She was bent over, hugging her knees, in the red light of the fire and at that moment I couldn't say what her face was expressing, but possibly it wasn't expressing anything and that was what made it beautiful. Looking further round I could see the stone girl shaman standing on her mound beyond the tent intently watching our clearing. She seemed like a reflection of me, two silent observers, me and Chachkan.

Even when I limped past them into the tent when I got cold, or sat down beside them to warm up, they paid no attention and Sasha didn't interrupt his story. They were so absorbed in the warmth of their evenings that everything else might as well not have existed. I could see they were being drawn together, but could never have imagined what was going to happen. Although, even if I had guessed, would I have been able, or wanted, or have dared to do anything about it? No. So I just watched and marvelled at how unfathomable the road is, and how strangely it sometimes shuffles people's fates.

Now they've gone, after trying to cook that inedible porridge. The two different kinds of grain couldn't be cooked together, and what use were rations like that going to be to them? "You like reading signs, Grand," I said pointing to what they had left behind in the pot. "What does this signify?" "You can interpret that yourself, Titch. It tells us that those two are beyond reproach."

I nodded and did not seek clarification of his new concept: I knew what he meant. "How will they get there?" "The road will help them. It's like hitchhiking. The main thing is to be open and to spread happiness."

After the descent they will find themselves back at the river and will walk along the bank. They will meet a group of schoolchildren, advancing towards the summit in an orderly single file, all of them with thumb sticks and with mugs on the side of their rucksacks as if on parade. The children will tell them it is less than a day's hike to the village. They have come from it today but they were given a lift in UAZ jeeps as far as the first steep ascent. There won't be anything they can scrounge from them, and they will continue on their way.

They will cross the river over a three-log bridge, then stop and eat blueberries from the bushes. These will be growing right beside the trail so they will help themselves. This will take up two hours and they will come to their senses only when they see that night is drawing in. They will grab their rucksacks and start running downhill, but after half an hour will see a good camp site with a table under cover, a bonfire like a hearth, and a couple of tents already pitched there. They will approach, say hello, and stay there for the night. The tents' owners will be a group of tourists from Tomsk who will give them a meal and vodka and tea to drink in return for Sasha's inspirational tale of our tribulations: the trail we followed which missed the pass through the mountains, and the Lake by the glaciers.

When they leave in the morning, deciding that by evening they will be on the outskirts of the town, they will leave their container of uncookable cereal, preferring to travel light.

The four of us woke up one morning to find snow on the ground. The glade and forest were suddenly hushed, no birds, no wind. The Lake placidly reflected the dawn sky but the snow was in no hurry to melt. I screwed up my eyes in the blinding brightness, scooped up a fistful of the snow and tried it with my tongue. It tasted good, sweetish, like the water in the Lake. In the distance, on the mountain, a crow cawed.

The bushes suddenly parted and three men in red overalls emerged into our clearing. I don't know who was more startled, us after not having seen anyone for so many days, or them, never expecting to find anyone here. After a moment's hesitation we got over our surprise and talked.

They were mountaineers heading for a glacier beyond the mountain pass and had already been waiting several days for snow. They told us that was the only way you could get through the pass and now the snow had come. We looked complete idiots for having reached the Lake by the least obvious, highly circuitous route which, if it was used by anyone, was the province of local hunters, and shepherds driving their flocks to the summer pastures.

"You really like doing things your own way, Grand," Nastya said when the climbers had gone off to mount their assault on the glacier. "That is how the road would have it, and no doubt there was a reason," Grand replied. "We have benefited both from this place and from the way we came here."

"I wouldn't have minded giving it a miss," Nastya said. "At least now we know there are people nearby and we can stop pretending to be a lost expedition. I take it we're leaving now?" "You know why we're here." "Well, we've been in these forests quite long enough. I was expected back long ago. People will be worried. You do as you please, but I'm going back." Grand shrugged and said, "You are free to do as you wish. It will mean only that our paths diverge forever."

Nastya made no reply and went to the tent. Uneasy guilt feelings stirred in my heart for a moment, but only for a moment. I knew that sooner or later this was going to happen. It was just that now they were being open with each other.

The day continued normally except that Sasha was behaving oddly. He kept hanging around me, looking at my face but recoiling from direct eye contact. He finally brought me a branch of honeysuckle berries and made his speech while I was gratefully devouring them.

"You know, Titch, I need to be heading home too. My holiday will be over soon and I should get back to work. And also I have to hitch my way back." "Right," I nodded with my mouth full, getting a sense for myself of the path he was embarking on.

"Well, and then... you know... Nastya hasn't got a tent, so how could she go back alone? At present we're, you know...

sleeping in mine because she hasn't... well, you know..." "Got a tent," I prompted, swallowing the last berry. "Right." He nodded. "So?" "Well, you won't mind if I er... If I go with...?" "Your tent?" "Well, yes. Well, no. With Nastya!"

"Go ahead. No problem." "Well, you know... You won't mind?" "What's it to do with me? I'm in no hurry to go anywhere. And I don't have a tent either." He went off as if he'd just done a heavy day's work. I stayed behind on the shore throwing stones into the Lake.

So I didn't say goodbye to them that evening, and didn't come out of the tent the next morning. What could I have said to you, friend? Safe journey!

Dusk is falling again. How many times have I experienced that now beside this Lake? Once again the bird which accompanies the setting sun flies out over the water with its shrill cry. This evening, however, is warm and I sit out until it is dark. The sky turns grey, then thickens, freezes, and the stars bore their way through. I'll go to the tent now and wait for Grand. He isn't back yet, but that is quite normal. He always comes back after the moon is up.

There is a huge pile of wood by the fire, enough for several days. Why does he need so much? I make out the pot with what remains of the porridge, covered with my bowl, hobble over to the tent, lean down and see it is open. The flap is thrown back and Grand's rucksack is missing.

It would be untruthful to say tears poured from my eyes. No, my cedarwood sense of tranquillity is not that easily broken. I stood thinking about the situation, trying to awaken my emotions through thought. What should I do now? Somewhere in another part of my brain I was thinking, "So that's why he gathered so much firewood. He must have been concerned for me." I heard a rustle in the tent and climbed in, found a lighter and clicked it.

Little tailless mice scatter in all directions trying in their panic to run up the walls. "Shit! For heaven's sake, shoo! Shoo! All of you, just get out!" The mice in their terror can't find the tent flap. I grab my things, shake my sleeping bag. More and more mice cascade out and scuttle around. I start trying to catch them and get them out but it's not easy. Then one mouse finds the flap, runs out and squeaks to the others to follow. Now there is just one left, but it is huddled in the far corner and in its terror doesn't know what to do. We go round in circles, trying to avoid each other, we thrash about until I hear another squeak. The first mouse has come back and the straggler rushes towards her. Together they scamper away. With a single tug I close the flap, retreat to the corner and suddenly, in the silence that descends, clear-eyed and desperate, consider my isolation.

"Hey, Titch! Aren't you scared?" "The forest is still and dense. I am of no interest to the Lake. All the mice are gone and will not return. I am not afraid." "Hey, but Titch, you've been left all alone." "I have the forest, I have the mountains, and soon the moon will rise and be reflected in the water, lighting up the icy peaks. Beneath a black sky there is the Earth, on it, like a tumulus, there is my tent, and inside it there is me, the only thing for miles around that can call this forest a forest. In the town there are millions like me, but that does not make me happier there."

"Titch, you are lame and have little to eat. You're not good at lighting fires and don't know the way back. What will you do tomorrow when the sun comes up? Hush, listen. A raven is cawing on the rocky mountain." "Yes. That is my kind Cara not forgetting me even here."

I must have dozed off or been dreaming. The frenzied girl shaman is dancing round the fire with a tambourine, now raising it to the skies, now lowering it to the ground. I hear drumming and singing, and muttering, sometimes soft, then louder, and seem even to hear the ceaseless rhythms of a mouth harp. She leaps and spins, and scraps of cloth and the ribbons of her complicated costume fly about her in the wind. I watch enchanted. I watch in a daze, trying to make out her facial features contorted in ecstasy. It is She, our Chachkan, come to life out of the stone. She jumps over to me in a single leap, leans over my injured foot and tugs something out of it or from nearby. I clearly see a small black serpent writhing in her hand, but only for a moment before she jumps over to the fire and casts this black thing into it. I lower my eyes to my ankle and cannot help laughing. A dozen tailless mice are dancing on their hind legs next to me in time to the music of this frenzied ritual.

I laugh and wake up. Through the walls of the tent I can see the campfire burning in our clearing. I look out and see Grand sitting there and he actually is quietly playing a mouth harp. A pot is suspended over the fire. I had forgotten food could smell like that. A pot of boiled potatoes and stew. I go to him but somehow instead of words of joy there comes from me an outburst of hysteria. "How could you leave me? How could you just abandon me? You're all traitors! All of you! The lot of you!"

"Titch, what are you on about?" He stands up and impulsively wants to put his arm round my shoulders. I don't want that and, ashamed of my tears, tear myself away, turn aside and wail.

"I told those mountaineers we were staying and why, and they invited me to go with them to their base for food. It was a couple of hours to the base and they've got a bathhouse. I told you, the road will help us. When you're better we'll go down there and have a good wash." "A wash..." I murmur dreamily, as if hearing the word for the first time.

I sit looking into the pot, and from just the sight and smell of his stomach-filling stew and the heat of the fire I stop feeling hungry. The fire crackles. Stars shine through the great paws of the cedars. The breeze is still and it is very quiet.

"Why have you gathered so much firewood? Are you planning to spend the winter here?" "I was going to commune with the spirits but as I was walking back from the base everything felt so good and peaceful. I didn't want to go hunting them. The world around us is enormous, Titch, and we are so small, puny and alone. We're all trying to go somewhere in this world, but if you look to the heart of things, you see that none of this is real."

"What do you mean it isn't real?"

"It just isn't. There is a boundless dark sea all around, and that gives you a sense of awe. Imagine, Titch: it's summer, it's hot, it's evening. There's a pool of yellow light on the veranda and a smell, the smell of the heated earth which is cooling as night closes in.

"Standing in the lamplight on the veranda, with the soft rustle of the wings of moths, you peer out into the garden and it seems as if it doesn't exist. What is around you is a dark sea, and the garden isn't there. Nothing else exists, only you, snatched from the darkness by a circle of dim lamplight. 'What sparks are those I see flickering?' you will ask. 'Fireflies or stars?' Stars,' I reply. 'Fireflies.'"

"Yes. I understand," I say, nodding my head, and for the first time I really do understand him.

Everything was like a dream, only it wasn't a dream. The nearby Lake was still and the glaciers were reflected in its bottomless depths. The sky was cold and black but we felt no chill and forgot the food. We sat and soaked up all the emptiness, and the good spirits of that place, my good brothers, surrounded us and were almost tangible.

We went to the tent and for the first time slept holding each other tight, and we were warm.

We left two days later. My foot was better and walking was easy. At the base we met a new group of climbers gazing mournfully at the glacial precipices in the hope of seeing dark clouds bringing snow. "Without snow there's no point in going up to the pass," they grumbled. We were in a hurry and didn't wash.

We moved on and it seemed to me that the road was familiar. We spent the night in the forest, next to a flooded meadow. We crossed it swiftly, following the path closest to the trees which grew round its edge.

We crossed streams and descended an almost sheer track. Our next overnight stop was by a river and, as we discovered in the morning, a bare hundred metres away from the site with the table under cover.

The place was deserted when we reached it. The dark planks of the bench and table, with rusty bruises around the nail heads, looked forlorn, a dull echo of the civilisation we had left behind and to which we were now returning. Near the site of the fire we found the plastic container with the incompatible grains which our friends had abandoned. We sat for a time before going on, down into the valley.

Mars, The Red Star

The Russian steppe, night time, and we are being driven at speed in a red car with rounded contours. It is a right-hand drive Japanese Daewoo and if I peep round the back of the driver's seat I can see the illuminated speedometer on the dashboard, only it's better not to. I really won't do that again. May God and all his messengers of light protect us. We are travelling so fast we seem to be flying. It would be good to have something to hold on to, but there is nothing.

"Why aren't you talking, Sergey?" the driver demands of Grand. "Let's sing! 'Moans my heart... moans my heart...!'" he bursts forth with a voice so powerful I am pressed down in the back seat from where, as if peering up from the bottom of the sea, I can observe only a scrap of black sky through the rear window and a large red star suspended in it.

God forbid that you should find yourself hitchhiking in the night with a drunk at the wheel. We have no one to blame but ourselves. We accepted the lift so now we must stick it out to the end because, in any case, we have no choice.

We didn't immediately see the situation. We were even pleased because we really needed a lift. Night was falling and we had gone barely any distance away from Novosibirsk. We hadn't made 50 kilometres and found ourselves in steppe so desolate there wasn't a birch tree to be seen. Far away on the horizon huge green radar dishes, which looked like eviscerated tortoise shells were rotating. It was a creepy place to be and we had no wish to be stuck there overnight. We had just decided to walk on a bit and start thumbing when suddenly this little car as red as a Christmas tree bauble and with tinted windows shot out of the filling station and screeched to a halt for us. The driver lowered his window, looked at Grand and laughed. Grand looked at him and laughed too, as if they were two old friends, as I thought they were. I laughed too.

"Fancy seeing you here!" the driver said, still laughing. "Well, come on. Get in and let's go." "Let's go," Grand agreed and opened the rear door. Before I could say anything I was bundled in along with our rucksacks and the car roared off. The driver turned to Grand and they continued laughing. He didn't look at the road.

"Hey, guys, it's great to meet you! We'll travel along together all the way to where I live, all the way to Omsk. You guys from Omsk? No? I am. I'm from Omsk. I've got a house there, kiddies, and the wife waiting for me. 'I've a wee wife a-waiting and she's waiting just for me...' She's been waiting three days for me and I didn't come back. I went to see my brother-in-law in Novosibirsk and I've been away for three days now. I had a wild time, guys, a really wild time. A man's gotta do... But now it's time to go home, if we make it, touch wood, eh guys? Isn't that right, eh? 'I'll be back home soon, back to my sources. Kiss the wife and tend the horses.'" He laughed again but by now I was silent. Grand gave a kind of nervous chuckle.

"What's your name, man?" our driver asked. "Sergey," Grand said. "And I'm Sasha. Call me Sash! How about you, Seryozha, do you know what a yesaul is? You've probably forgotten the meaning of the word. Anyway, Seryozha, a yesaul is a guy like me. Yesaul Ulanov, Captain of the Cossacks."

I'd worked out by now that they didn't know each other. May the powers of light protect us! Just as well the road here was running through steppe, flat, long, no side roads. Fly while you can! And we were flying.

"Whaddya say, Seryozha, how about we sing?" Yesaul Ulanov barked. "'Oh, boundless steppes of Russia...'"

I pressed myself down in the rear seat between the rucksacks. I didn't sleep. I kept an eye open.

I'm back on Yakimanka and Tolya is in a bad mood as he surfs the Internet, clicking his mouse and grumbling, pre-empting any desire others might have to make a nuisance of themselves. "Managers, Managers. The only people this country seems to need are managers." "Are you looking for a new job, Tolya?" I enquire from my gallery. "No, I'm studying the demand for new employees. I'm studying Russia."

Tolya works for a mobile phone company and is well paid by the standards of our commune, but he is an eternal oppositionist. I shrug my shoulders and get back to my book. "Managers, managers... nothing but bloody managers." I hear him squeezing a plastic beer bottle.

Yakimanka, Yakimanka. On Yakimanka old Artemiy sits night and day by the central heating radiator, rolling his own cigarettes from tobacco so rough you have to take a deep breath before you run into the kitchen and back out again. I had always supposed he was Roma's grandfather, but nothing of the sort. Artemiy has different grandchildren who come every quarter to pay Roma his rent of forty bucks a month so the old man can smoke his tobacco and sit by the central heating radiator.

"Isn't that a bit stiff, Roma?" Tolya asked him. "The old geezer takes up no space at all. You're turning bourgeois." "They don't bring him any food," landlord Roma retorts. "Half the money they give me goes on feeding him." "That poor old man only gets half?!" Tolya taunts him. "Oh, Roma, you sticky-fingered bourgeois!"

Old Artemiy, our commune's scarecrow, a symbol of times before any of us were around, sits in the kitchen, slobbering on pieces of newspaper and rolling his smokes with dirty, arthritic fingers. He inhales with a look of concentration on his face.

"Heh-heh," he laughs, squinting at me. "Khe-khe-khe," his laughter changes into a smoker's cough.

What does our Old Artemiy know, what does he remember? What nook of forgotten history is preserved in that bald head of his, that skull with the skin stretched taut over it? I tried to find out one time, but the old man said nothing and only bared his toothless gums from behind his smokescreen. "Heh-heh, girlie. I know why you keep asking all these questions," he finally wheezed. "Khe-Khe, girlie, I know everything. You're one of our blue bloods. If things had turned out different you'd have been living here on your own and we would be running errands for you. Khe-Khe-Khe." "You can't get anything out of him, just a load of nonsense," I growled, retreating from the kitchen in confusion. He chucked a few bricks after me: "Our lady countess, for Christ's sake! Khe-Khe-Khe!"

"Well, Titch, you walked into that, eh? He's got you sussed." Tolya laughed an evil laugh. "I've long had my doubts about you. I guessed as much! You're a member of the bourgeoisie, Titch, there's a class enemy skulking inside you to this day. Now you and your blue blood have been exposed once and for all!" "Oh, give over." I am Titch, a well-intentioned daughter of our latest Time of Troubles. What's my lineage got to do with anything?

We took off in a screech of rubber, like racers, with the wind whistling in our ears, a round red car eating up the expanses of the steppe at a hundred and forty kilometres an hour. "'From behind a distant is-land like a sho-oal of fearsome sha-arks...' Why aren't you joining in, Seryozha? Show me some respect!" bawls Yesaul Ulanov. I shudder and raise myself up a little. The same darkness surrounds us and the bleak expanse of Russia judders and rushes beneath us. "... there come sai-ailing with the cur-rent Stenka Ra-zin's painted barques." "I'd rather you told me about the Cossacks, and kept your eyes on the road in the meantime," Grand suggests.

"Ekh, the road, the dust, the mist!" the Yesaul intoned. "What are the Cossacks, Seryozha my brother? What were the Cossacks for Russia and what are they for our Russia today, I ask you? They are everything! The only link left holding Russia together as a nation. From olden times and up till now, to our own days. What is there of the past that is truly alive? From that great, great distance what is alive, I ask you? Nothing! Only the Cossacks remain. That's who we are – the Cossacks! We've been there from time immemorial, from aeons ago. It was we took Siberia with Yermak Timofeyevich, raised fortresses, kept the frontiers inviolable, drove off the Tatar scum, drove off the German scum, and held these lands against all comers. Without the Cossacks there would be no Siberia, without the Cossacks there would be no Russia either. That's what I have to tell you, Seryozha. What have you to say to that? Can you deny it? If you deny it, speak out, man!" "Times change, Sasha."

"I am not Sasha to you. To you I am Yesaul Alexander

Nikiforovich Ulanov, understand? They change, do they? Well... Of course they do. But we were the Cossacks, and as the Cossacks still we stand: for Rus, for the Fatherland, for the Holy Orthodox Church! Hurrah! Do you know how long the Cossacks have been guarding the borders of Russia? For all eternity, and we still are! Yes, Sergey, you can take it from me, we'll yet defend our Russia, our mother, to the last man any time, any time she needs us! 'From behind a distant is-land like a sho-oal of fearsome sha-arks...'. Come on, Sergey, sing along! 'There come sai-ailing with the cur-rent Stenka Ra-zin's painted barques.' Come on, now the chorus! 'There come sai-ailing with the cur-rent Stenka Ra-zin's painted barques'."

The red ball flies along the highway like a bullet fired from a gun. I'm cringing at the bottom of it, looking up at the sky where a big, blazing star is hard on our heels.

We've have taken off, broken away and now we're flying. "Hey, world, stand aside!" We live in crazy times, my friend, where eras and empires follow one after the other as our drunken driver stares into the impenetrable night. I was born in one country and live in another, and God only knows what's coming next. I only know it's nothing to do with me.

"You're apolitical, you're infantile, Titch," Tolya kept nagging me on Yakimanka. "You sit up there in your gallery reading and don't give a toss about anything." I smile and say nothing. Lenka and Sasha say nothing as they kiss mutely on the bed. Tolya is in the throes of a bout of righteous indignation. "What an unbelievable generation of airheads is growing up! They don't give a toss about anything. You don't want anything, you aren't going to change anything."

"Tolya, what are you getting so het up about? Everything's fine as it is." "That's what's so bad, Titch. Let's face it, what are you? A courier! We live in a country of managers and couriers. Oh, gods, bring me poison!" I feel the urge to give Tolya a round of applause.

What are you expecting from me, friend? I would like to have been born in your era. Then we would surely be able to talk to one another heart to heart.

Three brothers had I, three older brothers. The first founded a business and became rich. The second had two children and all he could think about was how to make ends meet. The third disappeared from our family's view as soon as he was any age at all. Three brothers had I, three older brothers. Just like in a fairy tale.

I loved my brothers devotedly, as a puppy loves the hands which give it sugar. They were a whole lifetime, a whole epoch older than me. They were going to school when I was born, and started families when I went to school. We never had anything in common. In my memories they are fine young men, the embodiment of manliness; in their memories I am a bundle of snot and tantrums bereft of brains or understanding, whose only function was to be a nuisance to them as they lived their important adult lives.

The gift I got from my brothers was to love anybody older than myself, and fate cast me up on Yakimanka. For my fellow members of the commune, hippies, stonewashed jeans, rock on the earliest cassettes, the Afghan War and the Young Communist League were features of their youth, not history like they are for me. For all that, they were still lost souls, searching for and ready to give all their love to whoever came along. I understood them, and that is exactly what they needed. Those around me on Yakimanka did not remember me as a child, but even so for them I was Titch, the eternal younger sister of all of them.

Once upon a time there were three brothers, Kiy, Shchuk and Khoriv, and they had a sister, Lybed. Just like in a fairy tale.

Your life long ago became reality but mine is stuck in a state of suspended attraction to you.

Oh, time, how inexplicably you allocate destinies! Where

is justice if everything good seems to be in the past, and all that
is left in the epoch of my own generation is to scrape out the
burnt leftovers?

Max cast Aquarium up on Yakimanka, the same highly
mysterious Muscovite Max by whose will I first went to live
there. He brought a whole stack of cassettes, said nothing to
anyone, and left them on the piano. "In the past I used to store
all the junk up in the gallery," Roma said. "But now you're
there, Titch, we'll have to chuck it out." "Why chuck it out?
You can store it with me. He may just have forgotten them."

I hadn't understood Aquarium's music before and didn't
like it, but these cassettes had been brought here by Max, and
everything Max did had hidden meaning, or so I liked to think.
I kept the cassettes and listened to the music. A week later,
Lenka and I were skipping about to one of their hits whose title
was '2-12-85-06' and racing each other to the phone to dial the
number. One time the phone was answered by a tired, cross old
gentleman. We said nothing and stopped calling.

I listened so much to their songs that I started seeing
chaotic, poisonously coloured dreams of hills and rivers, I
started rambling incoherently and all but talked in rhyme.
Max had accomplished his mission – I had discovered Boris
Grebenshchikov, the guru of a generation, and if you could only
become initiated into that generation by being poisoned by BG,
I cheerfully gulped down the poison.

It is a great torment to love something that happened
before you existed. When Boris was singing his best songs, if
I was born I might as well not have been. Nowadays he's a big
old sad gentleman with a beard and narrow eyes, and back then
when I would have wanted to love him, I didn't even know the
word. What justice is there?

I picture the women to whom he dedicated his songs as
beautiful, enigmatic, a little drunk, a little sinful, and that only

makes them seem the more beautiful to me, and makes me all the more aware that they are not me.

Oh, time, how inexplicably you allocate destinies! Where is justice if it is so easy to love something you don't even remember, and so difficult to love what is close at hand.

Although, then again, who says I don't remember? One of my brothers would sing "Under a Blue Sky" in the disconsolate tones of an abandoned cat, sitting on our kitchen balcony in the hope that our neighbour would come out and talk to him. I remember that. During the day he locked himself in his room and put on Aquarium. I understood none of it, but would sit by his door and weep over their songs, as magical as they were incoherent. At kindergarten I didn't play with the other children but wandered off into the bushes and sang them to myself, almost swooning.

By the time Aquarium arrived in our commune my brother had forgotten his songs and BG had gone to Tibet. The mossy, decaying trunk of Russian rock music was covered in thin, vigorously sprouting shoots and my pimply peers were joyfully hoovering them up. It's what is called a generational difference.

Oh, time, how inexplicably you allocate destinies! But if we want to talk about justice, friend, we will see there is nothing to talk about. The world outside the windows of Yakimanka was a glossy neon world, and if there was anything about that I didn't like, where was I to find a different one? You, my brothers, didn't have one either.

Tolya related that he came to Moscow in the 1990s, paraded about on the barricades, drank vodka and hugged tank drivers. He told me he was a long-haired hippy then. He and his friends intended to confront the tanks naked, covered only in flowers, and bring about the hippy revolution, but either they couldn't find enough flowers or they got blind drunk too early in the day. "What was it you hoped for, Tolya?" "Oh, Titch, you're not old enough." He gestured dismissively without even looking at me.

"'Yesaul, Yesaul, why abandon your steed? Why not put down your mount in its hour of great need?' Why aren't you singing, Seryozha? I'm not your bleeding radio!" "Tell me rather something about yourself, Sasha." "Ekh, Seryozha, why tell you when very soon we'll be home and you'll see everything for yourself. I'll take you to my home and to the bathhouse! You're helping me and I'll help you. People should be good to each other but today there aren't many good people around. The moment I saw you I knew, these are just the people I need, I'll certainly make it home with them, but without them... It's not good to be driving on your own. Your thinking's clouded, and the first cop you meet will pull you over. The bastards can sniff you out a mile away. So you're helping me and I'll help you. What, isn't that right? Ekh, Seryozha, it's not far now and soon we'll be home, if we don't die first."

You don't know whether to pray or not to bother. The Red Star scuds through the black sky close on our heels.

The way it happened was this. Right at the end of my shift, the owner of the travel agency where I was a courier found out where one of her top customers was. She was pushing through visas for him to take a whole group to India and needed his signature on some crucial piece of paper. We'd been trying to get hold of him all day until she finally discovered he was at the theatre and immediately sent me off to intercept him.

Rushing out of the office, I bumped into Sasha. He had finished his jobs for the day and was heading back to Yakimanka, but I knew that with him I'd be able to get into a theatre or a museum or anywhere else. As a courier Sasha Sorokin was a gift from the gods. He could have nipped down to hell, completed his delivery and been back out before the smell of sulphur had time to settle in his hair.

There was a crowd in front of the theatre and the performance was obviously expected to be sold out. We announced at the staff entrance who we needed. The name worked. It was a new theatre and labyrinthine, with gleaming laminate floors and white corridors full of people. They took us to the upper circle and left us there, promising that so-and-so would show up at any minute.

"Titch, do you know what he looks like?" "I think so." In fact I did recognise him, although he had only been in our office once when I was there. He breezed into the upper circle and started shooing everybody out. There were heavily made up middle-aged ladies with fat legs in gleaming stockings under short tight dresses who protested they were journalists. Sasha and I tried to interpose our request, but he shooed us out too and disappeared. The 'ladies of the press' began indignantly to leave. Sasha gave me a wink and we sneaked back in and stood over to one side.

The lights went down and the evening began. It was a performance by Buddhist monks. They chanted in eerie, unearthly voices, their brass cymbals clashing and ringing and their thunderous rhythmical mantra filled the auditorium. Sasha and I were stunned as well as deafened. Spectators in the stalls were sitting on the floor in the lotus posture and swaying in time like the shallows of a lake.

After fifteen minutes or so the door to the circle opened. Our target entered, followed by a number of other people and a couple, the male resplendent in his attire, the female insignificant, like birds. Our customer was fussing over them, getting them comfortably settled.

"Sasha, look!" My knees gave way. I recognised the man who had entered last as BG. He was just like he looked in all his recent photographs, a big, broad man in a brightly coloured jacket with a spade-like Tutankhamun beard. He and his lady remained standing, their faces composed and serious. When the chanting was over and the Buddhists in the stalls started their ceremonial prostrations, BG turned and left. My customer followed and, but for Sasha, I would have lost him that evening.

I remember thinking that if he looked so much like his photographs now, he must have been exactly the same as in his photographs back then. "Titch is in love!" Tolya hooted. "Titch is head over heels in love like a schoolgirl. For heaven's sake, he's got a daughter older than you!" "Tolya, pack it in. What do you know!"

I repaired to my gallery. "You'll wilt up there!" Tolya protested clownishly. "Want a beer?" "No." "What's up? Have you gone teetotal? Oh, Titch has given up drinking! You'll dry out like a radish! Time for you to retreat to a nunnery, a Buddhist one – Ommmm," he hooted. "See what's become of our gentry!"

Artemiy had stuck that label on me, Tolya had blabbed and now the whole of Yakimanka had heard. I got strange looks. In no time at all they would all be thinking it was true. I might even myself. When it comes to lineage, who knows...

My father had dreamed of hussars. He loved talking about their light blue uniforms and gold epaulettes, their bravado, moustaches, and the popping of champagne corks. Frantic races across the steppe at night like flashes of blue flame, unbuttoned uniforms flapping in the breeze, epaulettes and aiguillettes like sparks in the wind. Frantic racing, perpetual racing, and only that star, that red star up there, shining out of the blackness.

Another car overtakes us at high speed. The driver yells something, mimics the tightening of a loose screw at his temple and points backwards. Yesaul Ulanov attempts to understand, lowers the window. He too yells, can't understand, so starts swearing. The driver in the car gets pissed off, gives up contemptuously and rockets away from us. The Yesaul looks around puzzled.

"Okay, guys, seems we have a problem." He drives over to the verge. We get out. A rear tyre is torn to shreds. "Change it!" the Yesaul barks. "Seryozha, have you ever changed a tyre?

Nothing to it. Dead easy. I'll give you the tools, tell you what to do, and you can change it. I'm too drunk to change a tyre."

Grand pulls on the gloves the Yesaul has given him and takes the jack. I hover around. The Yesaul goes to the car and comes back. "We're down on diesel too, guys. My car gallops on diesel. Not enough to make it home. Need to find a tractor. I've got foreign currency..."

He surveys the dark steppe. Somewhere in the middle of it points of light flicker in the windows of what is presumably a farm. "Forward!" Yesaul Ulanov commands and, withdrawing a bottle of vodka from the glove box, leaves the road to head off into the blackness of the steppe. Grand and I attend to the wheel. The night is chilly. We have just finished when the Yesaul returns.

"The wretches, they're holding out for more!" he shouts and curses as he comes up. "How simple everything was under the Soviets. You gave someone a bottle of vodka and they let you take as much diesel as you needed, but now 'This isn't right, that isn't right...' Ekh! Okay, guys, pile out. I'll drive over there. I haven't a bent kopek. Perhaps I can talk them round. If you get a lift, goodbye, otherwise we'll drive home together." We barely have time to pull our rucksacks out before the car roars away over the weed-choked field and races, bouncing up and down, towards the distant lights.

We stand on the road. It's cold and barren and dark. We have roused ravenous mosquitoes from the ditch and nearby stagnant puddles. There is, in any case, nowhere for us to sleep. We stand. Then we dance. Then we run around in circles. Suddenly from the direction of the farm we hear engines revving. Two pairs of yellow beams bump over the black earth, one towards us.

We wait motionless to see what will happen next, but much closer than the headlights and engines we hear the lowing of cattle and dogs barking. Almost at once a small herd of calves, sheep and lambs, mooing and bleating, spills out on to the road.

Half crazed by running in the night, they stumble across the strip of asphalt and disappear into the darkness on the far side. The last across is a bullock with a white star on its forehead. It is being herded by a small but vociferous dog. The bullock halts when it sees us and moos in our direction, but the dog chases it on and they too disappear into the darkness.

One pair of headlights is already close, while the other is doing U-turns in the field. A minute later, Yesaul Ulanov is with us again. "What's this, guys, nobody give you a lift? I'm telling you, there are just no good people around any more. Oh, guys, we have a firm bond now. You're helping me and I'll help you. There's no parting us now, no way. In you get!" I'm dumped in the rear seat again. For an instant I resent it, but only for an instant. Who cares. At least it's warm and there are no mosquitoes.

"I talked them round and they filled me up with diesel. We shared out my bottle on the spot, and they had some hooch of their own." "What's going on over there?" Grand asks. We look across to where yellow beams continue weaving an intricate pattern in the black field.

"I introduced a bit of discipline. I said to him, why aren't you working? Why hasn't that field been ploughed?" He says, "Absolutely right. It hasn't been ploughed for donkeys' years. Any time now it will turn into swamp," and damn me but off he went and there you have it. But why are you looking so glum, Seryozha? Let's get singing again and cheer you up. 'Oh, from behind a distant is-land...' Come on, sing!"

Oh, the Russian soul, so unfathomable, so boundless.

Yesaul, Yesaul, Yesaul Ulanov, in the murk the red star rushes onwards. The untamed steppes exhale the scent of wormwood; our eternal Russian, boundless steppes breathing wormwood, the night, and an inebriate yearning from which we cannot wake.

"You don't know anything about life, Titch," Tolya continues to instruct me. "You don't know anything. This BG of yours was the ruin of Russian rock. Think about it, Titch. Rock is fate, it is struggle, it is like a revolution, something people die for. Victor Tsoy died, Sasha Bashlachov died, so why is he, your Grebenshchikov, still alive and kicking?" "Tolya, what are you talking about? He doesn't sing any more." "When rock becomes big business you get pop. We live today in an era of pop. But actually, you're right, rock died a natural death. The era of managers is coming, and managers don't listen to rock. And this is the era you are going to have to live in!" "What about you?" "Well, what about us? We've already seen it all. It's you I'm sorry for. Where are the young punks who will wipe us off the face of the earth? There are none!" "Nutter," I shrug and go back to my book.

When I came across Kerouac I was unspeakably happy. I read him and felt his stuff had been written by a mate in the Yakimanka commune I just hadn't run into yet. Not so improbable, there were plenty of people in the commune I never met. I dreamed of going to America, hitching on American roads, of reaching the mountains, the warm, solitary, misty mountains of California. I dreamed deliriously of meeting Jack, and when I heard he was dead and all this had been written – ohmigod, it *couldn't* have been written so long ago – when I heard that, something inside me just collapsed.

Once again, I was trying to live in an echo of the past. The America Jack Kerouac wrote about was long gone. It was killed in Vietnam, burned out by grass. It had become flabby and bourgeois, stuffed its cheeks with hamburgers and gone to Hollywood.

We live at the junction of two eras, friend. From here we can see clearly enough what used to be, but who can tell us what is coming next?

The dashing hussars of my father's imagination trample the

wormwood in a black field. One of his grandfathers was killed in Stalin's purges and everyone carefully forgot him. Another was 'expropriated' as a rich kulak farmer and they fled their home at night in a cart, losing some things and hastening to leave others behind. Who will gather up all the loose ends now and where will they find them? My father had a grandmother who told him how much like her brother he was, a young officer who died in the First World War. He was serving in the Tsar's Lifeguards. She remembered everything about him and told my father, and my father told me, but there was a lot he didn't remember. Now it's all lost, our roots, the traces, but in my father's mind the dashing hussars still wear jingling spurs and sip golden wine.

What do we know? What have we seen and what have we yet to see? The last times are coming, friend, and all you can do is get blotto on beer. "You don't know life, Titch. You are infantile and dreadfully boring. You've got to change, Titch, it's time you changed." Tolya has his back to me and is kneeling by the windowsill with a board in front of him on which he is carefully smoothing the modelling clay for his next picture.

"Who is going to change me?" "Anyone. Why not me! Why not, Titch? Do you want me to make you into a human being in two shakes of a lamb's tail?" He evidently finds the idea so inspiring that he immediately bounds over to the gallery. "Let's live together. If you like I'll shack up with you right now. We can live together and if you don't like it, we'll stop. But you might like it! You'll be a human being and Roma will give us a couple's discount. How about it, Roma? Will you knock a bit off the rent?" he asks. Roma has a policy of charging couples a bit less than two singles. It's not that he's concerned about demographics, he just thinks a couple take up less space, which has some truth in it.

"How about it Roma? A discount?" "Everything has to be consensual." "Of course it does. No sweat!" Tolya is jubilant.

"How about it, Titch? Shall I come up now? We'll soon make a human being of you!" He clutches at the gallery and puts a foot on the locker. People in the room are laughing.

"Get lost!" I retort, pushing his face away and slamming the door. You sometimes can't tell when Tolya is joking. I hold the door shut. "Rapunzel, show me your little face. Why are you fearful? I'm not going to eat you." He tugs at the door but I'm holding on tightly. "Titch, come to me. Hello-o." He waits. Then, in a different voice, "What is it? Are you offended or what?" There is silence in the room. "That's just silly." Silence. I hear him moving away. "Come out, Titch. I won't touch you, okay? I was only joking! We're friends, okay? Do you hear? Peace!"

I stay silent and don't move but let go of the door. I'm on all fours, in the dark, and it's as warm as a womb in my cubbyhole above the ceiling, in the gallery. So what if you don't understand me, friend. What's that to do with me? I hear Tolya sit down heavily by the windowsill. Then I hear him squeezing his plastic bottle. It sits by the foot of the piano, a brown plastic bottle of beer. As he drinks it crackles.

Quietly, very, very slowly and quietly, I grope in the corner for a candle and lighter. Roma tells me off for lighting candles in here. Don't worry, Roma, I'll be careful, I really will. I asked him once whether he would take me on the road with him. "No," replied Roma Jah. "Why not?" I asked surprised. "I won't be in the way, and I so much want to go to the seaside." "I understand, Titch, but I'm not going to take you. You have to appreciate, for me the road is the only place I can be alone."

Yes, Roma, I understand. I light the candle and fix it with a drop of wax to a jam jar lid. I wonder, if Roma were to knock at the door of my gallery whether I would open it. There's no sound from down below, though.

Curling up like a little animal, I hunch over a book. I don't read it. Instead I watch the paper swelli under my tears.

The lighted place in the darkness of the steppe is a traffic police post. Yesaul Ulanov cuts his speed. I peep out from behind his shoulder. "They can sniff you out," the Yesaul mutters, suddenly quiet. "They sense you, the devils." I can see the sleepy face of a young traffic cop when the Yesaul suddenly rams his foot on the accelerator. The car jerks, roars and takes off like a missile. "Now let's see what they're made of!"

A siren wails behind us. I turn to see glaring headlights. "Put yourself in my place, Sergey. What am I going to say to them: 'Okay, guys, I'm drunk'? What am I going to bribe them with when I have no money? I left my driving licence in Novosibirsk. The last time, just two weeks ago, I forgot it at my brother-in-law's and had to go back for it. Looks like I'm going to have to do the same again this time ..."

He laughs. What is he laughing about? I am scared to look back in case I suddenly see not just headlights but the faces of two cops bellowing through their windscreen. "Let them try," the Yesaul sniggers. "I've got a turbocharger!" I feel better. Looking back I see their lights really are falling behind. "They won't keep that up for long. I know. This is not the first time I've been here. I'm just giving them a bit of fun. What of it? They're bored. It's really boring for them at night."

The sirens can still be heard. The Yesaul starts getting annoyed. "See what they're after, eh? They want to make some easy money! The kind of people you meet nowadays! No one thinks about other people any more. Me, me, me all the time! They're wolves, not human beings." "Come on, Sasha. It's not like that at all." "It's not like that, isn't it? Well, let me tell you, if that had been my son in my place he wouldn't have given you a lift. No way! I know that for a fact. It's obvious from just looking at you that you haven't got any money, so he wouldn't have stopped. He's young – younger than you, I'd say – but the way he is... I can't think who he's got it from, the little brute. All he thinks about is money, fancy gear, and picking up skirt...

He hasn't got an idea in his head. What kind of generation is growing up, Sergey, eh? I ask you! Where's it all going to end? He wouldn't have given you a lift, and why not? We need to help each other out on the road, am I right? The road is all of us in it together. You help me out, I help you. We're all harnessed in the same team, aren't I right?"

"You're right, Sasha, but keep your eyes on the road. It's just life. Life is always that way." "Well what I say is..." The sirens fall away in the darkness and we calm down. I snuggle between the rucksacks again.

"No way am I going to drive into town, Sergey," I hear the Yesaul whisper conspiratorially. "There's a police post there where every last dog knows me. They're bound to stop me and I don't need that. I can do without losing my licence. When I get closer I'll stop and have a good sleep." "But for now we need to keep driving, Sasha." "Right, right..."

Oh, my gods, this night will never end.

I'm half asleep, half waking. I see my own, dear Yakimanka, a big old house where the history and the people come and go and will come and go. Only the house will stay the same, and who now remembers who lived in it and when, or who might have lived in it if things had been different. This vast old house is our Yakimanka with its archways, its high ceilings and its cavernous stairwells. The house is alive. We ourselves do not know just how alive.

Half asleep in someone else's car, I see the house, or perhaps not the house. I drive through its gates in my motor car, step down, run quickly up the porch and throw open the door.

No, in the dream I'm not Titch. I'm the last descendant of an illustrious family. I see shining floors covered with thick runners, a broad staircase. Behind glass doors is the old-fashioned lift whose gates you have to push back. That's unmistakeably it, only now it's gleaming with varnish and bright light-bulbs. The hall porter is sitting at a large brown desk reading a newspaper, pushing it in under the green lampshade. He is wearing a dark blue jacket and has a peaked cap on his bald head. He greets me.

"Hello, Artemiy. Is Papa home?" "He's upstairs in his office, milady." The hallways are wide, the furniture massive, huge windows are draped with heavy curtains. I advance to the large, shiny double doors behind which I know I shall find my father. When I throw them open he'll be there in his blue dress uniform with gleaming epaulettes. But I'm called back.

"What is it, Artemiy?" "An officer has arrived." I go down. A traffic cop is standing there in a dazzlingly white uniform like the street wardens wear in old Soviet films, with a strap across his chest and holster at his hip. Saluting, he says, "You have parked your car in the wrong place. I am fining you."

"How can that be?" I ask in consternation. "I left it in my courtyard." "No, you have *not* left it in your courtyard." "Let us go and see how that can be," I say, following the cop. He opens the front doors and dissolves like a white cloud in the darkness, because it's already night outside. I take a step forward and a glossy raven flies up from under my feet.

"Car-ra! Car-ra! Car-ra!" she caws three times. I survey the courtyard. There are cars parked in it now, children's climbing frames and a sandpit. I turn back and see behind me the tattered entrance to Yakimanka, in the depths of which Roma's commune lives.

"Car-ra! It's me, a lonely fragment of a Time of Troubles."

"Don't you believe it, Sergey, don't you believe it. It's all going to change." "Of course. It's changing already. Even now everything is changing." "Well, what did I say? Of course, Sergey. Look, that girl of yours has woken up." Yesaul Ulanov gives my crumpled reflection an amicable smile in the mirror. "What is it with her that she never says anything and keeps staring at the roof? What's your name? What is it you've spotted up there?"

"I'm not looking at the roof. I'm looking at the sky." "And what's up there?" "A star. It's so big and red. Look, there, to the left. It's been visible all night." "A star? Oh, right, that's Mars. It's August, so Mars is visible. Go back to sleep now. When we arrive we'll wake you up. You have the word of Yesaul Ulanov. With me you're as safe as houses. Go back to sleep. Well, what do you think, Sergey, shall we sing some more? Can we really have run out of songs to sing?"

I lie back in the seat and something clicks. I see everything at once and from above: the steppe, the night, wormwood, blood-red Mars, and us in a red car. The car rushes along, the road rushes by, and all our immense, immense country is asleep...

"Volga, Volga, loving mother," a voice thunders above the road. "Mighty talisman of Rus," it soars higher and higher. "Let my bride drown in your waters, that our men fight fast and loose."

May all the gods of light forfend!

The Woodchuck

Our commune is like the Flying Dutchman. Like an old, empty, creaking ship on the boundless black waves it is sailing headlong into the unknown, full of ghosts and memories. Roma and I are together in the single lit room. We two are the only living souls in an apartment full of ghosts and memories, old smells and unexpected sounds from the corridor. Everybody else has run away but we remain.

"It's fine, Titch," Roma Jah says, smoking. "Sooner or later everybody gets out of substandard accommodation like this. When they get a few bucks together and find work they want to live like human beings. Some leave and others come in their place. Everything changes. It's fine. It always happens."

He's sitting by the windowsill, his back pressed against the ribbed radiator, huddled from top to toe in his very long, ginger scarf. It's a cold autumn and we're feeling the chill.

"What are you going to do now, Roma?" "Wait for new people. They'll come." He knocks his defunct pipe out in his hand. Everybody ran away when Roma Jah and I were on the road. We heard that Tolya did eventually find a girl with a Moscow residence permit and went off to live with her. All that Lenka left behind were strange books, cheap jewelry, make-up and a lot of small items of uncertain purpose. She herself was scooped up and carried off by her unbridled femininity. Sasha Sorokin made it back from the road, that I know for a fact, and he can still sometimes be found in the vicinity of that same entrance hallway where he used to be a courier. He answers his mobile but has not come back to live on Yakimanka. Even old Artemiy has disappeared, and I've been afraid to ask Roma where he has gone.

When I got back, of all our old neighbours only Sergey the Violinist was still here, in a room parallel with my gallery, and Sonya Muginshteyn had her new brown upright piano in the room next door. But even they, even they, you sensed, were thinking of leaving Yakimanka. Sonya came back to spend the night here less and less often, and Sergey gave Roma notice he was intending to move, only there was something holding him.

Now even they have gone. I still sleep in the gallery although there is no need to, but I can't imagine sleeping anywhere else. And for all that, Yakimanka, my kind Moscow cradle, you gave me one last gift. You arranged my last adventure here in the shape of Sergey the Violinist who, as soon as I came back, started visiting our room, sitting near the gallery, and saying nothing.

He would come in, sit down, and begin to sigh without respite. He was awkward, bespectacled, had a broad square face and body, big ears, bad teeth and a dark mark on his neck caused by his violin. He would adopt a very intense expression, not look at me, and not know what to do with his hands with their broad palms and stubby fingers with short, white, flat-ended nails. When I once asked what he had come for, he replied adenoidally, "I want to get to know you, Titch. You are so strange. I really can't make out what kind of person you are."

He called me Titch, but was embarrassed by it and tried to swallow the word. Despite that, he never called me by my proper name. He said he wanted to understand me, but after that spoke never a word. I did feel sorry for him and would have been pleased to have someone to talk to, but he didn't respond when I spoke to him, and if he did would blurt out something beside the point, or start telling me something in a dull, incoherent manner before again falling silent.

I was still strange after the road, disorientated and totally unsure how I should live now. I wanted either solitude or understanding, and wordless Sergey could give me neither. Neither would he go away until it was time for Roma and me to retire for the night.

"Well, ask what you want to know and I'll tell you." He sighed loudly. I found him ridiculous but spoke kindly to him, in order not to laugh. "Sergey, smile. You look so glum." For the first time he raised his face to look at me. "Dear Titch, you've changed so much this summer," he said regretfully. "You're completely different..." "I saw the world in a different light," I replied flatly. "Someone probably showed it to you in a different light," he suggested archly before looking away again. "It was just the road," I said.

Roma Jah came in with the teapot and poured a glass for himself and one for me. He offered one to Sergey, sat down and started playing the guitar. Sergey said nothing, but I could see his curiosity had been piqued.

"So you really went hitchhiking?" he finally asked. "What of it?" "Well, it's just it seems so... out of character for you.

You're so... vulnerable. Getting into other people's cars, not having a home of your own, meeting strangers... People are all sorts, Titch. Were you really never scared?"

"You're afraid of something you don't know. When you don't know, you make things up and frighten yourself." "That's why I really want to know you, but you don't tell me anything." "How can I tell you? Let's go hitchhiking and you'll find out for yourself."

Roma struck a bum chord. Sergey had a hangdog expression but lacked the courage to refuse. We agreed to make an early start, and he immediately left the room. Roma Jah shook his head. "You need to think what you're doing, Titch. That's not for everyone, and he is a mole." "He should have thought of that himself. For some reason he agreed."

Roma shook his head again. With each additional road trip he became wiser and accordingly more and more placid, did Roma, the landlord of our commune. But the deed was done, and the pre-road trip butterflies in my stomach could not be stilled. A faraway smile lit up my face, my eyes began to shine, like Grand's crazy eyes. It took me a long time to get to sleep that night. I lay and stared the length of the room through the window to see the stars and the gentle glow of the Moscow sky.

Oh, Stalker, Stalker, why is the Zone drawing you back again?

We are footloose and fancy-free wayfarers on roads without end, friends of long-distance truckers and drivers, their amulets, talismans, their guardian angels. Even the cops leave us alone. They know us for who we are and where we are going. We may not know that ourselves, may laugh and gesture into the sun, but the cops know. They swear, shrug, hand back our ID, and send us on our way. There is no stopping us, but why that should be they don't know.

We are legion, dots scattered along the road, romantic followers of our guru Jack Kerouac, members of the same mendicant order, and the motto on our crest could read, *In via veritas* or, more simply, "The Road Is Always Right". Our destinations differ and the routes we take, but we are as one in our sense that only here, on the road, are we truly free.

We are twenty years old, give or take, do not yet have a past, do not look to the future, and in the present have only the road ahead, the asphalt, and the jubilant knowledge that everybody else has lost track of us.

We emerged only recently. We are still only starting out. We are on a high and embrace our road, anticipating its gifts, not knowing where it will lead us.

And you, capricious road, now smiling, now incensed, how are we to detect the moment when your mood changes? You are life, and destiny, the unique instance of all possible combinations. Right here, right now, with this person, and we know no alternative.

What an ordeal our way back had been! A wearisome ordeal, as though the mountains and the Enchanted Lake did not want to let us go. If up to the Urals we were on a roll, after them our way was difficult but it was too late to do anything about it. Why that was, what caused it I have yet to understand, but at the very beginning of our progress Grand said, "The road is a continuous test for us. It is always waiting to see our reaction. We are always facing a choice, and what happens next depends on each step we take."

"But what about luck?" "Luck on the road is not a matter of chance. It depends directly on you yourself, how open you are, how 'beyond reproach', how capable of transcending yourself, of accepting and loving everything around you. That will determine how easy and enjoyable your way will be. Ask yourself whether at this moment you're loving what's around you."

I looked around and shrugged. We were walking in Omsk, the weather was great, the rucksack wasn't feeling too heavy. I supposed I was loving it all, why not?

We went to the market. Grand decided to buy food. He left me looking after the rucksacks and disappeared. He had left me in a corner near empty stalls where nobody needed to come and with two rucksacks, each of which was up to my waist, yet within five minutes some lanky character showed up and started telling me how much he liked tourists.

"I was a tourist once myself. The Caucasus, the Khibin Mountains, the Sayans. I travelled all over the place, but now those years are gone. I am completely past it." As he said all this, he assumed a suitably mournful expression, although his face, haircut and everything about his lithe figure indicated that here was a man who took very good care of himself. His hair was still impeccably black, with a single bleached strand flopping over his forehead. Above his silkily gleaming black shirt, flirtatiously open at the collar, lay a flat gold chain.

I had seen him in the distance, while he was still a couple of rows of stalls away. He was quite a height and towered over the stallholders. I noticed him because he was so unlike the kind of people you usually find shopping for groceries at the market.

"I'm past it and need to make money," he went on. I tried to deduce his intention in approaching me from his expression. "Make money, feed the family. I used to have my own business but then we had the currency default, one thing and another. I work as a shipping agent for an Irish restaurant now." To prove it he incongruously shook a goodly bunch of leeks.

"Ah, youth!" he sighed. "You must let me buy you a meal. There is a place over there, nothing special but clean. Everyone knows me there. It's on me." For some reason I was reluctant to go and eat with him. I played for time, hoping that when Grand came he would decline to share our company with this oversized ex-tourist.

But he didn't. The three of us took ourselves over to the diner, bringing our rucksacks. Our new acquaintance ordered food, and vodka for himself. While we ate he talked. "You should get married," he said, looking Grand unblinkingly in the eye. Grand only smiled. "Get married and get on with having children. They will be there to support you later on. Myself, I married at nineteen and already have a son helping me. I've got a daughter too. What a stunning little daughter I have!"

Grand was not directly facing him and his smile was fairly non-committal. I could tell he didn't believe a word of it and, like me, was trying to work out what all this was leading up to. Our man started getting into his stride and telling us about an accident he and his family had been involved in. His mother-in-law had been killed and after that his much loved little daughter had developed a stutter. He didn't know what to do about it. His face was flushed, his neck too, and the part of his chest you could see through the unbuttoned collar. A swollen vein was throbbing under his cheekbone. We listened in silence and when we had finished our meal he produced a wad of banknotes.

"Tell you what," he said, "Why don't I give you five hundred roubles? Money always comes in handy when you're on the road." We exchanged glances and started protesting rather feebly that we couldn't possibly, but our benefactor was emphatic. It was a wad of fifties. He counted out ten, put them on the table and looked at us. "My name is Pyotr," he said. "Perhaps you'll remember me one day." He downed what was left of the vodka and left.

After waiting long enough for him to get out of sight, Grand stood up and said quietly, "Let's get out of here". He swept up the money, crisscrossed the two rucksacks over his head and rushed out of the café. I looked longingly at our sugar daddy's untouched meal and helped myself to the remaining slices of bread.

We fled from the market and made our way through back alleys, doubling back on ourselves. We changed the fifties in kiosks, buying trivial items. Grand was constantly looking back, focused and purposeful, but nobody came after us.

We left the town as unproblematically as we had entered it. The driver of a foreign car who picked us up asked loudly and incredulously where we were going and why we chose to travel this way. "I can't understand you," he said. "I like comfort and independence." "This is independence," we replied. "The freedom to go where you like and sleep where you like." "No! It's far better to have your own car." "Property is unfreedom," Grand said, and the driver laughed.

He had a sturdy black Jeep which was spacious, soft and quiet. Sounds sank into the beige leather upholstery. The way he drove meant you had no sensation of the roadway beneath the wheels and could forget about everything outside the windows. It was like flying. In the blacklist of vehicles renowned among hitch-hikers for never, or only exceptionally, giving lifts, Jeeps occupy the number one spot. To every rule, however, there are exceptions and this was one of them. He shrugged off our questions about where he had come from and where he was going. "Compared with you, just across the street." Then he started talking about all the countries he had visited. He talked a lot but in a great rush, and gaps suddenly appeared in his tales. As if forgetting what he was about to say, he would fall silent, carrying on after a pause from the same place.

At the boundary between two provinces he stopped, leaned back in his seat and said, "That's it. I'm not driving any further. I need to sleep." "Aren't you going to Tyumen, then?" "I'm going to Sochi. From Irkutsk. Do me a favour, I've been driving for eighteen hours. It was good talking to you, but there are limits." We dutifully got out. He stretched and started doing some relaxation exercises. The road was empty, the sky cloudy, and it was evening. I miserably breathed in the damp air.

"Get you a meal?" he asked, heading for the café. We'd already put on our rucksacks but were tempted. Grand shrugged uncertainly and looked across at me. I thought he felt it was awkward to refuse and wanted me to do it for him. "No," I said firmly. "We're in a hurry to get to Tyumen." "As you will," the driver said, shrugged and walked away.

We went back to the roadside but got no further that night.

"Turn, look them in the eye and say to yourself, 'Stop!'" "And what will happen?" Sergey asks, looking at me anxiously. "Everything depends on your *intention*," I reply seriously. "If it's strong a vehicle will stop for you." "I just say 'Stop' and nothing more?"

I feel mildly irritated. It's quite early and we've just come out. "No, you have to raise your hand as well. Get it?" He shrugs uncertainly. "Let's get started, then. It's best to put the bag down. No, not too far away or you won't be able to find it again. Put it beside you. Now turn to face the traffic, look the drivers in the eye and say: 'Stop!'"

"Stop!" Sergey says obediently. "You don't have to say it out loud. It's an order you're transmitting. You can do that mentally. What matters is that you should want it. It's a good idea to raise your hand or they won't know what you're standing here for. And smile."

"Should I have my hand open or closed?" Gods give me patience! Now I'm glad I took Roma's advice and came here by train. He said that if we wanted to hitch, it would be better to do it on the way back or we might spend all day getting here and not have time to get home. Sergey is not someone it would be a bundle of laughs being stranded with on the highway at night.

We stand there and Sergey dutifully holds out his hand. He's in front and I can't see his expression. I try not to think about him and focus on the vehicles. It's the hottest part of the day, there's a lot of traffic, but they all drive by without so much as a glance in our direction. Oh, road, could you not just send us one car to take us straight back to Moscow? A nice long-distance one. Actually, no. This mole would learn nothing from that. I'm going to have to put up with getting covered in dust with him on the verge.

What a great, happy feeling this is! Even the wind, that special highway wind that gusts with every vehicle which passes, pleases me, even if it does sometimes snatch the cap from my head. The smell here is so familiar and dear to me. It's just Sergey... He is a sorry sight, standing there with his arm limply outstretched. In the morning he was in the kitchen waiting for me, looking ready for inspection, all washed and ironed and the only thing missing was the customary bunch of flowers. Instead he had an empty travel bag in his hand. His tone of voice and his eyes suggested he hadn't slept all night. We fare-dodged on the train. He had actually done that before in his life. In the city he was gallant and pretended to be my boyfriend. He talked enthusiastically about a forthcoming tour of the chamber orchestra he was playing in now, and tried surreptitiously to take my arm. I found that comical, removed my arm and put my hands in my pockets. I felt bereft without the familiar rucksack on my back.

By now his spirits are failing and he is starting to regret having got involved in all this. He stoops with embarrassment and is almost certainly worrying now about what the driver in each car is thinking of him. He needn't worry. Nobody is paying us any attention or they would have stopped. Before you brake, you need to have opened your heart. How can I explain that to him?

"Sergey, ask yourself what you're offering these people. What do you have that you're going to give them?" "What? But I asked you if we have to pay? You said we didn't and I've brought almost no money with me." He turns to face me, upset. "I'm not talking about money, I'm talking about you." "What about me? What do you mean? Is there something wrong with the way I look?"

He examines himself and nervously brushes down his trousers. I feel that wave of irritation rising in me again. "Sergey, there are three rules you must remember if you want to hitch: we don't owe anyone anything; nobody owes us anything either; we are fun, and that's why people give us a lift."

I see uncertainty in Sergey's face. Have I convinced him? We'll have to wait and see, but if he pays anyone, I'll kill him.

It was raining in the morning so it was after midday when we emerged. We stood there for a long time without getting a lift. It was a boggy area and the road surface was incredibly cracked and rutted with potholes. The vehicles were swerving all over the place to avoid them and had no time for us. We walked on to find a smoother part of the road but it didn't help.

Eventually, an old dirty white Lada stopped. Its driver told us God had spoken to him. "He told me you were good people. He said, 'Give them a lift and take them to the city because they are good people.' What God tells me to do, I do."

He told us one should desire nothing and have no ambition because, if God so willed, everything would come to us. "God has promised me He will resurrect my father and my sister's husband. Where are you from yourselves, not from Tyumen? Never mind, even you will hear the tidings when the Lord performs this miracle."

It was night in Tyumen and he dropped us off at the turning for the city. There were trees on our side of the road and a brightly lit petrol station on the other. We crossed.

It was well lit and empty. Our footsteps resonated crisply on the concrete apron, echoing back from the service station's dome. Out of the shop came a little drunk geezer in a T-shirt, tracksuit bottoms and flip-flops. We recognised him as a trucker and he recognised us as hitch-hikers. Looking pleased, he headed our way.

"Where are you going? Why, we're going that way too! Come with us. We're parked over there, three trucks. We've already got one of yours, a kid going from Vladivostok to Petersburg, and now we'll have you as well. There's room enough and it'll be more fun with us all together."

"Where are you going yourselves?" "All the way to Moscow." "When are you aiming to get there?" "We've got a full load. Right now we'll be crossing the Urals, then drive on to Chelyaba, so we should be in Moscow by Friday." We could hear the pride he took in his slow, heavy truck.

"Okay, we'll be right back. We'll just get some water and come over," I said. "Come on now! We've got everything already. We're just going to cook up some *pelmeni*." "We won't be a moment. You go on ahead." "Okay. You'll find us with no trouble."

He went off. We cleaned our teeth in the filling station toilet, got water, and retreated to the other side of the road to hide in the freshness and shade of the trees. We pitched the tent among marvellous ferns. I really didn't want to spend five days in the company of truckers, and also didn't fancy sharing with another hitch-hiker. I thought we'd get to Moscow faster by car. Grand just shrugged.

The next morning we found we were near a factory. There was heavy traffic but we struggled for half a day without going anywhere. It was hot and dusty and the trucks driving into the plant were deafening. We eventually had to recognise that just standing there and thumbing wasn't going to work, so we started running up to every truck which stopped at the factory entrance and asking them to move us on away from here.

"Just take us into town, anywhere. We'll make our own way from there," we pleaded and eventually a KamAZ truck driver nodded without looking at us. Equally silently, without once looking at us, he drove us through the city, let us out on the roadside and, waving straight ahead, grunted "Sverdlovsk is that way". We were happy.

In the evening we got a lift in a new Lada. "I can't take you far. Sorry," the driver apologised. "I live quite near here." We nodded and expressed profound gratitude nevertheless. 'Not far' proved to be around two hundred kilometres. The whole way our driver evidently felt like a host trying to look after unexpected visitors. He asked what kind of music we liked, and selected only those songs. He gave us a plastic bag with chicken, vegetables and bread, urging us to eat the food or take it with us because he was home now and wouldn't be needing it. He asked us very politely about our travelling and didn't ask everybody's standard question of why we did it. On the contrary, after hearing our enthusiastic explanation, he said respectfully, "Yes, it is a good thing to travel like that. You get to know the land, and people, and you get to know yourselves." We nodded in delight. We couldn't have put it better ourselves.

"Well, this is where I live," he said, passing through a small village. "But I'll just show you a lovely spot. You'll enjoy spending the night there." He drove a little beyond the village and stopped. There was an unscythed meadow with tall, dry grass, and a stream about a hundred metres from the road.

"This is a good place. I come here swimming in the summer. There's fishing too," our driver said as we parted, adding, "You know, this is actually the first time I've ever given anyone a lift. All sorts of people try to hitch-hike. I'm nervous of stopping, but just yesterday I read in the paper that it's a kind of sport. Good luck to you, guys."

The night was cold and starry, the stream dark and silent. For the whole night nobody drove along the road, so we were able to forget about it. It was as if we were back in the mountains, alone and far away from other people. Coming out of the tent and looking up at the stars, I thought this really was a gift to us from the road, and that now I truly did love everything around me.

"They sometimes make signals. Have you noticed?" Sergey asks, turning round to face me. I'm pleased. Perhaps he will work up some enthusiasm now he's started noticing their signals. "What sort of signals?" "Some of them circle with their fingers like this." "That means they're turning back soon." "Others point left." "That means they're just about to turn off the road." "And they wave." "That just means they're pleased to see you." "Come again?" Sergey asks in puzzlement.

Ekaterinburg was a delight. After edgy, marshy Tyumen it was a joy to burst into the summery warmth of such a splendid, beautiful, sunny city. The driver who brought us, knowing it was our first time there, drove us on a sightseeing trip through the main streets, telling us all about the old buildings and churches. Afterwards we walked back to the centre, ate ice creams and walked along the river embankment. It was 1 September, the beginning of a new school year, and the holiday atmosphere was everywhere. We walked oblivious of the weight of our rucksacks.

In a pedestrian subway there were guys bumming. A lot of them. One boy with a guitar was singing while his girl took a cap round the onlookers. Others stood around nearby looking disaffected and talking loudly. They surrounded us, asking where we had been and inviting us to stay with them. Grand meticulously wrote down the address of the local crash pad.

"You aren't really intending to go there, are you? " I asked when we moved on. "Yes. I want a wash. We've already turned down two gifts from the road. It wouldn't be right to pass on a third."

We found ourselves in a remarkable apartment. Exactly how many people were staying there was probably a mystery to everyone, including the landlords. I identified them solely on the basis of their opening the door more frequently than other people. The landlady was a girl even shorter than me, blonde, with hair as matted as felt. Her husband was tall with large, sunken eyes which didn't smile, even though he told a lot of jokes. He wore a beige panama hat and looked like a very tall, brooding gnome. Their child was weaving its way in among everyone, a small, independent being with curly blond hair. I confidently classified it as a girl, before discovering he was a boy. He treated everyone as equals, completely unfazed by age difference.

Every square metre of the apartment was occupied. People were getting washed in the bathroom. Both rooms were living a life of their own. People went out onto the balcony to smoke. Even in the hallway there was a small group of people, but the real crush was in the kitchen. There some were cooking while others were eating. Music was being played through speakers built into a broken-down guitar hanging on the wall.

What all these people were doing here, why they had come, whether they knew what they were doing or why they came was beyond my comprehension. It was plain they were not all renting these few square metres of accommodation as we did on Yakimanka. They evidently came as visitors and stayed for several days. We were welcomed in just the same way as everybody else, that is, completely naturally and without curiosity, as if we were regulars.

Grand got into conversation with the owners and was very soon promoted to the status of philosopher. A circle of listeners formed round him, asking questions which Grand answered in detail. I found myself redundant and sat some distance away with world weariness in my eyes. Every now and then Grand would turn to me, his eyes asking, "Do you love what is around you?"

With each hour that passed, however, I found the apartment more depressing. The slaphappy indolence drove me to despair until I felt I was ready to reply to his question with a resounding, "No!" This slovenly partying, the indiscriminate friendliness and lack of curiosity, the aimless, lazy lifestyle with its pretensions to be seeking a meaning for itself seemed as tacky as a spider's web and I just wanted to get back on the road, to freedom. It was only in moving on that I could now see any sense.

"Why are you leaving?" the landlord asked Grand. "Gosha here came in from the road and thought he'd just stay overnight. When was that? Well, he must have been living with us for the best part of a month now."

"My life is about moving on. I can turn aside, see something new, but I can't see sense in stopping." "What does make sense? There is no sense," Gosha boomed from somewhere up near the ceiling. He was an athletic-looking giant with a happy baby sitting on his bare back. "There is no sense," Grand replied quietly and with a smile, "but there is a goal."

I had had enough and started pestering him to leave. "You're separating yourself off from them when you should be loving them, and then you'd understand them," Grand told me when, catching him for a moment in the hallway, I voiced my opinion in an irate whisper.

"It's usually the other way round! Usually you understand first and love afterwards." "Well, the opposite is the right way," he said and walked off.

Towards midnight our hosts took us for a tour of the city. Some hangers-on followed but gradually fell away. Cool, night-time Ekaterinburg was quiet, transparent, and as unreal as a film set. We trudged through backyards, sometimes clambering through holes in fences, and suddenly emerged into a square flooded with street light, ran across it and again disappeared into the darkness. At the end of each excursion we might see a unique flowerbed shaped like a baby hippopotamus or a totally unique crevice in a wall. I very soon lost my bearings and could barely move my feet from exhaustion. The whole thing felt like a dream which had been going on too long. The child on the landlord's shoulders had fallen asleep with his head resting on the panama.

When we got back, everyone who was still able to stay awake assembled in a room to read aloud from the Strugatskys *The Snail on The Slope*. Communal reading was evidently a local custom. It was already morning. I went off, curled up in my sleeping bag, and to a rhythmical communal murmuring on the other side of the wall started looking at the stars. They glowed with a phosphorescent light and were painted on the ceiling.

How sluggishly our hitchhiking went after that! We trekked through a small town called Kamensk Uralsky on foot without getting a lift at all. Just outside the town the traffic cops gave us a lift after we had stood a full hour by the roadside. We came to a halt in the Urals, spent a night in the mountains, then went on foot in search of a good position. A good position needs to be neither on a downhill nor an uphill stretch and where are you going to find that in the Ural Mountains? We finally got a lift in another Jeep with people from Perm but, as we didn't want to go to Perm, that lift didn't take us far.

We were driven through Bashkiria by a geezer with whiskers and his wife. We had been worn out by Ural mountain passes and fell asleep. Through my sleep I heard a conversation: "The Great Spirit of Ways and Roads protects you, but you do not notice it," the wife said to her husband, and I thought I must already be dreaming.

We bypassed Ufa, but would doubtless have had to walk straight through the middle, only the beneficent Spirit of Ways and Roads smiled on us and we got a lift in two MAZ trucks transporting bottles. You can't fit three people in the cab of a MAZ. Grand and I were separated and cheerfully went our separate ways, talking between trucks over the walky-talky to the accompaniment of the musical tinkling of the empty bottles in the back.

They dropped us off in Tatarstan, and we realised we had won a two-hour time shift off the road. That was enough to get us to Naberezhnye Chelny with a morose, taciturn driver. He dropped us off at the turning to the city, ten metres from a police station. Our rucksacks and general bewilderment attracted the cops' attention. An officer sternly inspected our passports and residence permits, checked our faces against our photos, and chewed his moustache. Just to be on the safe side, he ran our names through the national wanted persons database.

That was when I discovered Grand's surname: Grandovsky. It had never occurred to me just to ask him. Now it's practically the only thing I know about him.

By the time we got away from the cops it was already dark. There was no chance we would be going anywhere that night. We moved away from the road but didn't find any good sites so pitched the tent in a field on neglected, uneven ground. We were concealed from the road by a huge power station pipe and a stone plinth with the name of the ancient town of Yar Chaly. As we were pitching the tent I looked around at the dismal industrial landscape and wondered what there was here to love.

One day we encountered a thirteen-year-old boy who had no luggage, shabby clothes, and furtive eyes. He jumped down from a KamAZ truck near where we were standing and walked away backwards, thumbing. He disappeared round a bend. Someone gave us a lift soon after but, when they dropped us off, we saw the same kid dancing along fifty metres in front of us. We stopped and I turned to face him. He soon got a lift.

We kept bumping into each other all day, sometimes overtaking, sometimes being overtaken. Grand paid no attention to him but I started watching him closely. I started seeing him as a competitor and my determination to get a lift first came close to a race. I knew instinctively he had his eye on me too. After another lift I saw his face in an approaching truck. He was eating an apple and gave me a wave. I felt my gall rising.

It was already evening when we jumped down from a truck and went into a café full of truckers. We sat in a corner with our rucksacks propped up against the wall. We were tired and hungry. Grand bought some food and ate it with a smile on his lips but I felt like a cornered animal. I just wanted to disappear. Everybody around us knew what our game was and I felt they were weighing us up and deciding not to take us with them.

Another trucker came in together with the kid. They were talking loudly. The driver ordered a meal for himself and the boy, then joined a group of his friends and began talking to one. I had my back to them and could hear everything. "Maybe you can take this waif. He needs to get to Yaroslavl and I'm only going as far as Nizhny Novgorod."

After a time they pushed back their chairs and made for the door. The boy was now with a different driver. I stared at his back, and even in the way he walked I saw something smug. At the door the boy turned and it seemed to me stuck out his tongue. I could have thrown something at him.

"Smile," I heard Grand's voice at just that moment. "Smile!" His face began to emerge for me out of a fog of hatred. "Tell me, do you love all that is around you at this moment?"

Explain to me, road, why I am here right now with this person who looks like a scarecrow, and what I should do? How can you love someone it is impossible to love, be tolerant towards someone you just want to punch?

"Sergey, it's three hundred kilometres to Moscow, we have nowhere to sleep and we don't have a tent. Do you want to get home tonight?" "Yes." "Well it's not very evident! You're scared of cars! Look how you're standing. Where is your wish to get a lift and provide someone with agreeable companionship? What sort of expression have you got? Who's going to want to give you a lift looking like that?"

Soon we'll have been stuck here for three hours and no one has even slowed down. Maybe it's just the place we're standing. You do get hopeless places on the road, I've been told. Sergey makes me feel like I have a huge rucksack on my shoulders, much heavier than anything I've ever had to carry before and which makes it impossible for me to get a lift. I have pins and needles in the arm outstretched towards the road, my feet are tired and I don't know what to do.

"You're an actor, Sergey. Do something to make your audience respond to you!" "I'm a musician." "Don't musicians have to know how to hold their audience's attention?"

He is silent. He is snivelling. Waves of fury break over me and it takes an effort to restrain myself. I sense his weakness. I want to hit him or scream something at him. I move towards him. He raises his face and looks hounded and pathetic. I close my eyes.

When I was in kindergarten there was this boy. I don't remember any of the other children, but him I remember perfectly. I rarely played with anyone there. I was a quiet and totally unremarkable little girl. My only naughtiness was that I really enjoyed pinching this boy. When we were on a walk I would go up to him, take the striped straw hat off my head, shove it in front of him and say, "How many stripes?" He would say nothing. I knew he couldn't count. "How many stripes, how many?" I would ask again, jabbing my finger at the hat. The boy would say nothing, look down at the ground and begin to sob. That was when I pinched him. I did it every day. It became an addiction for me, and for him a nightmare.

I remember the wave of pleasure that rose in me every time. I could feel my power and hold over him, and his weakness and incompetence. No exhortations or shouting from the carers, no summoning of my parents, no punishments could deter me. Made to stand in the corner, I picked plaster off the walls, looking round to catch his eye among the other children, and noticing that he was looking warily in my direction. I knew I left dark bruises on his skin, but I also knew he was scared of me, and my exultation over that was stronger than all other feelings.

He was rescued by our teacher. The wisdom of her decision would have done credit to King Solomon. She made sure I was always and everywhere paired with this boy. Henceforth our cots in the rest hour were placed together, we had our meals together, and held hands when taken for walks. What really mattered for her was to ensure that we sat at the same table in class when we were being taught to count. The boy found this very difficult, while for me it was easy-peasy. I saw him struggling, sighing with the effort of trying to identify the changing number of sticks in the piles. It annoyed and disgusted me, and to my own surprise I started teaching him.

I had lost my trump card. Without thinking, I had given it away and by the time I realised what had happened it was too late. I was ashamed of helping him, ashamed of sitting next to him, and started avoiding him. No friendship blossomed between us, but a sense of responsibility took root in me. I had been burdened with this boy, and whatever I might think about it, I had no option but to carry him.

I could swear it is that selfsame boy looking at me now through Sergey's eyes. I have the exact same feeling: here is my burden and I have no choice but to bear it. I would like to turn away and leave him to it, let him trudge all the way back and get himself a taxi home, but, dammit, we are sitting at the same table now, friend, and together we are going to sort out those sticks!

"Sergey, look! There are people in those cars," I say quietly. "They are all kind people. They need you to like them.

It's up to them now whether we get home this evening or not."
"But I don't know them, Titch." "What of it! Just love all of
them anyway!"

Oh, road, help me to do that too: to love someone I find
it impossible to love, to forgive someone I just want to punch.

I thought our journey would never end. It was a cliff, a sheer
rockface we had to scale, pulling ourselves up a metre at a
time by our hair. No long-distance vehicles came along. We
got lifts from people going in our direction ten kilometres at a
time. We crept forward from one spot to the next, intersection
by intersection, milestone by milestone. The weather was
nothing to write home about either. In the vicinity of Kazan,
having already crossed the Volga, we found ourselves in such
a hurricane we couldn't stand upright. We had to get out of the
wind. It was blowing in our backs and we almost ran down the
hill to a place where there was less wind but no cars.

I was silent and sullen. When Grand said, "Smile!" I
couldn't manage even a grimace. Rage was building up in me
at our haplessness and helplessness. Despondency smouldered.

"Why are you so uptight?" Grand asked. "Weather not
suiting you?" "I grew up near here," I told him for some
reason. "We passed the turning to my town not long ago, and
my brother often drives along this road to Moscow, to pick up
goods. He has a Gazelle van."

"Do you want to avoid meeting him?" "N-no." I reflected
for a moment. "It's not that I want to avoid him, I just know
he wouldn't stop. My brother isn't the kind of person to give
lifts." "You know, our road will come to an end soon," Grand
said after a pause. "If the road is not smiling on two people, it's
probably best for each to carry their own destiny. How do you
feel now about us splitting up?"

I said nothing and looked away.

In the rain no one wanted to pick up two wet hitch-hikers. A sturdy truck finally stopped for us. Only two were allowed to be in the cab, so I was stowed away on the shelf and told to lie low if any cops appeared.

The truck was being driven by a Lithuanian who spoke Russian with an accent but very much liked doing so. He told us how great it was to go on assignments in Russia. It paid much better than Europe so, like him, a lot of truckers were keen to drive here. He set Grand off on his childhood memories, and he talked about how he used to travel to Lithuania when he was little and how much he had enjoyed being there. Their conversation became very man-to-man and I wanted to contribute something from my shelf. I remembered my parents too had lived there for a while, but then also remembered that was because my father was a serving officer who instructed soldiers in the art of firing missiles. I decided to keep quiet.

It was warm in the cab and I could see the road from above. It moved towards me like a ribbon and seemed to pass right through me, every kilometre carrying away a bit more of me. I started to feel dog tired. Moving on, moving on and never stopping, the succession of faces and places, and there were so many of them, both places and faces, and what's the point, what's the goal? Today I'm going somewhere, tomorrow I'm leaving, but where is the place I am eventually going to arrive at?

In one diner some truckers joined us and asked the usual questions. They asked why we did it. What was the pleasure, what did we get out of it? We gave them the same answers: it was interesting to see new places and people, and Grand added that we just liked moving on.

"Well, why don't you come and work as a trucker if you like being on the road so much," they said. They were hulking young guys who had arrived on the autobahn, and what every hitch-hiker knows about autobahn drivers is that they never stop to give lifts. "No, it's something quite different," Grand said quietly, and I agreed. "You're strange people," they replied. "We at least get paid. Like hell we would go on the road if we weren't getting paid."

"It's no surprise they don't understand us," Grand said afterwards. "They and we are at opposite ends of the spectrum, but for all that, we and they are travelling the same road. We and they together are the road. Do you see now why we have to love everybody?"

His smile just got bigger and bigger and he looked happy. Something had obviously occurred to him, but right then there was nobody feeling more disconsolate than me. That hateful question: 'Why?' which was so capable of devaluing everything, hovered over the world for me and I found it very unclear how one should live a good life. I tried to imagine how and what people live by, and could not. All the values that seemed self-evident in cities, after just two months on the road ceased to be meaningful. Looking back, I could see how they could all be arranged like links in a chain, explaining one thing by another. I tried to trace it back. Perhaps somewhere you could see what really makes life worth living, but I couldn't find the ends. Education led to a job, a job to money, money to prosperity, prosperity to a family, a family to children, children to... Where was the ultimate goal? After all, I knew now that you can live without money, without a home, without supplies. What really matters is to radiate joy and be good people. But turning to the world, I saw that everything in it was arranged differently, and I wanted to stand and face it, close my eyes and shout very loudly indeed: "Stop!" To make them all stop, and then ask just one big question: "What's this all for?"

A lot of time has passed since then, and although I don't know the answer to this question for sure, I sometimes think I am getting closer to unravelling it. It's as if something suddenly opens inside me, everything becomes crystal clear and I have no more questions. Then I remember Grand's smile in the diner and his words, "We and they are travelling the same road. Do you see now why we have to love everybody?"

This happened for the first time in late autumn, long after the adventure with Sergey. He had moved out but Sonya Muginshteyn still occasionally came back to collect her remaining items. Then one day when she came, she unexpectedly invited me to a concert she was playing at. "We will be a trio," she said. "Come if you're interested."

I was surprised and intrigued. In all our life on Yakimanka Sonya had never been known to invite anyone to her performances. But that life was over now, and everything was overgrown with weeds. Now such a thing was possible, and I accepted.

The concert was being held in someone's apartment. I was given a slip of paper with the address and the host's name. He was called Wulf Markovich, and I tried to memorise that on my way to the apartment on Leningrad Prospekt.

I arrived at the address and found myself in an entrance with enormous flights of stairs and tall, narrow doors. The perspective in such an entrance dizzies the hero of "The Cranes Are Flying" as he looks upwards, and now I too felt dizzy. The door I was looking for was already open, and Wulf Markovich, short, wiry, with curly hair, was waiting for me with a smile.

"Come in, come in, make yourself at home, no need to take off your shoes, no, really. Here you're welcome to keep them on." He was amiable and archaically courteous. No other guests had arrived yet so I received the full force of his hospitality. A child of the gallery on Yakimanka, I felt overwhelmed and tried to make myself as inconspicuous as possible. He took me through to a room, indicated an enormous tray of apples and urged me to help myself. On the other side of the wall, rehearsal was in progress.

"Do you also have musical connections?" he enquired

delicately. His big, dark eyes shone mildly in a face overgrown by curly beard. His body was frail, the weary body of a professor of physics, but those wise eyes enchanted and held me.

"We're all connected with music in one way or another," I said, embarrassed by the loud crunch from my apple. Wulf Markovich was delighted by my reply and nodded in response. I quickly took in the room, crammed with furniture and bookcases and lit by a soft half-light from two table lamps under faded orange shades. This room, a private library, the repository of knowledge from several different fields, also belonged inalienably to a professor no less than the body of the person in front of me. His eyes, however, knew more than you can learn from books.

I inspected the large photographs on the walls: the reflection of a building in a puddle (with only the puddle in the photograph); a maple leaf on a wet pavement; the light of electric street lamps in damp air, seemingly somehow taken at a high shutter speed. They testified to the eye of an artist and the hand of a professional. In the centre was the portrait of a handsome young man and a thin, sweet girl.

These were not typical family photographs where the subjects are posing and smiling artificially to camera. The people depicted were alive: the young man was sitting in a deep light blue armchair, turning to look at something off camera, while the girl looked as if she had just this minute sat down beside him on the arm of the chair. She too was turned half away and looking at the same thing. She had black hair which fell from a slender shoulder and tumbled down her back to below the waist. She had strikingly long, narrow eyebrows, a dark skin and a warm smile; her features were gentle, discreet, loving and trusting so that they immediately evoked a liking for her. The youth was a little older and had similar looks: equally dark skin, the same smile, and dark eyes in which, despite the paucity of light in the room, I could see something unknowable and unclassifiable which instantly put me in thrall to him. Tenderness, sincerity, a longing for warmth, almost forgotten and covered in dust on Yakimanka, awoke in my inner depths, called forth by his eyes. It was love at first sight, if it is possible to fall in love with a photograph.

My intuition told me this was Wulf Markovich's son, and the girl was either his sister or his wife. For me, it did not matter which: right now she too was as much a part of this man as the light in his eyes. But where were they, I wondered. Were they by any chance at home? Something melted at the thought that I might get to see that face and those eyes in the flesh. No, they have gone, the answer chillingly suggested itself and told me everything.

Just as the flash on a camera hauls objects out of darkness and we see them, literally, in a different light, so I suddenly pictured these people in the photograph differently. Who they were, how old they were, what their relationship was when the photo was taken, no longer mattered. They had ceased to be live human beings with their own history and emotions and were removed in an instant to a place where the concept of time and space was absent, as were all other human measures. 'They have gone' meant both this moment and forever. 'They have gone' could mean to the bread shop or into oblivion. They had just gone. They were not here and now, and hence they didn't exist at all. There was only this photo, those eyes and smiles. The people had ceased to be and instead had become art.

All these thoughts flashed through my mind in an instant, and Wulf Markovich, following my gaze, was already telling me his son was a photographer. All these photos were by him, and he only regretted there were so few. "In the next room you will see more. There are more of them in there," he added, breaking my trance.

The audience arrive, a lot of old people, and young people who are all, like me, friends of the performers. They take their seats in the adjacent room which has so many photographs on the walls it looks like a museum, and the trio come out: piano, 'cello, violin, all girls, Sonya's classmates. They are introduced by their teacher, who describes the music they will be performing, before thanking Wulf Markovich for hosting the evening which "will give the students an opportunity to play themselves before the examinations".

"These evenings," our host says, standing by the door next to the young performers, "are a joy for me, but they take place only because of my son's initiative. It was his idea that live music should be played within these walls, and by tradition I would like the first piece to be played for those who are always present in this house."

We didn't clap. The girls took up their instruments and played something as emotional and melancholy as his words. Wulf Markovich carried on standing in the doorway, listening, with a smile on his lips. His expression became fixed, then twisted, and his head was trembling a little. I listened and something inside me opened wide, like a pair of great doors, and the wind from the darkness came in through them.

"They have gone," I repeated to myself, and understood the wisdom which shone in the eyes of our host. It became clear where the boy and girl in that photograph were looking and what was 'off camera'. I felt myself lose love as fast as I had gained it. I remembered the emptiness and solitude of the mountain Lake, the solitude of a small human being beneath the abyss of the sky. I remembered Grand's smile. I looked at Sonya, sitting at the piano with her back to me, at the tall, thin 'cellist and plump, rosy-faced violinist, still just a young girl. I took in the visitors, looking motionlessly ahead with fixed, serious expressions. I looked at the host whose eyes were red and glistening with tears. I asked myself, "Do you love everything that is around you?" and that question 'why?' retreated. We all just were the same; we all just were going to die.

I knew I was crying too. I was listening not to the music but to the howling of a dark wind rushing through open doors. I knew it was for only a moment, but I knew also that after that moment I would no longer be the same person.

Passing through a town in the evening when everyone has finished work, darting like a shadow or a migratory bird from other lands, taking all a town has to give before again hitting the road. How I loved those expeditions! We would buy food, then turn up in the city centre, eat ice creams in the main square, and watch the careworn adults and indolent young people. We were not like any of them. For everyone we were a riddle and didn't belong, and that was an agreeable, a very good feeling, seeing ourselves in that light. Afterwards we would go round the nearby taxi drivers and ask them how to get out to the highway to the next town. The drivers would quickly size us up and tell us. They were the only people who treated us almost as their own. Our attitude towards the road was the same as theirs.

We were in no hurry, though, to leave. The towns were the knots that held our road together and we wanted to get to know each one and drink in our fill of it. Grand was interested in everything: the kremlins, the churches, squares, streets, people, ancient crests and history. In some towns we went to the museum, and in the cloakroom the old lady attendants stared at our rucksacks in perplexity. We walked around until the people went back to their homes and the town started falling asleep and oh, how wonderful and tormenting it was to stroll in the deepening darkness, to see the windows lit up, the people silhouetted, and think that they all had a home in this city while we had no home here or, in reality, anywhere else and yet were at home everywhere. That knowledge made me want to get back on the road, to get away, to be once more alone with the road. In the town you don't belong, you are a stranger, but on the road you are free and everywhere at home.

Towns were points along our way, places we were aiming to reach. Yet they were not the reason we were on the move, and neither was being on the move an end in itself. The goal lay somewhere beyond all that. I knew that when we were in the towns. Suddenly everything that weighed me down fell away and the meaning I was searching for was revealed. It was only a moment, these epiphanies of mine. They arose from the contrast between the life of the city and my own, and it was impossible to hold on to them. When, during the day, we were once more standing by the roadside and once more thumbing to no effect, fatigue again overwhelmed me and again chaos crowded in.

You taught me, Grand, to see and hear; you taught me that the world is more than we can know. Behind shadows limitless possibilities of human perception rose up; behind the warm wind in the trees I heard voices from other worlds. I learned, heard and saw, but as we approached the end of our hitchhiking something told me that when it was over Grand would be no more, our game would be over, and for me the world would never be the same again. I would remember that a shadow is not just a shadow and the wind is not just a breeze, and that I myself am not just what I see but something greater that exists behind all this. The old world was gone and with it the old meaning of life.

You changed my world, Grand, my friend, but what answer do you have for me now when I ask how I should live my life in the years to come?

Completely shattered, we sit down on a mound a little way from the road and gorge ourselves on one apple after another. Sergey bought a kilogram of them in Vladimir.

"Why did we choose this place to hitch to?" he asks. "I've wanted to come here for a long time." "Did you like it?" "Yes." "But we didn't go in anywhere." "I saw everything I wanted to."

Vladimir is a slumbering town, quiet and luminous. It retains its history and is itself a bit like a museum. The streets are like picture postcards from the seventies, and even the buses are of a kind you never see nowadays anywhere else. There are ancient churches in the town centre and the Golden Gateway. A lop-sided signboard over the sagging porch of a beer bar promises 'Drams', and wooden, slanting stairs lead down to a cellar from which you seem to catch the breath of a still feudal, pre-Petrine Rus. It's a sunny day, clear and windy, and the shining birch trees shed their leaves readily into expanses which open far and wide above the River Klyazma.

You don't need to go far outside the city on the ancient, rickety bus to leave behind the much hyped white stone walls of the kremlin and descend by an inconspicuous path to the plain. After the asphalt it is a relaxing pleasure to walk on soil, open, without crops, fallow. You smell water and the river gleams ahead. You see it. You walk quickly and silently to the white cloud which has settled here on the bank. It is the Church of the Intercession on the Nerl which, like a sorrowful celestial she-elephant, looks for its reflection in the eternally placid water.

"Perhaps we should have stayed back there a bit longer. We aren't really doing anything here." "We're not doing nothing. You're getting used to it. If we'd stayed it would be evening already." "It is evening already."

He's right. Damn! The air is becoming opaque and the sun is creeping towards the horizon. "Do you like it around here, Titch?" "It is beautiful," I concede. "Everywhere is beautiful." "No, I meant is this a special place for you for some reason? Coming here seemed to matter a lot to you." I poke a stick from an apple tree into the ground beside me and look at the road. "I didn't make it to this town this summer, and I really wanted to."

We had passed through Kazan and Nizhny Novgorod. It took us two days to reach Vladimir. We just wanted to get home by then and decided not to go into the town. What a terrible bypass though! At first we thought it was just little used: the road was so empty and overgrown. Then we came to the roadworks. A plume of dust rose in the air. Trucks carrying gravel were driving on the verge, asphalt was being drilled up, there were traffic jams of trucks and cars in both directions. Everyone was in a foul mood. Who was going to give a lift to hitch-hikers? We walked through it all, choking in the dust, then stood thumbing for an hour before a kind white Lada-6 with a local driver took us away from that hell.

Three hundred kilometres to Moscow. In the past, especially in the Urals where even the road maps use a smaller scale, that sort of distance would have struck me as trivial, but now I had no confidence we would get home by nightfall. With these thoughts in my head I felt suicidal, really wretched.

"The road will end for us soon," Grand remarked cheerfully. "I know." "You're very gloomy these days. Smile! We've already turned down the gifts of the road, at least we shouldn't scare it by looking like that." I do try to smile but feel I may start bawling at any moment.

"Let's play towns," he suggests. "I say 'Voronezh', and you have to say 'Zhitomir'. You know it? Right! Let's go!" "I don't want to," I say in a flat voice and shut my eyes. "I do not want to," I repeat, pronouncing each word distinctly, focusing on them one by one and, as a result, depriving them of all meaning. "I don't want to," I say, coming back to reality. "I'm sick of everything, the road, people... What are we going to do, Grand? We're moving slower and slower and every kilometre just makes me feel so cheesed off. There's nowhere left for us to go and we're never going to be happy like this again."

"Nowhere to go? Why are you talking like that?" I can see him looking at me very seriously, as if diagnosing the symptoms of a disease. "I'm tired," I say quietly, "tired." "Turn round."

He takes me by the shoulders and turns me to face away from the road.

In front of me I see green grass, quite, quite green, shining in gentle sunlight. A meadow. The ground slopes away from the roadway and further down there just has to be a river. Willows with rounded crowns extend in a row, bowing to the earth. I look harder and, through the green branches, seem to see the sparkle of water playing in the sun. I realise I'm already walking down through the grass and, understanding, suddenly lie down, embrace the Earth, feel her touch on my skin and almost cry, so complete is the happiness sweeping over me.

At this moment I see at a glance all my road, from above and afar, in the past and now, and everything I see is a miracle. Every driver who opened a car door for us showed great kindness; every person we met showed great tolerance and joy. A feeling of gratitude pours forth like the peaceful river, warm and dappled in the sun. I remember every driver, even if not their faces because usually they were sitting with their backs to me, but they pass before me and to every one I want to say again, "Thank you".

We and they are one, and all of us together constitute the road. Do you love what is around you?

All of this is borne in on me instantly, and I turn over on my back, look at the sky and smile at the clouds.

"Samara," I hear Grand's voice. I picture him sitting two steps away from me and smiling. "The Volga," I answer.

"Ufa." "The Belaya."

"Ekaterinburg." "The Iset."

"Omsk." "The Irtysh."

"Novosibirsk." "The Ob."

"Krasnoyarsk..." "Hey, that's not fair! We didn't go to Krasnoyarsk!" I laugh, get up and sit facing him. "Grand, this is so wonderful. What an immense, immense country we have!" I want to tell him everything I've just realised, but instead jump up and yell in jubilation, "Come on, come on, we'll miss our lift!"

I almost run to the road. I stand there, thumbing. A few cars go whistling by, but I no longer take it personally. A MAZ appears. Before I have time to reflect that they don't usually take two because there aren't enough seats, he has slammed on his brakes and come to a halt on the verge about ten metres away. I run up to him as fast as my legs will carry me, throw back my head and yell into the cab, "Moscow!"

"You need a lift straight to Moscow?" "Yes!" "I'm only going to Podolsk. Can you go on from there?" "Sure!" I nod, open the door and throw in my rucksack. "Just a moment, there's my friend too," I say, already clambering in.

"Aren't you on your own then?" The driver is chubby and for an instant reminds me of my brother. "No, there's two of us," I say and stick my head out the window, looking back at the meadow, the road and peering back further, down to the willows. Grand is nowhere to be seen. "Just a moment, he's here somewhere, must have gone off for a moment, of course."

"I haven't got time to wait for you, I'm already behind schedule. If you want to wait for him, climb out now." "No, no, just a moment..." "Well then, are you coming?" "Just a moment..." The road is empty. There is no movement in the grass.

The truck lurches, snorts, moves off, and the whole scene jumps and begins receding. I watch spellbound. Will at least a twig move? What if he really has just gone off for a moment. But no. Zilch. It's as if he'd never been. "Your friend'll catch up with you. You wouldn't both have fitted in here anyway."

Shaking like the picture on a broken TV, my very own piece of road disappears behind a bend. I can no longer see it even in the rear-view mirror. "Let's get introduced then. My name is Igor," the driver says after a pause.

We're completely worn out. Evening is drawing in and I can see I need urgently to save the situation for both of us. Otherwise we'll have to go back to the town and stay overnight at the station. I'm not going to risk hitching at night with Sergey.

"Go and sit over there, Seryozha," I say. "Where?" he asks in puzzlement. "Move away and sit down." "Hide?" "No, you need to be visible. Stop thinking about the road, relax, do something. I don't suppose you brought your violin with you by any chance?" "I've got a flute. I haven't had it long. I'm still only learning." "Excellent! Sit over there and play."

Sergey goes off, sits down in the dusty grass and pulls out a wooden flute. He starts blowing, tuning it, runs up and down a scale. I feel the heavy rucksack being taken from my shoulders and can now devote myself wholly to the road.

"I've only practised one song so far. Shall I play it?" he shouts. "Play anything at all. Just don't look my way, please!" "Okay. It's about a woodchuck." Cars go rushing by as I hear the familiar tune.

"Smile, look them in the eye and say to yourself, 'Stop!'" I murmur, only moving my lips. "It's easy. I'm just about to succeed. Come on, sweethearts, do me a favour, I really don't fancy spending the night out here."

"Through many lands I've wandered and my woodchuck came with me..." The tune forms itself into words in my head and I smile. I smile and turn to look at Sergey. He is playing, concentrating, his eyes half closed and looks a completely different person: happy, inspired... "And gay I was and happy, and my woodchuck came with me..."

I turn back to the road and I feel it: right now I love everything around me.

Its tyres screaming, a strange vehicle that looks like a Gazelle, only bigger and squarer, brakes sharply. I run over as fast as I can, look inside and say, smiling, "Give us a lift, please?"

"Where are you going?" "To Moscow, but anything's a help." "Sure, hop in." The driver, a young, pleasant guy, nods. Familiar rock is playing on the CD player and that makes me happy. I open the door and say, as I'm clambering in, "Just a moment, there's my friend too."

"Aren't you on your own, then?" "No." I look out the window. Sergey is sitting in the grass, oblivious. I can't hear the flute because of the loud music in the van. "Okay, where's your friend? There's room for everyone."

It really is a spacious van. In the cab, between the driver and passenger seats, there is access to the rear area, which has enough room to swing a small cat. I look quickly round in the semi-darkness and again look out the window.

Sergey is sitting motionless, by now looking at the van. He does not budge and seems totally bewildered. He is back to looking like a square peg in a round hole. I suddenly feel a great urge just to say to the driver: "Okay, let's go". He can carry right on sitting there if he can't even work out that our lift, our one and only lift which can be right here and now, has arrived. The road has smiled upon us and we need to respond in kind. Let him stay there. He wanted to learn all about hitchhiking. How better than on his own?

"Right, shall we go?" the driver asks. I look at Sergey, and still hesitate. Then I open the door and call him. He runs up, climbs in, and immediately goes in the back. He is so out of it, he even forgets to say hello. The van shakes and moves off. I look in the rear-view mirror as, shaking like the picture on a broken TV, the scene recedes and our piece of road disappears behind a bend.

"Let's get introduced then, since we're going to be together till the small hours," the driver says, turning the music down. "My name is Sasha."

Quiet, dark, chilly Yakimanka. Your days are passing and

fading. Roma Jah is sitting at the piano and inscribing new rules for you in felt-tip pen on a piece of wallpaper.

"Roma, there's nobody here yet. Who's going to read that?" "They'll come, Titch. They'll come." I sigh. The piano gleams dimly in the light from the bare lightbulb. "Roma, did anyone ever play it?" I ask. "Other than Sonya?"

"I remember my mother playing, when I was little. My grandmother played it well, but that was before my time. It belonged to her." I want to ask more about them, his forebears who once occupied these rooms, this house, but I keep quiet. The silence of Yakimanka quells me, so I lie and listen to its corridors.

I seem to be walking through them. They are dark and ghostly, and as I walk I see that all the doors have been thrown wide open and the slanting light from street lamps is falling on the black floor. There are no people, no memories of them. The furniture is shrouded in white dustcovers, but then I hear a tune. Our piano is sighing – sad, slow sighs.

I go to where the sounds are coming from, to the open door of our room. The window is open too and the piano has been moved to the middle of the room. It is gleaming and out of its ghostly white keys Cara flies up and perches near the ceiling on the window frame and caws, swaying, "It's Me, Car-ra, the last dream of Yakimanka."

I shudder and open my eyes.

"Well, Titch, dozing off?" Roma asks. "Quite right, it's bedtime. I'll switch off the light and lie down too."

The piece of wallpaper lies on the piano covered in writing and a corner has curled up towards me. In large red letters I read the final admonition of The Rules, which have changed a little:

"ALL OF YOU, LOVE ONE ANOTHER.

MAY JOY BE YOURS, AND EVERYONE NEAR YOU BE HAPPY."

Translated by Arch Tait

Tatiana Mazepina

TRAVELING TO PARADISE

To Egypt by Land

> *"There are two ways to live: it is entirely proper and respectable to walk on dry land – to measure, to weigh, to look ahead. But one can also walk on the waters. Then one cannot measure or look ahead, one must only have faith. Lose faith for an instant – and you begin to sink."*
> Mother Maria Skobtsova, 20th-cent. Christian ascetic

I had left the house hundreds of times, walked past the pond with its little central island, down the overgrown crooked lane to the light-rail station. I had left the house hundreds of times on my way to university, to work, downtown... Today, 29 December, I am leaving it once again but this time I have a different purpose. I walk across the small square in the direction of the pond; the weight of my backpack forces me to look down but at the same time it gives me wings. I lift my head and it seems to me that I see, or maybe I really do see there, beyond the horizon, the sharp minarets of mosques rising proudly and invitingly heavenward. Pale blue, lavender, grey. I can already hear the muezzin's call to prayer.

I am going to the Middle East. Eastern Turkey, Kurdistan, Syria, Jordan, Egypt...

Step by step, day by day, country by country I will walk along and come to mosques and minarets that I can see even now. To come walking is not the same as to come by plane. And even though I won't be walking very much, my chosen means of transportation will afford me the opportunity to not just fly by, dash past or drive through, the opportunity to experience my journey to the fullest. I'm going by random cars: hitchhiking.

To live as our Lord commanded, even just for a short while, even for not very long, even for only a month, to place everything in His hands, everything, my very being, really everything I have. To give myself completely. To accept the priceless gift of His care, to accept that His will is upon everything. What is free will anyway when you place everything in His hands...

But it's time to begin my story.

Chapter I. In a Turkish family

Early in the morning, the ferry brought me from Russian Sochi to Turkish Trabzon.

At night, the ferry still on the home shore, I look towards the line that separates sky and earth, towards that other world that I want so irresistibly to reach but still do not dare believe I will. I had spent five days in Sochi waiting for the ferry that, like everyone else, was celebrating the 2009 New Year. And every day brought the same disappointment: my call to the port was invariably answered with "There will be no ferry today. Call tomorrow."

I got on the ferry in the end, but was nearly convinced that my native land would not let me go, that it would keep me tied to itself just as it held the boat, and that the dream of minarets in that other world would remain only a mirage.

But this morning I'm on deck breathing in the salty sea air with great pleasure and that other world is already in sight! The horizon parts – in front of my eyes lies the land of Turkey.

* * *

I am standing in line for a visa. With my big backpack I am a conspicuous presence among the crowd of identical suitcases on wheels. Masking her shyness with arrogance a Russian woman asks me:

"Where are you going?"

"First to Erzurum, then to Diyarbakır."

The woman's seriousness changes to surprise and she exchanges glances with her grown-up daughter.

"Are you traveling alone?!"

"Yes."

"Don't you know that it's very dangerous to go to Diyarbakır now?"

"But maybe not as dangerous as they say on TV," I say, expressing my usual skepticism towards the media.

"It is, of course, only right that you should wear a kerchief," she notes with a studied air of expertise, and she turns back to the other women, a more grateful audience for her fantastical creepy tales.

Diyarbakır is the capital of Kurdistan, but no Turk will let you call it that. The Kurds express all too clearly that they have long wanted to establish their own state, and in response the Turks ban the Kurdish language and music and build military bases with large Turkish flags fluttering red and bold above them. All across Turkey, Kurdistan is known as a land of bandits and terrorists. But I know it isn't so. Two years ago I was there with friends.

I am much more worried about the Turks. I have heard one too many unappealing reports about the behavior of Turkish drivers towards women traveling alone. Though the reports have been mainly about Turkish truck drivers working in Russia; and everyone knows it isn't right to judge a whole nation based on those who come to your country to make a living.

* * *

I've finally found my way out of enormous Trabzon and am now on my way to Erzurum. I haven't had breakfast yet, and I don't even want to. I should look at the map but I don't feel like it. I better figure out how to wave down a car, why bother? I just want to walk and walk. To look around me at the pink and blue five-story houses and breathe the special smell of Turkey which I know so well and which awakens sensations, ideas and experiences I gained during my trip two years ago.

I feel so fine that I decide: "I won't go by car today. I'll just walk." Hitchhiking is not really so easy: you have to talk with the driver in who knows what language. I did write down a few Turkish words in my notebook but that's not really enough.

A big truck with a trailer, slow and tired, stops in front of me. The door opens and a 40-year-old Turk with a black moustache asks me something in Turkish.

"Erzurum, Diyarbakır," I say the only words that come to mind.

He waves his hand inviting me to get in the car.

In the cab it turns out there are two drivers. The one who hailed me moves to the sleeping area – a place in the back of the cab where the drivers sleep. The other, in his sixties with a grey moustache and a three-day growth of beard, sits behind the wheel. The truck moves swaying slightly. I look ahead at the road and it feels like I'm still walking, except that now someone is carrying me.

The drivers calmly continue their trip as if a young foreigner with a big backpack hadn't just joined them in the cab. Where is she going? What for? They picked me up not out of greed (which I fear), not out of some other personal interest, but simply because why should someone walk when you could give her a ride. Indeed, very simple.

I open my notebook to tell them who I am and where I'm going. "Russian" in Turkish is *Rusum*, "to travel" is *gidiiorum*, "road" is *yol*. The drivers become curious and then concerned: am I maybe hungry?

You know, sometimes it seems like you've never eaten anything tastier. This is probably what happens when you're truly hungry. And maybe when the food is simple and natural, for instance, cheese, fresh bread, olives. And maybe, when you share this meal with people you met just half an hour ago and for some reason feel that there is no one dearer people to you in this world.

A hair of the Prophet Mohammed

I'm walking again, now on a road trodden through the snow. Tall, wind-swept snowdrifts, and no more smell of the sea. The sea is far from here, this is mountain country.

It's already dark when my mustachioed companions bring me into Erzurum. Plaintively furrowing their eyebrows, they pleaded that under no circumstances I hitchhike to Diyarbakır. They even took me to the bus terminal. And what did I do? I immediately went to the edge of town and I'm now standing by the roadside, hitchhiking fearlessly and without success. People rarely pick up hitchhikers in these parts and there is no one hitchhiking anyway. For some reason, no one wants to go to "the land of bandits and terrorists", especially not at night. Yet, here I am.

Eventually, a car stops in front of me. Yes, I'll make it to Diyarbakır today after all! I'm in a hurry: the goal of my trip is to get to Jordan and Egypt, and I need to get across Turkey and Syria as quickly as possible. Pleased with my success, I get in. The driver is a 25-year-old Turk. He understands quickly that he won't get anything out of me besides *ben gidijorum Diyarbakır* – "I am going to Diyabakir." He starts the car and drives back to Erzurum! Oh well… I won't make it to Diyarbakır tonight.

It happens often when you're travelling that a local offers to help, asks a lot of questions and then, having satisfied his curiosity, discovers that he can't actually do anything to help you.

This guy has already spent twenty minutes trying to understand why I'm going to Diyarbakır, why on my own and in what capacity. Soon he'll make me learn Turkish. With the help of my notebook I'm learning the language quite intensively. Five times I wrestled with the thought of just leaving him there. I'm annoyed: I want to get a ride not a chat. "And why does he care? So annoying! He isn't even going to Diyarbakır! Is he just interested in talking to a foreigner?" I'm pressed for time: today I should already be in Diyarkabir. In the end, the guy calls someone and passes me the phone. I hear the voice of a man speaking Russian:

"Hi! Where are you going?"

"First to Diyarbakır, then on to Syria."

"On your own?"

"On my own." I sigh and shrug my shoulders expecting warnings to start falling on my head.

"And what is the purpose of your trip?"

"Are you with the police or what?"

"No, no…"

The Turk takes the phone back and listens carefully to his Russian friend, while I cast an eye towards the door handle and then back to the Turk. I notice his eyes: serious and slightly sad, those of someone who is genuinely concerned. I forget about the door… What drives this guy? Why didn't he just let me be? Did he not believe me in the end when I said that I know what I'm doing? Why didn't he leave me, why didn't he just go home to his family, to warmth and dinner?

The guy tears himself away from the conversation and looks at me, a look full of compassion and care, concern and anxiety. I can't hold back – rays of happiness replace the lightning-bolts of anger on my face. In response he breaks into a luminous smile that chases away the storm-clouds of anxiety.

I take the phone back.

"The guy who picked you up," says the translator, "is inviting you to his home for dinner.

"And then he'll bring me back here? It will be even harder to find a ride later on."

"No, he's inviting you to spend the night at his house. Tomorrow he will take you back to the road, if you like."

"OK."

The Turk immediately starts the car. At last we introduce ourselves. His name is Nurula. Before he starts the car he turns to me with the words:

"Mama, baba…"

Baba in Turkish means "father".

He shows me the ring on his finger. He is married. He does this to dispel my concerns and fears, unaware that he'd already done so wordlessly.

* * *

Several women came out to meet me. At first it was impossible to figure out who was related to whom and in what way.

On the way home Nurula picked up his elder brother Ahmed from his antiques store. In his long beige coat and a checkered sweater Ahmed looked impressive and impeccably elegant.

The women help me take off my backpack. As I unlace my shoes, I look out of the corner of my eye and can't see all the way to the end of what looks like a huge apartment. The women stare at me point-blank unceremoniously.

They lead me along the corridor. The living room is at the other end. Nurula goes in with me, while the women remain on the threshold. The living room is skillfully and tastefully furnished with a table of dark wood, sofas and chairs with elegant gold-painted legs. The walls are bright yellow. Three men are sitting there. The oldest of them is about 55, the second one around 40, the third very young. They are busy with their own conversation; I sit on an unoccupied ottoman and pretend to observe my surroundings.

"Hello!" The youngest of the men addresses me politely in Russian.

I turn around, surprised.

"Hello! Was it you on the phone? Are you Russian?"

"Yes. But from Dagestan. I study here. Where are you heading?"

At last I can explain everything in detail. At the same time I interrogate Ramazan, my interlocutor.

Nurula wants to show me something and he calls me up to a glass display case. Inside there is a black square bundle wrapped in velvet, inscribed with Arabic characters.

"This is a hair of the Prophet Mohammed," translates Ramazan.

Nurula begins opening the bundle, but the oldest of the men stops him.

"They cannot show it to you," explains Ramazan. "They only open it during important holidays."

The women are preparing dinner but they can only show their hospitality from behind the threshold. Nurula takes the plates from them at the door and brings them to the table. Another brother appears, his two children run among us dodging the outstretched arms eager to pat them on the head. Eventually I am introduced to the men. It turns out that the eldest is the father and the second-eldest is the Islamic scholar Mohammed Said, a friend of the family. I blush embarrassed by my initial lack of politeness.

Before dinner I manage to meet the mother of the family. I go out from the living room into the hallway where a woman in a white shawl comes to meet me, her arms reaching out for a hug, her face radiant with welcome. She says something in Turkish, hugs me, then reluctantly but dutifully lets me join the men.

During dinner there is general conversation. At first quiet, like the trickle of a small stream, then as loud and free as an overflowing river. The scholar asks about Russia. It turns out that he has twice been to Kaliningrad. A friend of his, a Duma deputy, lives there. For young people's religious education he had invited representatives of different religions to lecture at one of the colleges. Only Muslims responded to his invitation.

I ask lots of questions about young people in Turkey. I say that on first impression they don't strike me as very religious. And that it seems that there are far fewer genuinely devout Muslims – those who pray every day – than those who are devout merely in name. The scholar and the others assure me that the devout make up no less than ninety percent of the total. I find that hard to believe.

Ramazan goes on translating conscientiously and I keep forgetting about the food. The father keeps pushing forward different dishes, coaxing me to eat more. But the conversation itself is the main dish, a delicacy that we cannot get enough of. The scholar, Ramazan and I speak the most, with the older brother and the father sometimes interjecting, and the middle brother and Nurula listening in silence.

One, two, three, four, five, six men and I am the only woman.

The wives and sisters cautiously look in from the doorway but then hide again shyly.

They would have certainly had dinner with us were it not for the male guests: the Dagestani and the scholar.

Ramazan translates for me:

"The women also want to listen, so they will be allowed to come in."

One after another they come into the living room. The men make room for them at the table but they try to maintain some distance and some even remain behind the threshold.

"This girl looks a lot like a Russian girl," I say pointing to one of the little girls wearing a bright pink scarf and raspberry-colored sweater.

Ramazan translates. She smiles and nods.

"She is Circassian," explains Ramazan. "During the

war between the Russian Tsar and the Imam Shamil many Circassians settled in Turkey."

Cautiously and timidly the women ask why I am traveling alone, don't I have a husband or father or brother to travel with me? I explain as best I can that I can do very well without them on the road but refrain from adding that it's easier and more interesting this way.

Finally, at one point in our warm, sincere conversation, when it's already hard to believe that we're seeing each other for the first time and that I'm not a member of their family, the elder brother comes in and says that they have just telephoned their spiritual teacher and that he has granted them permission to show me the hair of the Prophet.

The house storms into action. Women fuss about. Ramazan gets up as the upcoming event is explained to him. He automatically takes out a knitted white cap from his pocket and puts it on.

The women give me a skirt to change into for the ceremony. They tie my headscarf properly. One of them suddenly gives me a ring from her finger: a turtle studded with precious stones.

"No, no!" I protest. But her eyes express such trust and such openness that I put the ring on.

The valuable parcel is placed on a small table in the center of the living room. People sit staggered around so that everyone can see. Among them I notice some new faces. This is too important and rare an event to miss.

I can't help asking:

"Isn't it forbidden to worship objects or images in Islam?"

"This is not worship." Ramazan points to the head of the family. "They are keeping this hair as a sign of love and respect towards the man who was sent by the Lord." Ramazan translates my words and the father nodds confirming that it is an act of love.

They put me close to the precious parcel. Off to one side

is the older brother Ahmed and the middle brother on the other side. Seven-year-old Ahmed is also here.

Everyone sings a greeting to the prophet:

"*Salalahu aleihi va saliam*! – Peace to him and praised be Allah!"

The two brothers start unwrapping the parcel. Under the velvet cover there is a colorful shawl, then another one beneath it, and another, and so on... It seems that all in all there are more than a hundred. I'm no longer afraid I'll burst out laughing because I now have a happy smile on my face. If this happiness hadn't already been inside me I would have breathed it in from the air all around. Happiness illuminats the faces of everyone present.

The shawls finally end and caskets begin: a biggish one with a smaller one inside, then an even smaller one. And finally there it is: a glass flask with a few dark hairs from the Prophet Mohammed's beard.

The eldest brother raises it high. Then he passes it across his son's brow. He catches the little daughter of the middle brother darting in and out among the adults and passes it across her brow as well. The father says something and the elder brother turns toward me. I obediently bend my head and the flask gently touches my forehead.

I look at their faces.

However beautiful the voice of each individual performer, when many voices blend in the choir it makes my heart stand still. Songs sound even more wonderful when sung in the name of the Lord.

The hair of the prophet is just a pretext, a wave of the conductor's wand for hearts already filled with love and ready to overflow.

Nurula wouldn't have left me there on the road in a million years. Why? Just look at his mother and father standing there. Or, I should say, standing before God – and that's the real point.

Awfully sweet Kurdistan

In the morning Nurula came by, sad because there were no more bus tickets to *Diyarbakır*. He could do nothing but take me back to the same place where he'd picked me up yesterday.

Nurula said goodbye quickly and hurried back to his car as if afraid to see the Kurdish terrorists attack and kill me on the spot.

Towards midday, strangely enough still alive, I had made it halfway to Diyarbakır.

Once the passing drivers saw that none of their warnings about terrorists were working, they went on with more reasons for fear:

"There is no road to Diyarbakır."

"The road to Diyarbakır is closed."

"The road to Diyarbakır is snowed in."

Here I am standing on the outskirts of a smallish town, rather worried. I almost believe that there really won't be a way to go further. The road does indeed go through a mountain pass. The mountains surrounding me, covered in white duvets, assert themselves eloquently.

There are almost no cars.

All of a sudden I see a silvery car, a foreign make. I extend my arm, and it cautiously, as if fearfully, stops.

The driver is a young man, about 25, Turkish, in a business suit.

"Do you speak English?" I ask.

"Yes," he answers with a surprised-fearful, childishly sweet expression.

"I'm going to Diyarbakır, could you take me there?"

He gets out of the car, opens the trunk and shamelessly checks me out as I'm putting in my backpack.

Finally we set off. He turns to me, eyes full of wonder, eyebrows furrowed:

"Tell me," he says, pronouncing the unfamiliar English words slowly, "how did you end up here, all on your own?"

"I'm traveling. I'm from Russia. I'm on my way to Diyarbakır. I'm hitchhiking."

"But that's very dangerous. You may run into very bad people."

"But I ran into you."

"You're lucky."

Oh, I know! How many times Russian drivers told me:

"Hitchhiker? No one will take you!"

"But you did."

"You just got lucky this time."

They believe they are the only ones capable of doing a good deed.

Soon we start talking. His name is Ozgiur and he is driving to Diyarbakır, where he lives and works. It turns out that he is only half Turkish; his other half is Kurdish. It is perfectly appropriate that he should be the one taking me from Turkey to Kurdistan.

The whole way we talk about Ozgiur's job which puts him at odds with his religion since he sometimes has to drink alcohol at company events. He tells me about his family, about his parents, who are devout Muslims but who have never forced their children to be devout as well. Ozgiur wants to travel because he hasn't been anywhere outside of Turkey. He has no time because of work, which "isn't very interesting but in three years he will be a senior manager and after five more…"

We only stop once, for lunch. Ozgiur orders several dishes for me and only one for himself, which he won't even eat because he isn't hungry.

Diyarbakır welcomes us with the light of streetlamps as evening sets in. Ozgiur gives me a tour of the city. He invites me for coffee and traditional local sweets. He spends a lot of energy trying to convince me not to go any further, to spend the night here, in a hotel, where he would even get me a room. I don't want him to spend more money on me. I'd stay if Ozgiur invited me to his house but he doesn't, which puzzles me until I realize that he is simply afraid I would misunderstand him. I had the same problem at Nurula's parents' house in Erzurum. Why hadn't the men in the living room paid any attention to me, a stranger and a guest? Because according to the rules of Islam, men are not even supposed to speak with women if they are not bound by family ties. Why did Ramazan look at my hands when talking with me? Because he wasn't supposed to look at my face or make eye contact.

Ozgiur is also afraid of offending me. In appreciation of the tradition and the religion responsible for this attitude towards women I don't mind sleeping in the open air. There was one thing I could not refuse – Ozgiur was unbending – he insists on buying me a bus ticket to Mardin, the next city in Kurdistan and very close to Syria.

Wishes fulfilled

Now I am in the very center of Kurdistan; it surrounds me from all sides, even touching my clothes. I am traveling in a bus crowded with Kurdish men and women. They have a different language, different facial features: bold noses and darker skin than the Turks. It's time to remember all the warnings that haunted me all the way here.

I'm lost in my thoughts: what a long road I have covered today, from Erzurum to Mardin where we're just about to arrive. But thanks to the eloquent darkness in the window, the clarity of my thoughts about the day is replaced by vaguer thoughts about the night. "Of course, I'm grateful to Ozgiur for the bus ticket, but… if I'd hitchhiked and someone picked me up it would mean he's a good person. And a good person would have invited me home. When you are in someone's car you are already his guest. On this bus I'm nobody's guest… Where will I sleep tonight?"

A Kurdish man of about thirty-five turns to me shyly:

"Where are you going?" He suddenly asks in English, rather haltingly.

"To Mardin, then to Syria."

"And where are you from?"

"From Russia."

"Oh! From Russia!"

Soon we're sitting on the floor, a large tin tray in front of us covered with plates of food: yogurt, fried eggs, rice with meat, homemade bread. For the first time on this trip I'm eating on the floor.

It turns out that the Kurd from the bus is a schoolteacher. He, of course, wants to know where I'm planning to spend the night. When he learns that I plan to sleep in a tent he thinks for about half a minute and says:

"My mother and I are going from Ankara to see my brother in Mardin. If you don't mind, I would like to invite you to his house."

In the darkness of the poorly illuminated streets we step out of the bus, my expectations for the evening already infused with the warmth of my travel companions' hospitality.

The three of us walk home together and have a lively conversation. I remember all the warnings about Kurdistan and smils to myself quietly.

Chapter 2. Arabic Christianity

Neon crosses

Will I really have to sleep in a tent in Syria? Have I not been surprising my friends with stories about how Syria is the most hospitable country in the world, that you need only raise your hand on the road and the first car will stop? That you need only make eye contact and people will immediately invite you for tea or lunch, or offer you a place to spend the night.

The day is ending and night is taking over covering the sky with a black blanket moth-eaten by shining stars. Night finds me on the highway from Aleppo to Damascus. The highways are alive with cars racing at high speed, hurrying to finish the day in the warmth of their own homes. And my outline barely visible in the dim light of streetlamps is too weak to tear them away from their thoughts of home.

At some point I turn around to face the traffic and notice the inviting red rear-lights of a little truck which has stopped to pick me up. Syria is Syria – you only need to raise your hand...

The driver doesn't speak a word of English and this is my first day in an Arabic-speaking country. With what words could I thank him? Involuntarily, I smile broadly. How can he express hospitality and good wishes? A small illuminated shop by the side of the road is selling hot chocolate. The driver slows down.

I'm holding a big cup of chocolate. I carefully take a sip and immediately burn my tongue. Waiting for the chocolate to cool, I concentrate on holding the cup so it doesn't spill on the bumpy road.

I want to enjoy this tasty treat down to the last sip but the very last drops end up on my light blue jacket.

The driver and I exchange understanding looks and laugh merrily.

I take out my notebook and illuminate the Arabic words with the help of a flashlight. Somehow or other I have explained something to the driver. And it seems I have understood some things too: we are going in the direction of Hama, a city on the road to Damascus and Jordan. The driver's name is Salim, and it even looks like I'll have a place to sleep tonight.

* * *

The road tricked me again: it lulled me to sleep in Salim's car. When I open my eyes I see huge crimson crosses glowing on the walls of village houses. I turn to Salim:

"Christian?!"

He nods and smiles.

Of course, I knew that there were Christians in Syria and I'd been curious to meet them. With wide-open eyes I look at the crosses and the reindeer with branching antlers harnessed to sleds.

My plan was to travel through Syria quickly and I didn't intend to look for Christians. With Christmas only two weeks past, how can I be surprised at such an unexpected gift?

Salim took me to the house of his older brother. The whole family came out to greet me. You can recognize Christians by two signs: women with uncovered heads, their luxurious dark hair is an unexpected treat for the eyes; and a second sign: they offer wine with dinner which is even more unusual in an Arab country. Since there was still some time left before dinner I asked to wash my hands. The female half of the family fussed over me. One woman drew me a bath, another one took my formerly light blue jacket (now darkened with brown stains). They gave me shampoo, soap, a towel. The women spoke ceaselessly in Arabic, smiling, gently touching my arms above the elbow.

The door to the bath closed. I hadn't even hoped I would be able to wash in privacy.

Once again, a tin tray spread with dishes is set in front of me. I am supposed to eat all of it but I don't have a chance to swallow one bite as I first have to satisfy the hunger of those around me, patiently answering questions from all sides.

The younger daughter, eighteen years old, speaks English. Her name is Hanouf. I can't come up with the answer to one question before she's back with another:

"When are you going further?"

"Tomorrow."

"No," she says sternly. "Tomorrow you'll be with us."

"Really?" I thought for a second. "Well, OK then."

* * *

In the morning, I hadn't even opened my eyes before Hanouf's parents came into the room. How long had they stood behind the door, waiting for me to wake up and give them the green light to enter?

The father sits on the divan, a smoking cigarette in his hand. He has black hair with a streak of grey and a black moustache which looks very good on him. He forgets about his cigarette, smiling with his moustache and looking at me from time to time while asking a half-sleepy Hanouf to translate. It occurs to me that he may have decided not to go to work today – what is going on in his home is too exciting: a real live foreigner! Today is a holiday for him.

The mother shows her welcome in a more practical way. Again a tray with food appears and large round flatbreads are being warmed on the stove in the center of the room. Five minutes later they offer me warm bread. They push towards me small plates with fried eggs, yogurt, hummus: a tasty dish made of mashed chickpeas. They carefully watch so that I keep eating. Two pairs of warm loving eyes stare at me as I eat.

Though the parents want us to stay, Hanouf and I leave to explore the neighborhood.

Nose to nose with a priest

Despite the fact that all continents appeared on earth many eras ago, you have to rediscover the world again and again. Or rather, how wonderful that you can rediscover it again and again! To see with your own eyes, to explore with your own hands, to disprove all the things people so love to say against one another.

You've probably heard about the relationship between Arab Muslims and Christians. But have you heard about Christian Arabs?

You couldn't call this village anything but Christian. Orthodox and Catholics live here side-by-side much the same way. "My" family – Salim's – is Catholic.

Hanouf and I walk in the direction of the church – only the Orthodox church is open during the day. Without Hanouf I wouldn't have been able to guess that it's a church. No domes, though there is a small square-shaped bell tower. The whole building looks like a tall house.

We go in, cross ourselves, each in our own way: Hanouf from left to right, I from right to left.

It was unusual inside too – benches as in Catholic churches, no gilding and not many icons. But I recognize familiar saints in the images.

"Would you like to go see the priest?" Hanouf asks once we're back outside, pointing to the house next to the church.

"No-o-o," I answer shyly.

Instead of going to see the priest, we go and visit two Belorussian girls. Their mother married an Arab and moved with her children here when the girls were still young. Now they are both married and have three children between them – these blond-haired kids are running around. The husband of one of the sisters and his mother are sitting inside. Right away they offer us tea and crackers.

Taking advantage of the situation and my native language, I bombard the Belorussian girls with questions, which they answer gladly until we hear the call to prayer.

"The priest is here to bless the house," says one of the girls. "It's a tradition every Christmas."

Before I could ask how one should behave on such

occasions the priest entered the room preceded by his own singing. Tall, imposing, he was wearing a black robe under which you could see the contour of a round belly; he had a dark brown beard and curly ringlets and behind his glasses he resembled a huge soap bubble. And his pure joyous singing resembled the play of sunbeams on a soap bubble. And just as a soap bubble bursting flies apart in all directions, the priest liberally threw holy water at all of us. At some point, the priest turned towards me and...the holy water sprinkler in his hands and the prayer on his lips both froze. Puzzled, he turned to our hosts and asked something in Arabic. Eventually, with a bright happy smile illuminating his face, he sank into an armchair. Break-time.

They offer him tea but he doesn't notice watching those present and asking about this and that. We start a conversation with the help of one of the sisters. I talk about the Church in Russia, ask him if he's been to our countryIn the end, duty calls. The priest takes up the holy water sprinkler and his prayer fills the house even more fully than before. And I, hearing Arabic singing from the mouth of an Orthodox priest, try to convince myself that this is in fact quite real.

Cross and Kaaba

"OK, we need to turn back," Hanouf said all of a sudden, although the village street looked interesting further on.

"Why?"

"This is where our village ends."

"And what's down there?"

"Muslims."

"Let's go there."

"No!" Hanouf protests fearfully.

"Why?"

"I've never been there alone." She means, without a man.

"And what are you afraid of?"

"Wait," she agrees and makes a few steps towards a crowd of Arabs standing by a shop on the Christian side. A tall, broad-shouldered young man approaches us.

"This is my cousin," Hanouf introduces him. "He'll go with us."

The guy smiles bashfully.

There is no border between the two villages. Houses with *kaabas* begin where houses with crosses end. *Kaaba* is a cube-shaped temple in Mecca, the main place of pilgrimage for Muslims.

Today is Friday – the holy day for true believers. Almost all the shops lining the road are closed. From the mosque, through a loudspeaker, comes the call of the Imam.

Here I attract even more attention than in the Christian village. I look back at Hanouf and suddenly I also experience fear building a wall between me and these people. People whom days ago I completely trusted with my own life. And whom I'll trust again tomorrow.

"Don't you have friends among Muslims?" I ask Hanouf.

"No."

"Are there no Muslims in your school?"

"We have different schools: we have our own school and they have their own."

"Does it ever happen that a Christian girl marries a Muslim man?"

"No! Never!"

Unlike Hanouf, her cousin is completely calm. He is shaking hands with someone.

"Does he have acquaintances here? Muslims?" I ask.

"He was shaking hands with Christians."

At a mechanic's shop like the one in the Christian village, a handful of men – Muslims and Christians – are talking. They are likely discussing important business: how to fix a carburetor, or whether it makes sense to overhaul the engine. They seem to be oblivious of any silly fears, rumors, or feuds that have been started by someone for some unknown reason.

The Syrian Church

In the evening, Hanouf's father takes us to another nearby village, which is bigger and has four churches.

We drive up to the huge Orthodox church, which was built quite recently. Its white walls glow in the violate twilight.

The large carved wooden door turns out to be locked.

"It's very beautiful inside!" Hanouf makes me even more sorry that we cannot go inside.

Instead, we go to the old Orthodox church and find a wedding service. The priests recite the rites and prayers in Arabic. I recognize the word for God, which in this language is still "Allah".

I look at icons with Church Slavonic inscriptions in the little church shop. A man comes in and we begin talking in English. He apologizes for his Canadian accent:

"I worked there for a long time."

"What did you do?" I ask, already guessing the answer.

"I'm a priest."

I smile broadly:

"And could I ask you for a blessing?"

"Yes, but I don't like it when people kiss my hand."

"I won't do that."

He blesses me, and meanwhile another man comes in. There is no need to ask him about his profession: his robe speaks for itself. Hanouf says something to him, and it turns out that he is the senior priest of the church that was closed.

"Let's go!" Hanouf calls.

"Where?"

"The priest has agreed to show us the new church."

I'm holding the cup, plate, and spoon for Communion. I've never held anything like this before.

"These inscriptions are in Old Church Slavonic," I say to the priest. Like the "Canadian," he too speaks excellent English.

"Read it to me," he says and so I do.

The inside walls of the church are as white as the outside. But here within they shine even more brightly, flooded by the electric light.

"Are there many worshippers here?" I ask, looking at the vast space filled with benches.

"On Sundays the church is full."

There aren't many icons on the walls, and the priest tells us that most of them were brought from Russia.

We walk out of the church.

"And where did you study to become a priest?" I ask.

"In Lebanon."

"And where is your patriarch?"

"Constantinople."

I don't know how long we would have gone on talking if Hanouf's father hadn't been waiting for us in the car.

In the end I can't hold back and ask:

"Listen, are you really an Arab?"

"Yes," he smiles, understanding the reason for my question.

No matter how difficult it was for me to comprehend this, I carried undeniable proof: the Gospel in Arabic, a gift from the priest.

The village of brothers and sisters

Hanouf has two older sisters and a younger brother. Salim – the guy who brought me here – already has three children, even though his wife is not yet thirty years old. Hanouf's father has about ten brothers and sisters. A big family needs a big house, which is why homes in this village can be adjusted to increase in size. No magic is involved. On the roof of each of the houses there are concrete pillars. When a son brings a wife, and they need a place to live, they build another floor using those pillars. There's no need to split up, families can stay together: one big family in one big house.

We visited an uncountable number of houses as we walked through Hanouf's village: Hanouf's aunt, her grandfather, cousin, her best friend from school... In each house they wanted to feed me, to offer me at least some tea, some tangerines, some cookies. They were so earnestly hospitable, so genuinely happy to meet me that I found myself again and again agreeing to just one more visit. It turns out we didn't skip a single home in the whole village.

Hanouf has so many relatives that there's not a single part of the village where she can't turn her head to say: "Oh, there's my cousin (walking, standing, running)."

Even when one steps out of the house he is still within his family as family members surround him on all sides. All around you are your own people.

* * *

It was already dark and we were on the way home when we stopped at the house of yet another friend of Hanouf's. This friend studies at the university, and she has an older sister already graduated. They also have an older brother. He came out to meet me wearing a white shirt, black pants and a serious expression. He works as a lawyer.

"This is my girl. We're engaged..."

"How old is she?"

"Twenty-two."

"And you?"

"I'm thirty."

I look at this handsome grown-up man, silver hair already streaking his dark head, and he's only just engaged! Knowing local tradition I know that his fiancée has not yet become his wife in any sense.

Hanouf's father got married at about the same age.

Hanouf and I and one of her uncles are strolling on the already-sleepy village road.

"I would also like to go with you," he smiles.

"Come along," I answer and smile back.

"First," he said, "I need to bring up my daughters."

"And how many daughters do you have?"

"Three. The oldest is eight and the youngest is not yet one."

I look at him; he doesn't look younger than forty.

"And how old were you when you got married?"

"Thirty."

"And why so late?" I finally ask my long suppressed question.

He looks at me with surprise.

"What? I first had to earn money, build a house. I first had to prepare everything for my future family. And only then could I finally get married."

My eyebrows go up as if this is the first time I hear about this approach to family life.

Chapter 3. Venerable Jordan

In Turkey, at the house of the schoolteacher in Mardin, I had jotted down lots of Turkish words from a book he gave me, even though I would part with Turkey the next day. Now I don't want to deprive myself of the pleasure of dreaming how I might one day live in Turkey. In Syria I decided that I'd definitely return and live here, even for a short while. Here people surround you with such sincere care and love that you want to come back.

"They live in poverty. For them a foreigner is a novelty. Their concern is no more than curiosity." Some people would probably be satisfied with this simple and convenient explanation.

The bright and spacious building of the Jordanian customs office shines with cleanliness. I present my passport. The customs officer cannot keep from smiling, even if it reveals the gaps in his teeth.

"Is this your first time in Jordan?" He asks almost laughing, exultant.

"Yes."

"Excellent! Welcome! Would you like some tea?"

Two years ago I was shocked by an offer of tea on the Syrian border. Back then, they didn't even ask, they simply brought us tea. While they stamped your passport why not have a glass of tea in the boss's office? Tea is traditionally a hot sweet drink which is drunk from a glass. The Syrian office had a shabby couch and dusty floor. The Jordanian customs office is different, but the offer of tea is the same.

Accelerating goodness

Huge shiny Jeeps drive up to the customs building. Slowly, some Jordanians get out of the cars. Only later do I learn that they are not Arabs but Bedouins, a different nationality: darker skin and stronger facial features.

Their white robes reach down to their feet, and they wear red-checkered headscarves. Their unhurried movements convey an awareness of self-worth. Jordan is a rich country. Although I've heard countless positive comments about Jordan I still wonder: "And what if people here are not as hospitable? And what if they won't pick me up when I hitchhike?"

Passport in hand, I walk in the direction of the last customs booth. Once I show them my entrance visa, I'm in Jordan, and I'm here for the first time.

The customs official notices me from afar. He follows

me attentively and even calls for reinforcements from another booth.

I notice their impeccably-fitting military uniforms, their berets playfully pushed to the side. Most of them wear neatly trimmed moustaches.

"*As-salem, va rahmat Llahi, va va barakyat*! Peace be with you, mercy and blessings of the Lord!" I greet them loudly.

"*Va-aleikum assaliam*," they answer, brows furrowed, forgetting to smile politely.

I understand their surprise since they only ever see Mr. and Ms. White in big tourist buses accompanied by guides and interpreters. And now they see someone going on foot! And a girl! Alone!

I show my passport and begin to move on.

"Where are you going?" One of the border policemen stops me.

"To Amman."

"And where is your bus?"

"*Mafi. Ana mashi*. There is no bus. I am here on foot," I answer in Arabic.

"*Mashi*? One hundred kilometers! On foot? One hundred kilometers!

"*Tamam*. Fine."

To me this is *tamam*, while they just blink helplessly. I take pity on them and explain:

"*Shvaye-shvaye mashi, seiara.* A little bit on foot, and then by car."

The poor customs officers experience a wave of relief. They cheer up:

"So wait then, we'll get you a cab."

"But I don't need a cab. I need a free ride."

"OK, OK." The customs officials are ready to agree to anything just to prevent me from going on foot. "How's that possible anyway, to go on foot… all the way to Amman?"

I lean on the fence so that the gazes of the border policemen, fixed on me from all sides, don't knock me over. As soon as I raise my eyes they look away, like tiny mouse-thieves scattering across a room when someone suddenly turns on the light.

In the end, they call me up to a tall black Jeep. I say a warm goodbye to the customs officials.

Inside the Jeep, there are three Arabs. One of them leaves us rather quickly. The driver has a big bushy beard, a great rarity in both Jordan as well as in Syria. An Arab businessman is sitting in the front seat. He is wearing a white shirt, a leather jacket, and sunglasses. His phone rings and he answers in fluent English.

"I'm sorry they stuck me in your car," I address him cautiously.

"No problem, it's fine," he answers and turns back to the windshield.

Some time later he casually asks me where I am going and why, but without any keen interest. Then he falls back into indifferent silence.

We arrive in Amman. The twilight enveloping the city brought on similarly murky thoughts: "Arriving in an unknown city at night…where even by day… you can't find a hostel… And in a car the customs officials put you into, you didn't even stop it yourself…"

"Where should we drop you off?" asks the businessman as if reading my thoughts. "Where will you sleep?"

"In a tent. I just need to find a park. You don't happen to know of one?"

"I do," says the Arab as if it were an everyday occurrence for some random foreigner to ask about a park where she could spend the night. "There's one not far from here, I'll show you."

And so, despite my assurances that I only need walking directions, the Arab releases his driver and accompanies me, taking all his briefcases and laptops with him.

"I could invite you to my house…" he volunteered in a low hesitant voice.

"No, thank you," I refuse, seeing clearly that his offer was merely polite.

We find the entrance gates locked.

"It's OK. I'll find another entrance, thanks," and I rush to say good-bye to the businessman who has so kindly wasted his time with me.

"If you wish, you may spend the night at my house," he offers again, unexpectedly.

I fall silent, trying to guess the reason of his proposition.

"You can have some dinner, take a shower," he adds. "If you so wish…"

"Of course, I'd be delighted, but won't I be a bother?"

"Not at all."

"Are you sure?"

"Absolutely."

"All right then!" I answer, genuine gladness on my face, impossible to conceal.

"Then we need a cab."

We leave our things at his house and drive to dinner in Joseph's car. Joseph, that's the Arab's name. We eat fried potatoes with chicken and vegetables, and we drink Pepsi. He doesn't let me pay for it.

It turns out that Joseph is from Lebanon and works in Amman, where the company rents an apartment for him and his family.

Without a trace of indifference this time, in fact, quite the opposite, Joseph asks me with sincere curiosity about Russia and the countries where I've been.

That evening I managed to expand the boundaries of my journey to cover yet another country as Joseph told me of his beloved Lebanon with much enthusiasm!

Then he allotted me a separate room and even made

up the bed, despite my assurances that I could do it myself. He kept coming up with more things to do for me as if he derived some kind of pleasure from it. Like a child who has just mastered a new skill and can't get enough of it. It was so fun for him!

Bottles filled with sand

I'm looking at the Israeli shore glowing with bright yellow lights; the lights of Egypt are shining a bit further, to the right. I am in Jordan. Between us lies the Red Sea, but the heavy warm blanket of the night has covered the red and turned it to black. The sea is softly tossing in its sleep, the waves splash unhurriedly onto the shore, mumbling and snuffling drowsily.

* * *

This morning I arrived in Aqaba, a city on the border of three states. I got picked up by a mini-bus on the outskirts of Amman where Joseph had left me. All the other passengers paid for the ride, but the driver kept reassuring me that I was riding for free.

I am walking in the very center of a wide boulevard. Jordanians are sitting on benches under the trees, together with their friends and families. They don't pay any particular attention to me. They see too many tourists – this is a well known international tourist resort. Largely because of this I've decided not to stay here for very long. Too many shops, restaurants, and streets full of green cabs. It's hard to make friends in such a city.

All I need is to find the office where I can get my free visa, since I've arrived in Aqaba – a "free economic zone," as the Jordanians themselves call it. I'll leave the city as soon as I get my visa.

A souvenir stall on the corner is selling bottles filled with multicolored sand. Behind the counter stands a young shopkeeper in dark glasses. He is expertly pouring purple mountains, brown camels and orange clouds into a bottle.

My attention is immediately arrested by these mountains, camels, and clouds, and I can't tear myself away.

"Hello!" The shopkeeper greets me loudly and cheerfully, in English, fully aware that he's got me hooked. I can see myself reflected in his dark glasses: a potential customer.

"Where are you from?"

"Russia."

"Oh! Russia, Moscow! You can put down your backpack, have a seat and you can watch."

"No, no, I'll be going, just for a second." Naively making my apologies, I am still unable to tear my eyes away from the exquisite sand filling up the bottles.

"Are you alone?" Knowing he's got me hooked, he reels me in easily with his casual but interested tone.

"Yes."

"Come on, put down your backpack."

I take off my backpack and sit by the little table, gazing wide-eyed at the Jordanian's work. He is pleased by my attention, and continues to envelop me in a web of standard questions: where from, where to, how.

A minute, two, three, and now he, having taken off his glasses, is the one staring at me. I simply told him where I'm from, where I'm headed and, most importantly, how I've been traveling.

"I can't believe it... Would you like some tea? My treat," he adds. "My name is Ibrahim. What is your name?"

He calls an assistant and asks him to bring us some tea, then hurriedly turns his gaze back to me, and I see a completely different expression than before. He now speaks quietly and not as insistently as before, so I answer his questions more willingly.

"Why do you wear a headscarf?"

"Well, your women wear headscarves, so, out of respect for tradition…"

Judging by his reaction, Ibrahim has never yet encountered a foreign woman wearing a headscarf, nor such an explanation.

As invariably happens in Muslim countries, we end up talking about religion. Ibrahim believes in the absolute truth of Islam but when I ask if he prays the *namaz* he answers in an uncertain and unsteady voice:

"No."

He can't explain why. As we continue our conversation wholly engaged, a young Arab around twenty-seven comes up to Ibrahim's table with a slow and arrogant gait, obviously going for the European look: blue jeans, black sweatshirt, blue baseball cap, sunglasses. A thick gold chain seems to gleam only in order to draw attention to his dark tanned neck. He gives me a nonchalant sideways glance and says hello to Ibrahim who enthusiastically starts telling this guy about me and our conversation.

The guy's name is Khalil. Hearing that we've been talking about Islam, he sits down to join us. He has an excellent command of English and with unexpected openness begins talking about what religion means to him, about his studies of the Qu'uran and his thoughts about what is written – all this without a tinge of arrogance or condescension. He speaks without a break, looking at me and holding eye contact, seemingly afraid that if he loses eye contact I will disappear like a mirage in the desert before he gets a chance to have his say.

Like Ibrahim, Khalil is convinced as to the absolute truth of Islam, and in speaking about it he resembles a man who has just discovered a treasure and wants the world to share in the joy of his discovery.

"And what about you? Do you observe all the teachings of the Koran? Do you pray?" I ask, full of hope. On my second day in Jordan I'm already asking these questions with hope, rather than with the certainty of a positive answer as I had in Syria.

Echoing Ibrahim, Khalil answers:

"No."

"Why?"

He drops his head, then suddenly raises his eyes as if I were the one expected to answer and not he.

"I don't know," he says. "I feel that the less I pray, the more I become alienated from God, but there is nothing I can do."

Then he glanced back at me:

"I don't understand why I'm telling you all this. It feels like we've known each other for a long time. I have never said this to anyone before."

I feel my cheeks burning and look at Ibrahim as if he could offer me a way out, and suddenly I remember:

"I need to go to the visa office."

"I have a car," says Khalil.

"Ibrahim says it's not far from here."

"I have a car all the same."

Shops, restaurants, hotels flicker past in the car window. At the office they tell me to come back tomorrow. I'll spend the night in this city after all: Khalil's parents have left for England while his brothers and sister are at home.

"How many brothers and sisters do you have?"

"There are ten of us all together."

"Ten! And you all have the same mother?"

"Yes. My father married when he was thirty, and my mother gave birth to the last child when he turned forty."

The brother

The large house was a mess of the sort only twenty and thirty-year-old sons can create when their parents are on vacation. One sister cannot cope with this chaos on her own, especially when she lives elsewhere and visits only in order to cook for her brothers. This is what she is doing when we arrive at Khalil's – a girl around twenty, with beautiful facial features. She welcoms me very warmly and despite my insistent offers does not allow me to help.

We sit down to dinner. Khalil introduces me to his younger brother Sufiyan. Another one of Khalil's brothers comes into the room. The first thing I notice about him are his huge arms with bulging muscles. Well, well! I wonder why he needs such muscles.

"This is Iyid, my brother," Khalil introduces us.

Iyid carefully studies me and smiles with sad-looking eyes, or maybe I'm just imagining it.

"What's your name?"

"Tatiana."

"Wha-a-t?" He frowns uncertainly.

"Tatiana."

Later he tells me he misheard my name as *santyana* which in Arabic means the part of a woman's underwear worn on top, and he was confused.

"Where are you from, Tatiana, Germany?"

"No, from Russia."

"A-a-ah!" He exclaims significantly.

I would find out about the meaning of this reaction only later, in Khalil's office. He works as a tourist guide. When his boss heard I was from Russia he chuckled slyly:

"From Russia with love?"

I already have some idea what this implies, but I still ask:

"What do you mean?"

My slightly indignant tone change the atmosphere. The boss doesn't answer. Although, of course, it isn't really his fault that the majority of women working in the Aqaba nightclubs (not as waitresses) are from Russia.

Iyid's scornful tone is most likely for the same reason, but it doesn't last long. Khalil goes to fix his car and Iyid begins showing me photos on his laptop.

"This is my older brother, he lives in England. Our parents have gone to visit him. This is my second brother, he lives in France. And this is my crane. I work on a crane in the port."

"You need such big arms to work on the crane?"

"No," he smiles. "I work out. And this is me in Egypt. I really love Egypt."

"Do you go there on vacation?"

"Yes. It's warm there."

"Like it's cold here?"

"Now it's cold here, it's winter."

One of the most entertaining things to do while travelling is to scare the locals with stories about Russia. To tell Austrians who can cross their country in five hours, for instance, that in order to get from Moscow to Vladivostok it takes six days by train. Or to tell a Lebanese person, who lives in a country of four million people, that in Moscow alone we have ten million.

Later, Iyid and I go for a walk on the beach, and as we stand on the dock, I look into the blue water of the Red Sea and wonder whether to go swimming or not. I tell him that some Russians swim in winter.

"We go down to the river, break the ice and jump into the water."

If I could have photographed Iyid's face at that moment it would have been the most unique shot of the entire trip.

Khalil comes back late that evening. We hang out with Iyid. He has an excellent sense of humor and we laugh the whole time. Still, it seems to me that for some reason his eyes are sad.

* * *

"Can you whistle?" Iyid asks me as we were walking out of the house early the next morning.

"Yes, but not loudly."

"I can't whistle at all, so I always ask my friends to hail cabs."

Iyid wants to show me the office. A green cab whisks us to the center of the city.

"Can I ask you something personal?" I ask him on the way to the office.

"Yes, sure..."

"You have very sad eyes. Why?"

He doesn't answer immediately.

"I have many sad thoughts. And I think them all the time."

"What kind of thoughts?"

"If I tell you about them I won't think them anymore."

"So wouldn't that be better?"

Most likely not, because Iyid doesn't answer.

Such a familiar situation: when melancholy lives inside you for a long time, in the end it becomes a source of pleasure and you won't give it up for anything.

Once I have the stamp in my passport we go for a walk.

"Let's go to the beach," Iyid suggests. "I'll show you my sand bottles."

"You can make them too?!"

The table is covered with these wonderful handcrafted objects, but there's no one to look after them.

"Nobody looks after them?" I ask in disbelief.

"No. But no one will take them. I leave them like this even overnight."

"And what if someone wants to buy something?"

"They'll give the money to them," Iyid says and points to some venders nearby. They are his friends, and offer us some of the sunflower seeds they are selling.

"I'll make one for you, OK?"

"Why don't you sell your little bottles like Ibrahim?"

"You make too little money this way. And I have to pay for the gym. I work out for a couple of hours almost every day.

After Iyid makes me a present for me we take a walk along the embankment. To the right the noise of the sea seems to gently push us towards something.

"So why do you spend so much time at the gym?" I ask. "Is it really so important?"

However hard we try to talk about something general and simple the conversation keeps coming up against locks impossible to open, and I see that there is no way to free him of his sad thoughts, no way for him to let them go.

Iyid stops and leans against the low stone wall. I sit next to him but he turns away and crosses his arms on his chest as if holding on to something inside. In a little while he says:

"Because I want to be strong. I think that there is strength in this. I am really weak. Part of me wants to cry, but I can't cry because I'm a man."

I see his face and I hear his pain. Talking about this brings tears to his eyes.

"Several years ago I had a girlfriend. I loved her very much, I did everything for her. But she turned out to be… She was just after money. We went to nightclubs, I began drinking. I stopped praying. In the end I began taking drugs because of her. The last thing she made me do was get this tattoo… I never want to trust anyone ever again… And I think that I'm terribly weak. That is why I go to the gym."

I touch his shoulder. Iyid straightens up and I jump off the wall. We slowly walk on. I take his big warm hand and it feels like I'm holding a child's hand. The warm clear rays alight in his eyes. The keys and the lock click goodbye to us from the low stone wall left behind. All is well, there's no need for them any more.

The funny Dead Sea

Today the sun rose for the tenth time to illuminate my road. But am I on the road? I spend every night at someone's home and this usually becomes much more than just a roof over my head. It becomes a home in itself, hard to leave every time. I've never been hungry on this trip and I've not spent any money on food yet.

I already have more than ten new numbers in my phone beginning with un-Russian 0s and 2s. Every day I receive text messages from my new friends. They worry about how I'm doing and regret that I only stayed with them for a short while. They are all people whom I've met during this journey. I even have a Jordanian brother now! He writes more often than the others and in almost every message says how grateful he is to have met me and that he will never forget me.

So am I on the road? Or am I at home, a home with dimensions larger than I could ever imagine?

I'm striding along a paved road; to my right is a village. Beyond it lie the Jordanian mountains: low, with peaks painted in pink, orange and red. The sun paints them every day with its hot touch at sunset. They are its trusted harbingers and even in daytime they carry a promise of the unusual color feast of the sunset.

I look at these mountains, at the sky, at the desert to the left of the road. All this is mine, native to me. So many times I have heard people say to me with complete sincerity: "Make yourself at home!"

Like on the first day of my trip, when on the road from Trabzon in Turkey I was picked up and carried, so I'm still carried by people.

* * *

The driver takes me to within fifteen kilometers of the Dead Sea before he has to turn. But that's for the better: I need to find out where exactly on the shore the hot springs are. After swimming I'll need to wash off the salt in their warm fresh water so that I don't dry up to a crisp from all the salt.

I'm walking along the side of the road looking back at the one-story concrete houses stretching out close to the road and thinking, "How can I meet someone in this village who speaks English well enough to explain how to get to these hot springs?" On a road to the side of the main one a car slows down and a young Jordanian man in his early thirties with skin the color of chocolate gets out and addresses me in excellent English:

"Hello! What do we Jordanians say when we meet a foreigner? Welcome! Can I help you in any way?"

Of course, I'm not going to lie to him. The hospitable Jordanian knows where to find the hot springs but agrees to tell me about them only after I have tea at his house and meet his family.

My new friend's name is William. Not only he tells me all about the hot springs, but also offers to take me there.

We leave the car on the side of the road and walk through a field of tomatoes. I look carefully at the smooth surface of the sea opening out before us trying to discern what is unusual about it. Only when we get to the beach do I notice the enormous rocks covered with a thick salt crust like white icing. The sea rolls onto them in licking waves but the waves do not, like cows or elk do, lick the salt off but rather leave the rocks even saltier.

The beach is completely deserted. William brings his family here so his wife can swim just wearing a bathing suit rather than the long shirt that Muslim women wear on public beaches.

I've heard many a horror story about the danger for one's eyes of even tiny drops of water from this sea. So the first thing I do is head off with a mug to a stream of warm fresh water coming down from the mountains.

With a mug of water in place of a first-aid kit waiting on shore and with William waiting for me a little further off I can finally explore the most unusual sea in the world.

The water is not at all summery – this is January after all.

At the bottom there are stones encrusted with salt. I discover just how sharp they are when I get back to the beach, my feet striped with crimson marks.

I have to work hard to keep the waves from knocking me off my balance. I have absolutely no desire to fall into this awful water – there's so much salt that the water tastes bitter more than salty. Eventually I find myself in water up to my shoulders and I lie down carefully stretching out my neck to protect my eyes.

It is indeed impossible to sink. But you can't really swim, either: your legs keep getting tossed up like a floater. It's more comfortable on your back: you sit on the water as if in a large armchair. It's so funny! Hop! With one easy push you turn on your own axis. Hop! You turn in the other direction. You spin like a top, and just like a child watching a spinning top can't conceal its joy and delight, so I too share my impressions with William, not in words, but with a ringing laugh.

The sun apparently wants to follow my example and have a swim. It's already slowly sinking into the sea. Or maybe it just wants to look closer and see who's having such unabashed fun there laughing and tumbling in this big salty puddle.

As the day's ending I can't refuse William's invitation to spend the night in his house which makes the hospitable Jordanian sincerely happy.

At home, especially for me, his wife prepars a dish of chicken with rice. For dessert they offer me their wedding photographs. I open the album – it is empty. What's this? I opened it from the wrong end: here albums, like books, begin with the end. Though, it's the end for us but for them it is the beginning.

In the morning William persuades me to go have a look at a beautiful mountain valley not far from their village. Our conversation turns out to be more interesting than the view.

"Tell me," asks William, "is it true that in Russia there

are people who put their old parents in the care of special institutions?"

"That is true," I answer. I don't go into details, knowing that here it's impossible to abandon elders or sick children, that it's impossible to leave the neediest people without help.

William asks about the relationship between men and women. News about our "freedom" in such relationships is renowned even in these parts.

"I was engaged for a whole year," says William. "And all that time I did not even touch my future wife. And I am happy it was this way."

William actually practices his religion. When the time to pray comes he leaves me and goes to pray.

So what can I say about this striking "freedom" in male-female relationships? Or about the old people's homes and the orphanages? How can I explain this to him? And I tell him about how the moral and religious foundations in our country were completely destroyed and only now are being restored.

In parting, William hugs me tight:

"You are the most surprising individual I have ever met." And he adds with a secretive air: "You are like a sister to me now. Think of me as your brother."

I smile to myself as William tells me something that I already know.

Chapter 4. Unexpected Egypt

First meeting

The ferry takes me across the Red Sea that separates Eurasia from the African continent. We are about to arrive in the Egyptian town of Nuweiba and I will step onto African soil for the first time in my life. But I'm not expecting anything good to come of this.

Egypt is one of the few countries where hitchhiking is officially prohibited. I've heard dozens of stories from friends about roadblocks where my friends had to get out of cars that had picked them up. Inside the car you have to hide from the police, to play "cat and mouse" with the police, as my friend Anton Krotov put itt.

Locals are prohibited from inviting foreigners to sleep at their house. By the same token it is prohibited to invite foreigners to visit.

Sleeping in a tent is prohibited.

All these prohibitions are supposedly aimed to improve security for tourists. In fact, obviously, they ensure income for the tourist business.

I don't expect anything good from Egypt. Will I be able to hitchhike there? Or will it be a constant cat-and-mouse chase and I'll get sick of it and quickly regret having come here?

These restrictive laws are not even the main drawback of one of the world's most visited countries. The tourism network has ensnared the country and people's minds so completely that Egyptians now perceive white people exclusively as walking fat wallets.

"The prices are automatically raised two or three times for tourists," they told me about Egypt. I'd also heard plenty of stories from friends who exposed these frauds by being able to read the Arabic prices and pointing it out to the sellers.

"They ask for money for the smallest service. Even for things you don't need and they'll go on pushing them on you."

I'd also heard any number of frightening rumors about the prevailing chaos and messiness in Egypt.

"Even in Jordan," my friend Igor was telling me when we ran into each other in the port, "if they see some weirdo on the road driving in a slapdash way they say, 'Oh, he's got to be from Egypt.'"

* * *

Two or three hours ago to my question: "When will we leave?" the driver replies: "In half an hour," and later he repeats the same thing.

"In fact, the bus won't leave until it is packed to bursting," explains Igor, a seasoned traveler used to the way things work in Egypt.

Finally, the last passenger who wants to go to Cairo gets on. They are carting a huge wheelbarrow filled with a mountain of trunks.

"But there's no more room on the roof." I look puzzled at the packed roof-rack.

"What do you mean?" Igor is also surprised. "It's practically empty."

Indeed, through some miracle and a few ropes, the driver and his helpers manage to tie on all the luggage of the last passenger. But just as I was hoping for our imminent departure, a huge cardboard box falls from the roof onto the pavement with a loud thud. The driver and helpers look on impassively. Then they decide to see what's inside. The box contains nothing less than a TV set. Somehow no one is particularly worried. No big deal.

Cairo sketches

There are only a few truly large cities in the world. It's just not easy to get an accurate count of the population, to separate the city from the suburbs, and so a few of the world's biggest cities fight to be considered the largest and most populous: Shanghai, Istanbul, Buenos Aires, and Cairo.

Cairo! It's hard enough for me to live in Europe's biggest city, Moscow. And now Cairo!

I'm walking along sidewalks thick with pedestrian traffic on Tahrir, one of the main streets in Cairo. On intersecting alleyways the cars are parked so close together it's impossible to squeeze between them, they seem to be leaning in for not-so-tender kisses.

No turbulent river could compare with the noise rising from the madly rushing street traffic. And the noise gets even worse when the traffic jams. Car horns are used much more in Egypt (as in most Arab countries) than in Europe or Russia. Is it simply that the desire to communicate is stronger here?

I observe the language of traffic with amazement while still on the highway. The driver wants to pass: HONK! Giving a warning, apparently. But then once he's already passing and even with the other car: HONK! As if to say, hey, I'm passing you, look out. And then once he's passed: HONK! As in, everything's fine, see you later. A tractor by the side of the road: HONK! A man walking: HONK! A donkey: HONK!

So now just imagine what happens in a city teeming with taxis when none other than a *foreign woman* is walking along the side of the road. All the taxi drivers salute me and offer their services, not suspecting that I can't stand the noise.

Along the sidewalk packed with all sorts of traders, pedestrians and parked cars, a motorcyclist goes speeding by. How is this possible when even pedestrians can barely make their way through the crowds? The motorcyclist doesn't take his hand off the horn. Still, everyone is so accustomed to this sound that the motorcycle dude has to apply his finest driving skills.

And then right behind him a guy on a bicycle comes rolling by with a large wooden construction filled with freshly baked bread on his head. How can he keep hold of all that while pedaling at the same time?! And how can he find his way among the dozens of people walking, standing, sitting? The guy asks people to step aside.

"Ps-s-s, ps-s-s, ps-s-s," he hisses softly. And people, oddly enough, make way for him.

Road theme, continued

Traffic lights and pedestrian crossings are rare. How do you cross these streets, clogged twenty-four hours a day? You just have to throw yourself into the stream; at least the current's not too fast. You won't get knocked over although cars don't really stop either, they'll just continue to move on slowly waiting for you to make your way through and jump back out onto the sidewalk.

And even when there are traffic lights... In Russia I never walk on red and here I wait just as patiently for the green. When the little green man appears I walk with him even though the cars continue driving across the black-and-white pedestrian walkways. Fortunately, I've learned to get by even without the stoplights.

Metro

Because of constantly rising prices in the Moscow metro I'm anxious to find out about the price of metro tickets in Cairo. I breathe a sigh of relief and surprise when I see that it isn't much: one pound (this means five rubles).

On the platform, here and there you can see placards with the image of a woman: there are special train-cars for women only. There are no men in these cars, well, if you don't count the occasional brazen salesmen offering all sorts of trinkets for which women worldwide seem to have a weakness.

I rode in these cars several times. It seemed like the women would burst out laughing any moment.

Women can ride in the other cars too, especially if accompanied by a husband or male relative. I also noticed a couple of single women. Apparently they're not too fond of the chicken-coop either.

The AFT House

In Cairo I didn't stay in a hotel. In this unusual city I had a chance to stay as a local rather than a guest.

My friend Anton Krotov, a true traveler, writer and founder of the Society of Free Travelers, thought up a new way of exploring the world. Instead of just travelling in the sense of getting there and going through, you rent a house or an apartment in an interesting country for three or four months. You live in this interesting place and make short trips to the environs.

So in late December 2008, Anton rented an apartment in downtown Cairo and filled it with a whole crew of interesting people and travelers, myself included. The place was on the sixth floor of an ordinary building with Egyptians living in it, a hardware store on the ground floor and a mosque right around the corner. The call of the muezzin and the Friday sermons resounded through our apartment. It was just a pity we couldn't understand a word.

Culture

On the first day Anton led me out onto the balcony of our apartment. The very center of the city – Tahrir Square (after the main street) – was indeed only steps away. The roofs of the tall buildings surrounding us were piled with trash.

"There you go, take a nice long look," laughed Anton. "Only the tallest buildings are clean. All the other ones get dumped on from the windows of the surrounding buildings."

Coming out of the building I often had to jump over piles of trash left by people taking out their trash to the dump. You either have to jump over it or walk around it.

Subway tickets are cheap but not always so easy to get.

One man pays while the next one is holding his money

ready, and I'm third in line. When it's my turn to buy a ticket, an Egyptian man nonchalantly shoves his money to the cashier right under my nose. Discouraged, I look back at him while another guy does the exact same thing. It's just my perception of the situation that I was next in line: they don't have this concept. Or at least I never picked up on any signs of its existence.

Cairo Museum

I always used to think that my favorite museum was the Tretyakov Art Gallery. Now I'm not so sure anymore.

In front of the famous Museum of Egyptian History there is a papyrus plant growing in a small shallow pool, its leaves spread out like the fingers of a hand. It's one of the few papyrus plants left in Egypt. In his book *Ra*, Thor Heyerdahl, the famous Norwegian traveler and ethnographer, writes about how difficult it was to find Egyptian papyrus to build a papyrus boat.

"Miss! Ma'am! Mister!" Swarthy Arab sellers surround you as you exit the museum.

"Papyrus! Papyrus! Original papyrus!" They are hawking large "papyrus" posters with images of the pharaohs, pyramids, and symbolic maps of Egypt.

"Ten pound!" They fix you with an anxious gaze while you patiently make your way forward.

My friends and I wonder what they actually make these "original papyrus" from – probably just dried palm leaves.

I have the good luck of getting a guided tour of the museum. Otherwise I'd have a hard time getting oriented among the five thousand pieces on exhibit.

An hour, two, three, four... and my eyes are still wide-open, my lungs still giving out sighs of astonishment.

The Cairo Museum amazes with the wealth of its historical

treasures, despite the fact that it is also the most burgled museum in the world.

I was there at the very end of my journey and nevertheless decided that I would have come to Egypt just to visit this museum.

Food

An apt observation: in cheap countries you spend a lot more money than in expensive ones. When everything is expensive you don't buy anything. But when everything's cheap you don't hold back and buy everything on sale.

I've never tried fresh-squeezed orange juice in my life. Until now. Two pounds – ten rubles in Russia, or around 30 cents – and the shop-keeper picks one orange ball out of the pile, a second, a third, slices them in half and into the maw of his squeezer. A minute later, the juice comes pouring out in a cheerful, fidgety stream into the thick transparent glass.

And the fruit cocktails they make there!

I've already made short work of my cocktail but I still remain standing by the kiosk to watch the nimble hands of the cocktail-master at work. A white (probably milk-based) beverage pours into the bottom of the glass, then yellow (probably mango juice), then strawberry. The whole thing is crowned with a headdress of banana, apple and strawberry slices carefully arranged and lined up against the sides of the glass. But why does the vendor have a small plastic bag? Oh! He pours all of this beauty inside. It turns out this particular cocktail has been ordered to go by a woman wearing a dark-red burqa. So the decoration process was just to give her aesthetic pleasure?

Kosheri! A mysterious word, right? Amazingly, the ordinary hotel tourists who come to Egypt don't know this word. So why am I bringing it up? The *kosheri* spot is another place I love to observe the vendor's dexterous work, unable to keep from drooling.

I get my portion to go (this is cheaper, by the way): so the vendor produces a plastic box, puts in a pile of rice, different kinds of pasta, peas, deep-fried onion and all of it bathed in a thin tomato sauce, plus two other sauces in small plastic bags. I am holding a warm box giving off a tempting tasty aroma.

Two pounds! Ten rubles! And you're full.

You find yourself trying to convince yourself over and over that you're hungry again.

All she needs is a hookah

All of the ground-level floors along the street are occupied with shops. Sometimes the shop-windows move apart as if to let one into the cave-like semi-darkness. A tea-room! Small tables only big enough to accommodate a few small tea-glasses and two pairs of elbows. You never see any women in these places. But they never go without men. To accompany the tea and conversation there are hookahs and backgammon.

I love tea but in Russia we don't drink just plain tea. So first I go peek into my favorite shopl, the one selling sweets. What a pity we don't have anything like these sweets in Russia. Enormous round metal trays present finely sliced baked goods of every possible variety. Sweet and very rich. Sometimes with pistachios, their green color highlighted dramatically against the golden-yellow background. They are really lovely but you have little time to admire them before you eat them up.

I'm carrying a plastic plate with these Eastern sweets, enjoying its weight. This time I take a table outside. The waiter brings out a glass of hot sweet tea and a glass of water to wash it down with. Casting glances at my solitary feasting, Egyptians promenade past. I don't pay attention to anyone and peacefully enjoy my treat.

"There she is! Look at her! All she needs is a hookah," a familiar male voice rings out loud and slightly indignant nearby.

It's a friend from the AFT apartment coming back from his trip round the environs.

"What, can't I sit here?" I say apologetically for no apparent reason, also smiling in response, and invite my friend to join in my exotic feasting.

Religion

The spot! Half of all Egyptians (men) in Cairo have a dark plum-sized spot right in the center of their swarthy brows (the percentage of spotted men is much lower in the rest of Egypt).

Like a medal, this spot is a mark of particular piety and religiosity. Muslims touch their foreheads to the floor several times during the *namaz*. So they develop this sort of callus. But why don't other, no less pious peoples have such spots, like in Afghanistan, Syria and Saudi Arabia? We put this question to a number of Egyptians. And hear several different explanations in response:

Egyptians have softer skin than other nationalities.

The prayer rugs in the Cairo mosques are made of very rough material.

Egyptians are more fervent than the others: they don't just touch their heads but bang them against the floor while praying.

We have our own explanations too. Egyptians probably just paint the spots on their foreheads. Maybe to demonstrate their piety. The second explanation: the prayer rugs in the mosques are not rough but just dirty.

Anton suggests the third and most convincing: due to unsanitary conditions, some kind of fungus is widespread on the mosques' prayer-rugs and leaves its mark of devotion on the Egyptians' brows.

In fact they don't need any proof of their religious devotion.

The space in front of the mosques, completely occupied with the faithful on Fridays, bears eloquent enough witness, and that's not even all of them – they simply all can't fit inside.

Women

The most freethinking city in any country is always the capital. As concerns religion an indicator of this pattern can often be found in women. The capital cities of Muslim countries usually have a higher percentage (in comparison to the provinces) of women with uncovered heads. In Egypt everything is different: it's nearly impossible to see a woman without a headscarf on the streets of Cairo. If you do run into one she's either a foreigner or a Christian.

The Coptic Quarter

More than five hundred years before the Catholic and Orthodox churches were formed the Coptic Church already existed. On Sunday I go to a church in the famous Coptic quarter. There are many bare-headed women there. Here and there you can see big stone crosses on the wide domes of enormous cathedrals. I go into one phenomenally big church that is empty; another one is empty too. Sunday and no service?! Finally, I find a girl who agrees to take me to a church where there is supposed to be a religious service. Side streets, narrow passageways, a few steps down – the service is being held in a small lower church.

No more than ten women are sitting on wooden benches, with no more than five men seated on the other side. Without thinking I sit down on the left-hand side, the one with more space. Shortly thereafter someone, probably a novice, comes up and asks me to switch my seat to the ladies' side.

The service lasts around two and a half hours, like in an Orthodox church. The priest says something in a singsong voice in a language I don't understand. Finally, they move from words to action. Another priest, different from the one conducting the service, comes out to administer communion. He looks like he has a higher rank.

To my shock, I discover that the churchgoers take off their shoes before communion and that for some reason everyone gets snow-white, embroidered and lace-edged handkerchiefs. Finally, the parishioners move towards the communion chalice shaped as a little house-box containing bread from which the priest breaks off hefty chunks and hands them to the parishioners. The men come up for communion first, the women only afterwards. After the bread, the people go up to the deacon for deep spoonfuls of holy wine. This is when those handkerchiefs come in handy: the parishioners wipe their lips with them.

At the very end, the people come up to the priest who gives them bread and his smile. I'm pleased: not because it's finally over but because I've got here after all.

Matchless silence

The January sun is beating down mercilessly. And I don't have a drop of water on me. I'm so thirsty it seems like my entire body has been squeezed dry. I'm alone in the midst of the Sinai desert.

At the last post where I'm stopped the frightened policemen yells after me:

"Where are you going?"

"To Saint Catherine," I name the village at the foot of the famous Moses' mountain.

"That's a hundred kilometers," they attempt to appeal to my good reason.

"No problem," I smile.

"What if I really do have to walk the whole way?" I think,

my smile fading. My confidence that I'll get picked up by a car evaporates with the remnants of moisture in my body (for some reason I hadn't brought any water with me). I'd already turned around a few times at the sound of a motor. Tall tour buses rush by without even slowing, blasting me with the wind from their speed.

Well, I'll just keep walking then. Maybe there's a special meaning in this. After all, the Israelis walked a long time before they reached Sinai and earned their wondrous prize: the wonderful Ten Commandments.

A car picked me up in the end but not for long. There are no cities in this part of the country, but there are Bedouin villages. One of these Bedouins, wearing a long white robe and a beautiful white headscarf, is giving me a lift. We turn off the road in order to visit his friends who treat me to some life-saving sweet tea.

Soon I find myself back on the road, alone with my thirst.

From time to time I lift my head heavenward and its cool azure assuages my unbearable thirst, at least slightly. At the same time I am glad that after the dark months of Russian winter I am finally able to meet face-to-face with the sky, free from the storm-cloud barrier.

Behind me, I hear the hopeful hum of a motor. I lift my arm at the new white foreign-made car. It slows down but drives past and disappears around a bend. Although the people inside signaled something to me. "Maybe the driver just didn't want to brake on an uphill?" I think hopefully and start running after the car feeling the air grate against my dry-as-sandpaper tongue.

The car really is waiting for me, but it turns out to be a taxi: the Bedouin driver is taking an elderly German couple to Saint Catherine. Without much faith in success I make my request. Surprisingly, the driver agrees. And in response to my question about water he hands me a full bottle of water.

Though the four of us chat cheerfully the whole way to Saint Catherine, I keep thinking that the Bedouin may have not understood me and will probably demand money in the end.

The driver, whose name is Suleiman, leaves the Germans at their hotel and turns to me:

"You're probably hungry?"

I nod involuntarily and the Bedouin orders four different dishes for me in a roadside café. He watches me trying to manage it all.

"I'm taking a group of Romanians up the mountain today, want to come along?" He suggests and adds right away, "Absolutely free."

I had the earliest wake-up call in my life that night – 00.40. Suleiman came to pick me up at the campsite, where he'd also fixed me up with his friend for free.

The evening before he'd invited me to look at the stone with "Moses' eyes." I couldn't understand what this meant until I saw the enormous chunk of cliff, taller than me, with oblong depressions. Legend has it that this is the very stone from which Moses drew water for the thirsting Israelis. How? Well, how did I manage to meet a tourist guide in one of the most touristy places on the road to Saint Catherine who started taking care of me quite selflessly?

The sky is alight with myriad yellow stars as if a million eyes are following me. Twinkling as if winking. I smile at them in grateful response.

The road leading up to the mountain looks a lot like a busy city street, a bit like the Arbat in Moscow. People move in masses, constantly turning on their flashlights, shouting, screaming, laughing:

"Camels, camels!"

Aside from English the Bedouins here have also learned good Russian. For the Russian tourists who usually can't speak English.

The group of Romanians is moving too slowly. I overtake them, agreeing to meet Suleiman at the last café on the way, a coffee shop, as they call it here.

Nearly at the top of the mountain there are some steep, tall steps. A young Bedouin overtakes me.

"Can I lend you a hand?" He asks in Russian.

"For money?" I smile, remembering all the stories I heard.

"No."

I accept his help. At the last coffee shop I say good-bye to my helper and sit down on a bench covered with a colorful blanket, waiting for Suleiman to arrive with his Romanians.

There come loud cries: "Blankets, blankets!"

These are coffee shop workers offering to rescue the tourists from the cold while lightening their wallets.

I'm so sick of hearing "camels" and "blankets" that when some Bedouins ask me where I'm from I answer in an annoyed tone:

"Not telling."

"From Russia?" One of them guesses. He is strong, tall, and is wearing a headscarf.

"No," I say, shamelessly denying my homeland.

My attempt to go incognito quickly becomes a joke. A Bedouin with a headscarf comes up to me. I expect him to try to sell me something.

"You don't have a Russian accent," says the Bedouin, paying me a compliment without knowing it. "But you're from somewhere near Russia, no? Where from?"

"I'm not telling."

"OK, OK. As you wish. Let's say you're from the Moon."

I show my appreciation for his sense of humor with a bright smile.

"Do you work in the café?"

"Yes, this is my coffee shop."

"How old are you?"

"Twenty-six."

"And do you like your work?" I ask expecting him to complain about the endless streams of tourists.

"Yes, I love the peace and quiet. There is no one here during the day."

I take in his burly appearance, sports pants and a worn grey sweater, and I can't believe it's him saying these things.

"What's your name?"

"Joseph," he answers. "Would you like some tea? My treat."

"It's too expensive here," I say not having heard his last words.

"My treat," he repeats.

The sweet aroma of the strong, life-giving drink rises up along with the steam. Once again it saves me from thirst, and once again in an unexpected way.

After I greet the sunrise on the peak, I come down to the coffee shop and Joseph again treats me to a cup of tea. He invites me to come inside the little store. Tired foreigners hurry after their guides while at the same time pricing souvenirs. I am meanwhile sitting on top of one of the most touristy spots in Egypt holding a cup of hot tea. The steam from the tea melts along with all of my silly fears about Egyptians' incorrect and selfish behavior.

Joseph lives on top of the mountain six days a week, and on his day off he goes down to his village. Today happens to be Friday.

"We can go together," he offers. "I know a different path. It's beautiful but not easy."

"All the better." I agree without a second thought.

We leap from stone to stone. I look back at Joseph:

"So why aren't you offering me your hand?"

In touristy places like this Bedouins and Arabs usually try to seize any opportunity to take white women by the hand.

"If you need a hand you'll ask," Joseph answers.

I look back at him again with astonishment.

We go to see his brother. Once again I am holding a glass of tea, this time made from hibiscus. His brother then leaves to run some errands and we stay behind to guard his goods.

"Look," Joseph points to the peak of one of the mountains surrounding us. "There's a chapel up there. There are a lot of them here. Monks used to go up there a lot to pray. Now they're almost always closed."

"So do you pray?" I ask expecting a negative response. In these touristy spots the foreigners often infect the locals with their materialism and Western values.

"Yes," answers Joseph.

"Five times a day?"

"No, not always. Sometimes I don't pray for a whole week. I don't want to lie to you... And sometimes during prayer I think about what I need to buy for the shop. That's not right either."

I look back again at this Bedouin who spends six days a week on top of this mountain. But he spends those six days on a mountain that is far from ordinary.

We come out to the start of our difficult journey. Below us, the buildings of the St. Catherine monastery lie like rectangular boxes.

"How long will it take to get there?" I ask.

"Two hours."

The sun is still high.

"Let's sit here for a bit," I suggest.

"All right."

We sit down on a big yellow rock at the edge of the mountain. I sit face-to-face with the sky. I feel like I'm seeing it for the first time. To the right the peak of Moses' mountain looks eloquent at us. Everything is seeped in matchless silence. There is not a single sound coming from below, so it seems as if the world below does not even exist. And you don't feel like going back there, all the possible fullness of life is here, in this proximity to the matchless azure silence. I look back once again at the mountain thinking of Moses and the Ten Commandments. Yes, in this silence you could hear many things!

Ring of oases

Sahara means "desert" in Arabic. This morning I am heading there. On the map the road I'll be going by resembles the ribbon of a river. But in fact, there are no rivers all around for hundreds of kilometers in every direction.

The first oasis I'll reach – Bahariya– is indicated on the map by a few little palm trees. But what will it look like in reality?

The paved road that leads from Cairo to the southwest is empty, evidently because it runs through the desert. Maybe it's not too late to run back to Cairo, heed all the warnings about the oases being far off and hard to reach? I sit down on my backpack by the side of the road. The road is empty ahead and behind me. To the left and right lies empty desert.

* * *

"If the road is paved, there have to be cars on it. And if there are cars, then you'll get picked up," Anton instructed me. Having been in complicated countries like Afghanistan and Sudan he really knows what he's talking about.

The two astonished Egyptian drivers exchange glances. They have seen lots of different kinds of tourists, of course, but probably none of them has ever tried to stop their big old truck.

No, they fail to understand the point of my words *shvaye-shvaye mashi, seiyara* – "a little bit by foot, car." When it's time for me to get out I have to take a few pieces of dry bread from them which they push on me against my will. They pour the remains of their water into my bottle mixing my bought drinking water with their tap-water which is dangerous for untrained foreign stomachs. One of the drivers goes for his wallet.

"*Lya-lya*! – No, no!" I almost screamed.

They exchange glances but once again there's no arguing with them. I'm forced to take fifty pounds, around two hundred fifty rubles (about nine dollars) and in Egypt you can buy a lot more with that money than in Russia.

By midday I am in the oasis of Bahariya. The simple clay huts alternate with palms whose dull branches barely give off any green. Apparently there isn't enough water in the oases for them.

I look for the next clump of palm trees in the mist of yellow desert on the map – Farafra. Found it... then drive right past it in the evening darkness.

The next day, just past Farafra, a pick-up truck driven by a sturdy young Arab comes to a screaming halt. It turns out he's driving to Kharga, the penultimate oasis, where his uncle's family lives. I'll get to cover a significant distance! But my joy can't compare to Muhammad's, the name of my new friend. He immediately invites me to meet his relatives. And it seems he's hurrying to get us there faster so that he can provide me with all the necessary hospitality in the proper fashion.

I'm met by their entire enormous family. The only one missing is the father. But the mother, around sixty-five, is there with her numerous adult married and unmarried children, grandchildren of all ages, all the way up to near-adults. The oldest, thirty-year-old Mahmud, speaks a little English. The impossibility of communicating through words is compensated for by our irrepressible desire to make friends.

We sit for a long time in the living room. They bring in supper especially for me – the others have already eaten. A few of them join me in eating, slightly embarrassed. Then tea is served. Despite the fact that it's after midnight and I'm tired from the journey, despite the fact that we don't even have a common language, we simply can't get enough of this communication and our laughter won't quiet for even a second.

Even if I remembered the law forbidding Egyptians to invite foreigners into their homes I'd probably not believe in its existence and that anyone could possibly observe it.

Chapter 5. The Valley of the Nile

Sugarcane

I'm sitting by the fireside – red coals smoldering in a metal tank – surrounded by a big Arab family. The mother sits opposite, watching me, and crinkles of joy run across her tired dark face.

Her thirty-year-old daughter brings two sticks. She hands one to me and starts gnawing on the other one. I wonder in horror whether I have to do the same.

The whole family responds with gleeful laughter at my perplexed and frightened expression. With her teeth, the woman peels the bark off part of the stick, breaks off a piece and hands it to me. It's sugarcane, of course. My mouth fills with sweet juice. Now they look worried and signal to me that I have to spit out the pulp.

The mother can't hold back her feelings, she comes up to me and places her work-rough hand on mine looking at me with her clear eyes. She doesn't say anything. But does she really need to?

She has a little tattoo on her forehead: a tiny cross. The whole family, indeed the whole area around here is Christian. This time they're Orthodox.

* * *

At the exit post from Baris, the last village in the ring of oases, the poor policemen are quite perplexed not knowing what to do with me. But happily, a big new van soon appears that is driving to Luxor. The driver is amazed to find a white tourist with no money, but to the sincere joy of the policemen he agrees to take me.

"*Muslim?*" he asked, pointing to my headscarf.

"*Lya, masykhi.* – No, Christian."

"*Ana masykhi.* – I'm a Christian too," says the driver, pointing to a small copy of the Gospels in its familiar blue cover, sitting on the dashboard. He asks whether I might like to come for a visit – maybe joking, maybe serious. It's not hard to guess my answer.

The final 120 kilometers run through unchanging yellow desert. Finally the desert parts before us and we approach the Nile. As if waiting for us the sun starts leaning down over the horizon which opens out into a blue full-flowing river. Meanwhile, the palms flanking it and spreading their luxurious juicy-green branches against the transparent blue sky, sing a silent hymn to the celebration taking place: the closing of yet another day on Earth.

* * *

The driver takes me to see his sister. The wooden door of the apartment shows an image of Christ walking inside. In a glass cabinet are porcelain statues of the Virgin Mary and saints. The sister starts bustling about animatedly.

After supper we go to the local church. At least twenty women have gathered for an evening meeting with the priest whom I don't notice at first behind the podium.

On the way to see their mother, the sister introduces me to her friends and I greet them all politely, carefully pronouncing the unfamiliar *markhaba* – hello. I've already screwed up a few times with the greeting *as-salaam aleikum* – who would have known that it's only for Muslims, that Christians don't use it?

Europeans in Africa

The next morning, my hostess takes me to see the famous Luxor church. We take a bus with a closed cab that does not seem intended to carry people. This church has a whole gallery of small sphinxes and large statues of pharaohs traditionally depicted in ceremonial step and clutching their seals, sometimes with little statues of their wives at their feet.

Luxor is bursting with tourists of all possible nationalities other than Russians. Hurghada is not far away, but why would they want to take any time away from the sea, the beaches and hotels?

Ignoring all the inviting calls I walk along the embankment and look at the even blue canvas of the river. My eye is accidentally caught by some interesting knick-knacks in a souvenir kiosk and the young Arab vendor is there right away. He starts a conversation in decent English, invites me inside.

"But I'm not going to buy anything," I warn him right away.

"Of course, of course. Where are you from?"

"Russia."

The guy looks me over with greater attention.

"Would you like some tea?" He suggests once I'm inside and looking at the funny little drums and unusual one-stringed instruments.

The vendor brings out a chair and some hot sweet hibiscus tea. When we're already making friendly conversation, Ahmed – that's the vendor's name – suddenly asks:

"So why are Russian women so easy?"

I blink helplessly.

"European girls too," Ahmed explains, "but the Russians... When I heard you were from Russia I thought..."

Hurghada, frequented by Russians, is very near to Luxor. But in order to find out about Russians' behavior in other countries you don't have to go to where they are as their fame extends far and wide.

Later, in Luxor, I notice the special reaction to the mention of my homeland. Once I even asked a riddle:

"I'm not going to tell you where I'm from. But I'm from a country whose women are known to behave pretty badly when they come here."

"I think I know where you're from," the Arab answered. "Are you from Russia?"

* * *

On the way from the souvenir shop I am once again attacked from all sides by all sorts of offers. The most tempting of them is to go down the Nile on a *felucca*, a small sailboat. And even though money is very tight I can't resist the temptation and agree, won over by the discount.

But when I find myself in the *felucca* with the boatman, the price rises from ten pounds to forty.

"Ten pounds is the price if you can find three more passengers," the swindler explains raising his eyebrows naively.

Angry, I leave. But I swiftly get caught again by another tempting offer.

"*Khamstashara ginei*? – Fifteen pounds?" I ask the twenty-year-old boatman for the fifth time.

And he answers for the fifth time:

"*Aiva.* – Yes."

"And you won't ask for more afterwards?" I finally ask him directly, in English.

"No."

One-thirty p.m. I note the time so that the boatman will take me for a whole hour and not skimp.

Four-thirty p.m... I hang from the boat with my hand trailing in the cool transparent water.

"Look," Ali points at a brown object floating nearby. "It's

a crocodile." I don't have time to be afraid before he starts laughing, showing an even row of white teeth, a bright patch highlighted against his darkly tanned face.

"They're just palm branches."

I splash water at him and laugh along with him.

He's twenty-three and has a fiancée whom he's known since early childhood. Their parents agreed a long time ago that their children would marry when they grew up. Now he just has to pile up some money and he'll be good to go.

We sail to the opposite bank and go to find something to eat. Ali won't let me pay for the *kosheri* but I treat him to some tea. We can't stop chatting. I feel like I live in this city and that I just went off this morning with my older brother to work – taking tourists around on our family *felucca*. And that for some reason there aren't any tourists right now so we enjoy our time together, just the two of us, having fun, joking and chatting. We splash each other and fearlessly swim around in the Nile. What do we have to fear when we've grown up on these riverbanks? This river is our homeland, it has watched over my whole life, and I am dear to it. How could it be otherwise when I have seen myself in it every time I look into the water to see directly into its eyes. When evening comes we return home. Mama feeds us *foul*, and I help her feed the animals and mix up the bread dough for tomorrow. I walk down to the river to get water, fill the clay water-jars to the brim; when I tire I dip a mug into these same water-jars drinking down huge gulps of the fresh water with its familiar dear scent, and then I go to bed. Today has been a good day.

On the threshold of Africa. Aswan

Ali tries to convince me to stay:

"Where are you going to go so late at night? Stay, you can leave tomorrow."

"No, I'm going now. If I have to I'll sleep somewhere on the way."

For some reason I really want to go to Aswan right now. I head off towards the exit from the city. Luxor disappears along with the last rays of the sun. In the darkness mixed with the light of streetlamps I stand on the main road that leads to Aswan, Egypt's southernmost city. There aren't any roads that go further, just the water-route to Sudan.

Will I manage to cross any distance at all today? Will I manage to find a warm place to sleep? There's nothing to do but once again, for the umpteenth time, to hand over my whole life into the hands of He Whom I trust implicitly.

An empty tour bus delivered me to Aswan at three a.m. Lucky for the policemen, this bus was driving past their post and generously agreed to take me along for free. Otherwise these guardians of public order, shocked by my appearance, would have had to let me get into some other random car since I categorically refused to go back to Luxor.

Aswan greets me with a warm southern night as if the true Africa were pressing me to her breast. Despite the late hour the streets are filled with people and the souvenir shops are open. I'm surprised, though this suits me. Where better to look for a place to stay than among people? I go down one of the main streets, walking past the cheery souvenir kiosks.

"Hello, hello!" a young Arab shopkeeper hails me.

This time I won't try to avoid conversation. I'm right: a stool and a glass of hot tea are quickly produced for me. A few of the merchants, mainly young guys, crowd around me, asking questions and expressing surprise. One of them is already offering a present: a little scarab-beetle, one of the symbols of Egypt.

"Where will you spend the night?" asks the guy who first noticed me.

"In some cheap hotel," I answer, seeing that none of my "admirers" have thought to invite me home, or are just shy.

The same Egyptian, very forthcoming, offers to accompany me. One hotel turns out to be closed and we go into another one.

"Hello, you are looking for a room?" The employee sitting behind the desk quickly gets down to business when he sees me. Another young, rather well-fed Arab stands next to him, elbows on the desk.

"Yes, I want your cheapest room."

"Of course, forty pounds."

"Oh, no, I'd like a room for fifteen."

"We don't have rooms for fifteen," the well-fed Egyptian butts in; he is evidently the boss. The man behind the desk falls silent.

"But I will only take a room for fifteen," I shrug.

"All right, we'll give you one for thirty with no shower."

"But I'll only take one for fifteen," I start putting on my backpack.

"My last offer – twenty."

"I only have fifteen pounds."

"I'm afraid we can't help you."

I turn towards the stair and my astonished companion follows me.

In the stairwell the fat guy chases me down with a serious, somewhat angry expression on his face, although he began the conversation calmly and wasn't at all desperate to keep his customer.

"But where are you going? You won't find anything cheaper!"

"Well, I'll spend the night somewhere else."

"Where?!"

"Well, probably in somebody's house."

"Whose?!" He is really surprised.

"Well, your place, for instance."

The guy stares at me wide-eyed.

"Well, OK," he says finally.

Now it's my turn to be silent.

"Only, don't get any ideas," I decide to make myself clear. "I just need a place to stay, and that's it."

"I'll give you a room," he says and directs me down the hallway to one of the hotel rooms. "Here."

It's a little room with a bed, bedside table, dresser, shower and toilet.

"Oh, well, I feel bad, I'll give you fifteen pounds all the same."

We're sitting in the dining room. Right now no one else is around. The young manager still hasn't managed to overcome his amazement.

"Wait," he says.

In a minute he comes back with a plateful of cheese, bread and jam. I don't wait to be asked and start eating.

"Do you know what this is?" He waits for me to eat everything before asking this question. "This is breakfast. But it's not included in the price of the rooms for twenty pounds."

"Ah, I see. Thanks!"

His eyes are still wide-open in amazement. But who does he find so amazing? Probably himself.

Funny cordon

"*Lya, lya, lya* – No, no, no." I yell at the ambulance driver and in desperation add in Russian: "Don't do this."

But to my dismay he wants to rescue me all the same and brakes at the roadside police post. I get out of the car with a distressed and displeased grimace. The driver watches me go guiltily and with sympathy as if accompanying me to the scaffold. "It's not your fault, brother," I want to tell him: "It's not your fault that I don't know how to say in Arabic: a little further or a little closer but not at the police post."

The gazes of the policemen flock to me like moths to a

flame: a single foreign woman with a backpack climbing out of
an ambulance at 1.30 a.m. I hoist on my backpack and in my
despair start walking into the darkness thickening beyond the
police post knowing full well that this is senseless.

"Hey! Ma'am! Please!"

The same old story for the hundredth time.

I have to play "cat-and-mouse" with the police every day
and very nearly every fifty kilometers. They manage to catch
me pretty often but I tear away from their claws every time.
Sometimes it's easy, sometimes it's hard, but it's always fun.

So even now I can't hold back a grin when I find myself
surrounded by about eight hefty soldiers with automatic
weapons blinking helplessly and discussing something amongst
themselves. I recognize the Arabic words *mit vein* – "where
from?" which one of them says to the other, evidently about me.
And I shock the poor policemen even more by saying in Arabic:

"*Min Rusiya.* – From Russia."

"*Tatakalyam arabik*?! – You speak Arabic?!" Their
eyebrows shoot up.

"*Shvaye-shvaye.* – A little."

"*Shvaye-shvaye.*" Cheered up tremendously they repeat
after me.

The first fright passes – I'm a foreigner but at least not from
another planet, I even speak like a human being, in Arabic, that
is. Their faces grow warmer and the policemen become brave
enough to start questioning me.

I hear the familiar *le* – "why", which apparently relates to
my most recent mode of transport, and start giving them my
usual spiel:

"*Ana seikha. Min Rusiya – Tyurki, Ordon, Syuriya, Mysr.*
– I'm travelling. From Russia to Turkey, Syria, Jordan, Egypt."

"*Mashi*? – By foot?"

"*Lya mashi. Mashi shvaye-shvaye. Ana seiyara beduni
fulius.* – Not by foot. A little by foot. I go by car with no money."

"*Beduni fulius,*" one of the policemen repeats this unusual combination, all the more unusual coming from a foreign girl.

"*Aiva, seiyara beduni fulius. Lya taksi, lya bus, lya shorta, lya mushkele.* – Right, by car for no money. No taxi, no bus, no police, no problem."

The last two phrases provoke a flash of delight, but it goes silent suddenly. The boss is approaching. All the bosses at all the posts look suspiciously alike as if they all had a special subject at school: rules for police-boss behavior.

They're always dressed better than the others, but never in uniform. The relationship between the boss and his soldiers recalls that between a grandee and his vassals. He often sits at a desk somewhere in the shade if it's daytime, or inside if it's night. If he wants to smoke someone takes out a cigarette and gives it to him, and someone else lights it; if he gets thirsty yet another guy goes running for a Pepsi. The boss accepts these services as his due, with a self-important and arrogant look. It all reminds me of kids playing at being king. One sits on the throne while all the others serve him. Until someone thinks up a coup.

The boss often knows English. But this doesn't really help us come to any understanding. This time too he commands:

"A bus is on the way, you're going to Luxor."

But Luxor lies behind me, I've just left the city.

"I'm not going to Luxor, I'm going to Aswan."

"No, you're taking the bus to Luxor!"

"I don't need a bus, I need a free car."

"There are no free cars!"

"So how do you think I got to Turkey, Syria, Jordan and Egypt from Russia?"

The boss has no answer for this and after giving his subordinates some kind of orders he leaves. The soldiers look at me with sympathy, expressing clearly that they'd be happy to help but do not have the authority to act against the will of their boss.

Like an enormous hedgehog with splayed spines, swaying from side to side, a tractor comes crawling by, its trailer filled with sugarcane.

I point to the treat:

"Oh!"

One of the soldiers tears off, still holding his gun, catches up to the tractor, yanks off a piece of cane and starts peeling it vigorously with his teeth on the way back. Pleased, he offers me a piece of the white sugarcane which I take right away. The policemen and soldiers watch me attentively like nannies pleased they have a treat for their "charge."

Suddenly, an empty tour bus appears and generously takes me on board for free. Before boarding I turn back to my automatic-weapon-bearing yardkeepers:

"*Shukran! Masalyam!* – Thank you! Good-bye!"

"*Masalyam!*" They yell after me waving.

* * *

But the game heads in a new direction every time.

I've never been kicked out of a car before, though this didn't prevent the policeman leaning in the driver's window from interrogating him tediously and at length about how a foreign woman got into his vehicle, where she is going and... At one point I suddenly started speaking loudly in Arabic:

"*Mafi mushkele! Tammam! Yelle, yelle!*" – There's no problem! Everything's fine! Let's go, let's go!"

The discouraged policeman didn't know what to do with a foreign woman unexpectedly speaking Arabic and he had to let us go.

Afterwards I learned to cover my face with my hand as we approached the police posts. When the policemen see only a headscarf they obviously take me for a local woman.

Sometimes I break the rules shamelessly.

With a firm stride I walk past the post towards the road and the unknown. For the first few seconds, the policemen can't believe their eyes. Then they wake up and start calling to me:

"Hey! Ma'am!"

I don't turn round, I keep looking ahead and imperceptibly increase my speed heading towards a saving turn I can see lying ahead. Just a few more steps and... The voices grow quiet, I disappear from the soldiers' field of vision and they evidently decide I'm merely a vision not to be chased down. They probably just repeat to themselves: "*Auzu bi lliakhi min ash-shaiti radzhim* – I turn to the Lord away from sly Satan."

But the "cat" doesn't always let the "mouse" go so easily.

One time I walked past a post under cover of dense night. But slightly further on I ran into an ambush: a patrol car on the side of the road. I decided to convince the two policemen who came leaping out that I did not in fact exist. Not responding to their cries I proudly and fearlessly moved off into the darkness. But when I decided I was already safe the timid hum of a motor came from behind. Turning back I saw that a police van filled to bursting with policemen and soldiers was creeping along behind me in first gear.

Knowing that I had no chance I nevertheless kept going, choking with laughter. Finally, I decided to have mercy and stop. The policemen came pouring out onto the road and began moving towards me cautiously while I held onto my sides chortling and swaying rhythmically to and fro. After a few seconds of extreme confusion, finally some of them became infected with my laughter and smiles flickered to life on their faces one by one like streetlights in twilight. I laughed out loud wiping away tears from my eyes.

* * *

The posts in Egypt are located every fifty kilometers; it seems I managed to spend time at all of them. Each post has between five and thirty policemen and soldiers. No enemy could sneak past them. At least, no foreign girl with a backpack, that much is for sure. As for the rest, *inshallah* – as God wills it.

On the road by the posts there are barrels standing like chess pieces; cars can't get past the posts at top speed because they have to navigate between the barrels. This rusty dented barrel, painted in the colors of the Egyptian flag, is none other than a symbol of Egyptian statehood.

You can draw conclusions as to the military preparedness of the menacing forces of Egyptian law and order from the uniforms alone: ill-fitting pants coming apart at the seams, boots with scuffed backs, sweaters stained with *foul*.

At the post in the village of Baris the policemen call me into their concrete shelter with one wall missing. They pour sweet cane syrup out of a plastic bottle into a metal bowl. Everyone breaks off a piece of white bread and dips it into the syrup which drips onto the ground, their pants and sweaters.

"*Khalas*! – I'm done!" I pat my belly.

"*Le*? – Why?" They push the bowl towards me suggesting that I eat more.

* * *

It's no wonder that tiny little Israel took over the whole Sinai Peninsula in just a few days. These guys are brilliantly sloppy and, it seems, utterly unsuited to do battle.

A van shows up at the post near Baris and agrees to take me. Five kilometers later, though, I get stopped at the next post. And when I'm all ready to start making a fuss they explain to me that I forgot my map at the last post and they radioed ahead and asked them to hold us. Ten minutes later my familiar policemen come driving up to return what I'd forgotten.

"*Shorta mushkele*? – Police problems?" they ask handing me the map and remembering my recent complaints.

I smile without saying anything acknowledging my error.

The van takes me away while the policemen line up on

the road and wave goodbye to me. Their guns swing uselessly at their sides bringing to mind little boys who have run and played all day and are tired; now their mothers will stick their heads out the window and call them home. We had a good time playing. It was awfully fun. Too bad we have to finish the game and part ways. But maybe not forever.

One more familiar faith

I leave Aswan in darkness again. What am I looking for with night coming on? The moon lies in the velvety dark sky with horns raised. It feel tired, lie down and admire the stars probably thinking about something personal. The moon is lying down! I can't tell whether it's waxing or waning the way I could if I were looking at the moon in my own country. In Russia the moon is always on guard, always standing up, while here it's lying down. I tear myself away from it but I keep looking up to check if it's still reclining.

The tall dark-green grass ripples by the roadside, playing with the warm southern breeze. Where will I spend the night? The cars don't notice me in the darkness and if they do see me they are just surprised. Aswan is a tourist city and the drivers probably think that I need an expensive comfortable tour bus.

All the same, an old car slows down. There's a whole family inside: mama, papa, a fourteen-year-old daughter and nine-year-old little boy. The women don't have headscarves, so they must be Christians. I wonder which kind they are this time. The girl speaks English, putting together the words memorized for dictation with difficulty.

"You're Christians?" I ask.

"Yes."

"Orthodox or Catholic?"

They have a hard time answering, searching for the right words.

"Protestants?" I guess.

"Yes," answers the girl.

So now I have met with representatives of all three main Christian confessions. I give my usual answer to the question of where I will spend the night: "In my tent." The father falls into obviously perplexed thought. Finally, they decide to take me to their village church, where the elder will most likely allow me to spend the night.

"You see," the head of the family explains, "we're forbidden to invite foreigners into our homes."

"Of course, of course," I reassure him.

It's clear that his perplexity continues. From the back seat, where I'm sitting next to the boy and girl, I can see the mother's concentrated profile fixed on the father. He probably feels this profile too even if he can't see it. The mother says something gently to the father and he turns towards me.

"But we'd still like to invite you to our house if you don't mind, of course."

"I'd be delighted!"

No perplexity remains, the tense atmosphere disappears. The mother, son and daughter all start talking at once, laughing. The father happily speeds up.

"What do you usually eat for supper?" At the house, the girl translates her father's question.

"Whatever there is."

In the middle of the living room, at a big table covered with a white tablecloth is a large platter of hamburgers (god knows where they came from!) We fold our hands and pray. The father thanks the Lord for having brought me to their home and asks that He show them the important message they are meant to convey to me.

The next morning, when I'm already leaving, the father hands me a slightly worn book with a colorful cover.

"This is the New Testament in English," the girl explains.

"I've been dreaming of having a copy."

I'd given away my own copy a few days ago to that Orthodox woman in Luxor, the one who took me in and treated me to sweet sugarcane at the campfire.

* * *

The road from southern Egypt to Cairo seems to run alongside one long endless village. For this reason every time I get out of a car I find myself in the thick of Egyptian life.

"Hello! How are you?" Little boys yell to me from their village cart hitched to a donkey.

"Where you go?" A group of young men walk up to me in business-like fashion.

Often someone invites me over for a cup of tea, worries that I'm hungry. They exchange e-mail addresses with me and promise to write.

The police keep refusing to let me on my way, consult with each other for a long time before finally cranking up their dark-blue clunker: it has two seats up front for the driver and one more person, then a little truck-bed behind with no doors and wooden benches. Despite their insistence, I throw my backpack in the back. My attendants sit down next to me. I pick up a stick of sugarcane from the floor and start awkwardly peeling it with my teeth. One of the policemen takes it from me and in a few seconds hands back a white piece all prepared. I gulp down the sweet juice looking back at the palms bordering the grey road behind us. Or the road ahead?

Conclusion

It's ten minutes walk from my friends' place in Tahrir to the airport-bound bus. What a shame it's so short. I get the crazy idea of shaking the hand of every Egyptian in the city. But you can't shake hands with all eighteen million.

They're about to announce the flight. I understand that it's almost impossible to leave. Can you really leave paradise so easily? Can you say: "Thanks for everything but it's time for me to go… I have stuff to do at home."

Of course I have stuff to do. Important and necessary stuff. But how can you leave paradise? A place where you are surrounded with tender care twenty-four hours a day. Where it's impossible to feel lonely for even a second. Where people give you gift after gift with selfless and sincere warmth and goodness. Where the sky does not abandon you in daytime, shining with clear blueness, or night, showering you with sparkling gems whose weight you can sense even if you can't touch them.

Where does this all come from? What did I do to deserve this?

When I left home exactly one month ago, and set off into the world, I left more than just my familiar comfortable home, my warm bed and regular meals, I also left the ubiquitous striving to plan, calculate and organize everything in my life the way I think it should be, the way I think would be best. But nothing at home had ever worked out the way it had during this month on the road. Why?

Here on the road, I stood in the dark on a path made through the snow in the outskirts of Erzurum, or near the rustling reeds of Aswan, bearing eloquent evidence of the roadside swamp, and I didn't know where I would spend the night, whether there would be any supper after a whole day of active movement; whether I would be safe. I didn't and could not know. I couldn't organize or plan anything. As a last resort, I would turn round to ask. And He Whom I asked would delightedly extend hands filled with gifts to me – hands He Himself was tired of holding back. These hands are always extended, and I turn to them so rarely. And no wonder because I'm not used to being in paradise.

I'd travelled so much before. I'd accepted these gifts so many times before. But never before had they been so generous. Why?

Well, because they aren't going to just fall on your head from the sky. They need hands into which He places them. Here, in these countries I'd gone through, I could see for myself how open palms were raised five times a day in order to accept and fulfill His will. You know this will when you give yourself entirely into His hands.

But it's time for me to finish my story.

March – November 2009

Translated by Ainsley Morse & Mihaela Pacurar

THE DEBUT PRIZE
FOR YOUNG AUTHORS

www.pokolenie-debut.ru

Debut launched its international publishing program in 2009. Three anthologies of Debut winners in English translation have been published. French, German, Spanish, and two Chinese editions have come out while Italian and Serbian editions are under way.

The prize was established in 2000 by Andrei Skoch, the founder of the Pokolenie Foundation for humanitarian projects. Debut is coordinated by the Booker-prize winning author Olga Slavnikova. A huge database of texts by young writers has been accumulated.

Awarded annually the Debut Prize is the largest and most authoritative Russian project today spotlighting young talents. Every year Debut receives up to 50,000 submissions from across Russia and worldwide. This new generation is declaring itself with increasing confidence in all literary areas.

"These emerging writers throw around their technical mastery, richness of perception and uniqueness of experience with a confidence that's almost terrifying.
This is not a collection to miss." – *Booktrust*

"There is clearly a very varied and committed range of young writers in Russia. They provide new perspectives and deserve to be heard." – *Fest Magazine* (Edinburgh)

"Meet Russia's young, exportable writers ..." – *Publishing Perspectives*

"Debut... a project of awe-inspiring ambition in a climate ripe for dystopian fantasy..." – *The Guardian*

GLAS NEW RUSSIAN WRITING

Contemporary Russian literature in English translation

www.glas.msk.su

The premier showcase for contemporary Russian writing in English translation, GLAS has been discovering new writers and rediscovering under-appreciated past masters since 1991.

Based in Moscow, GLAS has published anthologies grouped around a unifying theme (e.g. revolution, fear, childhood, women's views) as well as books by single authors.

With more than 100 names represented, GLAS is the most comprehensive English-language source on Russian letters today -- a must for libraries, students of world literature, and all those who love good writing.

Latest titles

Vlas Doroshevich. *What the Emperor Cannot Do.* **Tales and Legends of the Orient.**

Michele A. Berdy. *The Russian Word's Worth.* A humorous and informative guide to the Russian language, culture and translation. 2nd rev. ed.

The Scared Generation: **Vasil Bykov's** *The Manhunt* and **Boris Yampolsky's** *The Old Arbat*.

Mikhail Levitin. *A Jewish God in Paris*. Three novellas.

T.J. Perry. *Twelve Stories of Russia: a Novel I Guess*. 3rd. ed.